KISMET

A Story of Love, Friendship, Obsession and FATE

The debut novel

By Dawn Knight

Published by Knightlite Publishing
paperback fiction

Knightlife Publishing
10736 Jefferson Blvd., #417
Culver City, CA 90230
www.knightlifepublishing.com

Knightlife Publishing paperback edition 2000
Cover designed by ByronnCo Designs
Manufactured in the United States of America

ISBN 0-9678660-0-6, LCCN 00-190646

Printed in the United States by
Morris Publishing
3212 East Highway 30
Kearney, NE 68847
1-800-650-7888

Dedicated to all who are trying to get to

"the next level,"

where-ever that may be in your life.

Remember to take the time to be quiet,

sit still and listen to your inner voice;

the Holy Spirit, which lives within you.

It is God who speaks to you through your heart,

and when you listen to Him,

rewards are bounteous.

dk

kis•met

Fate; fortune

Chapter One

Kilamunjaro ~ *lil ghetto boy*

The dark, smoky pool hall was the ideal escape from what had gone down less than an hour ago. Kilamunjaro, or *Killa* as he was known, blended perfectly with the other lost souls who had no desire to be found.

The scar-faced man wearing a black leather trench coat sat coldly at the bar. He caressed his goatee with his right hand and fingered an empty shot glass with his left. His permed, shoulder-length mane lay in waves under the black brimmed hat that donned his head. It was tilted forward so that the brim nearly touched the bridge of his nose.

Not visible was the .357 Magnum that rested inside of the back of his pants, its handle exposed for easy access. Equally invisible was his sick, twisted mind.

He sat quietly at the empty bar while thoughts of Danielle Johnson danced in his head. In his daze, he envisioned caressing her long, black, shiny hair and looking into her bright hazel eyes while they made love on a deserted beach. He dropped gentle kisses on her soft, honey-colored skin as they shared bold lovemaking beneath the moon. In this fantasy she was his wife and they were on their honeymoon in Jamaica. It was a vision he often entertained.

"Hey, Big Man, let me get anotha' shot of Hennessy for the road," he said to the owner and bartender of "The Pool Pit."

The bartender's attention was fixated on the small thirteen inch TV that sat at the end of the counter. The frail, slightly hunchbacked man was thoroughly enjoying a women's boxing match. Impatiently, Killa slammed his glass onto the counter, getting the old man's full attention.

Larry, the bartender, was tired. Tired of working, tired of dealing with the cocky knuckleheads that frequented his establishment and tired of life. The Pool Pit had been his lively hood since Killa was twelve years old.

The seedy establishment had served as Killa's school away from school. He spent all of his time watching and learning the older pros' hustling techniques, especially Black's. Black was the shit. He could con a dog into meowing. Black was his idol, but it didn't take long before they became enemies. Killa was good at the game and his skill level eventually surpassed Black's. Black hated him and ultimately tried to kill him for it.

I was the king. Nobody could beat me, he remembered proudly.

"Here you go," Larry said, placing the full shot glass onto the worn, wooden counter. "And here's your tab. The total's forty eight dollars even." He dropped the check next to the glass with hopes that Killa would soon leave.

He's a real troublemaker, Larry thought, trying hard not to set off Killa's raging temper. He knew that it didn't take much.

"I can read, fool. Just sit tight."

What did he think? That I'mmana try'ta bail on my tab?

Killa abruptly snatched the tiny, yet powerful, glass of Hennessy from the counter and drank the liquor down in one smooth gulp. It tasted sweet as it left a burning sensation in his chest.

He thought of Danielle and compared her to the liquor. He craved to be with her, but the fact that she was not his made his chest burn. She was on his mind every minute of every day. Danielle was everything a man could want and she would be his. Soon.

As he daydreamed about her beauty, he reached into his right pocket for some cash and inadvertently pulled out the medallion that had once hung around his neck, then glanced quickly around the room to make sure no one was watching. He knew it wasn't likely since the place was practically empty.

There were three old dudes chewing on cigars and playing a quiet, intense game of pool. Marla, the oldest working stripper on the planet, was giving her girlfriend a lap dance, and a Mexican couple in the corner was making out so tough that Milton got a hard-on just watching. He wasn't worried about old Larry. He'd seen and heard it all, but never knew a thing.

Killa grabbed a napkin from the counter to clean his gold medallion, but the blood from J-Money's throat had dried into Queen Cleopatra's eyes and refused to come out. He gave up, slipped it back into his pocket and exchanged it for a fifty-dollar bill.

"Keep the change, Big Man," he said slamming the money onto the counter.

Larry picked up the fifty, examined it and glanced fearfully in Killa's direction. Wordlessly, he placed it into the cash register despite the specks of blood sprinkled across its face. He didn't dare utter a sound.

The liquor did Killa a world of good after his episode with J-Love.

That fool actually sat in my face and denied that he owed me money, Killa recollected.

J-Love was shocked as hell when he showed up at his front door. Apparently, he didn't think Killa would find out where he lived but he was wrong. Killa recalled the scene vividly.

When the tall, unattractive girl invited Killa in the front door without asking any questions, he knew it would be an easy mission. Upon entering the apartment he examined the small, scarcely furnished living room, quickly soaking in every detail.

The worn sofa and love seat sat in a L-shape on the tan stained carpet. All four of the white walls were bare, except for the stains and cracks. They had obviously seen many fights where someone had been slammed against the wall. The splattered blood that they tried to clean afterwards did not totally vanish.

"Hi, I'm Kesha, Jay's girlfriend," she announced proudly. "Go on an' have a seat an' I tell Jay you here. What's your name again?" She asked as if she had in the first place.

"Munjaro."

"Aaight," she smiled revealing two fangs, which grew from each side of her top gum. Just as Kesha began her walk to the back room to get her man, he yelled,

"Who's at the door, Baby?"

"Somebody name, Mun-jar-o," she yelled back.

"Who?" he asked suspiciously before coming to see for himself. When J-Love saw that it was Killa he played it calm and cool. He even offered him a marijuana blunt, which Killa passed on.

J-Love was disgusting with his oversized belly and hairy arms and back. You'd think he'd keep a shirt on at all times with a body like that. His girlfriend wasn't any prize herself. She had yellow, gapped buckteeth, untamed hair, big bugging eyes and sagging tits. *The perfect couple.*

J-Love thought he was safe because his girlfriend was there. He was well aware of Killa's reputation, but somehow felt he was exempt from his vengeance. He pretended to have no idea why Killa had hunted him down and showed up at his door, as if he had no memory of their loan agreement.

"So what's up, man? Uh, I paged you yesterday but you didn't get back," J-Love lied shamelessly.

The truth was he'd been avoiding Killa. J-Love had been holed up in the house, in fear, with Kesha for two whole days. Kesha didn't complain about the rare event of him being at home. She'd been going off on him for weeks about being in the streets all the time instead of home with her and their newborn daughter. J-Love went along with her and played the role.

"You know I love you, Baby, I told you I was gon' slow down," he'd said, and she bought it. She had no clue that he was a fugitive from the neighborhood.

Killa just sat and stared with an intimidation that made J-Love want to shit his pants. He couldn't believe it. He had fronted J-Love money as he did many times before – for him and many other neighborhood fools trying to come up. The difference between those times and this time was that J-Love was late with his payment.

Killa thought J-Love knew the rules. No grace periods, no payment plans. He didn't believe in late interest either. He'd seen many times before when a nigga was late with his money and because the interest had built up so high, he never could come up with enough to pay it back. Killa never let it go that far. If the bitch didn't have his money, it was death. There was no more chopping off fingers or burning out eyes with cigarettes. Besides, that was Hollywood bullshit. He did try those methods of intimidation back in the day, but it always ended in murder. He knew better than to leave room for a three-fingered, one-eyed bastard to get revenge whether they paid him or not. That was one of many rules he'd learned while earning his degree in The Art of Pimpin', Playin' and Hustlin' from Tha Streetz University.

J-Love's girl left the room to tend to their crying baby. He sat nervously on the old, dusty velour couch and lit the marijuana blunt that he had offered Killa earlier. Dauntingly, Killa rose from his chair, then stooped-down, facing eye to eye, his fearful quarry. He stared into J-Love's yellow eyes for several seconds before saying in a low and threatening tone, "J-Love, I'm here for my spread or yo' head. Which is it gon' be?"

J-Love shook his head from side to side, shrugged his fat shoulders and coughed out a nervous laugh.

"Whatchu talkin' 'bout, man? What money?

That was all Killa needed to hear. Before J-Love could blink, Killa slit his throat with a nine-inch switchblade. He was a done deal.

With J-Love sprawled at his feet gurgling up blood and gasping for air, Killa patted him down and searched his pockets. He emptied the contents and, to his disbelief, discovered a wad of hundred dollar bills. *Punk ass biyach.*

J-Love tried desperately to hang onto Killa, his left arm flailing helplessly in the air, as Killa tried to fight him off. He used the last of his seemingly superhuman strength grasping blindly in a futile fight for his life, as his hand latched onto the gold chain around Killa's neck. Despite its thickness, the platinum gold chain snapped and fell into the pool of blood in J-Love's lap.

Ol' boy put up a good fight for somebody strugglin' fo' they life. Killa couldn't help but admire that. He'd enjoyed watching him. His dick got hard seeing J-Love suffer, but since he didn't want to be smiling over his bloody corpse when his girlfriend came back, he grabbed his jewelry and fled.

Killa didn't want to kill J-Love. He was once one of his best customers. But when J-Love didn't show at the drug spot where Killa negotiated business, Killa bribed Smitty the Smoker to tell him where he lived. Smitty was the neighborhood's walking Thomas Guide. He'd sell his mama to get high and he knew Killa had that good shit.

When Killa got to The Pool Pit, he sat in his candy apple red Cadillac Seville and carefully counted the money that came from J-Love's tight pockets. Come to find out the fool had over a thousand dollars. He only owed Killa five hundred.

What a ignant jackass. Only a sucka would go out like that. If he was a true nigga he would've paid me and kept his pulse.

Killa began to feel the fear and the sadness that he dreaded. It was the same feeling that crept over him when he killed in the past. He let the feeling overwhelm him the first time. He became paranoid and hid in a motel room until he felt sure he was safe.

He didn't know if it would be the cops, or his Creator, but he knew in his gut that he would be punished for what he had done. While in hiding, he was haunted so intensely by the events that took place, that he'd contemplated turning himself in to the police. It was months before he was finally able to stop looking over his shoulder.

But that was years ago. Through denial, he'd since learned to control and manipulate the paranoia and the guilt and, in time, all emotion that he felt made him weak. All emotion, that is, except love and jealousy. He was in love with Danielle and painfully jealous of her husband Drew. Those feelings sent him into a rage if he dwelled on them for too long. Anger was his strength. He allowed it to consume him until he was high, then he'd violently unleash it onto his victim. They never survived.

On an average day, Killa would've stayed at The Pool Pit and hustled a little pool, but this was no average day. Aside from having just committed first-degree murder, he wanted to get home and clean up for his date with Danielle.

She'd be home from work soon and he wanted to *surprise* her with a visit. After two long months of watching and waiting, the time had come.

When Danielle gets a taste of my irresistible charm and good looks, she'll dump her punk ass husband and become my wife. Yeah, me and my wife Danielle – 'til death, do us part.

Chapter Two

Danielle ~ *Prisoner's Princess*

A sigh of relief escaped Danielle Johnson's pouty lips when she realized that six o'clock had finally come. She looked around her small, cluttered office and debated taking work home with her.

Nope, not tonight. Tonight is my night, she told herself.

Without a second thought, she picked up her durable, yet classy, steel briefcase, grabbed her Prada handbag, which went perfectly with her shoes, and walked out, locking the door behind her.

The stares and whispers were already in motion, but they no longer concerned Danielle. She'd come to terms with the fact that no matter what you do in this world, there would always be someone who had something to say about it, good or bad. With an air of confidence and assurance, she walked through the many mazes of cubicles without acknowledging any of her co-workers' childish smirks and giggles. She wanted badly to put the whisperers in check, but knew that a confrontation would only make matters worse.

"Goodnight, Scott. Don't work too hard now," she said, teasing her friend Scott Freeman as she approached his spacious, though crowded, cubicle. She stopped in to say a brief good-bye, but found him tangled in spreadsheets and engrossed in a heated business call.

On an average workday, Dani would be working late right along with him, but today she just didn't have the energy. As Scott lifted his index finger in the air as if to say "hold on a minute," Dani flashed her broad, pearly white smile, waved good-bye and mouthed the words "see you tomorrow." She knew if she waited she'd risk being reeled into whatever Scott was dealing with, she didn't want to take that chance.

I'll talk to him tomorrow, she thought, succeeding in fighting the guilt she knew would convince her to stay if she let it.

There was more whispering as Dani walked down the seemingly never-ending corridor to the elevator to freedom.

"Goodnight, everyone," Dani said, as she passed the clique of murmuring secretaries. "See you tomorrow," she added, flashing her wide Julia Roberts-like smile. Dani was going to kill them with kindness to show them just how foul they were being. It was obvious by the looks on their faces that they were already feeling remorseful.

"Goodnight, Dani," they chanted in unison, seemingly pleased that she'd given them the time of day. She had no interest in having anything other than working relationships with the women. She could tell from jump that they were gossiping busybodies and wanted no part of it. She thought it a shame that these people didn't have anything better to do than to create imaginary soap opera dramas about people they knew nothing about.

Finally reaching the elevator doors, Dani pushed down arrow and leaned her toned five foot ten inch frame against the glass wall behind her.

Despite her glum mood, her outside appearance always said, "I feel wonderful." Dani wasn't much of a primper, but being well groomed was something she was almost anal about. Today she was wearing her usual business-casual attire, which consisted of gray and black pinstriped Capri slacks with a matching blazer. Underneath her jacket, she wore a silk, maroon, v-neck camisole and on her size-eight feet, a pair of strappy Via Spiga sandals, the exact color of her blouse.

Her jewelry was understated. Her usual one-carat diamond studs dazzled her smile and her rock of a wedding ring, which she never took off, was perfectly accented by a platinum gold bangle. Her hair was slicked back and wrapped in a tight bun, her usual style for the office.

Her husband, Andrew, always complained about her hair being confined in a ponytail, especially when the "tail" was hidden within the coils of a scrunchy. She could still hear him lecturing, "you have it, so flaunt it." *What's up with men and long hair anyway?* Danielle wondered. She thought the obsession was ridiculous and chalked it up as "a man thing." She couldn't wait for the day she could tell her girl, Tai, who also doubled as her beautician, to cut it all off. But, who was she kidding? She knew it wasn't going to happen anytime soon. As much as she pondered getting a flyy haircut, she didn't have the nerve. Not only because Drew would shit bricks, but because, with the exception of bangs, she had never had her hair cut in her life. She knew that no matter how much she threatened to Drew that she would chop it off, she was just as attached to her long, thick locks as he was.

Dani waited impatiently for the elevator, pressing the down arrow for the umpteenth time, and took solace only in the fact that she was the only one there. The last thing she needed was to be surrounded with phony small talk.

Her once fun and exciting job as a regional account manager at Kravitz Advertising Agency had become a chore. Since Andrew had been away, Dani was spending more and more time at the office. She was so far ahead in her workload that her boss, Marty Kravitz, began to assign her projects that he felt weren't getting the proper attention.

The gossip around the office wasn't far behind. The rumor was that Dani and Mr. Kravitz were having an affair, which was supposedly why she got special projects and stayed late every night. It didn't help matters that Mr. Kravitz had an obvious crush on her.

Dani cringed at the thought of anyone, let alone her, having sex with her boss. Although his Armani suits and his Gucci shoes were fashionable, his appearance remained that of a Sesame Street character. His white, woolly hair reminded her of Albert Einstein, yet the worst part was that those same hairs protruded from his ears. His teeth were hideously crowded and Dani was convinced that if he flossed, he would find the beef that they were looking for in that old Wendys' commercial. Dani shuddered at the thought. At one time, his spontaneous visits to her office to "see how she was doing" were appreciated and welcomed, but that was until she caught him giving her *the stare.*

Mr. Kravitz had shared an elevator with Dani at the end of a late evening. After they exchanged the usual end of day chit-chat, she faced forward to exit the elevator.

She was parked on level three that day. She noticed that he was getting off on P1, two floors below, so she politely turned to her left to say a final goodnight. To her horror, she found her boss standing in a zombie-like daze and drooling profusely onto his gray Hugo Boss suit. He resembled a very damaged stroke victim, which terrified Dani. It was a memory that would be lifelong.

"Mr. Kravitz, are you okay!" She remembered shouting at him nervously. She shook his arm until he finally snapped out of it.

"Are you okay?" he asked.

"Am *I* okay?" Dani asked, confused about the whole scene.

"Yes, you were yelling in my ear and shaking me around like a rag doll."

Dani felt embarrassed. *Was I tripping?* She looked at him, puzzled, but shook it off and let the elevator door finally close behind her. She hadn't thought of the incident in the elevator again until the *next* time it happened, and the *next* time. Her womanly intellect and intuition told her that *the stare* was simply what it was. A stare. He stared at her the way any old, perverted man stared at a woman. She knew he was harmless and didn't feel threatened, but she did feel uncomfortable.

She dared not mention it to Andrew. She knew that it would be an invitation for trouble. Andrew had that "let's deal with this in the parking lot" mentality and Mr. Kravitz was definitely not up to the challenge.

No, instead she dealt with it just as she had everything else. She would pray about it then put it to rest in her journal. The answers to her prayers were often revealed during meditation. She was spoken to through her subconscious, which told her to simply tell Mr. Kravitz that his attention made her uneasy.

It had been easier than she'd expected. When she'd surprised him in the privacy of his office, the tables had been turned. That time, *he* was uncomfortable. After Dani explained how his staring made her feel, he acknowledged his rudeness and even apologized. She never saw *the stare* again.

She wanted to share her personal victory with Andrew, but knew he would miss the whole point and be mad at her for not telling him about it first. Being her protector was important to him and she loved him for it, but she was a big girl and had to learn and grow through her experiences. In order to do this, she had to actually deal with them and not pass them on for someone else to handle. She also knew she had broken their pact of "no lies and no secrets," but it was for his own good so she felt no remorse.

Not long after she'd dealt with the most recent situation with Mr. Kravitz and his fixation on her, the gossip started. Office gossip was always prevalent at Kravitz Advertising, but it had never been so heavily directed towards her. At first she shrugged it off and figured someone decided they didn't like her shoes that day or maybe her fragrance. But after a full three weeks of conversations that stopped as she approached and stares that easily said "she think she all that," Dani wanted to know what the deal was. She wanted to know why all the looks and the muttering and she knew exactly who to ask.

"I didn't tell you because I assumed you were above it," Scott explained after he confided to Dani that the latest bit of hot gossip was all about.

"Dang, Scott, I thought you and me were better than that. Did you at least get my back when they were ripping my good name to shreds?" Dani feigned a look of hurt and disappointment. To be honest, she didn't really care and was only teasing her nervous, apologetic friend.

Sweat began to drip from his curly brow and because of the moisture, his glasses repeatedly slipped from his nose. He then dabbed his forehead with the ever-present handkerchief in his shirt pocket.

She found it amusing that Scott would think she was actually mad at him behind such bullshit. *Psssh, puleeez.*

After several, long minutes of grilling him about his loyalty to her as her friend, she let him off the hook with her usual, "I'm just playin' witchyou, boy."

His face instantly relaxed when he said, "I knew that."

"Unhhuh. Sure you did." She laughed. She often teased him that way and she found it incredulous that he fell for it every time.

The arrival of the elevator snapped Dani out of her gaze into past events at the office. "Finally," she muttered, relieved that elevator had come. Doubly pleased that it was empty, Dani stepped inside. She'd gotten a good parking space in front today and was happy to not have to be a part of the after work traffic jam in the underground lot.

"Hold the elevator, please!" yelled an inappropriately dressed Paula as she squeezed between the closing doors. Dani had no intention of lifting a finger. Paula was not one of her favorite people and it was no secret. She smiled nervously when she realized whom she had accompanied on the twelfth floor elevator. The tension in the air was thick and Paula was obviously uncomfortable with the silence.

"So, Dani, you have any special Thanksgiving plans?"

"Yep, spending time with my family," Dani answered without looking in Paula's direction. She had already noticed the low cut polyester dress that was two sizes too small and the fishnet stockings. She didn't intend to put herself through the visual agony again.

"Oh, that's nice. And, how *is* Andrew?"

Dani turned to her with a glare that could kill. She then looked her up and down disapprovingly and rolled her eyes. Even more mortifying than Paula's attire was her make-up. Her clumped mascara made Dani wince. *She's a regular Tammy Faye Baker.*

Paula's ghostly, pale skin against her jet black, curly hair gave her a zombie-like appearance. The blood red lipstick didn't help matters either. She looked as if she'd just eaten a plate of raw flesh. Sadly though, Paula didn't know it. She thought she was the finest thing on earth and would dare you to argue.

"*My husband* is fine, thank you," Dani said in the same tone she'd used with Paula at the company picnic three months ago. Dani stared at Paula as if to say, "I dare you to say somethin', bitch. Make my mothafuckin' day." Dani didn't have to verbalize it because Paula got the message loud and clear.

The elevator doors opened as if on cue.

"Right," was all Paula managed to say before all three of them – herself, her hair and her makeup hurried out of the suddenly uneasy environment.

It was beyond Dani how Paula could feel so comfortable asking her about Andrew. At Kravitz's annual picnic last August, Paula got drunk and did her best to try and get onto Andrew's dick. After she had hounded him all day, Andrew finally got fed up and confided what was going on to his wife. He didn't want to get Dani fired by making a scene so he let her handle it.

Although the incident was three months ago, Dani remembered the scene vividly. Because she had gotten into Paula's ass that day, the flashback usually gave Dani a sort of twisted pleasure, but not today. Memories of her and Drew were all she had now and she wasn't taking them lightly.

Dani had learned a lot from Drew through the years. One thing was not to let a person mistake your kindness for weakness. Dani had come a long way. Once a shy and non-confrontational young girl, she'd quickly metamorphosed into a strong, independent woman comparable to a cunning lioness when necessary.

The thick brown smog and the film of gray clouds were the perfect setting for Danielle's overwhelming sadness. *California is supposed to be the sunshine state,* she thought as she looked at the sky. Consumed in thought, she walked over to her shiny, royal blue, convertible Jaguar XK8, profiled gloriously in front of the busy business complex, and carefully placed her briefcase into the almost empty trunk.

She then sank comfortably into the soft leather that embraced her when she got in the car. She was overcome with an angst to get home, confident that today would be the day she'd get a letter in the mail. Without looking back, she drove away from the curb and into the unknown, which always lurked.

Dani felt as though she was one with nature, cold and gloomy. She couldn't help but notice people in other cars singing along to music without a care or talking casually on their cell phones. She wondered if they were truly happy. *Probably not,* she decided with a shrug.

She waited for the green arrow for entrance to the visibly congested 405 freeway, switching her radio dial from a Power 106 traffic mix of Eric B. and Rakim, a young L.L. Cool J and EPMD to a smooth R&B station where Mary J. Blige crooned , *Missing You.*

Sing it, Mary. You know exactly how I feel gurl, Dani thought as she surrendered her sadness to the beat of the song and bobbed her head to the hard-hitting bass.

Temporarily comforted , she headed home on the highway in a fog of memories. Her most vivid was Andrew's last day of freedom and her first night of abandonment. While she sang along with Mary, she wished heavily that Drew would be waiting for her. As if he'd never left in the first place.

Chapter Three

Andrew ~ *What Goes Around*

Andrew Johnson lay restless in his cold jail cell, counting the days until he would return home to his family. He longed for the goose-down pillows and crisp designer sheets that he'd become used to retiring on each night. But not more than he longed for his wife, Danielle. The hard, cardboard mattress and fluid-stained blanket was all he had to embrace him now.

At two a.m., Andrew was wide-awake. He hadn't had one decent night's sleep since he'd been confined to the LA county jail two and a half months ago. The night's darkness carried screams of terror and pain and the echoed moans of those who had accepted their surroundings in defeat. The thick stench in the recycled air smelled of fear and hopelessness. Drew felt like he was in a bad dream that wouldn't allow him to wake up.

He still couldn't understand why he was there. Sure, the charges against him were clear. Felony, narcotic distribution. But he was innocent. Andrew had long ago left drug dealing to the ignorant, the blind and the greedy. He'd made a gang of money in the game and by making a series of wise investments over the years was able to retire and live forever in a life of luxury. But now he wondered if he had actually gotten away with anything at all. He knew from the beginning that there would be a price to pay for the genocidal acts he'd committed in the past, but he would always put the karmic consequences in the back of his mind.

How the large packages of heroin were found in his truck was still a mystery. He went over the scene again and again in his mind to find a hidden clue, but always came up empty. The cops didn't plant them. He wouldn't have believed it if he hadn't seen the drugs being torn from the leather seats of his brand new Chevy Tahoe with his own two eyes.

After his rights had been violated he was sure the bogus charges would be dropped. That the search and seizure laws would work for him. After all there was no just cause for their pulling him over in the first place, let alone rip through his truck like savage beasts. But he soon found out that they had received several "hot tips" regarding his alleged heavy drug trafficking and had all the paperwork they needed to support the legality of the shakedown.

The trial was heartbreaking for Andrew. The courtroom was filled with his family and friends. Everyone was sure that he'd be acquitted. That someone would come forward to exonerate him of the erroneous charges. But it didn't happen. Instead, there were witnesses who claimed Drew "served" them the drugs on a regular basis. Crack heads and heroin addicts who were obviously paid for their efforts. And then there were the police officers who stood up before a mostly white jury, supposedly his peers, and told their tale of finding the drugs hidden inside of the seats of his new SUV.

Crock of shit!

After the jury deliberated for just two hours, they returned with a guilty verdict. A tense air filled the courtroom and outcries from Drew's supporters were heard loud and clear, but they did him no good. He was disgracefully handcuffed and escorted from the courthouse to jail. His new home.

Since the trial at which he was sentenced to three years with one and a half years served, he struggled to figure out who set him up. Who would go to such lengths to have him locked up and take a loss on that much profitable heroin? He hadn't a clue, but he was determined to find out.

The obviousness of a hidden motive was eerie. Someone wanted him out of the way, but why? And why keep him alive? Because if anyone knew Drew, they also knew not to cross him. He had a dream team consisting of his attorney, his boys from his old neighborhood and his wife, Dani. He was also in the process of hiring a reputable super-sleuth private investigator. *By any means necessary.*

He knew that nothing good could come from his being taken away from his family. He had dark dreams that loomed with danger and often woke him in a sweat filled panic. Something told him that if he didn't get out of jail now and figure out why he was falsely imprisoned, he would eternally regret it.

"Hey man, shut the fuck-up!" shouted the resident of a neighboring cell. He was tired of hearing the screams from his neighbor who was being brutally defiled, again, by his new celly. Despite the threats of his celled neighbors, the screams continued followed by a chorus of horrific cries.

Andrew clutched his blanket and tightly shut his eyes in an attempt to lock himself into his own existence. He silently chanted a barrage of personal pleas to His Father.

Please forgive me God for all of my past mistakes and wrongdoings. Please protect my family and shield them from danger, Lord.

He then focused his mind of Psalm 91 and chanted it over and over again.

We live within the shadow of the Almighty, sheltered by the God who is above all gods. This I declare that he alone is my refuge, my place of safety.

He had never depended on the God his mama raised him to love, honor and obey, but he decided that this was the time to put Him to the test. At the time he did give reverence, it was because if he didn't, his mama would've gotten that ass. But when that ass got too big and tall to get gotten by his mama, he abandoned God for the streets. The streets offered a much more immediate gratification for loyalty, in his eyes. He had to learn by losing his best friend in a drug war that it would eventually lead to a dead end if he didn't change his ways.

He was grateful that the concept of God was embedded in his brain from childhood. Thankful for the years of being a church usher, attending bible study and being involved in the youth ministries. Had he not had God buried in his heart, he would be a sitting duck. As much as he appreciated his lawyer, his boys and his beautiful wife, he knew it'd be God who'd come through, and ultimately save him. He thought it very possible that this was punishment for past crimes gone unpunished, past sins gone unforgiven. He felt so vulnerable, yet fought the tears that tried to invade his outer self.

Stay inside, where you belong, he told them, just as he had many nights before. *I have to get outta here by any means necessary. I just have to.*

He used his thoughts of being free to soothe his nerves enough so that his body could rest. His body and mind needed sleep, but his spirit was on constant watch. Every day in the hellhole they called LA county hell was a battle that had to be fought, mentally and physically as well as spiritually. Whatever was coming after Drew was in the unknown, and until it came to light, he had to be prepared on all levels.

Drew's attorney, Jonathan Jacobs, came to see him the next morning to discuss their request for an appeal. They wanted to file the appeal as soon as he was sentenced, but Jacobs explained that because he was considered an open and closed case, he was at the back of the line for a court date. He also told Drew that he would be scheduled for transfer into a state penitentiary sometime the following week. The prison was so crowded that there was no room, not that Drew was in any hurry. As hellified as the county jail was, he was sure the state penn was way worse.

As far as Drew was concerned, Jacobs was the bomb attorney. The best. He'd been his attorney for two years and in that short of a time had freed Drew from several legal predicaments. But this was the worst jam he'd ever been in, and he wasn't as sure as he'd been in the past, that Jacobs could work his magic.

When Drew was released into the visiting area, Jacobs was sitting there busily preoccupied with paperwork. The sight made Drew crack a smile on his, otherwise, normally stern face. He admired Jacobs' bookworm persona and his ability to look the part to make things happen.

The visiting area was wrapped with thick, protected glass windows, black phone receivers, and divided by thin partitions, which offered no privacy.

"I hope a brotha's got some good news today," Drew said into the worn phone receiver. He stared into Jacobs' sincere, intense brown eyes through the thick glass window.

Jacobs was all about winning and it showed in the way he dressed, spoke and poured his heart and soul into his work. He was a young, Black, pretty-boy, and had only been out of law school for three years. Despite his freshman level of experience, he was smart and hungry to be top gun in his field.

"Andrew, I do have some good news." He held up a document that boldly confirmed an appeal date for Andrew Philip Johnson, inmate E77954. "We go back to court on December seventeenth." Jacobs was obviously pleased with the accomplishment, but displayed a look of concern. "You know that gives us just over a month to find some hard evidence that those drugs didn't belong to you. Have you thought of anything yet that could be of any help?"

Andrew painfully shook his head and wondered if anything concrete would ever point to a reason behind his twisted circumstances.

"Naw, I'm still stuck, but did you ever get in touch with that private investigator that you told me about?" Andrew was anxious to get this "so called" ghetto sleuth on his payroll. "The Shadow," as this infamous PI was called, had a reputation for getting to the bottom of things.

"Actually, I did. We're meeting tomorrow morning at my office." I'll fill you in on the outcome when I return on Friday. If anybody can solve this mystery, it's The Shadow. I'm sure of it. We just have to hope we can get him to take the case. From what I understand, The Shadow is very particular about his clients."

Jacobs had all the right contacts and was able to get a meeting with The Shadow. He had worked with him before and knew well of his work. What he didn't tell Drew was The Shadow was never seen by anyone and meetings were rarely held in person. He usually had a go between to field his clients until he decided to deal with them personally. When and if he did decide to meet with his potential client, it was always in a Catholic Church's confessional booth, with the privacy window closed.

In addition to those bizarre stipulations, the fee was paid up front or no deal. Complicated stuff. Knowing Andrew as well as he did, Jacobs knew he wouldn't handle his business that way let alone trust a mysterious outsider with his life. He didn't want to exhaust Drew's hopes, so he kept those details to himself.

"The Shadow *will* take the case," Andrew said confidently. "Make sure he knows that money is no object. The retainer Dani paid you last week should be more than enough. But there is no money until I get my evidence and I want to know ahead of time before you pay him and how much."

"I'll do my best. But you keep thinking about who would want to do this to you. We don't want to put all of our eggs in one basket. Your freedom is depending on –" Jacobs was cut off in mid sentence. Their time limit was up just like that and Andrew was promptly escorted back into his personal hell.

Back in his jail cell, Drew thought about his chances of being released. He thought about reuniting with his family and how much he'd realized that they were his emotional lifeline. He felt an unbearable emptiness that could only be cured by their presence in his day-to-day life. Dani was not only his wife, she was his best friend. He thought about the times they would go to the park and shoot hoops. Even though some of her shots were off, she'd protest to his taunting by claiming that she was the bomb point guard in high school. He'd never admit this to her, but she wasn't half bad. For a girl.

Chapter Four

Keera ~ *Home is Where the Heart Is*

"Excuse me, Miss? Is your name Keera Sanders?"

An attractive man with milk chocolate skin and deep brown eyes dropped into the empty seat beside Keera and opened his copy of *Sports Illustrated* magazine. He exposed her in a sexy swimsuit shot on page forty-seven and she blushed instantly.

"Yes, I'm Keera." She wished that she had worn a baseball cap and sunglasses. She acknowledged that the brother was fine as hell, but the fact that he was looking at a picture of her practically naked, in her presence, was embarrassing.

"Hi," he said, flashing a bright smile and extending his hand for an introduction. "I'm Thomas, a friend of Chance's. I think we met before at his pool party this past summer.

She recognized the name better than the face. Chance always mentioned him when he spoke about hanging out with his friends in Miami. Thomas was his newest road dog, and she was glad to have been able to put a face to the name. Keera took a closer look and realized that she *had* met him before at her boyfriend's party.

"Oh, yes, I do remember you. How're you doing?" She was pleased that he wasn't one of her overzealous male fans.

She came across them often and they freaked her out every time.

"I'm good, I'm good," he said, nodding his head to confirm what he had said.

"Well, I certainly hope you're on this flight to LA so you can join us for Chance's birthday celebration tonight."

"As a matter of fact I am," he said, admiring how beautiful Chance's longtime girlfriend really was. Curls of auburn hair lay softly upon her shoulders. Her mocha complexion glowed healthily and her eyes had an unmistakable sparkle that seemed to come from within.

Her long legs and sleek torso rested comfortably into her chair. Her demeanor spoke nothing of edginess that paid her an unexpected visit.

"Great," she replied, noticing that he was checking her out. "Chance is picking me up from the airport. He'll be so surprised when he sees that we were on the same flight from New York."

Keera became nervous. She didn't want to leave any room for suspicion. She had a man and she wanted that to be known.

"Yeah, he'll trip alright." He answered smugly, as he knew something that she didn't. Not wanting to overdo the small talk, Thomas excused himself. He saw that she was trying to make a point regarding Chance, but he was hardly interested in her. He'd only met Keera once before, but he knew of her well.

When he first noticed her on the plane, he didn't want to impose on her privacy. Instead, he sat quietly two seats across in the luxury of his first-class seat. Toward the end of the flight, he pulled out his *Sports Illustrated* magazine, which fell open to a page where Keera Sanders posed provocatively in a leopard print thong bikini. Thomas felt it was a sign and an opening for an introduction. Satisfied with the outcome, he wanted badly to return to his seat.

"Well, it was very nice seeing you again."

"Yes, it was," Keera replied hoping he would go back to his seat. He had begun to make her nervous.

"I guess I'll see you at the birthday bash." He flashed her a friendly smile.

"Definitely." She shook his extended hand and watched as he returned to his seat. She couldn't help but wonder what he was thinking. She had an eerie feeling about him, but she couldn't identify the source of it. He was handsome, friendly and a friend of Chance's. *I'm trippin'.*

Dismissing the whole incident, she relaxed in her leather recliner, one of the amenities of first class air travel, and peered out the window. Thoughts of Chance flashed through in her mind. She hoped this trip to LA would be the fun, relaxing trip she intended for it to be. For both of them. They hadn't spent quality time in weeks and she was anxious to be with him. They'd been fighting for the past few months, heavier than ever in the six years of their relationship.

The fact that he lived in Miami and she in New York made things even more difficult for them as a couple. Chance was in the National Basketball Association and was the star forward for the Miami Beat basketball team. It used to be that during his off-season, he would spend every moment that he could with Keera. She had more flexibility in her schedule, although she was constantly working. When they'd met, both juniors at UCLA, Keera had just started modeling. Chance had encouraged Keera's modeling career. They would spend countless nights in each other's arms, fantasizing about the day they would both be big stars. Keera's career took off quickly, as did Chance's.

They both stuck it out at UCLA and graduated despite the temptation not to. Many pots of gold dangled before them but they held their ground. Both had families who expected no less than a college degree and neither could live with themselves if they let their folks down. Once that goal was accomplished, Keera's successful modeling career landed her in New York, while, Chance had been drafted by Miami's hot, young team.

Things remained wonderful for a time even though the relationship became a long distance one. But things slowly began to deteriorate. Chance became jealous and accusatory about her activities, which led her to believe that he was the one cheating. Things had cooled off, yet they weren't nearly as close as they used to be.

Keera wondered if it was over. She wanted to do everything she could for it not to be. But regardless of her desire to remain Chance's woman and someday become his wife, she knew that it had to be something that he wanted as well. She planned on having a long talk with him this weekend. She would wait until Sunday when everything had wound down.

She tried to convince herself everything would be fine. That it would all work out. If only she believed it.

Keera had to admit that she missed life in Los Angeles. Floss Angeles, as she liked to call it. Modeling had taken her all over the world, but when it was all said and done, nothing compared to home. She loved New York with its never-ending energy and unparalleled habitat, but she was definitely a Cali girl to the bone. The air was foul. Most of the people were superficial, and everything from real estate to a decent meal was overpriced. But, despite all of that, it was the place to be.

"Excuse me. May I have another Mimosa, please?" Keera asked the flight attendant who hoped to someday be in her shoes as a successful model.

"Of course, Ms. Sanders. Right away," she said, pleased to serve the beautiful supermodel.

There's nothing like first class air travel. Keera enjoyed the hand and foot service. She closed her eyes and anticipated the wonderful Thanksgiving weekend she was about to enjoy. She would be with her daddy, her friends and her man, all in one trip. It was a rare treat that she would enjoy to the fullest.

At LAX's arrival-gate forty-seven, Chance stood tall and sexy. Keera quivered with excitement as soon as she saw him. Instantly she felt as if they were back in college. She'd had a huge crush on Chance before they were formally introduced and eventually started dating. Every time she saw him, she'd get major butterflies. Some things never changed.

He smiled broadly as she approached him. His charm and charisma were magnetizing. He gave her a warm hug and a tender kiss on the lips. The entire terminal watched as they greeted each other affectionately, including the paparazzi, but Keera didn't care. She was in her own world.

"These are for you, Baby," Chance said, handing her a bouquet of multicolored roses. His eyes held her captive, piercing through Keera as if he were internally examining her.

"Thank you, Sweetie, they are so beautiful," Keera said, as she inhaled their fragrance.

"Not nearly as beautiful as you," he said sincerely. He leaned in and kissed her again only this time with heat. It was unlike Chance to be so affectionate in public – especially in the eyes of the press – but Keera didn't complain.

Because she'd packed lightly and brought only carry-on luggage, they were able to go directly to the black stretch limousine parked in the loading zone, directly in front of the exit.

"Your chariot, madam," Chance said, one arm behind his back and the other arm outstretched.

"Thank you, sir," Keera said, taken aback by Chance's behavior. Not only was he surprisingly affectionate, but his chivalry was just as refreshing. He took from her hand the bouquet of roses and helped her into the car. She enjoyed this new Chance and decided to go with the flow. She was certain that if she mentioned it, he would find some way to turn her compliments into an argument. In the real world, instead of taking Keera's words as pats on the back, they'd be interpreted as slaps in the face.

"Happy birthday, old man," she said jokingly. "How old are you today anyway?"

"I'm the same age as you, grandma."

"Oh, are you twenty-three, too?" she joked.

"Is that the age we're claimin' today? Twenty-three? Well, all right, Miss Twenty-three. Where are we headed?"

"Well, we have a reservation at Crustacean for dinner. I was starving so I called from the plane. You know I can't stomach that airplane garbage they serve."

"Crustacean sounds perfect. Only you would know that I've been craving lobster all day." He beheld her with his eyes and she smiled back with hers. "Wendell," Chance voiced into the intercom to the driver, "head over to Crustacean on Sunset. We'll be having dinner there this evening."

"Crustacean it is," pronounced the portly, bald headed limo driver. The middle aged white man couldn't wait to get to the donut shop, which was across the street from the trendy seafood restaurant of destination. He lived for glaze twists and chocolate old-fashions.

Chance pressed the button, raising the privacy partition.

"Now you're all mine. I've been missing you girl."

"I've missed you, too, Chance," she closed her eyes and kissed him tenderly on the lips.

He received her by parting his lips slightly and warmly welcoming her with his tongue.

They took advantage of the car's exclusivity until interrupted by Chance's cell phone.

"Hello? Hello? Damn cell phones," he muttered after being disconnected from the caller.

"Are you sure that wasn't your other woman?" she asked teasingly.

"Never that. You're my one and only."

"Unh huh, good answer."

Keera had gotten so caught up in the moment that she had forgotten all about Thomas, Chance's friend from the plane. She didn't remember seeing him as she left the airport, but then again she wasn't exactly looking.

"Oh, Baby, I forgot. Your boy, Thomas, was on the plane with me today. I thought he'd stop and speak being that he *is* here in LA for your birthday party."

Chance looked dumbfounded. "How do you know it was Thomas? You two have never met."

"Yes, we did. Remember your pool party? Not that I would have recognized him. He came over to me and introduced himself." She left out the part about her picture in Sports Illustrated and about him checking her out. She didn't want any unnecessary drama jumping off.

No fighting, no fighting, no fighting, she reminded herself.

"Oh, yeah, that's right. The pool party. What'd you guys talk about on the flight?" Chance asked next.

"You, mostly."

"What about me?" he asked defensively.

"Nothin', Baby, dang. Just a little about the party and that was about it. Don't trip. Can't nobody take me away from you," Keera said lovingly. She was trying to get Chance back into that affectionate state that he was in before she mentioned Thomas. She was sorry she had done so.

"You know I love you, right?" He asked in a way that Keera hadn't heard in a long time.

"I love you, too, Chance. Is everything aiight?" Keera asked tilting her head to one side, trying to read him. He seemed to have gone to another place.

Chance caressed her face with soft, wet kisses. "I'm perfect. Especially now that I'm here with you."

She moaned in pleasure as he continued to kiss her softly. He then reached for her breasts and got down on his knees in front of her. She knew she was in trouble. While he kissed and sucked on the left breast, he stroked the right with his big, strong hand. Keera grasped his head with both hands and massaged his scalp, pressing his face deeper into her bosom.

Next he slid his tongue to her belly button and stroked gently, yet lustfully. He knew it drove her crazy. Keera opened her legs invitingly. Slowly he moved further down and pulled down the waist of her pants with his teeth until they were no longer prohibiting her freedom. She slipped her right leg from the bondage of her pants and spread her legs wide. His mouth was warm and soft and his tongue took full control of her body.

Keera moaned and swayed her hips to the motions of Chance's hands. He gripped her bottom and pulled in and out to the suction of his lips. Her hips were raised from the seat and her pelvic cushion was soaked with ecstasy.

"Oh, Chance," Keera said breathlessly. "It feels so good, Baby."

She was lost in his seduction. He was a very generous lover and always made sure that she was pleased. She wanted him inside of her so badly that she began to grab at his pants. He knew that she was ready for him so he strategically pulled down his sweatpants while he kissed between her legs.

Keera eased him up and guided him into her slowly. They kissed passionately as their bodies became one and danced together in rhythmic motion. She embraced Chance with both legs clasped around his back and pulled him in deeper and deeper. They went around and around until neither one of them could stand it.

"I'm cummin', Baby, I'm cummin. I'm cummin," he breathed into her ear.

"Oh, Chance, I'm cummin', too, I'm cummin', too."

At once they both exploded in orgasmic pleasure and held each other tight.

"Don't move," he whispered. "Don't move, please don't move."

Keera couldn't help but giggle at his request. He had been reduced to a little boy begging for mercy. He had been drained free of his manly juice. Chance nuzzled his face into Keera's breasts and took a deep breath. She kissed him tenderly on his forehead and stroked the back of his head.

"I love you, Chance."

"I love you, too, Baby. Now and forever."

This is how it's supposed to be, she thought. She wanted to ask the driver to skip dinner at Crustacean and to instead drive around for the rest of the night but she knew that they couldn't. After dinner, she had planned a visit with her dad. They haven't talked in weeks and she missed him. And, her triple treat was hooking up with Dani and the girls for Chance's party. She had a long night ahead of her, but it was a night that she wouldn't trade for the world.

Chapter Five

The Boutique ~*dangerous interludes*

It was Tuesday evening and the ladies; Tai, Saudia and Jody were enjoying their girls' night out ritual. In anticipation of Chance's birthday party that evening, they had their hair done while they drank champagne and enjoyed the food that was delivered by Grits n' Greens, the diner up the street.

"If I don't snag me a ball player tonight, I'm gettin' a boob job," Tai announced with a neck roll and smirked lips.

Tai was the owner and operator of a small hair salon in the city of Inglewood, which she called "The Boutique." She stood over her swivel chair and worked the flat iron over Jody's thick mane.

"Tai, I'm through wit' you. How you gon' let a man or lack thereof drive you to a plastic surgeon? That shit is dangerous. Don't you watch the news?" Saudia asked, annoyed at Tai's constant barking about getting breast implants.

"I'm not doin' it for a man, Saudia. I'm doin' it for myself, thank you. Besides, it's not dangerous anymore. That was back in the day when they used that silicone shit. It's perfectly safe now."

"Humph," grunted an unconvinced Saudia with a smirk.

"Personally, I couldn't go through with it," said Jody, deciding to join into the debate. "God didn't give us these bodies for us to chisel and reshape." Of average height and pencil thin, Jody secretly wished for a body like Saudia's healthy, hourglass figure. She never understood why Saudia was always on a diet.

"Well, what about exercise and going to the gym? Isn't *that* reshaping? Tai asked, trying to defend herself.

"Oh, come on now. That's a whole different thing," Saudia interjected. "Exercise is a totally natural way to go if you want to change something about your body. There's nothing wrong with it. My point is that you shouldn't go under the knife just because some fool doesn't respect you in the morning. Big boobs, or none at all. If you put yourself in a position to be disrespected, it's gonna happen regardless."

Saudia had gained ten pounds after the twins were born. She never thought that after years, the weight would still be there. Her round butt and full breasts made her appear heavier than she actually was. She was never comfortable with the added weight, but she had eventually accepted it.

"It's gonna happen regardless," Tai mocked Saudia in a childlike voice. "Saudia you've been pretty uptight lately. When's the last time you had some, girl?"

"Actually, last night," Saudia giggled, "and it was the bomb!" Saudia grinned devilishly. Her healthy figure didn't keep the men from flocking.

"Ooh, with who?" Jody wanted to know.

"With Sam, who else?"

"Married Sam?" Tai exclaimed. "And you talkin' to me about being in a position to be disrespected? Ha! You are too much, girlfriend."

Tai shook her head as if to say, "that's a shame."

"Pu-leeze. Sam is just my sex toy and anyway he and his wife are…"

"Getting divorced!" Tai and Jody chimed in unison, followed by bellows of laughter.

"Y'all make me sick. Tai, hurry up and do this bird's hair so we can go. Hell, I wanna meet me a ball player, too."

Saudia threw both hands in the air as if "raising the roof" and rhythmically swayed her body from side to side. She entertained the thought about meeting a tall, handsome stranger at the party – until she thought about her two five-year old twins, Damon and Daria. *It'll never happen,* she thought. She knew that if anything, it would be just a sexual relationship as all the others had been. She had yet to meet a man who would step up to the plate to take the place of their absentee father. *Fuck him. I hope he chokes and dies on a chicken bone.* She remembered bitterly that he loved to eat fried chicken. Death was the only excuse she'd accept for Dead Beat Darryl having abandoned them.

"I see I'mma have to keep an eye out on both a y'all tonight. Ol' huzzies," Jody said, in her usual mothering tone.

The truth was she wasn't thrilled about clubs and the whole party scene. This time, she made an exception because it was Chance's birthday. Since she became heavily involved years ago with Reverend Davis' church, Best Baptist, she gave up lots of things she'd enjoyed in the past. Her changed state of mind had even driven a wedge between her and her now ex-husband, Marcus. Still, she was confident that when the time was right, her prayers would be answered and he would come back home to her and the kids, where he belonged.

"We gon' find you a man, too," Saudia said, her tone serious. She eyed Jody, one eyebrow slightly higher than the other. "Lord knows we can't let you wait around for Marcus all your life."

"Marcus? Please Saudia, I don't want that man. I mean I'm happy to have the kids, but if I could do it all over again I would've never married him. Unh unh, we're just two different types of people with different wants and needs," she lied.

Tai and Saudia gave each other knowing looks. They knew better.

"Saudia, turn on some music, gurl. I need to get in the mood for tonight. I'm gon' definitely get my party on." Tai did her version of the Bankhead Bounce.

Saudia got up and turned on the radio. "Me, too. I'm so happy we're all going out tonight. We haven't done this in a long time." Switching from station to station, she settled on The Beat, a hip-hop station.

"Hey-y-y-y!" They sang out as they heard the chorus of one of their favorite songs and began dancing to the beat. Even Jody faked the funk.

The doorbell and loud knocks at the rear door startled Tai. She wasn't expecting any clients because she reserved the evening for her and the girls.

"You want me to get that, Tai?" Saudia asked waiting patiently for the conditioner to be rinsed out of her braids. She was so happy she just had to be rinsed and dried. No more pressing combs or flat irons for her.

"No, girl, I got it. Maybe it's Dani and Keera. They said they'd meet us here around eight o'clock but they could be early."

"Just a minute!" Tai yelled to whomever was on the other side of the wooden door. She smoothed down one more lock of Jody's hair before placing the hot flat iron gently in its holster.

Curiously, Tai opened the door and was instantly comforted to see her girl, Queenie, standing there.

"Oh my God, get in here!" she screamed, pulling Queenie inside and locking the door behind her. "When did you get to LA?"

"Hey, everybody!" Queenie sang out after giving Tai a hug. Before they could completely exchange their heart felt embraces, Saudia and Jody had joined in the reunion with their good friend. The hugs and screams, although loud and bold, couldn't have been a warmer welcome.

Queenie beamed with joy and was instantly filled with a comforting familiarity that she'd only now realized she'd missed.

"My plane landed this morning and I had to go straight to work from the airport," she said, settling onto the black leather sofa accentuated with leopard print pillows, where she was joined by Saudia. I talked to Dani earlier and she said y'all would be up here. She and Keera should be here in about an hour."

"Well, you sure look good, girl!" Saudia gushed, trying to ignore her envy of Queenie's petite figure. She always admired

Queenie's sense of style. Saudia envisioned herself twenty pounds lighter and wondered how she would look in Queenie's leather, strapless tube dress and silver sling back sandals.

"Queenie, you look better than good, girl, and your haircut is too flyy," admitted Tai. "Even if I *didn't* do it." She eyed Queenie disdainfully.

"Do you want some champagne? Or do you want some apple cider like Little Miss Sober?" Saudia pointed at Jody and smirked.

Jody stuck out her tongue. She was proud of her sobriety. And although it had once been a problem, she had no desire to drink.

"Anyway," Jody began, "what made you decide to cut your hair so short, Q?"

"I don't know. I always admired Nia Long's style so I decided to try it out." Queenie combed through her short, sassy hair with her fingers. People had always told her that with short hair she could be the actress' twin.

"The look definitely suits you. Maybe I should cut mine short. What do you guys think?" Jody asked.

They glanced at each other as if they didn't want to be the one to tell her.

Tai accepted the unspoken challenge. "I don't know if the world is ready for that yet, Jody. Maybe you should wait before trying something so drastic. You know how long your hair takes to grow back and you'll bitch about it for months. I can hear you now." She felt that a short cut would only magnify Jody's large, prominent nose, ears and forehead.

Jody was disappointed with Tai's answer, but shrugged it off. *What do you mean the world's not ready for that?* She wondered, but she didn't have the guts to ask out loud. She didn't really want to hear the answer. She knew she couldn't afford to maintain a short cut anyway. Getting her hair done tonight was definitely not the norm.

The doorbell rang again.

"I'll be right back." Tai sashayed towards the door.

"Well, I think it would be real cute on you, gurl," Queenie encouraged, waving off Tai's comment. "You would really rock a short hair style."

Jody instantly felt better. If anybody knew about looks and fashion, it was Queenie. She always looked together. She was the queen of style.

"Who is it?" Tai yelled. There'd been a rash of rapes in the nearby residential area and Tai wasn't about to invite trouble into her salon.

"It's Chris!"

Tai cracked the door slightly, making it obvious that he was not welcome. "What are you doing here?" she asked, her voice an irritated whisper. "I didn't page you. Go away." She attempted to close the door, but he stuck his boot into the crack just in time.

"Come on, girl. Quit trippin'," He looked at her like he was confused. "I want you to try some shit I picked up today. It's off the hizook, Tai. You gon' love it."

"Is it a *free* sample? Tai asked, her curiosity overcoming her wariness.

"Of course, Baby, of course. You know how we do it." He gloated over his ability to convince her so quickly. *I got mad skills,* he thought.

She glanced at the girls to find them consumed in music and conversation.

"All right, into my office. Quick." She let him in the door and hurriedly pushed the six foot three, two hundred-pound, well-groomed brother into her small, cluttered office, while hoping the girls didn't see him.

"Chris, don't be comin' over here without an appointment. I don't care what you have. It's just not cool."

"Aw, baby, I thought we was better than that." He moved closer to her and attempted to nibble on an exposed shoulder.

"Boy, get off me." She pushed away from him. "You ain't got it like that no more. Come on, let me see this *good shit* you talkin' about."

"Damn, you all uptight. Yeah, you definitely need this fix. Let me roll it up real quick."

He held up the large, plastic storage bag of weed. And, although the zip-lock bag held its' contents securely, it was not tight enough to contain the odor. It confidently stated "top of the line chronic."

Tai sucked her teeth in disappointment when she saw that the marijuana that she was anxious to enjoy, wasn't rolled and ready to smoke. "Damn, why you didn't have that shit ready for action? Go on and roll up a fat one. While you doin' that I'mma go check on my clients. And Chris, don't play, aiight. Stay put." She said in a tone that she thought was threatening.

"Y'all sound like ya'll in there partyin' and shit. Ain't you gon' introduce me? I peeped a couple o' fine honeys out there before you shoved me into this matchbox of an office." He frowned as he emptied the weed onto one of the many hair magazines stacked on top of Tai's desk.

"Are you crazy? No, I'm not gon' introduce you. You think I want everybody all in my business?"

It was no secret to Tai that a few of her girlfriends indulged in smoking weed on occasion, but Tai didn't feel comfortable with them knowing that she was a *serious* "bud head." She felt that their knowing would put a cramp in the business-woman image, which she so proudly clung to. "Anyway," she continued, "you're definitely nobody's type in there."

Chris was cute in a dangerous, roughneck sort of way, but she knew her friends would never give a drug dealer the time of day. She was confident that with one look, they'd instantly know Chris's story, so she kept him hidden.

"So, Queenie are you here to stay or are you going back to New York?" Jody asked, hoping she'd moved to LA for good. She missed Queenie since she moved back east to accept a Buyer position at Bloomingdales' department store two years ago.

"I'm happy to say that I'm here to stay. I've been back and forth from New York for the past month but my transition from the New York to the Beverly Center store is finally complete. Ya'll just don't know how good it feels to be home." Queenie leaned against the wall and took in The Boutique's new décor. She noted how much better she liked the black and gold color scheme as opposed to the dull gray that once was. *Very nice,* she thought approvingly.

"And we're glad you're home, too." Tai slid into the styling room and joined into the conversation as if she'd been sitting there the whole time. "You know we missed you, girl. You still get that employee discount hook-up, right?"

Tai placed the flat iron into the warmer to continue straightening Jody's hair.

"Oh, so you usin' me for my connections, huh?" Queenie joked. "Actually, I'm going shopping this weekend if you wanna come with. We should all go together. We'll shop 'till we drop, like old times."

"That sounds fun," Jody said, knowing she was broke. After paying her bills and buying groceries, she tithed the rest of her paycheck to the church. It was the same story every two weeks. If it weren't for Marcus' alimony, she wouldn't be getting her hair done or doing anything else extracurricular.

"I ain't got money like ol' times. I'm broke as hell," Saudia said bluntly. "But I'll come window shop. Get a hot dog on a stick from the food court." Saudia was always the comedian.

"Saudia, you are a straight fool! You better come hang out. You know you're the life of the party, gurl," Queenie said.

"Well, will being the life of the party get a girl a flyy outfit for free?" Saudia asked seriously.

"I don't know about that, but I did want to buy something for the twins since I missed their birthday last month. I know they're big."

"Yeah, they are big and gettin' bigger every day. I swear they eat like there's no tomorrow. They outgrow a pair a shoes in a month!"

Tai and Queenie silently thanked God they didn't have kids yet. They enjoyed their freedom, money and time, and used their friends' single motherhood experiences as motivation to wait awhile.

"Who was at the door, Tai?" Saudia asked, remembering the tall dark-skinned man Tai had rushed into her office. Saudia was always observing her surroundings. A habit she formed when she lived with Deadbeat Darryl, her psychotic, wife-beating ex-husband. She had to be on guard at all times because she never could tell when he was about to flip out.

"Oh, him. He's the guy who delivers my hair products. He's in there totaling my tab right now," Tai replied.

"Um hmm," Saudia said, suspiciously. "Don't let us interfere with your *delivery*. Go handle yo' business."

Tai got nervous. *She couldn't know the truth... could she?*

"I know you wanna go get you a quickie. Go on, girl. We'll wait." Saudia and Queenie laughed. Jody gave a disapproving grimace and wrinkled her nose.

"Please. I'm not *that* horny. But I do need to settle my account with him. I'll only be five minutes." Tai hoped they bought it.

"Go on, Tai. Don't pay Saudia any mind. She's just saying that because having a quickie while her friends wait in the next room is something she would do in a heartbeat." Jody looked at Saudia and winked.

Saudia returned the gesture by giving Jody the finger. One of her usual sisterly expressions of love.

"There's more champagne and apple cider the fridge and plenty of snacks in the pantry."

Tai hurried to her office. Her body was now literally begging for what Chris had *delivered* to her door.

While the girls continued catching up, Tai joined Chris in her now smoky office. Quickly closing the door behind her, Tai instinctively opened the window, and turned on the fan, in an attempt to clear the aroma of the burning drug.

"You know what? We should go out to the car with this," Tai said, nervously.

"Stop trippin', girl, and smoke the shit. I got people to see and money to be made and you standin' around actin' all paranoid." Chris had no more reason to be charming. As far as he was concerned he got in where he could fit in, therefore, he could be his usual abrasive self. He handed her the lit joint from which she instantly took a deep drag. She exhaled, satisfied with the lightheaded feeling that overcame her.

"Damn, this is the shit!" She exclaimed, taking another long drag. "I'll take my usual ounce."

Pleased that he had made such an easy sale, Chris pulled out the already packaged weed and threw it on her desk.

"Our usual arrangement, right?" Tai asked in a flirtatious tone.

"This is prime shit compared to my usual..." He stopped in mid-sentence, hypnotized by Tai's beautiful smile. His eyes traveled down her body and he felt a familiar warmth as he admired the way her nipples were vividly outlined through her thin cut off tee-shirt. He remembered the last time they had sex and how good it was. He didn't want to burn the bridge so he gave in. "Our usual arrangement is cool. This time."

Besides, Tai didn't know he had added a sprinkle of prime heroin to her supposed marijuana joint. He knew it was a sure way to introduce her to his new product and at the same time have her at his mercy forever. Tai went to her cash box and came out with Chris's usual fee. She smiled at him, pleased that he was still sprung.

Maybe I'll give him some after the party tonight, she thought as she eyed Chris and took yet another drag of the joint. *That is, if I don't meet somebody there with an offer I can't refuse.*

She smiled suddenly, wondering what the evening held for her and her friends. She had a strong suspicion that it would be a night none of them would forget.

Chapter Six

Danielle ~ *Goin' Through Changes*

Dani drove through the remote controlled gates into the townhouse community she called home. She reveled in the unbelievable beauty of the flowers and trees enveloping the grounds. Instant peace of mind consumed her. The moment she felt Mother Nature's warmth, she knew she was safe; safe from the unreal and the unknown on the outside. She'd always counted on Drew for her security. But he was gone and now she had to get into the driver's seat.

The lake just beyond the meadow was the best place to meditate. Dani's four-year old son, DJ, loved to feed the ducks any chance he got and she got a kick out of watching him. It was the perfect place to sit inside of happiness. If happiness was an object, Dani would imagine it to look like Las Flores.

Today, though, she didn't have to pick DJ up from school. Her grandparents, Willie Mae and Alfred, offered to pick him up since it had already been arranged for him to spend the night. The act was a blessing. As much as she loved her little boy, she looked forward to a little "me time."

To look at the property, one would never imagine that there were fifty townhouses hidden behind the plants and trees. The majority were nameless and existed quietly among her in their own little worlds. She was sure if any of them took a peek into her life right now, they would appreciate the things they probably took for granted, particularly, their significant other.

Dani hurried toward the Las Flores' mailboxes to get her mail. In angst, she unlocked the mailbox for townhouse number thirty-three and quickly shuffled through the small stack of mail inside. A smile of pure delight overcame her when she saw the envelope from the Los Angeles County Jail, inmate E77954. She sighed with relief. *This is better than Christmas,* she thought as she smiled to the heavens and clutched the envelope tightly to her chest. It was the perfect way to begin what she expected would become a memorable evening.

The letter was from her husband who'd been innocently jailed. She missed him like crazy and ached with nostalgia. She hoped to relieve some of her stress by burning up the dance floor later that night. God was smiling on her and she was definitely feeling the love.

Dani parked in her private garage, pushed open the back door and trotted up the stairs. She kicked off her shoes with two quick shakes and plopped down onto the soft leather of her living room couch. She threw the insignificant mail on the marble coffee table in front of her and took a deep breath. As she carefully opened Drew's letter, she exhaled and entered his world. It was short, but sweet.

Dear Danielle, I hope everything is everything with you and my lil' man. Of course, I am miserable without you guys but, otherwise, I guess I'm surviving. I still don't know how long it will be before I get to make a phone call so until then I will write every day. Because these fools don't know how to act in here, our phone privileges have been stripped. The mail here is funny too so I don't know how often you will get my letters. Just know that you are forever on my mind and in my heart. And baby, I love your letters. They're the only bright spot in my day. I don't want to go into how bad things are in here because I know you will worry but just know that your man is a rider and he will be okay no matter what. Send some more pictures of you and DJ, and Jasmine, too, if you can. Speaking of Jasmine, have you seen or talked to her since we last spoke? I hope her crazy mama don't start trippin' cause there's really not much I can do from in here. We should start looking into getting sole custody of her so we can take action when I get home. It'll be soon too, watch. I gotta go now, Babe. It's lights out and I can't write in the dark. I'll see you in my dreams.

Love Always, Drew

After Dani read his letter twice, she poured a much-needed Mimosa and turned on the stereo. The soulful sounds of Maxwell poured out of the speaker like a liquid massage. The soothing melody worked magic over her tense body.

She focused on the last part of the letter and realized that she needed to come clean with Andrew about the situation between her and Trixxy. Dani knew that he would be pissed if he knew that she had been practically raising his daughter since he'd been gone. Not that he didn't feel Jasmine shouldn't be with Dani, but he knew Trixxy would take advantage of Dani's kindness and her love for her step-daughter.

Before Andrew left, Trixxy refused to let Jasmine visit their home. Again. It was an off and on split personality episode with her.

"I don't want that bitch around my daughter. If you want to see Jasmine, you have to come over to *my* house," Trixxy said the last time Andrew went to pick up Jasmine for her usual every other weekend visit. The last time Drew had gone over to visit with Jasmine, Trixxy called 911 from another room and claimed he'd forced himself into her home and that he was threatening her life. The cops came quickly and picked him up. It was a big mess. *I still owe her an ass kickin' for that one.*

Needless to say, he hadn't seen Jasmine since. Dani's demands that they get legal visitation were not heard. Andrew was in the middle of his court case and was convinced that the court would laugh in his face if he asked them for help with getting custody of his daughter.

"We should at least get a lawyer," Dani told Andrew on several occasions. She'd located the best family attorney for their case and made them appointment for a consultation, but Andrew refused. He insisted that they wait until the outcome of his pending court case was revealed. He was confident that it would all end in his favor but ultimately it put him behind bars.

Andrew was shocked and disappointed, but Dani had been preparing herself for the outcome. Although she had faith in her husband's innocence, she had none in the judicial system. She stayed positive, prayed constantly, as did they all, but nevertheless he was convicted. He was torn away from his family to be wrongly and unjustly sentenced to three years, a year and a half time served.

Dani suspected Trixxy of having Drew set up, bamboozled and shackled until she realized that she was not clever enough, nor did she have the balls. The question of who did still haunts her. *It's not fair.* It saddened her to know that her husband was in jail and to see that it not only negatively affected her home life but also Jasmine's. *Who will save her now?* Not only had she lost hope in his being freed, but in getting legal visitation of Jasmine.

Trixxy was vicious towards Jasmine. Especially when she didn't get her way where Drew was concerned. She used Jasmine as a pawn to satisfy the venom she harbored for Drew and Dani. Trixxy could never accept the fact that after one of she and Drew's many break-ups that he finally decided to move on with his life.

Even harder for her to swallow was that he chose to move on with Dani. She was no longer Drew's number one, she was just his baby's momma. When Drew and Trixxy were involved, Trixxy had accused Drew of cheating on her with Dani. She didn't believe that the good friend of one of his homeboys had eventually become cool with him too. It was strictly platonic. And not to say that they weren't physically attracted to one another from the start but they both respected one another's commitments to other people.

Dani felt that it was by the grace of God that both of their significant others were revealed as cheating liars at the exact same time because the outcome, the two of them getting married, was destiny. Dani's reptile of an ex-boyfriend didn't put up much of a fight when he saw that it was Drew who he was up against when trying to stay in Dani's life. But Trixxy was a different story. Her self-esteem was lacking. She had just given birth to Jasmine and she had strong suspicions that Drew was cheating on her. They argued constantly about his hustling lifestyle, which more than often kept him in the streets until wee hours in the morning. To ease her insecurities and at the same time secretly punish Drew for his spending most of his time in the streets, she cheated on him with one of his underworld rivals.

The affair backfired on her when Drew's foe took no time in rubbing the videotaped sex-fest in Drew's face. The tape was dubbed and passed around all over the neighborhood until a copy eventually landed in Drew's lap. Needless to say, Drew was finally finished with her. Trixxy dug her own grave and to this day refused to lie in it.

Now, all of that was water under the bridge but the animosity between them remained. This was the very reason Dani was so surprised to get a phone call from Trixxy declaring "truce" shortly after Drew's false imprisonment. She apologized and practically begged Dani to forgive her for her foul behavior. She claimed to want to start fresh and wipe the slate clean for the sake of Jasmine. Dani was suspicious and even disbelieving on her adversary's newfound change of heart. She knew Trixxy despised her and wished nothing but harm on her, but at the same time she couldn't help but think of Jasmine. Instead of harboring her doubt, Dani convinced herself that God proclaimed a miracle in Trixxy's unexpected vicissitude. But Andrew didn't share the sentiment. He felt Trixxy was being manipulative and that she had a hidden agenda.

"D, until I get home, arrange to see Jasmine through my mother. Trixxy won't trip with her, she needs her too much." When he realized that Dani wasn't goin' for it, he continued, "Baby, you know how crazy she is and she knows that Jasmine is your weakness. The girl is the devil's spawn and I don't trust her. I promise when I get home we'll get things taken care of legally and she won't be able to do shit about it."

Dani agreed to comply only to avoid hostility between she and Drew. And, although she loved Drew and respected his view points on their issues regarding Trixxy, she communicated with her anyway. She felt strongly that Andrew underestimated her ability to take care of herself and to kick Trixxy's ass if need be. Little did she know that her forgiveness of Trixxy's demonic behavior would open the door for Jasmine to visit them on a regular basis. Dani had gone from "dat Biyatch" to "Jasmine's other mother" in just a couple of weeks. And, even though Dani felt that Trixxy's babysitting requests *so she could be free to run the streets* had grown ridiculously frequent, she could never find it in her heart to say no. She had a feeling that if she didn't keep Jasmine, Trixxy would find any old body – whether a stranger, an acquaintance or an undercover child molester – to do it. Then again, she wouldn't put it past her to leave six-year-old Jasmine home alone.

Dani could never forgive herself if something happened to Jasmine. In her eyes, Jasmine was a precious angel. She wanted to protect her and care for her because she knew that Trixxy didn't give a damn. *Every woman is not mommy material.* She knew she would eventually have to confess to Drew what had really been going on. *He would see my point,* she argued with herself. *Especially since nothin' has jumped off between us. Everything has been real cool. People can change after all,* she told herself, although in the back of her mind she knew better.

Drew's letter also made Dani wonder what their lives would be like when he returned. Of course she'd be there, but would she be the same woman? It had only been two months, yet already she felt like she'd captured a year's worth of maturity as well as a sense of independence she never dreamed possible.

Despite all of the chaos that surrounded her, Dani's son, DJ, initialed to stand for Drew Johnson, helped her to stay focused and strong. Her girls were always there for her as well. They hung out as often as they could, but they'd all pretty much moved off in their own directions.

One truth she'd quickly learned was that being a *single* mother was no joke. Drew's presence and influence in the home had been taken for granted. She reflected on the time she would criticize Drew for letting DJ stay up late; letting him eat those cookies that were off-limits just before dinner; or allowing him to get caught up in a game of Mortal Combat, when both of them should have been at the breakfast table. But now she sees that it was all in love, and that is what counted above all.

Dani truly hoped that once Drew returned, she'd never have to experience being a "single mom" again.

The after-effects of the Mimosa had set in and Dani wanted badly to take a nap. Tonight she would put aside her guilt about Andrew being in a cage and instead dance the night away at Chance's birthday party. Knowing Keera, the party's hostess and one of her best friends, the event promised a fun-filled evening. Dani knew she would need some rejuvenation if she intended to stay awake and enjoy herself well into the night, so she decided hands down on a catnap.

In her pre-dream state, she saw her life ten years ago. Back in the day she could party all night long and still get to work on time without a wink of sleep to speak of. Those days were a mere memory to her twenty-eight year old body. Lately, she was amazed if she could stay up past ten o'clock.

Clutching Andrew's letter, she went upstairs to her and Drew's fairy tale bedroom, which was fit for a king and queen. The square footage was enormous. Dani was in love with the picture window that offered an amazing view of Las Flores' landscaped grounds. There were so many trees and flowers Dani often imagined she lived in an enchanted garden. She stared out at the picturesque scenery on clear nights and gazed at the moon and the stars' formations.

Their king-sized canopy bed was inviting with its Laura Ashley bedding in Lilac and Black. The shrouds of sheer draping hung playfully over the dark wooded bed's four posters. The chase lounge near the window offered just as much comfort. The floor was covered with plush gray carpeting that appeared to have just been laid. Dani's "no shoes" policy worked well with the carpets' preservation. She stretched languidly across the canopy bed and rested Drew's letter on her chest before retiring into a land of dreams.

The steady chime of the doorbell jerked Dani out of her visions of her and Drew's reunion after his release from jail.

"Who in the hell?"

No one ever came by without calling first. The controlled access gate wouldn't allow for it. At least she thought. When she got downstairs, she looked out of her private peephole to find a disarrayed Trixxy at her front door. *What is she doing here?* Dani wondered. She had a feeling that she was too hasty in thinking everything was okay with regard to Trixxy. Something was very wrong. Dani's trepidation, when faced with opening the door, proved it.

Chapter Seven

Kilamunjaro ~ *BITCH PLEASE*

When he looked at her, he was disgusted. Once built like a brick house, Jackie had become fat and nasty. He watched her as she sat in their beat-up recliner eating a bag of red hot pig-skins and watching Judge Judy.

Danielle would never let herself go like that, he told himself, wanting more than ever to substitute her for Jackie.

"Is that all you plan on doin' which yo' self tonight?" Killa asked in an irritated voice.

Jackie glanced at him, shrugged her shoulders and turned back to Judge Judy who was embarrassing one of her court litigants. She was relieved to see that he was still on the Internet where he spent most of his time when he was at home.

The day he brought the computer home she never thought he would actually use it. She overheard him bragging on the phone that he got the computer as a trade for a twenty-dollar bag of crack cocaine. Jackie thanked God for that day. Killa never bothered her when he was on the computer. She knew that he was spending all of his time in sex chat rooms and was glad that he released his sexual energy there instead of on her.

"I got business to handle tonight, but when I get back we gon' settle some things." Killa said as he logged off of his computer. It was hard for him to leave the teen chat rooms.

They were where he spent most of his time lurking, preying and perpetrating that he was just another kid getting his jollies off on the Web after homework.

"And if you not here when I get back, stay gone." He knew she wasn't going anywhere. She never did. He was subtly giving her a way out without complications. He'd rather she leave on her own as opposed to him taking measures to *get rid of her*. He already knew that if she tried to stand in the way of his being with Dani, he'd have to kill her.

Jackie didn't utter a word. The only sound was from her smacking on pig-skins. She was still fixated on Judge Judy when Killa left the room to shower and change into his best suit.

Tonight is the night that me and my woman will finally be together.

He was nervous and excited. He thought nothing of the fact that Dani had no idea of who he was and that she didn't want to know, nor of the fact that she was married to Drew, one of the neighborhood's most respected and feared cats who no one else would dare to betray. But Killa felt invincible. He was confident that Dani would fall in love with him just as he had with her – on sight. He was the king of the world and no one could bring him down.

Every now and then, during moments of clear consciousness, he did wonder if everything would go the way he dreamed it would. He had to believe so because he didn't want to have to take the same measures with his precious Dani that he had with many others before her. He hoped for her sake that she was as different from them as he perceived her to be.

Back in the living room showered, suited, booted and reeking of Obsession for Men cologne, Killa couldn't believe that Jackie was still planted in front of the TV. But this time she was snacking on Oreo cookies.

"Bitch, get yo' fat ass up from in front of the fuckin' TV and clean up this fucked up house!" Killa yelled. He had to make sure he kept her in her place. Ever since most of his attention had been displaced, she'd had it easy. "If I come back and this house is still nasty, I'm kickin' yo' ass and yo' mama's ass. And there better be some food on the stove too."

Jackie huffed and slightly smacked her lips so that it wasn't too defiant, then raised herself off the couch where her size 18 behind left a permanent dent. She knew Killa meant every word and didn't want to go there.

Thank God he's leaving, she thought. She wondered why she even stayed, but even more so, where she would go if she didn't.

Killa was sure Dani was home from work. He'd staked her out enough times to where he knew her daily regimen by heart. He thought about the things he would say to her. *Should I buy flowers? Naw, too corny.* He became nervous and decided to stop and get a bottle of Hennessy. He needed badly to calm himself before he plunged into the crazy scene he'd plotted in his mind for months. It was such a die-hard fantasy that over time he'd convinced himself it was perfectly normal.

After a liquor store run and stopping at his hot dope spot to make sure business was as usual, he finally made it to Dani's place.

"Las Flores," Killa said in a tone of satisfaction and pleasure. He had inquired about renting one of the lavish town homes but was told by the snobby real estate broker, "No one rents in Las Flores. Everyone who resides in the community is a bonafide homeowner."

Her voice ran through Killa's head several times as he stared at the gate, which was the only barrier between him and his queen. The snooty realtor would be flabbergasted to see Killa rigging the security gate's master remote, to allow himself entry onto the private grounds. The sky was now pitch dark and allowed for a perfectly slick break in.

He had done it many times before and out of sight of the many security cameras, which hovered closely. Picking locks and getting around any electronic security device ever made was yet another trade he learned as a troubled and disturbed youth in the ghetto.

Now filled with a half bottle of Hennessy cognac and heavy doubt, he found himself approaching Dani's front door. He had never ventured this close before and was beginning to sweat. *What if she thinks I'm some lunatic and calls the police?* Killa asked himself, proving that his insanity was buried in denial. *The last thing I need is for the po-pos to be on my ass.*

Approaching the tall gate that surrounded the front patio of town house number thirty-three, he saw that someone had beat him to the punch. As he watched closely and peeked through the tiny holes of the wooden gate, he realized that Dani had another visitor. The girl stood outside on Dani's porch and knocked frantically on the door.

When Dani flung open the door he was instantly captured by her image. She glowed with radiance even though she didn't appear happy to see the strange girl at her front door. His heart was beating wildly now. He didn't expect to see her so soon. He wasn't ready. Unnoticed, he dipped behind a large bush, which allowed him to soothe his curiosity. Intensely, he watched Dani and the darker, bigger-boned girl, with the disheveled hairdo. He would make his move as soon as Big Bone made her exit.

Chapter Eight

The Boutique ~ *Ready 4 Whatever*

All of the ladies – Tai, Saudia, Queenie and Jody were having a good time at The Boutique as they caught up on one another's lives and shared their thoughts on what the evening would hold for them. Each had a different idea of what the night would be like.

"I'm going to hook up with a tall, dark, handsome and well-off stranger who will sweep me off my feet and treat me like a royal princess," Saudia fantasized."

"I'll take that same scenario," added Tai, experiencing a high like no other. After she smoked out with Chris, he promptly left and she'd been in a state of delusion ever since. It took all of her power to hold it all in and remain cool around her friends.

"I wouldn't mind meeting someone cool, but I'm not looking for love right now. I'm plunging head first into my career. The big bosses are really going to have their eyes on me now that I'm buying for the LA stores so I can't slip an inch," Queenie said. She had something to prove as a young black woman in the fashion world and she would make sure to make her mark.

"Well, as for me," Jody said after taking in what the others said, "I'm going to kick back, sip on a virgin Margarita and enjoy the scenery."

"Don't you wanna dance, girl? I know you won't last two songs before you get out on the dance floor to show off your moves," Queenie told Jody.

"It's been a long time since I've danced at a club. I wouldn't know what to do," Jody laughed.

"Just let the music take you there. You'll be fine," Saudia added. "It's been a while since I've been out, too, and I'm gonna eat, drink and be merry. Keera is hookin' up the grub, isn't she?"

"I'm sure she is," said Queenie. "You know Keera always goes way out, especially for Chance."

"O-kaaay! I can't wait!" shouted an anxious Saudia. She was going to be like a kid in a candy store.

Suddenly everyone's attention had turned to Tai. They noticed that she hadn't said a word. She'd been putting all of her concentration into Jody's French twist and had zoned out of the conversation.

"Tai, are you okay, girl?" asked a concerned Queenie.

"Yeah, Tai, you've been real quiet and you don't look all that good either," Saudia commented.

"No, I'm fine. I'm just trying to get Jody's thick ass hair into this up-do," Tai said, as she struggled to get Jody's hair into a neat roll. She had done it countless times before, but this time it just wasn't working.

"Ow!" screamed Jody almost jumping out of Tai's chair. "Watch those bobby pins, Tai. You're killing me here."

"Ooh, I am so sorry, JoJo. There. That ought to do it." Tai finally finished the hairstyle she had been battling with for the past thirty minutes. It usually took her less than ten. She turned Jody to face the mirror and she sprayed her down with a powerful yet sweetly scented hairspray.

"Tai, it's cute but remember I wanted the spiral curls to hang down in front?" Jody asked, as she primped in the large mirror, which reflected Tai's irritated glare. "Sorry, never mind then." Jody said, not wanting to get Tai started. Tai had some serious mood swings sometimes and Jody was scared of her when she turned into Ms. Hyde.

"No, Jody, you should get what you want unless the service is *free*. Is it free, Tai?" Saudia jumped in. She always felt that she had to stick up for Jody and hated to see people get taken advantage of. She watched it happen to her deceased mother all her life.

"Hell, no, it ain't free!" Tai yelled. "I got bills to pay like everybody else up in here." She began to feel ill. Her stomach was cramping uncontrollably.

"Jody, you know I'll hook you up. Don't trip." She looked at Saudia with a smirk that said "You always startin' something," and excused herself to go to the bathroom. "I'll be right back you guys. I think that food we ordered is getting to me," she said as she held her stomach and walked swiftly to the private bathroom in her office.

"Do you need anything, Tai?" Queenie called out after her.

"No, I'll be alright. I just need to take a dump." Tai called over her shoulder as she made her way through her office door.

The girls looked at each other and shrugged their shoulders.

"Way too much information!" Saudia yelled back just before Tai slammed her office door behind her.

Tai was a character and nothing she did or said ever surprised any of them. For someone in as good physical shape as Tai was, they each wondered why she always complained about this or that being wrong with her body. After the girls discussed it openly with Tai one day, they concluded that she was a hypochondriac who subconsciously just wanted attention. But tonight seemed different. Tai had lost her color and was exuding more than the usual "doin' hair" sweat that occasionally dotted her brow.

In the bathroom, Tai was bent over with stomach cramps. "Aw, shit. Damn greasy food," she muttered between moans. It was strange to Tai that one minute she was fine and the next in a twilight zone of bodily dysfunction. The stranger part was that at the same time she felt euphoric. It only took minutes before her cramps developed into diarrhea, but Tai didn't care. She felt like she was floating on a cloud made of marshmallows as opposed to sitting on a cold porcelain toilet seat. It was the most exhilarating feeling she had ever felt. Even better than sex.

She thought about Chris's visit and that maybe the weed he'd sold her was why she felt so good. *Now that's some good shit.*

As the euphoria overwhelmed her, the diarrhea and the vomiting had stopped. She cleaned herself up, but instead of returning to her guests, she sat down on the closed toilet. She was suddenly having all sorts of flashbacks in her head. She sat down to regroup but instead wound up crying, her face cupped by shaking hands.

All the memories she thought she'd banished from her psyche had returned to haunt her. Her father "touching" her when she was a child, being date raped when she was sixteen, and having sex with her monster of an ex-boyfriend, Calvin. He made her do the most disgusting things.

Tai looked around the claustrophobic bathroom and listened to the faint sounds of music, laughter and conversation coming from the salon.

"I am trippin'," she said aloud, finally getting a grasp of her sanity. She exhaled deeply and once again fixed herself up in the mirror. She knew she'd better go back out before anyone came to see about her. She couldn't explain what had just happened if she wanted to.

We all ate the same food so why didn't anyone else get the runs? She wondered as she primped in the sterile, yet feminine, bathroom's lit mirror. Confident that she was once again a vision of beauty, she joined the others while in mid-conversation.

"Tai, I was just telling Queenie about when we saw that fine ass actor Omar Epps in Ladera while he was filmin' "The Wood." Saudia informed. "Queenie, gurl, Tai is so crazy. She walked right up to him and told him –"

"I love you!" Tai interrupted Saudia to act out the scene for Queenie exactly as it had happened.

"Oh, my God. No, you didn't!" Queenie screamed. "What did he say?" she asked with wide eyes and an open mouth.

"Girl, he smiled that gorgeous smile and said, "Thank you, sweetheart" then he winked at me before he got into his boy's Expedition. He is so, so fine, y'all."

Tai was energetic and animated in her speech, but the girls didn't question her about her newly acquired disposition. In fact, they enjoyed the entertainment. They were each on their own high counting the hours before they'd be mingling with Black Hollywood's beautiful people at Chance's birthday party.

They weren't impatient about getting there though. They were kicking back and enjoying one another's company. Time was not an issue. All that was needed to complete the long awaited reunion was for Dani and Keera to arrive. Once they did, the evening was sure to be a smooth ride on a magic carpet.

Chapter Nine

Danielle ~ *Keep the Faith*

"Who is it?" Dani asked, knowing very well who it was.

"It's me! Trixxy!" She was in a panic and her voice quivered. "I need your help!"

Dani opened her front door to find Trixxy in a state of anxiety. Despondent, Jasmine stood by her side pulling at her dress, which was way too short for Dani's taste.

"What happened?" Dani asked urging them into the town house. Trixxy looked like she'd gone a few rounds with Iron Mike, and smelled heavily of liquor. Dani looked at Jasmine and realized that she was in distress.

"Jasmine honey, go upstairs and play with your toys while me and your mommy talk. DJ has some new video games up there. You better go and practice because you know how he gets when he wins all the time."

Jasmine giggled and hugged Dani. Her facial expression went from frightened to relieved in an instant.

"Can I Mommy?" Jasmine asked Trixxy, who stood there tapping her foot, demonstrating her impatience with Dani's concern for Jasmine's well-being.

"Girl, go on, shit! Go play somewhere, please!" Trixxy yelled to Jasmine, waving her away with her hand as if her daughter's mere existence was a thorn in her side.

Trixxy immediately turned to Dani who scowled at Trixxy's indelicate demeanor. Despite Dani's cold stare, Trixxy proceeded to explain the goings-on which had led her to Dani's front door.

"I need a favor, no bullshit," Trixxy said.

Dani wanted the whole story. She was getting a very uneasy vibe from the situation. Dani looked at her as if to say "and?"

Trixxy continued. "Me and a coupla' my homegirls were at the store over there on the corner," she extended her arm and pointed in the direction of which she spoke. "We were pickin' up some beer and mindin' our own damn business when these punk bitches from the neighborhood gon' come in and start clownin'."

Dani still had no words. She knew there was more.

"Anyway, one of them and my homegirl had got into it and shit and the next thing I knew they had all jumped on Keeshawn. I had to jump in and that's how I got all fucked up. Them was some big ass bitches."

"What does this have to do with me?" Dani asked, trying to get to the bottom line.

"I want to know if you can keep Jasmine for a little while so we can go handle this situation."

"Go handle what? What are you trying to go and do?" Dani thought about it. *Why do I care?* She knew Trixxy was younger than she was, but she was no out of control teenager. She was a grown woman with the responsibility of raising her daughter. In any event, that was not Dani's business and she didn't want to be pulled into Trixxy's turbulent life. "You know what? Neva mind. Just go on. I'm going out tonight but she can to my granmom's house. DJ will be happy to see her."

"Cool, girl. I'll come back for her in a little while."

"Trixxy, I just said I was going out. I won't be here in a little while."

"Oh, yeah. I'm trippin'," she answered with a perplexed look on her face.

"Just let her spend the night with my grams and DJ and I'll call you tomorrow when we get here. I'm only working for half a day so it'll be early afternoon."

"Aiight." Trixxy shrugged as she opened the front door to commence her adolescent affairs.

"Aren't you going to say goodbye to Jasmine? Dani asked in disbelief that Trixxy could be so indifferent about her own daughter.

"Oh, you can tell her for me," she answered casually.

"You know what?" Dani began, "You really need to grow up." Dani was pissed. "Be a woman and take care of that beautiful little girl up there. Don't you realize that she is a blessing?"

"Oh, like you perfect?" Trixxy responded. "Your husband is where? Oh, yeah. In jail," she added sarcastically.

"And what does that have to do with you not being a mother to Jasmine?" Dani asked, irritated that Trixxy had thrown Andrew's state of being in her face.

"Y'all livin' foul, that's what!" Trixxy said, getting in Danielle's face. "So now what, Judge Judy? Whatchu gon' do?"

"Girl, you better get out of my face before you get hurt. And that's real." Dani said as she sized Trixxy up, debating whether to give her the ass whoopin' of her life. They'd argued plenty of times before, but things had never come to blows.

I will beat her ass, Dani thought as she glared at Trixxy.

But then her thoughts went immediately to Jasmine who did not need to see her mama getting a beat down.

"You just better get outta my face," Dani said, as she reeled back slowly.

"That's what I thought," Trixxy said, satisfied that she had intimidated Dani into bowing out of the fist-fight she felt was way overdue.

"Girl puh-leeze," Dani said, waving Trixxy away and sucking her teeth. "Ain't nobody scared of you. If you had any sense, you'd realize that your daughter is just a holler away. She doesn't need to see this. Besides she just saw you get your ass beat before you came over here. Didn't you get enough?"

"I didn't get my ass beat," Trixxy insisted. "Besides, Jasmine is tough she's seen it all," she added, as if that were something to be proud of.

"If you didn't get your ass beat, why is your eye swellin' up like a water balloon? You're hopeless. I really feel sorry for you. You need to just let Jasmine stay. You don't want her anyway."

"Not in this lifetime. What? So you guys can be the big happy family while I'm all by myself? I don't think so." Trixxy's cell phone rang before Dani could reply.

"Yeah, this me." Trixxy then proceeded to walk away, leaving her daughter without saying good-bye.

Dani stood at the door and wondered why she wasted her energy on Trixxy. *She is selfish and childish and definitely not fit to be anybody's mother.*

When Trixxy left, Dani slammed the door behind her, expressing her irritation of Trixxy's invective behavior towards Jasmine. It was hard for her to allow herself to imagine what things are like for Jasmine when they were home alone together.

Trixxy had made it very clear that Jasmine was merely a bitter reminder of Andrew, but as much as she despised motherhood, she still refused to give up her parental rights and allow the little girl to live safely and comfortably in her father's home. Dani looked at her watch and realized that she had less than an hour to bathe and dress for her evening out. She took a deep breath and wondered if she should even go out at all. She could pick DJ up and spend the evening eating pizza and watching a movie with the kids. *No, I am not going to let Trixxy mess up this night out with my girls.* She laughed to herself knowing that they wouldn't allow it anyway.

Upstairs, Dani found Jasmine in the den fast asleep on the couch. She lay in front of a cartoon show clutching the handmade rag doll that Dani and Andrew had bought for her from the African Arts Festival one year ago. It was her favorite doll and she'd clung to it from the moment she saw it. Dani covered Jasmine with a blanket and turned off the TV, then left Jasmine to slumber in dreams that she hoped were better than the events she'd experienced earlier today. She did not quite grasp Trixxy's logic when it came to leaving her daughter to chase after some thug girls who disrespected her homegirl. *I don't get it.* She knelt down beside Jasmine and stroked her neglected hair, which was matted and clearly dirty.

I'll wash it tomorrow before she goes home 'cause I know that heifer won't bother with it. She then gave her a light kiss on the forehead and smiled, satisfied that there was a good chance that Jasmine could become a permanent addition to their home.

Patience, Dani, patience.

Chapter Ten

Andrew ~ *Lost in the System*

Another cold and miserable night in the contaminated rat trap known as the Los Angeles County Jail. Andrew knew that he could never get used to the vile conditions that had been forced upon him. He was pulling strength from deep within himself to remain sane through the ordeal that he knew for some obscure reason he was destined to experience.

Everything seemed unusually still tonight. Unusually quiet. It wouldn't last for too much longer. The guards would be around to do a bed count soon. It was amazing, the things the guards came upon while administering bed counts. They didn't give any advance warning either. Prisoners would be masturbating, getting head from their cellmate, giving head to themselves and all kinds of craziness.

Unable to sleep, Andrew couldn't help but dwell on the mystery behind his setup. He knew from Dani's last letter that she would be out tonight with her friends to celebrate Chance's birthday. When he first read of her plans, he became afraid. Afraid that something was waiting for her as well. Something was out there waiting to capture its prey. He didn't know why his gut ached whenever those thoughts entered his mind. For now he had to convince himself that he was just being paranoid because otherwise he would go mad with worry. For all he knew, paranoia could very well be the motivation behind his fear that the worst awaited for him and his family.

Interrupting his thoughts, one of the prison guards stood at Andrew's cell door jingling his keys impatiently.

What the hell does he want?

The guard did not acknowledge Andrew in the least. Instead, he stood tapping his foot and jingling his keys as if he was being kept from an exciting event taking place elsewhere.

Andrew sat up in his bottom bunk to prepare himself for whatever was coming. Just in case he was put in a position of kill or be killed. He knew it was not an impossible theory. He'd seen it happen many times before. Prisoners were at the mercy of the guards and the guards did not hesitate to make that clear.

The handcuffed man wearing the orange jailhouse jumpsuit swaggered toward the cell escorted by yet another jaded guard. Drew's former celly had been released earlier in the day and his replacement had arrived. He knew his privacy would be intruded upon sooner or later but hoped it would be later. It was bad enough having to exist in such conditions, but having to share the space that you'd manipulated yourself into believing could be worse, was unbearable.

The last man had been a gem with his unwashed ass and his deathly body odor. He was quiet but in an insane kind of way. Andrew was prepared to have to go to battle with the fool, but he was released before anything went down. Now he had a new celly and for the sake of his mental health, he hoped they would be on the same page.

Chapter Eleven

KEERA ~ *Never Gonna Get It*

After dinner with Chance, Keera had finally made it to her father's house where she relaxed in a pool of warm, sudsy bath water and mentally went over the details of tonight's party. Although Chance's birthday party was taking place in just a couple of hours, she wanted to be sure she hadn't forgotten anything or anyone. She would move heaven and earth if she could to make her man's birthday party one that he would never forget.

There was a knock on the bathroom door. Keera hoped it was her dad who wasn't at home when she arrived. Actually, she was surprised to find the house empty. Her dad, who knew she was flying into LA today, was usually home to greet her when she came into town. Even after he'd gotten married and started a new life, it was just like when it was only the two of them. Until tonight.

To Keera's dismay, her father had recently wed a woman named Mary. Keera privately called her Cruella because of her nasty disposition. Along with Mary came her thirty-three year old lazy son who still lived at home with his mama, and now *her* father. What her dad saw in Cruella was beyond Keera, but it was his life and she respected that. However, no one said she had to like it.

Keera turned down R. Kelly on her CD player to find out who was at the door.

"Daddy? Is that you?" she asked, eagerly waiting for the response of her father's gruff voice.

"No, Keera, it's me, Kevin. I saw your truck in the driveway and I wanted to say hello."

"Oh, hi," she replied, slightly irritated.

"Can I come in and talk to you?"

"Kevin, I'm in the tub! Can't it wait?" *Dang, what is up with him?*

"Oh yeah, I'm sorry. I thought you were just primping in the mirror or somethin', he said. "I'll be waiting in my room, okay?"

"Whatever," Keera mumbled, relieved to hear his footsteps fading away on the hardwood floor.

She turned her music up loud to deter him from attempting to talk to her anymore. The last person she felt like dealing with was Kevin, her big, dumb, sorry-excuse-for-a-man, stepbrother.

From the first time Keera was introduced to Kevin, she found him strange. Even stranger was the fact that his mother treated him as if he was five years old. She did everything for him; she cooked, cleaned and washed his clothes. It was ridiculous.

Kevin was a muscular man of slightly shorter than average height. Keera's six-foot frame towered over him. Until a knee injury pulled him out of the ring two years ago for good, he'd been a professional wrestler. He'd been unemployed since.

Glancing at the small travel-sized clock on the bathroom's vanity table, Keera noticed she was behind schedule. She drained the tub and grabbed the thick, teal towel, which hung perfectly folded over the towel rack on the wall. She quickly dried off and slid into a warm, leopard print, cotton bathrobe, kicked on matching furry slippers, then turned off the CD player. She slowly opened the door and peered in both directions before dashing across the hall into her bedroom. She didn't want to bump into Kevin until she was on her way out the door, if at all. She was certain he'd want to accompany her to Chance's party and she didn't feel like getting into it with him tonight. She had once given him a trial run as her bodyguard; needless to say, it hadn't worked out.

Keera had begun receiving perverted letters from anonymous admirers and she felt the need for protection. She'd approached Kevin since he'd once or twice proposed the very idea. He was in need of a job and he had the ability to crush somebody if need be so Keera felt the decision was faultless. The agreement was that he would move to New York and escort her to rehearsals and runway shows. Everything went well at first, but Kevin soon took things to another level. It had gotten to the point that if anyone glanced her way, Kevin would have them in a chokehold begging for their uncle. When he flipped out at a major designer's runway show, she had no choice but to send him back to LA. He begged her for another chance, but Keera put her foot down. She had to be more on her toes with Kevin around than she would just being by herself. Even with creepy admirers lurking in the wings.

The letters still came, but all of the other models attested to getting them as well. After a while she shrugged them off as "part of the territory." Now Kevin was simply a pest she hoped would get a life.

Keera was dressed in minutes. She wore the sexy red dress she'd been lucky enough to keep after working it on a runway for Donatella Versace. It was a spaghetti strapped, backless number that flowed easily with her every move. Her matching red pumps were hidden beneath the chiffon silk that stopped just at her heels. Her soft Auburn curls sprung wildly for now, but Tai would work her magic and style them into a classy chignon. Her makeup was light, yet sophisticated, and her fragrance was sweet, but daring. Keera was an unmistakable knock out.

The tap on the door caught her putting in her diamond teardrop earrings.

"Daddy, is that you?"

"It's Kevin again. Can I talk to you now?"

"Sorry, Kevin, I gotta run. I'm already late. I'll be here tomorrow though. We can talk then, okay?" she said through the bedroom door. She turned and eyed herself in the mirror.

"But that's just it. I think I should come with you tonight. What if one of those stalkers is out there?" Kevin asked, in a peculiar tone.

Keera wondered why he sounded so concerned, but didn't put too much thought into it. It was Kevin after all. King Dufus.

"Kevin, that's sweet, but it's not necessary. Chance will be there and he can protect me better than anyone. But thank you anyway."

She did one last turn in the mirror before dialing Dani's number to tell her she was on the way. The limo driver was out front and had been waiting dutifully since Keera was brought to her dad's house.

"Okay. If you're sure," Kevin said, obviously disappointed. He wanted badly to accompany Keera to Chance's party. He quite enjoyed mingling with celebrities and felt that if his wrestling career hadn't ended so suddenly, he would be famous himself by now.

"Oh, and Kevin? Do you know where my daddy is?"

"Yeah, he and Mother went to some play in Westwood. She surprised him with tickets this morning."

Hmmmph, I bet she did.

There was no answer at Dani's, but Keera knew she was there. She then paged her with her code 5000*12 to let her know she was on her way. Missing a much-anticipated reunion with her father, she sat at her old desk, which was still stocked with stationary and other supplies, and wrote him a short note.

Hi Daddy, I'm home but on my way out for the evening. I'm off with the girls to Chance's birthday party. Remember I told you about it last week? I heard you went to a play. I hope you had fun and I'll see you in the morning. Hugs and Kisses, Keera.

She wanted to add, *"And tell you bitch of wife "thank you" for purposely taking you out of the house tonight so that you'd miss me and that I'm gonna deal with her later."* If she felt her daddy could handle it, she would have passed on the additional message but she knew he couldn't. He seemed to be really taken with his wife and could find no faults. Keera left the note for her dad in his favorite recliner underneath the remote control where he would be sure and find it.

When she walked outside to get into her limo, Kevin was outside chatting with Wendell, the driver, who was still chowing down on glazed twist donuts.

"Bye, Kevin," Keera said, dismissing him with a limp wave.

"So, Keera, are you sure you don't want me to come? It'll only take me a second to change."

"No, Kevin, it's cool. I'll see you tomorrow." Keera was too through.

Kevin stood in awe as the limousine escorted his stepsister to her evening out. He gazed hungrily and wondered if she would ever see him, the same way he saw her. He wanted badly for the day to come where they could be together, not as stepbrother and sister, but as lovers. When he could stroke her hair and plant soft kisses onto her face as she slept.

He was tired of having to secretly watch her through keyholes and ceiling vents. He wanted to be invited inside. He accepted his mother's new marriage so easily only because he felt the union's soul purpose was to bring him and Keera together. He'd be a made man, if only Keera could see it, too.

Chapter Twelve

Kilamunjaro ~ *Mercurial Madman*

He didn't realize he was choking her so hard until it was too late. In his mind he had no alternative but to do her in. Trixxy refused to shut the fuck up. If she had stayed calm, she would've lived. It made no difference. When Killa was finished with her, she would've wished she was dead anyway.

Stupid bitch ripped my new shirt, too, he thought, as he looked down at his torn dress shirt and suit jacket.

If he'd known he was going to waste somebody tonight, he would have been better prepared. Worn the right clothes, driven a low-key getaway car – all of that.

At first, he was just going to threaten her and tell her not to fuck with Dani anymore. After he saw what he saw and heard what he heard outside of Dani's house, his blood boiled to the hottest.

The words were mumbled by the time they reached his perched ears but the tone was unmistakable. Trixxy and Dani were face to face with built up resentment and anger that was ready to finally dance. They were two neck rolls away from a rumble and tumble. Even though nothing actually happened, Killa felt he had to come to Dani's rescue.

He'd recognized Trixxy once she'd turned around and faced him on her way out.

Andrew's baby's momma.

She was from the neighborhood and her name was always attached to mad drama. She was talking on her cell phone and boasting about the fact that she had just put "that bitch Dani" in her place. After Killa heard this, he was out of control. He had to protect Dani because he knew of Trixxy and her reckless ways. She would come back for more someday and try something crazy. Naw, he wasn't having it.

When Trixxy went to her car, he was right behind her. When she opened her car door, he put his nine-millimeter to the back of her skull threatened that she quietly get inside. He climbed in after her into the backseat. The whole time she was steadily talkin' shit, smellin' like she'd just bathed in a bottle of gin.

Although she was drunk, she wasn't that incoherent. She knew her life was on the line and sobriety was soon her friend. She became very quiet as if she'd finally come to her senses. They drove to a desolate street beneath an overpass of the 110 Freeway. She drove real well with the gun to her head. She knew she was in for it when she got a good look at Killa's face and realized who he was. Suddenly her plans to get into trouble with her crew of hood-rats seemed minuscule. She was in deep shit and well aware of it. The screams and kicks that she thought would save her ultimately did her in. Killa had a reputation in the neighborhood and mothafuckas knew he'd do some crazy shit – anytime, anyplace. Especially for a price. He'd steal, kill, rape, whatever and everybody knew it. He made sure they knew it, so they'd remember not to ever fuck with him like they fucked with his big brother, Dimitri. Being a punk put him in the ground at Holy Cross Cemetery. He was only seventeen. *Seventeen mothafuckin' years old.*

Killa missed him painfully. They never played outside with the other neighborhood kids or hung out on corners instead of going to school. Not that they couldn't. Their mother wasn't thinking about them. They could be gone for days at a time and her life would go on like nothing was wrong. Dimitri was into school and getting good grades and Killa – Munjaro was his street name then – always looked up to him.

He was one smart nigga.

Dimitri looked after Little Munjaro the way their mother should have. Their dad was nowhere around and, as a result, their mother had a new man in the house every other week.

Dimitri and Munjaro were always playing and wrestling around. Munjaro looked up to his big brother in awe. He was "the man" in his opinion and he knew he could count on him for guidance. But Dimitri was no goody two shoes either. His big brother had lots of girlfriends. Munjaro was only ten years old, but he knew what a true playa was, even back then. That playa life was what eventually got Dimitri killed.

China, a girl who lived on their block, liked Dimitri big time. She always followed behind him after school, tryin' to give him some. China was only twelve years old and Dimitri wasn't with that. Too young. Dimitri had told her to get lost one time too many and, when China's feelings got hurt, she accused Dimitri of raping her. Killa remembered it like it was this morning.

One cold and foggy morning as they were on their way to school, Dimitri was surrounded by China's big brother, Troy, and his gang, the Del Reys. All young with something to prove. China was only twelve, but she was the biggest trick in the neighborhood. She already had two kids by two different fools on the block.

Dimitri didn't survive that day. They shot him five times in the stomach and once in the head. They wanted him to admit that he raped her. He died crying that he didn't do it.

Little Munjaro stood and witnessed the traumatic scene and they never even paid him any mind. In terror, he was able to slip away and run. He ran as fast as he could but soon he realized that no one had even come after him. He guessed that his brother's killers felt that he was no threat. They would someday know differently.

He had witnessed his own brother's murder and didn't speak on it once out loud. It was ten years later when he finally brought closure to his pain as only he could. Revenge was sweet when he finally did release his fury over Dimitri's execution. One by one he took them out – the ones that weren't already taken out by other consequences of living foul.

He got Troy first, but he was damn near dead anyway. The massive amounts of crack he'd smoked had him one foot in the grave; Killa just gave him an extra shove. He made sure they all knew it was Dimitri's little brother who was responsible for their suffering and that they were losing their life for having taken his.

His mother never got over Dimitri's death. She already drank all the time, but she started smoking crack no sooner than Dimitri's grave was filled.

Munjaro took care of himself when he saw that he couldn't depend on her. He hooked up with a hustling kid on the block named Domino and was soon selling dope on the corner. His mother was well aware of his illegalities, yet never once tried to stop him. In fact she reveled in it. The money was rolling in and it didn't take long before she started looking to Munjaro to take care of her habit and put food on the table.

Fuck her! Fuck China! Fuck Trixxy! Fuck all them ho's!

With every squeeze of Trixxy's neck, he thought about China. He'd taken care of her the same way. He'd relived the scene when he gave China her death sentence. Killa raped and tortured China for hours before he finally choked the life out of her. The whole time he was fucking her, he made her call him Dimitri and tell him how sorry she was for lying about being raped. He'd never forget the fear in China's eyes. It was the same fear that Trixxy had displayed just moments earlier.

During Killa's reflection, he frowned at one memory in particular after he murdered China in cold blood. Two days after he'd raped and killed China his dick swarmed with crabs. He itched so badly he couldn't stand it. He was almost tempted to put a match to his pubic hairs. He hoped that Trixxy was clean but doubted it seriously. He still remembered the stories from the homies about how she gave Craig herpes this past summer.

Nasty trick-ass-bitch. Bitches – Always tryin' to get the last word.

Killing Trixxy had been a breeze. She begged and begged for him not to hurt her. If she would've followed his instructions to shut the fuck up, she may have gotten away with her life. And a horrible life it would've been. Killa planned to leave her with emotional and physical scars that would've lasted a lifetime.

In the end, he'd left her bruised body in her beat up Volkswagen and walked to a bus stop about a mile away. She sat upright in the driver's seat with her head laying lifeless on the steering wheel as if she were asleep. *Now she's just another statistic. Another dead whore is how the cops will see it*, so he didn't worry about being hunted down. *No will care.* Killa had accomplished his mission. He made sure that Trixxy would never bother Dani again.

Chapter Thirteen

The Boutique ~ *Nothin' but love*

By the time Dani and Keera arrived at The Boutique, Tai, Saudia, Queenie and even Jody were in full party mode. Each was beautiful in her own right and had her own special reason to be pleased to spend an evening with good friends.

While Tai sculpted Keera's untamed curls into a neat, classy chignon, the others simultaneously primped, laughed and danced as they waited. As Tai smoothed over Keera's chic hairstyle, her mind drifted to thoughts of the next drag she'd take from the joint waiting in her office. It echoed seductively, calling her name out loudly and clearly.

She looked hot tonight. Her bold, blonde hair was cropped close to her scalp, enhancing her honey almond complexion. She was always experimenting with her hairstyles and colors and loved her latest choice.

Her dainty body was well fitted in a long-sleeved, backless, gold-beaded mini-dress. It's sexy, V-shaped, open back ended at the very spot where her back ended and her round rear began. Her classic slingback pumps added a perfect balance to the attention-grabbing garment. As usual, Tai made a statement that exuded her sexy and uninhibited demeanor.

***

Keera sat patiently in Tai's chair, her mind on earlier events. From her brief encounter with Chance's friend Thomas, during the flight to LA, having sex in the limo with Chance, then an enjoyable dinner at Crustacean, to the disappointment of not spending time with her dad and finally her disturbing encounter with Kevin. Keera frowned. *He is too weird for words.*

But now here she was with her extended family. Her girls. She looked around at her friends and exhaled a deep breath as she recognized how truly blessed she was. The scale that balanced the good and the bad in her life had tilted heavily toward the good. Damn the money and the fame. She had a wonderful father, a loving mate and a terrific group of friends who were as close to her as sisters. She closed her eyes and said a silent *'thank you'* to her Father in heaven. She hoped to always be as fulfilled as she was at this moment.

***

Saudia stood in the mirror primping and dabbing at her perfectly made-up face and hair. Her make-up looked so natural it was as if she wore none at all, yet she glowed like she'd been dipped in gold. Her wrapped braids lay in a neat bob against her gorgeously chiseled face, but she played with different ways to express them. She twisted them up in back, then tucked them behind one ear. Both looks were sexy. Ultimately she let her braids fall around her face once more in the original style where they hung just short of her shoulders.

She looked stunning in a black, off the shoulder, full-length evening gown with a slit up the side. Her five-inch heels provided the added height she'd always longed for. *If I could be five feet, eight inches barefoot, I would be bangin'.* Of that, she was convinced.

Saudia had always wanted to be taller than her average five-foot five height. She could visualize her full hourglass figure stretched to the slender proportions of her younger years. *I'mma start going to the gym right after Thanksgiving.* She'd been telling herself that one for three years in a row.

Saudia's mind wouldn't settle on anything in particular. The twins were safe at home in bed while being babysat by Simone, her neighbor's studious teenage daughter. All other concerns were on men, bills and work. Specifically, whether or not she would be promoted from receptionist to secretary of the A&R Department at Mayhem Records. There was a recent opening and she had not wasted a minute putting her bid in for the position.

Being her usual confident self, she decided that tonight would double as a celebratory night out. She didn't mention it to the others because she didn't want to risk jinxing her chance to move up the career ladder. Mayhem Records needed somebody with talent like hers that shouldn't be wasted answering telephones. Someday, she knew, they would recognize just that.

I look good tonight. If I don't meet my dream man at this function, then it's a hopeless cause, Saudia decided, her shoulders momentarily drooped in defeat.

Despite her confidence in career advancement, her thoughts were depressing in the romance department. Often thoughts of being happy with a new husband crept into her mind but would always conclude these thoughts with doubt and fear. Long ago, to get herself to a new level, Saudia had buried herself in self-help books and soaked in a lot of knowledge. She battled with accepting the realization that her accomplishments first began in the mind. Her thoughts were the forefront of her achievements. Until she did, she knew she would forever feel lonely and hopeless.

***

Queenie lounged comfortably on the sofa and flipped through the latest issue of *Honey* magazine, admiring the bold fashions displayed on its pages. She was surprised at how anxious she was about going to the Greenroom tonight. It was past time that she'd gone out strictly for fun, particularly since everything had evolved so firmly around her job lately. She was buried in work and hadn't come up for air in months. Her desire for male companionship was overwhelming and tonight would serve as her personal "welcome back to society" celebration.

Sporting a new short hairstyle and her usual gleaming smile, she looked and felt sexier than she had in a long while. She was going to work it tonight. Subtlety was her usual style, but tonight she would be daring. Queenie planned to open a conversation at the bar with a handsome stranger and invite a gorgeous onlooker to a brief interlude on the dance floor. Yes, tonight Queenie would transform into Queen Bee. In charge and taking no prisoners. It had been way too long since she entertained a male companion and she looked forward to the end of her dry spell.

***

Jody sat in the empty manicurist's chair and applied a clear coat of nail polish to her short, self-manicured fingernails. She was conservative, yet sophisticated, in her navy blue, silk pantsuit. Her freshly done hair lay bone straight, slightly bended under at the ends. It had grown since she had last had it professionally done about two months ago, and now reached the middle of her back. A big difference from the shoulder-length style she'd just grown out.

Even though she hardly wore make-up – only lipstick and a touch of mascara – she felt slightly uncomfortable being glammed up. She never thought herself attractive so she'd never felt the need to use beauty enhancers. *What's the point?*

As hard as she tried to fight her thoughts of Marcus, her now ex-husband and the father of her two children, it was a failed attempt. It had been three years since their divorce, yet she loved him as much as the day they were married. She cringed at the thought of his live-in girlfriend, Shelby. Jody communicated with Shelby regularly regarding the kids and as much as she didn't want to admit it, she found her too flawless. She was a beautiful person on the inside and out.

Jody wanted to be happy for Marcus. He and Shelby were painfully a perfect match. He was happier than Jody ever remembered him being when he was with her. It ate her up inside, but it was something she had to live with. She realized that no amount of praying could reunite her and Marcus as a couple. Their growing old together was not God's intent. She had to accept the fact that their divorce was a done deal.

Another revelation she had was that she wouldn't find a good man at tonight's party. A party filled with entertainers and sports stars was nothing but the devil's workshop as far as Jody was concerned. She had no intention of giving the evening any more credit than being an overdue night out with her girlfriends. She made a mental note to attend the special pre-Thanksgiving church service being held tomorrow, specifically to cleanse her system of the corrupt air she was sure to breath in at the club tonight.

***

Dani swayed to the music that pumped through The Boutique's airborne speakers. All she wanted to do was dance away her blues with a dance partner who could hang with her throughout the evening. No awkward conversation. No touching or sneaky feels. Just dancing.

She was comfortable in crème leather Capri pants and a cashmere halter-top, (crème as well) beneath a matching three-quarter inch leather jacket. Her beaded sandals refined the trendy outfit and added elegance, Dani's trademark.

Like Queenie, Dani had a flair for clothes, although both were unlike Keera who would prefer sweats and tennis shoes above anything, if she could get away with it. Dani always thought that it was ironic that Keera became a high profile supermodel despite her ill regard for being a fashion prima donna.

Dani adored her friends and felt blessed to have them to lean to during these difficult times in her life. She dreaded the thought of her Andrew being locked in a cage with murderers and thieves while she prepared to rub elbows with the rich, famous and ghetto fabulous, but she knew that his situation was a temporary one. In the meantime, she needed to be distracted.

This evening's escape would contribute to the balance she needed in her life. It would keep the scale from tipping over by carrying too heavy a load of worry and work, especially after the scene she had experienced earlier with Trixxy.

She could still see the relief on Jasmine's cute little face after she learned that her mother had gone and that she would be united with DJ over Grammy's house, Jasmine and DJ's affectionate term for their great-grandmother, Willie Mae. By the same token, Alfred, her grandpa, was called Papa. It was clear that Jasmine was happy with her newly arranged destination.

Dani would have a good time tonight as if her life depended on it. And essentially it did. As well as she knew her husband, she was sure he'd have it no other way.

Chapter Fourteen

Andrew ~ *Heartz of Men*

Drew's mysterious new cellmate entered the barred hell-hole without uttering a single word. Drew couldn't have been more pleased that the man was quiet. He hated fools who thought the size of their mouth equaled the size of their strength. Drew knew that the analogy couldn't have been more backwards.

Drew had since covered his ears with headphones blaring 2 PAC's "R U still down?" from a well worn CD. It was Drew's favorite of the CD's and tapes he'd either received from friends and relatives or in a trade with another music hungry inmate. Music kept his soul happy and it was legally accessible – one of the rare things he could do there without getting into any trouble. Speaking of trouble, Andrew's gut ached with bad thoughts. He was convinced that something was wrong on the outside. His nightmares had gotten worse and had grown strong enough to creep into his conscious thoughts, no longer hiding behind difficult sleep.

Tomorrow he would call Jacobs to find out about the private investigator they would hire. That is, if he could get to a phone. The jail had been on lockdown because of a series of riots and killings. Lockdown meant no privileges and lasted for however long his oppressors pleased.

He was surprised that some of the prisoners had lived so much of their adult lives institutionalized and that being on lockdown was no big deal for them. Their mentality was that of a much different world. A world that Andrew never wanted to know. An entire existence dictated by someone else. Day after day, hour after hour, minute by minute. He knew of men who didn't know what to do or how to act on the street because they were in jail more than they were out. It was a sad reality.

Drew also wanted to call his wife. He ached to hear her voice. He would always tell her that she was a diamond in the rough. She sparkled more and more every time he looked at her or even heard her voice. *How did I get lucky enough to marry my wife?* He believed it was destiny. Since the first day he met her he knew they'd be together, even if only as friends. Beautiful to look at, intelligent, stimulating conversation, scent always sexy. But above all else, when he looked into her eyes, he could see her soul. She was his soul-mate and he would die for her.

Andrew needed to get the hell out. Those drugs were not his and he was not going to give up on himself and let *them* win. *Them*, meaning the system and them, meaning whoever set him up. His boys were also working on his behalf right now. But sadly he found he really couldn't trust them whole-heartedly. *They were the main ones rollin' in my truck. It could be one of them who set me up,* he thought to himself. Doubt had crept in like the enemy that it was. He shoved away those thoughts, refusing to allow himself to go there. Somebody had to help him figure the shit out. He passed his lie detector tests. He had no prior felony arrests. *And I didn't fucking do it.*

He refused to give up on himself. He never had in the past, so why should he start now? Besides, he had a family to take care of and he truly missed his mama.

Chapter Fifteen

Kilamunjaro ~ *The Watcher*

Killa left Trixxy's raped and strangled corpse without a second thought, then caught the bus to his original destination. Dani's house. The bus ride offered the solace he needed to plan a proper introduction to Danielle. He was tired, but his arousal about finally meeting her face to face kept him wide-eyed.

Two bus transfers and a ten block stroll later, he had arrived. He slithered easily past the security gate, which surrounded Las Flores, and soon reached Dani's front porch.

Despite a rare case of butterflies, he enthusiastically fingered the doorbell. The time had come and he was eager to get things started. He was itching to tell Dani about Trixxy's demise. He was sure the news that he'd gotten rid of her, would capture Dani's heart completely.

The house was dark and he'd waited five minutes before he realized no one was going to answer.

"I know she didn't leave me," he said, as if she were expecting him.

His yearning to be near Dani was intense so he quickly resorted to "plan b".

He picked both door locks with ease, then effortlessly disengaged the home security system. He was disappointed that Drew had invested in what was in his opinion, one of the lamest alarms in the market. It was just another sign that it was meant for him to be there.

That nigga don't even know how to protect my queen. Dani needs a real man to take care of her right.

"Wheeeeew!" Killa let out a long whistle and rubbed his hands together greedily as he carefully scanned the living room. *The nigga do have taste though,* he observed. *And his pockets is fat, too.* Killa didn't realize how large Drew was really living until he stepped foot into his home.

Yeah, a nigga could get used to this shit. I always knew someday I'd be livin' like a king. I have finally found my castle.

The high ceilings gave the house a feel of endless space. Countless frames filled with Black art hung strategically on the living room walls. It wasn't the cheap stuff that Killa had seen peddled many times on the boulevard either. It was true art. The real deal. The tan leather couches were complimented by mahogany wooded tables. There were plants everywhere, but not too many. The polished hardwood floors in both the living and dining rooms on the bottom level were a statement of class.

The kitchen opened into the dining room, which was also immaculate with its blue marbled floor and matching tiled countertops. The large oval window invited rays of moonlight, which shone brightly into the breakfast nook in the west corner of the kitchen.

Killa felt strangely comfortable. Especially since he'd put himself in the position of possibly being arrested, or even getting his head blown off. After all, he was in Dani's home uninvited. And from what he knew about her, she didn't pull any punches. She was ruthless when necessary.

The neighborhood was full of stories about how she had to set straight a few of Drew's ex-broads during their early dating days. There were many who tried their hand at distracting Drew from his new mystery woman who had stolen his heart. But it was Dani he would be with and exclusively Dani. Ultimately, she made her point known and was not tested again.

As far as Killa knew, Dani could walk in at any given time and discover his inexcusable forced entry into her dwelling.

But she would understand. Especially when I explain to her how I fell in love with her from the first moment I saw her almost two years ago. And definitely after I tell her that I killed that bitch Trixxy. She won't have to worry about her no more.

Killa fantasized while looking at a picture of Dani on the mantel over the fireplace. It was among many other framed photos of what seemed to be her family and friends. *She looks so beautiful. So angelic.*

When he first saw her at Montel's wedding reception, his jaw dropped to the floor. She stood alone pouring herself champagne from one of many flowing fountains. After gawking for a few moments, Killa began to move towards her, but to his shock and disappointment, Andrew appeared out of nowhere and whisked her away. He watched them dance and whisper to each other after they'd moved to a far away table.

Before the night ended Killa learned Dani's name and that she was Andrew's wife and the mother of his son. On the block, in the neighborhood, Drew had always bragged about his mystery girl, Dani. Dani this and Dani that. Drew had gone from the neighborhood's Don Juan to Freddy Faithful. Everybody teased that she must have been a truly ugly bitch born with the best pussy in the world because Drew never showed her off like he did the other neighborhood tricks he used to date. But when Killa saw Dani, he instantly understood where Drew came from with the decision to keep her to himself.

Only a fool would risk losing her by bringing her around a flyy nigga like me, Killa bragged to himself.

The memory of that night haunted him until he took measures to dig deeper into the life of his obsession. Late one night, he followed Drew home from Rick's house, who just so happened lived two doors away from Killa. Discovering where they lived was just the beginning of his pursuit of Dani.

As he walked toward the winding staircase to check out the rest of Dani's house, he de-framed the photo he so admired and slipped it into his jacket pocket. *Now I can look at her whenever I want.*

He noticed the fully stocked bar in the scarcely lit room and managed to pour a healthy shot of cognac before continuing his tour. As he stomped up the stairs with his usual heavy footsteps, Killa daydreamed of living there with Dani.

Her kid can stay, too, if she wants, but he better stay out of my way. I'm going to be number one in her life.

Curiously, he entered the first room he encountered when he reached the top of the staircase. The first door on his right appeared to be the den. The room was furnished with a black leather couch and a recliner. In the center was a round, marble coffee table cluttered with women's magazines and children's books. There were more plants and yet another fully stocked bar for his convenience. He took full advantage and poured himself another stiff drink.

The entertainment center was enormous, covering an entire wall. It was fully equipped with a big screen TV, both a Playstation video game and a Nintendo 64, a complete stereo set and a DVD player. He spied a brand new Sega Dreamcast sat on the floor unopened, then inspected the scattered video games on the shelves and debated on whether or not he should help himself.

This shit is worth good money on the street, especially with Christmas right around the corner. But naw, I can't steal from Dani. That would be like stealing from myself.

He quickly moved on to the next room. His time couldn't be wasted dilly-dallying. On his left was a partially opened door. It was definitely a kid's room suited more for a little girl with its frilly curtains and bedspread and the dolls that sat erect on the shelves. He concluded that the room belonged to the little girl who was left here earlier by her now dead mother. Drew's daughter.

The room next door to hers was very obviously a little boy's room. There were bunk beds with race car bedspreads and a camping tent set up in the middle of the room. Killa assumed he had an adamant interest in sports as well for there were balls for every game imaginable scattered on the floor.

This lil' nigga got mo' toys than any kid in the neighborhood could dream of.

Next, he stared ahead at the last room on his right. His heart pounded and his hands were sweaty. He knew this was it, this was her bedroom. The place where she undressed and where she slept. *The bedroom that she will someday share with me.* He carefully opened the wooden shuttered double doors and gasped in awe. *This is fucking incredible.* He walked into the room in a state of awe and the large bathroom on his left called to him.

This bathroom is the bomb! I can't wait to get Dani into this big ass tub either! He thought to himself upon entering.

He wanted to make love to her like no other man had. His dick was hard just thinking about pleasuring her.

Finally, he examined her bedroom. *Nice. Real, real nice.* The canopy bed was big and inviting. He sat down softly on its edge and smoothed the comforter with his hands.

Real sexy. Oh yea, we gon' have a good time in this muthafucka.

Led by his hunger for more of her, he got up and started to go through the dresser drawers. The phone rang then, temporarily interrupting his mission. He stood frozen, unsure of whether or not to pick it up. Snapping out of it, he realized that he wasn't supposed to be there, let alone answer the phone. Relieved, he let out a deep sigh as the machine picked up.

"Hey, leave us a message and we'll get right back," said Dani's sexy, tape-recorded voice. Following the long beep, a man's voice spoke.

"Hey, Dani, it's Chance. I was just calling to see if Keera had been by yet. I was trying to catch her before me and my boys headed out. Aiight, then, I guess I'll see you guys at the Greenroom. Lata."

The Greenroom, huh?

Killa was familiar with the club's name, but had never been there before. It was a place he thought only celebrities and wanna be celebrities hung out. Apparently, it was time he found out for himself.

At least now he knew that Dani wouldn't be home for quite a while. And as far as he knew from trailing her for the past few months, she lived there alone with her son. With this new information, he could relax a little and take his time. He wanted to learn everything he could about Dani before meeting her. *What better way than to go through her shit?*

Killa had a ball playing around in her things. He felt her panties and rubbed them all over his face while he pretended to eat her out. She had the sexiest panties he had ever seen. They were sexy and classy at the same time. He noticed the dirty clothes hamper in her closet and did not hesitate to scavenge himself a pair of her unwashed panties. He stuffed those inside of his jacket as well. By now his inside pockets were full. Two pairs of panties – one clean, one not – a couple of pictures and a candle from her bathtub. Shrine material.

He continued to go through her things, smelling her clothes and admiring her shoe collection. Then he finally lay on her bed imagining her lying there with him. He removed his heavy jacket, his blue jeans and his checkered boxers. With her picture in his left hand, he simulated making love to her with his right. It felt so real. Like he was really inside of her warm body.

After pleasing himself three times and making sure not to leave evidence of his erotic behavior, he got dressed and headed back downstairs. Killa was pleased that each time he climaxed, his semen rested comfortably in the pair of her unwashed panties that were held tightly in his right hand. *Now our fluids have met and bonded. We are one.*

He wanted their first encounter to be a pleasant one and he reasoned that if she found him there, it would be far from that. *Time to bounce.* When he reached the first floor, he saw a door just off the dining room that he hadn't noticed before. He looked inside and found that it was an office. It looked to him like something off of TV. It had the feel of an African safari. He turned on the halogen floor lamp next to the door and dimmed the light just enough to get a glimpse of the room's contents. There were hanging pictures of giraffes and elephants and tall plants that resembled jungle trees.

On the hardwood floor lay a leopard skin rug, with a matching love seat and chairs that faced a large oak desk. There was also a computer, a phone and a fax machine on a separate table along the wall.

The big oak desk was home to everything from her kid's schoolwork to a family picture including Drew's little girl, magazines and bills. The small stack of bills stared him in the face and the telephone bill, which was on top, jumped out at him. It hadn't yet been opened but he stuffed it in his pants pocket. *She won't even notice it's missin'* Now he would not only follow her around, but with her telephone number he could call her any time he felt the urge. He was like a kid in a candy store after his little scavenger hunt was complete. Short of meeting Dani face to face, he came out like a bandit. Killa was now satisfied enough to leave. *Now where in the hell is The Greenroom?*

He had no idea, but he wasn't concerned because he knew the answer wouldn't be hard to come by. It was now just a matter of getting there, so he could once and for all be united with his one and only.

Chapter Sixteen

The Greenroom ~ *Ladies' Night*

The energy that surrounded the club was powerful. As soon as the ladies' limousine turned the corner it entered a dimension of magnificence. The line of shiny luxury cars and stretched-SUV-limousines moved slowly but surely towards the club's entrance.

They peered out of the limousine's tinted glass and observed the glittery scene. Saudia and Tai couldn't help but deliver jokes about scantily dressed hoochies and brothers in pimped-out gear. While the others laughed uncontrollably about the comedic cracks, Jody sat horrified. She trembled at the thought that she'd soon be bound inside of the devil's play place.

As the car inched forward, the women swigged down the last of their respective liqueurs and took final puffs of the sticky green marijuana-filled cigarettes, compliments of Keera.

"Anybody have any lotion, or body spray?" Keera asked as she touched up her lipstick.

"Yea, and gum too." Queenie added.

"Here." Dani answered, as she handed each a stick of spearmint gum and dabbed peach-scented lotion into Keera's palm. "Anybody else?" She asked as she lubricated her own hands with the lotion.

Tai, Queenie and Saudia all held out their hands like children waiting on to be inspected for dirt before dinner. Dani gladly obliged.

"What we do without our Danielle? My girl is ever-prepared." Tai quipped as she inhaled the lotion deeply and rubbed it in vigorously.

"Would you expect anything less?" Dani kidded.

"Jody, you all right over there?" Asked a concerned Queenie. She was well aware of Jody's club phobia and hoped she'd have fun despite it.

"I'm fine, just a little nervous," she admitted shyly.

"Aw, Jody you'll be fine. You're gonna have a good time." Queenie re-assured her in a sincere tone.

"Yea, I know," was all Jody could manage.

When they finally arrived at the entrance, they each graced the red-carpet with sophistication and class. Keera headed the line greeting acquaintances with double-cheeked kisses and friendly waves.

"You're beautiful as always, Keera." Charmed Brian, the Greenroom's infamous doorman.

"Thanks, Brian. And how are you tonight?" Keera charmed him right back. She flashed her radiant smile and gently held his cold hands into hers.

He kissed her hand and noticed Dani and the others standing behind her, all sparkling like diamonds.

"Hi ladies, long time no see!" He was excited to see Keera's friends. They were all so beautiful to him, especially Saudia.

"Hi Bri-an!" they chimed. They were all very fond of the young, well-dressed schmoozer. He was always very polite and courteous, which weren't common traits among most men in the nightclub scene. They "meet and greet" every night and most of the time it showed. But not Brian, he was a gem.

"Okay, ladies. I don't want to hold you out here in the cold. Go on inside and have a great time tonight. I know I don't have to tell you that it's *goin' awn* in there," he beamed. "For real though, it's like whoa!"

"Cool, is Chance here yet?" Keera hoped that he was.

"Yea, him and his crew got here about twenty minutes ago. He's probably already chillin' upstairs."

"Aiight, Brian. See you later, Babe." Keera then gave Brian another smooch on the cheek and breezed inside.

Dani, Tai, Queenie and Saudia cruised in behind her but Saudia couldn't get past before Brian stopped her for a hug.

"You know you my girl, right?" He gave her a warm hug and a knowing wink.

"Yes, Brian, I know, I know. Just holla' when you and the wifey break up," she whispered flirtatiously in his ear. Then came the affectionate smile followed by a light but lingering kiss on the cheek. Her eyes were bright and glittered like jewels. She left him salivating. For a minute he'd even forgotten where he was, he was so hypnotized by Saudia's essence. Non-existent was the clawing on his sleeves and taps on his back from anxious party-goers who wanted desperately to gain entry to the star-studded party.

On nights such as this, Brian was "the man." Aside from being on Keera's list or presenting a personally engraved invitation, without Brian's consent, one had no chance in hell of getting through the iron door.

There were small-scale, yet, well-known celebrity faces who Brian recognized and allowed an easy entry. Then there were "the regulars" who treated clubbing like a job, a life-style, and because they were in the know, were treated like underclass royalty.

Those who were indifferent about the Hollywood scene were usually the ones to get frustrated with the seemingly endless wait behind the velvet rope. They come to simply dance or exercise a rare urge to re-visit the "old days." They wouldn't think twice about leaving once their self-respect had been endangered.

And finally, there were those who wanted to rub elbows with the "beautiful people" and feel special for a night by association. Some became so intense about getting inside it was mandatory for Brian and his "guest list coordinator," Tanya, to be accompanied by two bodyguards. But regardless of the headaches and the tremendous pressure Brian endured, he loved every minute of it.

Inside, the club was off the hook. Everybody who was anybody in the ghetto-fabulous circles of Hollywood, not to mention professional sports, could be accounted for. The Black and the Beautiful were definitely in the house.

Guests included actors, singers, rappers, models, writers, music video and film directors, choreographers, sports stars, and of course the wanna be's. A "wanna be" was an industry groupie. They had no working role in any area of the entertainment industry, but badly wanted to be a part of the scene. They always know somebody, who knew somebody, whose cousin played on something, or played for someone who ultimately got them on the VIP guest list.

The dawn of the evening was occupied with champagne toasts, getting re-acquainted and networking among the few hundred guest. The club's fabric covered walls were a warm burnt sienna. The dim lighting gave it a relaxed ambiance, a sensation that some couldn't feel in their own home.

Although the place was packed, it still exuded a strong sense of intimacy. On the first floor were small, candlelit tables which were accompanied by deep burgundy velour chairs. For the larger groups, there were booths surrounded by velour sofas and oval coffee tables, suitable resting places for the abundance of drinks and food.

The center of the room was strictly for dancing and scores of people had already gotten started. The mixture of music, from hip-hop and R&B, to salsa, made the guests' heads bob and hips swing. There were buffet tables along an entire side of the club that were set up like a craft services cart on a movie set. They held everything from barbecued chicken to caviar. Unlimited Cristal champagne was served by ever-present drink waiters and a fully stocked bars with liqueurs were strategically located on both floors.

Upstairs, in the VIP lounge, the scene was quite a different one. Two muscle-bound bouncers stood at the bottom of the stairs allowing entrance only to those who wore a special silver wristband. There was a mixture of people included in this elite group. Some were Chance's friends, some Keera's and some were mutual friends and acquaintances of both. But all were enchanting.

In every corner a celebrity settled. Others comprised of behind the scenes movers and shakers, entourage members and plugged-in groupies. Hollywood kisses and brotherly fist pounds were generously exchanged, as were champagne toasts and energetic conversation. In the blind spots of security's vision, marijuana blunts were rolled, toted and passed and ecstasy pills ingested. The room was high with a reckless spirit, which was hypnotizing to say the least.

Keera, Dani, Queenie, Tai, Saudia and Jody were seated at their private table and having a grand time. Keera played the good hostess and flitted from table to table, but the table she shared with her friends served as home.

They had just finished their third bottle of Cristal and all were feeling playful, except Jody who sipped Shirley Temples with extra cherries. She was at war with the urge to have a glass of the expensive champagne being generously circulated, and so far she was winning.

Chance occupied a separate table right beside theirs. He and his friends laughed about events in the years past when they'd all been newly acquainted. Aside from Chance's brother Jeff, they were mostly friends of Chance's from his college ball-playing days. There were a few new friends in the clique as well including two rap stars, a popular actor and three ball players from other professional teams. They were all dressed to a tee, immaculately groomed and smelling sexy, the way a man was supposed to represent. The table was full of gorgeous, physically fit, financially stable brothas and Saudia, Tai and Queenie each had her eyes on her own personal draft pick.

"Keera, I didn't know Chance knew Rhetoric," Saudia said, her eyes fixated on the rugged, yet charming, rap artist.

"Yea, girl, they're real tight," Keera answered. "Would you like an introduction?"

"Hell yea," Saudia said, hungrily. He was just her type. Young, sexy and nothing but trouble.

"Well, while you playin' the datin' game, what's up with the cutie pie wearing the expensive gray suit and the killer smile?" Tai asked and casually nodded toward one of the other men at Chance's table.

"Who Jeff? Girl, puh-leeze, that's Chance's brother. You don't want none of him, and anyway that's his wife sittin' right over there." Keera pointed to the pretty, but homely, woman who sat alone at a nearby corner table nursing an apple martini.

"Why she over there sittin' by herself?" Dani asked. She had met Jeff's wife, Terry, a few times before and found her pleasant and friendly.

"Girl, they're probably fightin' again. It's sad, but they're havin' some major marital problems."

"Oh," Dani replied. "Well, she's better than me 'cause I would've stayed my behind at the house. Not sittin' up in somebody's face that obviously doesn't want to be bothered."

Jeff boldly had a fabulous time with his brother and his friends while his wife sat neglected and bored. "Let's invite her over," Dani suggested.

"I already did, girl, but she said she was sitting there waiting on Jeff to come over so they could *talk.*"

"Fuck that," Tai interjected. "Why she gotta wait on his sorry ass? He ain't even payin' her no mind."

"O-kaaaay? What she needs to do is to get her ass out on that dance floor and forget about that fool and his ego," Saudia added.

"Yea, I hate to say it, but the ego is gonna be magnified tonight since he's with his boys. He's gonna play the role even if he's not feelin' it," Queenie said, getting in her two cents.

"Well, she should know better than any of us. She's been his wife for five years now. She knows exactly what she's in for."

The girls sat and shook their heads with disapproval.

"Well, then, hell, forget that fool. What about him over there? He looks good enough to eat." Tai pointed more obviously this time at yet another man at the male populated table.

"Oh, him? That's Thomas, girl. He's cute, but he's not your type," Keera said nonchalantly.

"Why not?" Tai wanted to know. "Is he married?"

"Nope."

"Gay?" She asked, scrunching her nose disapprovingly.

"Nope."

"Then what's wrong with the brotha?" asked a now frustrated Tai.

"He's too nice. You'd be bored with him in two seconds."

"Oh," Tai said defeatedly, knowing that Keera was right. "Yea, y'all know my men gotta have that *edge*."

They all nodded knowingly.

"But he'd be a good match for you, Queenie." Keera said, looking at her friend with a devilish grin.

"Yeah, Q, he looks like your type, girl. He's real handsome," Jody said, finally adding something to the conversation.

"Well, actually, I did have my eye on him." Queenie sported a sly grin. "Okay. Introduce me."

Everybody looked at her with eyebrows raised.

"What?" Queenie asked.

"Nothing, Q." Saudia said. "It's just not like you to be so – "

"Willing," Tai said, finishing Saudia's sentence.

"O-kaaay? Let me get him now before you change your mind," Keera said, quickly rising from the table.

"Pssst. Don't forget about me, girl." Saudia gestured to Keera before she could plant herself at the other table. She whispered softly trying not to attract attention from the men's table. She was very anxious to meet Rhetoric. She loved his music and couldn't wait to explore the man behind it.

"Well, I don't know about y'all but I'mma try my luck on out on the dance floor. I can't get no action up here." Tai stood, straightened her short dress and promptly made her way down the stairs. Her mission – to find the eligible bachelor of her dreams, or at least one that she could have a memorable evening with – was on.

"Aiight, girl, but don't make us have to come look for you. Be good," Dani said. She knew Tai well and that she was good for taking off without saying a word to anyone. "Ay, we came togetha so we're leavin' togetha!" Dani yelled just before Tai made her exit.

Tai looked back with a sly grin before she disappeared.

"Oh my God, Rhetoric is lookin' over here," Saudia said, suddenly nervous. "How do I look y'all?"

"Gorgeous, as always," Queenie said.

"What about me? Thomas is looking, too," Queenie whispered.

"Both of you look fantastic. Like you just stepped out of a photo shoot," Dani said trying to ease their fears of rejection.

***

Jody sat and observed the activity that surrounded her. She thought it was shameful the way her friends picked out men as if they were steaks on a menu. *Filet Mignon or T-bone?* She was ready to go home and was sorry that she didn't drive her own car.

"I'll be back. I'm going to the bathroom," Jody announced. But they were all so wrapped up in Keera's conversation with Chance and the guys that no one heard her.

The bathroom upstairs was packed with primps and gossips. Jody decided to go down the stairs to the main floor and try her luck there. She hadn't realized how crowded the club had become since she'd been upstairs in the VIP lounge. She weaved through the crowds and finally arrived at the larger bathroom, which she found even more crowded than the one upstairs. By now her urgency to pee had gotten worse. She spotted a door marked "Office" just around the corner and decided to intrude. She hoped the room was empty and with a nice, clean bathroom inside available for her use.

"Yes!" Jody said aloud as she discovered the door was unlocked. She was even more shocked that there actually was a private bathroom inside. *God is good!*

Without trepidation, she walked into the dimly lit room with her need to use the bathroom at the forefront of her mind. She had absolutely no idea that she had been followed.

***

Tai eyed a clean-cut gentleman at the bar. He watched her with hopes that she'd come his way. *Ooh, a sponsor,* she thought victoriously. A sponsor was a name the girls adopted years ago for men whose main purpose was to pay for drinks from the bar. Tai was sure that this guy fit the bill. She moved slowly and confidently to the bar and wasted no time.

"Hi." She smiled and blushed seductively.

"How you doin' beautiful? I'm Walter, and you are?"

"Thirsty." She answered without apology.

He loved a blunt woman. He also thought she looked delicious and he wanted a bite.

"Whatever the lady is having, it's on me," Walter told the foreign bartender who seemed preoccupied.

Tai followed the bartender's gaze and noticed Lana Devoreau, an investigative reporter from channel four's entertainment new show, Hot Topic. She was a beautiful sister with wild curly hair, big brown eyes and flawless skin the complexion of butterscotch. Lana continued to primp despite the onlookers. She got off on the attention. She held her audience captive while she re-applied a coat of glassy bronze lipstick.

Tai wasn't impressed.

Puh-leeze, you are not all of that, honey.

She quickly dismissed Lana with a quick roll of the eyes.

"Bartender!" She yelled, above the music and loud chatter, "I'll have a Thug Passion, please!"

She then turned to Walter, flashing her Pepsodent smile.

"Thank you for the drink. That was very sweet of you." She had already given him the quick once over and decided that for starters, he was good for conversation over a drink.

"No, *thank you,*" he said, in a too deep baritone. "Bartender, please allow this beautiful lady to order on my tab this evening. Unlimited," he said proudly.

"Ooh, handsome and a big spender too?" Tai asked teasing him mercilessly. She already knew that he wasn't her type but he obviously didn't mind spending his money. She sipped on her drink, a Thug Passion made with Cristal champagne and Hennessy and Alize'. She then looked at Walter carefully as he spoke.

Damn this nigga's breath is of the hinges! Do you brush your teeth with feces, Muthafucka?

Tai couldn't believe how foul his breath was. It had now invaded all of her personal space and she was suddenly on the verge of fainting. Oblivious to his personal hygiene crisis, Walter continued to breathe words into Tai's face. The deathly stench worsened amidst sips of his Remy Martin cognac. He went on and on.

"I got a deal on the table that I'mma be signin' tomorrow morning, as a matter of fact," he said, smacking his lips together in a quick motion as if tasting his words.

Now Tai was really sick. She was sitting at the table with a frontin' wanna be. That was not her style. As she turned her head in search of uncontaminated air to breathe in, she saw Chris who looked damn good. Better than she ever remembered him looking before.

Did he get a haircut? Is it the suit?

She contemplated the motives for her attraction to him but would never admit to the reason. She ached for some of that stuff that he had given her earlier. Strangely, the weed she bought from him after their smoke out together didn't have the same effect.

"Excuse me. I see a friend that I must speak to. Oh, and thank you for the drink," she said as she dropped a ten-dollar bill on the table. She didn't want to give him any excuse to further pursue her.

Tai walked away in the same seductive manner in which she arrived. Walter's eyes followed her lustfully until she disappeared into the crowd.

***

Saudia and Rhetoric were deep in conversation at their own private, dimly lit table in the VIP lounge.

He is even more beautiful up close and personal, she thought, as he spoke enthusiastically about his upcoming CD.

"So, see it's 'bout be hot off da grill, ya' know what I'm sayin'?" His voice was rough, matching his style. He looked at her and licked his already moist lips. He had seen the look in her eyes many times before. *She wants me.*

Just as Saudia was about to turn on the charm full power, she was interrupted by Rhetoric being forced from his chair.

"Muthafucka, what are you doin' here? You said you was flyin' out tonight!" The girl was pissed off.

Saudia was startled, caught completely off guard by the interruption.

"Aw, Baby, cummon? It's my boy's birthday and shit. You know I had to represent," he said in a smooth tone. He seemed to be completely at ease with the situation.

The girl locked eyes with Saudia and gestured for her to excuse herself from the table. The longer Saudia stared she realized that the petite, long-haired, dark complexioned beauty was none other than Karma, the newest "it girl" in the female rap game. Saudia rose from her seat and excused herself politely. *I don't want no shit.* She had heard stories about Karma and did not want to be the supporting actress in her next drama. By now Keera and Dani had peeped the scene and had made it over to the now intense table.

"Hey, Karma, girl. What's up?" Keera asked, giving the young Ms. Attitude a hug.

"Same old thing, Keera. You know this nigga told me he was leaving for New York tonight?" She turned to Rhetoric and glared.

He returned the look by shrugging his shoulders as if he didn't know what the problem was. After all, he had only been chillin' with Karma for a few weeks and he didn't consider her to be his woman.

"I didn't know you guys were a couple," Keera said, looking at both of them expectantly. She didn't appreciate the disturbance that had taken place and wanted to nip it in the bud.

"Yea, me and Rhetoric been together for a while now. Ain't that right, Baby?" She popped her gum incessantly and turned to him with a deadly stare.

"Well, you know we been kickin' it and shit. We cool."

Dani and Saudia took a few steps back, sensing that Karma was about to erupt.

"We been *kickin' it?* And what do that mean? *Kickin' it?* You think I be fuckin' niggas just to *kick it!*" She got loud and attracted even more stares. Her neck rolled and her jeweled hands flew in the air with as much passion as her tone.

Keera gently took Karma's arm hinting for her to stay calm.

"Baby, don't trip," Rhetoric said. "You know how I feel about you."

"Then what was you doin' *kickin'* it all cozy like wit' *her*?" she said, in her thick New York accent, turning and pointing at Saudia.

"We was just talkin', that's all. It was business, girl. She work for Mayhem Records and shit."

Karma didn't look completely convinced, but she was satisfied that he'd made an effort to explain – enough to finally take a seat in the chair next to Rhetoric and crack a smile. Keera, Dani and Saudia took this as their cue to leave.

"Can you believe that shit?" Saudia asked.

"Girl, I am so sorry to have put you in the middle of that mess. I had no idea they were *kickin' it*."

They laughed heartily as they sat back down at their table. They looked around and noticed that Terry and Jeff were in an intense conversation at their table and that Chance and his friends had left theirs.

"Well, fuck you, too, Jeff!" Terry screamed, then stood and ran down the stairs in tears.

Jeff did not move. He just sat shaking his head in his hands.

Keera got up to go and see about Terry. "I'll be back, y'all. I'm gonna see if she's okay.

"Okay." Saudia and Dani answered in unison.

"Hey, where's Queenie and Jody?" Saudia asked Dani.

"Queenie is dancing with that guy Thomas and I don't know where Jody went. I think she went downstairs, too."

"Good, I hope she's having a good time. After that shit with Karma and Rhetoric, I'm about ready to go." Saudia said, upset that her conversation with Rhetoric was cut short.

I didn't even get a chance to charm the nigga, she thought, dissatisfied.

"Okay? I'm ready to go, too. I'm hella tired. I'm thinkin' I may even pick the kids up from Willie Mae's tonight instead of tomorrow after work. The way I feel now, I may not even go in."

"Kids?" Saudia asked, stressing the "s" at the end.

"Yeah, girl, didn't I tell you? Trixxy came over drunk and unannounced and dropped Jasmine off with me so she could go fight some girls who attacked her in the store."

"Whaat? That girl needs some serious help."

"It's really sad, Saudia. Jasmine deserves better."

"Are you guys gonna keep her from now on?"

"I'm gonna try to do something. Just pray for us please."

Queenie came back upstairs and sat at the table next to Saudia.

"Weeell?" They asked her in unison in hopes that she and Thomas had hit it off.

"Weeell, the man is as gay as he wanna be." She let out a heavy sigh, expressing her disappointment.

"Gay?" Saudia asked in disbelief. "Are you sure? Did he tell you that?"

"He don't have to tell me. I know, trust me." Queenie was not happy.

"Damn. Now I'm really ret to go." Saudia stated. "This night has been too much for me."

"Me, too," Queenie agreed. "I saw Tai on the dance floor, but where's Jody and Keera?

"Keera went downstairs to talk to Chance's sister-in-law, but we don't know where Jody went," Dani said.

"I'll go down and look for her. Poor thing. She's probably hiding in the corner somewhere, clutching her Bible." Saudia giggled.

"Saudia, you are so wrong," Dani scolded.

"I'll go get Keera to arrange for the limo driver to drop us all off. I'm sure she's leaving with Chance in his car."

Just then Keera walked up and sat down.

"Terry is in bad shape, you guys. She was cryin' so hard I couldn't understand a word she said. Finally I put her in a cab and sent her home."

"Jeff is still sitting over there. Are you gonna tell him she's gone?" Queenie asked.

"No. I'm sure he already knows. And if I go talk to him, I'mma end up cursin' his ass out for doin' her like that."

"Well, he looks upset," Queenie observed.

"And he should be. That at least tells me that he's human."

"Keera, are you going home with Chance 'cause we old lady's are about ready to go," Dani said.

"Yeah, you guys can roll in the limo. He's parked right out front. I'll walk y'all out. Where's Jody, Tai and Saudia?"

"Saudia went to go find Jody. She's been gone most of the night, come to think of it. And Tai could be anywhere. You know how she does it," Queenie replied.

"Come on. Let's all go downstairs and look for them," Dani suggested.

When Keera, Dani and Queenie got downstairs, they were greeted by an anxious Tai.

"Aiight, y'all I'm out." She smiled mischievously.

"We're leavin', too. You're riding with us, right?" Dani asked suspiciously.

"Actually, I have a ride." Tai said pointing to Chris who stood by the door making a call on his cell phone.

"And who is he?" Queenie asked, not liking the idea that her friend was leaving with some strange man.

"He's my friend, Chris. We go way back." Tai answered, hoping that her friends didn't recognize Chris from his earlier visit to The Boutique.

"So you know him, huh? Why haven't we ever heard of Chris?" Keera asked, sharing Dani and Queenie's skepticism.

"Yea, I know him. I wouldn't be leavin' with him if I didn't. Come on, y'all. Give me some credit."

"Well, he is *fine,*" Keera said, lightening her tone.

"Tru dat, tru dat," Dani added, while serving fist taps to her girls.

"So, since you guys approve, can I go now?" Tai asked, impatiently checking to make sure that Chris was still waiting. He had a tendency to be inconsiderate. She feared he would leave her considering his restlessness.

"I'mma call yo' ass first thing in the morning and you betta be at home," Dani said in an authoritative tone.

Tai gave Dani a sly wink and bid her farewells to them all. Chris was gesturing for her to hurry up and she didn't want to keep him waiting any longer.

Suddenly Saudia appeared, her eyes followed Tai as she rushed towards Chris.

"Where is she going?" Saudia asked, quickly recognizing Chris from the shop. "Strike the question," she said, too preoccupied to investigate the issue further. "I don't even want to know. You guys are not gonna believe this."

"What?" they asked simultaneously.

"Come and see for yourselves," Saudia said, as she led them through the crowded dance floor.

When the ladies reached the center of the dance floor, they could not believe their eyes. Jody was sitting on a handicapped man's lap while he twirled them around the dance floor in his wheel chair. Their jaws dropped to the floor in awe. Jody was laughing and moving to the beat of the music as if she hadn't a care in the world. The man in the wheel chair was well dressed in all black and extremely good looking. His upper body was well built and he had a beautiful smile.

Happy to see that Jody was having a good time, the girls found themselves standing on the sidelines cheering her on.

"Go Jody! Go Jody! Go Jody!"

They had also inspired others to do the same. Jody and the handicapped man were now in the spotlight. When Jody realized the attention they had drawn, she excused herself from her new friend's lap. She received cheers and claps as she walked over to her friends, red-faced. Her wheel-chaired friend followed her just as he did when he first saw her. He'd waited for her outside of the bathroom and charmed her onto the dance floor despite her having refused him several times.

He cleared his throat to get her attention.

"Oh, I'm sorry. Everybody, this is Daniel. Daniel, this is everybody," Jody offered a vague introduction.

"Girl, ain't you got no home trainin'?" Dani asked an embarrassed Jody.

"Hi, I'm Dani, this is Saudia, Queenie and I'm sure you know Keera."

"You're a friend of Chance's, right? Daniel Homby?" Keera asked. "You played for the New York Jets a few years ago?"

"That's me. The one and only. It's nice to meet you all. Especially you, Stephanie." He said, looking at Jody.

"Stephanie?" Saudia asked, verbalizing what the rest of her friends were thinking.

"Um, actually my name is Jody." She admitted to Daniel after her attempt at giving a false name was ruined. She gave Saudia a threatening look. "I apologize for being dishonest, but I'm not accustomed to meeting men in clubs," she answered truthfully.

"Especially men in wheelchairs, right?" Daniel asked with a chuckle.

"Oh, no, it's nothing like that. You're great." Jody blushed.

"Well, can this great guy get your phone number?"

The girls silently nodded yes to Jody as she looked to them to bail her out.

"Of course. Let me get a pen," Jody said, defeatedly.

"Here's one." Saudia said, pulling a pen from her miniature sized purse. It was the pen she had hoped to use to give Rhetoric her number.

"And here's a napkin." Queenie grabbed a napkin from a nearby table.

Jody felt trapped. She didn't want to give the man her number, but what else could she do? And he was a friend of Chance's so she felt obligated to give the real digits.

"Okay, here you go." Jody said, limply handing a smiling Daniel the napkin, which was now graced with her home telephone number. It was times like this she wished she'd invested in a pager.

They all said their "good-byes" and "nice to meet you's" to Daniel and headed out the door to the waiting limousine.

"Okay, you guys, I'll talk to you tomorrow. Are we still having bridge night at Dani's tomorrow night?" Keera asked, giving each of her friends a hug as Wendell, the chauffeur, dutifully helped them inside the limo.

"Yep. Everybody at my house at seven tomorrow. And remember it's potluck."

"Where's Tai?" Jody asked, noticing she was missing.

"Don't ask," answered Queenie. The others giggled. They knew Jody would have a holy fit to hear that Tai had left with a man.

"Okay, I'll see you guys tomorrow. I'mma go find Chance so we can go, too. Love you guys," Keera said, as she waved goodbye.

"Love you, too," they chimed.

As the stretch limousine pulled off, Keera trotted back inside the club to find her man. She hadn't seen him in a while and was curious as to where he'd disappeared.

***

Killa had a terrible evening. He spent hours outside The Greenroom trying numerous ways to be allowed entry into the well-guarded club. The security was extra tight and Killa had not been successful. He even went so far as to talk a guy, who held an invitation, into helping him with his supposedly flat tire.

When the poor man went into the lot where Killa's car was parked, he was banked over the head with a toolbox and his invitation was stolen from him as he lay unconscious on the ground. To Killa's dismay, the invitation had the guy's name engraved on it, which had to be accompanied by a valid picture ID. Even if Killa would have taken the man's ID to complete his scheme, he knew he'd never pass for the unconscious white guy.

He finally gave up trying and decided to sit in his car and wait for Dani to come out. He parked closer to the club's exit and fell into a Hennessy-induced sleep at the wheel long before Dani made her exit.

***

Keera couldn't find Chance anywhere. She asked everybody and no one had seen him. She even had DJ Merlin announce for him to meet her near his booth, but after twenty minutes he didn't show. She was pissed and at the same time worried. She was still receiving those threatening and perverted letters and the thought that someone waited for her in a dark corner remained in the back of her mind. On top of that, Chance had many crazed fans to contend with as well. She circled the large club and saying her good-byes to departing guests, she sat in a comfy chair and removed the shoes from her tired feet. *Chance, where are you, Baby? I hope you're okay.*

Meanwhile, Chance had entered the back door after having escaped to fulfill his urges. After entering, he quickly slipped into a nearby bathroom and proceeded to cleanse his privates of the odor that he was sure Keera would recognize. He took a breath and prepared to be interrogated by his girlfriend. He was sure she'd been looking for him, so he prepared to face her with another set of lies. He hated to lie to Keera. He loved her very much but he knew she wouldn't understand if he came clean about his fooling around. Living a lie was getting harder. He wanted badly to live his life truthfully. For now though, the charade had to continue and strangely he knew it wouldn't be for long. He spotted Keera half asleep in a chair near the now empty floor. He hadn't realized how late it had gotten and knew that his excuse had to be a good one. He exhaled another deep breath and approached Keera with his fingers crossed.

Chapter Seventeen

Danielle ~ *Leave a Message*

It was Wednesday morning, the day before Thanksgiving. Dani had already hit the snooze bar three times debating on whether or not to go into the office. *I really need to go.* Everyone else had the day off so it would be painless. The thought of actually getting some work done without constant interruption was appealing.

Dani experienced the worst sleep the night before. After being chauffeured home from the club, she took a quick shower and hopped into bed. Following an internal debate, she called Willie Mae from the limo and told her she'd pick the kids up on her way from work. Then she called Trixxy, who didn't answer the phone, to tell her to pick Jasmine up the next evening. It was two-thirty a.m. and Dani had decided that it was too late to drag those two out of bed.

She tossed and turned all night after an eerie dream about Drew. He was fighting for his life in an ambulance after being brutally stabbed or shot, she couldn't tell which. Topping off the bad dreams, her sleep had also been invaded by a prank caller. Her phone rang every half an hour, but when she answered there was no one on the other end. Finally after the umpteenth call, she turned the ringer off altogether.

After a few moments of silent thoughts and dream recaps, Dani finally got out of bed. Her first agenda was to call and check on DJ and Jasmine. Willie Mae said that they were still asleep and that she would see Dani when she came by after work. Next, she did a bed check on Tai just as she promised. To her disappointment, she was not at home. *Hmmph, I'll deal with her later.*

It took no time for her to shower and dress. Without DJ there to share her preparation time, she was out of the house in a flash.

The office was a breeze. Extra Strength Tylenol did wonders for her headache. *Too much champagne last night.* Her work was distracted by thoughts of Andrew and what was up with those prank phone calls. When she confided to Willie Mae about them this morning, she said it was probably a wrong number. Dani thought they were strange and stored it in the back of her mind for future reference. With Andrew gone, caution was key.

She worked for three hours, then decided it was time to go. The project at hand was for an important client, but if she stayed there any longer, the work would've suffered. She took her work home with her as usual where she would confer with Scott who assisted her on the campaign.

Dani and her girls decided that they would get together for a few hours tonight, kids and all. She spoke briefly with Keera and according to her, she and Chance had been in bed since they came home from the club this morning.

You go girl. Somebody needs to be getting some 'cause my sheets are as cold as ice.

Everyone was coming over to just hang out and chill. As long as Dani didn't have to drive anywhere, it was all good. She was exhausted. Tonight's get together, or Bridge Night, as they liked to call it, was supposed to be a pre-Thanksgiving potluck, but Dani hadn't confirmed with anyone about what was on the menu. She hoped not turkey and dressing. She was sure Willie Mae would cook enough Thanksgiving food tomorrow to carry them into the new year.

After Dani left the office, she stopped at the Beverly Center to shop for Thanksgiving gear. She shopped for herself and DJ, and also bought Drew a few things so he'd be stylin' when he returned home. He was a clotheshorse and would appreciate the gesture. *Spoiled rotten.*

She thought about shopping for Jasmine, but remembered that Trixxy refused to allow her to spend the holiday with her and DJ. She pondered on the fact that Trixxy hadn't called or paged her all day in regards to getting Jasmine. She'd left Trixxy a message to come tonight as opposed to the afternoon and Dani was sure Trixxy would give her grief, strictly out of spite.

It was now time to pick up the kids. Driving home from the Beverly Center was a chore. Bumper to bumper traffic down every street Dani tried. Inching along, she finally entered the freeway. She headed south on the 405 freeway and popped in the Isley Brothers' Greatest Hits CD and zoned. She was in one of those moods.

Now, on Crenshaw Boulevard, at the Coliseum Street light, she heard furious honking. When she looked over, she saw some lunatic in a Cadillac who smiled and waved as if she knew him. Dani turned back to face front when the strange man yelled, "*do you remember me?*" She couldn't translate what else he had said and she didn't want to.

Her curiosity got the best of her though, and she looked over at him again. She still didn't recognize him at all. She tried to be nice so she smiled and nodded hello. He gestured for her to pull over, but was left hanging. *I'm not pullin' over for nobody's stranger.*

To her, he looked to her like comedian Martin Lawrence's character Jerome from his defunct show "Martin." He wore a perm and he had rotten teeth as well. *I said, Jerome's in the house!*

Dani laughed as she pictured the outlandish character. When the light turned green, she looked at him, waved goodbye and floored it. She did about seventy miles per hour until she disappeared into the hills, leaving him in the dust.

Chapter Eighteen

Kilamunjaro ~ *Skandalouz*

I can't believe she dissed me like that. Killa was confused. He thought for sure that getting Dani's attention, while in traffic, would initiate a conversation. He at least thought she would pull over and chat with him for a minute. But instead she took off like a bat out of hell and while he was in mid sentence. He tried to tell her that he was a friend of Drew's. he felt that would make her comfortable and that she would want to talk. *I followed her all day for this?*

It seemed that after the dry run from the night before at The Greenroom, he was even more determined to meet her. He woke up at four a.m. in his car and found that he had missed Dani – and everyone else for that matter. He then drove straight to her house and parked.

He made several attempts to call her from his illegally chipped cell phone, but each time she answered, he lost his nerve to speak. No matter how cold it got while he sat in his car – all morning, he waited. He wanted to know her every move and he couldn't risk missing out on anything by going home. He dared her to bring another man around.

He didn't get to see her at the club but he wanted to make sure she didn't meet anyone who would threaten his position. He was nice to Drew by not killing him. He would get pleasure from his envy after he took his wife. But a new man wouldn't survive Killa's jealousy. He felt close to her as if they were already lovers. He wanted to love her and protect her from any harm. He was still very proud of getting rid of Trixxy and anxious to tell Dani all about it.

Killa was taken by Dani's beauty at first glance this morning. His view was from quite a distance but his industrial strength binoculars were quite helpful. She drove straight to her Beverly Hills office and when she got out of the car, his heart pounded.

She was dressed casually in a black and white Adidas sweat suit with matching sneakers. Her hair was pulled back into a ponytail and she wore dark sunglasses. Long ponytails drove him wild. He wanted to put his face in hers, anticipating the strawberry scented shampoo that was in her shower. He thought the smell was delicious, but not more delicious than he knew she would taste. He longed to help her with her briefcase, which seemed too heavy for her to carry, along with her purse and the several books, which filled her delicate arms.

Like a recurring scene from last night's Greenroom experience, the security guard would not allow him entry to the building. He said that it was closed for the holidays and only employees were allowed inside. So he waited, again, for the entire three hours she was inside. When she pulled off in her convertible Jag, he was right behind her debating on an opening line. In the mall, again, he trailed her. He watched as she bounced from store to store, pondering this item or that. There were too many people around, he felt, for him to make his move.

Finally, in traffic, he did a honking and waving routine, which got him absolutely nowhere.

Frustrated, he parked in an active McDonald's parking lot. Seeing Dani and having such close contact had gotten him excited. With her fresh in his mind, he unzipped his pants and felt the boldness of his groin. His nature was so hard from his fantasizing about Dani that he had no choice but to somehow satisfy his yearnings.

He reached behind his seat and retrieved a large container of petroleum jelly. He spread a wad of the lubricant onto his palm and stroked himself as he watched the kids play in the McDonald's play area. He noticed a little girl who could've easily been a young Dani. His strokes became harder and more intense in Killa's slippery hand. The vigorous rubbing sounded as if he were getting the real thing. His moans so high pitched they resembled those of a woman. Finally, he exploded as his thoughts of making love to the young Dani became too real.

He grabbed a towel from the back seat of his cluttered car and proceeded to wipe away the mess he had made. He kept the petroleum jelly in his car just for this reason. He often had to pull over to fulfill his sexual urges. The lubricant made the act of masturbation much more sensual. It also kept his hands from blistering as they had done in the past.

He decided to go home. *Maybe I'll get drunk and fuck Jackie.* Killa was still horny and knew that it would be a little longer before he and Dani got to a sexual stage in their relationship. To him, fucking Jackie was like fucking an elephant. *She is so fucking nasty.* He grimaced at the thought of her blubbery thighs, filled with dents and pockets of cellulite. Jackie had stopped caring for herself long before Killa met her. At least then, she kept up her appearance. Not anymore. Now, she rarely even bathed.

When Killa met Jackie, she was pretty, petite and always smelled edible. She was his biggest moneymaker on the street. He couldn't understand what turned her into the monster she was today. She'd blown up like Free Willie one and two. The only way he enjoyed sex with her was in the ass. He knew she liked it too, even though she screamed the whole time. Her screams turned Killa on even more than the sex. He felt if she was really in pain, she had the strength to free herself from him if she wanted to. As far as he was concerned, Jackie knew her place and she knew better than to mess with "the man."

Killa stopped at a nearby liquor store to pick up yet more of his favorite cognac. *Enough Hennessy and I'll ride her Free Willie ass 'til the sun comes up.* He made a mental note to remember the Vaseline. It seemed to help her blisters, too.

When he got home, Jackie was nowhere to be found. Killa entertained the fact that she'd left for good, until he found the note she had left on the refrigerator.

Munjaro, I'm up the street at the spot. Come get me when you see this note. Jackie.

"She must be outta her fuckin' mind," he said aloud. I'll come over there and drop off yo' shit so you can stay forever." He laughed.

He found a half-eaten meatloaf, some collard greens and mashed potatoes on the stove. *That's why her ass is so damn big. All she does is sit around here and eat. But she does know how to throw down,* he thought as he swallowed a spoonful of the still warm potatoes. *Shit, she should know it takes more than good cookin' to keep a nigga like me at home. She about to be replaced by my queen, Dani. She has everything I need.* He had gone ahead and fixed a full plate of food, then sat in front of the TV where he found a rerun of "Good Times" on cable. He ate his food heartily and then dozed off on the sofa. He planned to revisit Dani tonight after his nap and he vowed that this time nothing would stop him.

Chapter Nineteen

Andrew ~ *Losin' It*

Yet another day without phone privileges or mail, incoming or outgoing. Andrew had become restless about the situation and began to panic. Internally, of course. He had a reputation to uphold.

His nightmares continued. He thought they couldn't get worse, but they had. His sheets were soaked with sweat and tears. Silent ones.

His new cellmate had been quiet all day. He read books, listened to motivational tapes and meditated in silence. He was the perfect celly in Drew's eyes. He had enough problems as it was.

Andrew was anxious to get in touch with Jacobs. He was supposed to have met with the private investigator this morning and Drew's curiosity about the outcome was overwhelming. From what Drew had heard about The Shadow, there was no guarantee that the underworld's illustrious P.I. would take the job. This was Drew's fear and it was killing him that he was cut off from the outside world.

His dilemma had taught him many lessons in the past few months. Lessons that he never knew needed to be learned. A greater reverence for his God was first and foremost. He thought he had life by the balls until this wrongful imprisonment interrupted the flow.

Quite honestly, he thought he was "the man." He had a beautiful family, an expensive home, a collection of cars, he was large and in charge. He often thought about how everything he had, except his family, had been acquired by illegal activity. Drug dealing, armed robberies and carrying out professional hits. There was no shame in his game. If the price was right, Drew would work hard for the money. The strain that this lifestyle had on his sanity, let alone his marriage, was horrific.

Dani shared his grief because she was blinded by love in the beginning and turned her head to the actions that led to the fat bank accounts, the fur coats and the diamonds. They both grew to realize they were living wrong and he feared that the wrath was near.

They talked about it and Drew agreed with his wife that he would get out of the game. The problem was that the game wouldn't let him. It was too good to him. But when his best friend was killed in a drug war, his eyes were forced open. He got out and never looked back. Now here he was, years later, in jail for a crime he didn't commit. He had no choice but to put all his trust in his God to help him through, to protect his family, and ultimately, to get him home.

In the meantime, Jacobs sat home thinking of a plan. He needed to be prepared for his longtime client, Andrew Johnson's reaction to his spending The Shadow's large fee on his habit for Internet stock trading. It was a bad addiction from which his finances had tremendously suffered.

He had to lead Andrew on to believe that The Shadow had taken the job. That would give him time to make the money back and really hire the eccentric investigator. He also conned himself into believing that Andrew's appeal hearing would solve both of their problems. They would release Andrew, therefore leaving no reason to actually hire The Shadow. Jacobs felt he had plenty of time between now and the hearing to get the money together. He thought he had things all figured out. Hopefully, for his sake, he did.

Chapter Twenty

Bridge Night ~ *Just Kickin' It*

On Wednesday, the eve of Thanksgiving, the girls were in for yet another evening of bonding. This time it would be just the six of them, not counting the kids. Queenie, Saudia and Jody had all arrived at Dani's house at around seven o'clock. All, that is, except for Tai and Keera. Tai had a few last minute holiday clients to finish and Keera was spending her last moments with Chance who had mysteriously cut his trip to LA short to fly back home to Miami.

Everyone was in such a different mode from the night before at The Greenroom. As if it had been planned, each wore sweats, tee-shirts and sneakers. All were relaxed, comfortable and ready to dive into the food that Dani had prepared. She had called them earlier in the day to cancel the plans for potluck and instead cooked a batch of her scrumptious chicken tacos.

The kids, DJ, Jasmine, Damon, Daria, Xavier and Chelsea, were all upstairs enjoying themselves in their little carefree worlds. The thumping and laughing from upstairs in DJ's room was barely audible through the music that the ladies were enjoying just below. Saudia and Jody lounged lazily over each end of the sofa while Queenie relaxed in one of the deep leathered chairs in Dani's living room.

The drink of choice was Pink Panties, which consisted of crushed ice, pink lemonade, Bombay gin, a dash of Gran

Marnier and cool whip, was in the blender. The kids would get the delicious non-alcoholic version.

The grilled chicken breasts for the tacos had been cooked, seasoned to perfection and shredded. The Caesar salad was tossed and chilled and the aroma of the Black beans and Spanish rice was invigorating.

Queenie entered the kitchen where Dani was preparing the food to be served.

"What you need me to do?" Queenie asked, although she knew Dani's reply would be that she didn't need any help.

"Naw, girl, go on and relax. I'mma fix the kids' plates first and then I'll call you guys. You can start pouring the drinks, though. You know what I'm sayin'?"

Queenie laughed. "I can do dat."

"But you know, if you want to take over and get the kids' ready to eat then –"

"Handle your business, Mami. Handle yo business."

Queenie beamed proudly. She remembered when she and Dani were in high school and they would imagine how their lives would be when they were grown, although as far as they were concerned, they were already adults in a mental sense.

Dani had come a long way having gotten married and had a child. She hoped to someday say the same for herself. But not too soon though. She first had to make a name for herself in the fashion world. Then she'd meet a handsome, well-off man with no baggage and live happily ever after, Queenie's secret fantasy served as her escape on those lonely nights that she spent at home alone.

Dani walked through the living room past Jody and Saudia carrying a large tray with several plate of food on top.

"Dani, let me help you with that." Jody jumped up to assist.

"No. You came here to relax. I got this."

Even after Dani had started up the stairs, Jody just stood there. She felt certain guilt for not tending to her children, Xavier and Chelsea. *Relax, Jody. Let Dani handle it.*

She had to reason with herself to not go upstairs and fuss over them. Since Marcus left, all of her attention went to the kids. She recently noticed that her life revolved around them and began to obsess about the fact that her life had become lost within theirs. *Will there ever be another man in my life?* She couldn't see it. There was no more room. After the kids, her involvement in church and her job at the bank, there was nothing left.

"Where are Keera and Tai?" Saudia asked. She flipped through the pages of a recent issue of *One World* magazine and sipped on the drink Queenie just handed her. "Thank you, darlin'."

"You're welcome, lady," Queenie obliged.

"Tai is at The Boutique and Keera is saying her good-byes to Chance," Jody announced.

"Good-byes to Chance?" Saudia asked. "I thought they were both leaving on Sunday together. What happened?"

"Are ya'll talkin' about Keera?" Dani asked, trotting down the winding staircase.

"Uh huh."

"She's on her way. She just called from the road."

"And how does she sound?" Queenie asked, knowing that when Keera is upset with Chance, she was upset with the world.

"Actually she sounded pretty good."

"Good, 'cause my head is in no shape to be entertained by the wrath of Keera," Saudia complained. She loved Keera, but was in no mood for the drama.

"Well, I guess we shall soon see," Dani said with a half laugh.

Suddenly, Saudia grabbed the telephone, which sat on the end table to her left and placed it on speaker. She quickly dialed a number and got an almost immediate response.

"Boutique," Tai answered in a low, throaty tone.

"Girl, you sound like pure sheey-it." Saudia was in a playful mood. "When are you gonna be finished making your fortune for the day? We are about to grub and I can't promise you any leftovers. You know how I likes to do it."

"Saudia, you pig. You betta leave me plenty. I'm hungry as hell. I haven't had a break all day."

"Damn girl, how early did you get there this morning?"

"Six fuckin a.m. and I'm as tired as a whore on Sunset. The day before Thanksgiving is always a bitch."

"You raked in the dough today, Sistergirl. I need to start doin' me some hair. I know you make a grip, so stop frontin'," Saudia taunted.

Dani, Queenie and Jody sat in the background and laughed. Saudia could be a comedic fool when she wanted to be.

"Hell, I gotta pay for the Mercedes S500 profiling in front of my shop. Let alone run this money pit." It seemed Saudia had pushed a button.

"Okay, okay. Let me leave you alone cause you are obviously on one today. Just come through when you done. And how long did you say that would be again?"

"Damn, girl. I just finished my last client. I'm cleanin' up now. Is that cool with you, Ms. Rushmore?" Tai was irritated, but humored.

"Rushmore? Oh, so now you got jokes, huh? Aiight then, see you when ya get here, Mama. And we wanna hear every detail of what went down last night with you and your delivery man. Peace."

She quickly clicked the speaker off and laughed slyly.

Saudia always had fun missing with Tai's head. "You are so bad, Saudia. You knew you would blow that girl's fuse by asking her about her money." Queenie laughed.

"O-ka-a-a-ay? And then you went and busted her out about homeboy from her so-called past actually being her product delivery man at The Boutique," Dani shook her head. "Why would she lie about that anyway? It's not like her to lie. She's crazy and she'll tell you all her crazy ass business detail for detail. But now she lies?" Dani put on her mental sleuth hat and began to think. "Interesting."

The truth was that Tai was in a funky mood. She went through her stash in the wee hours of the morning with her drug buddy and personal dealer, Chris. She rushed from his house in such a hurry this morning that she completely forgot to have him replenish it. Now it was seven thirty at night and Chris hadn't returned one of Tai's pages. Even still, she waited desperately for his call.

"I'll find out what's going on with Ms. Tai Robinson. She is definitely hiding something," Saudia proclaimed assuredly.

"I don't know," Jody sang.

"Watch me," Saudia threatened.

The doorbell rang suddenly and interrupted the conversation about Tai.

When Dani opened the door and saw Keera, she instantly knew that things with Chance were not good.

"Hey, girl. You got here fast." Dani gave Keera a hug and opened the door wide enough for her to enter.

"I know, huh? There was no traffic so I cruised right on over."

Keera was putting on her game face for the girls. She knew they hated to be around her after she and Chance fought and she didn't want to make them uncomfortable. Just one of the personality quirks she was working on for the new year.

"Hey, ladies," Keera called, peering around at the girls who were as relaxed and comfortable as if they were at home. Keera wore her gray and black FUBU sweatsuit pants and tee shirt with the matching sweatshirt tied around her waist. The addition of her FUBU sneakers and baseball cap completed the trendy designer ensemble.

"Hey, Keera, how you feelin' today?" Queenie asked with genuine concern.

"I feel aiight. Me and Chance are fightin', again, but I'm so used to it now I'm not even trippin', she lied. "Are the kids upstairs?"

"Yea they're up there getting' their grub on."

"Oh, no wonder they're so quiet." Keera was used to being greeted by her friends' children with an abundance of hugs and kisses. "I'll wait till they finish then before I go up."

"What happened with you and Chance? I thought he was staying 'til Sunday?" Saudia wasted no time.

"It's a mystery to me, too. He woke me up early this morning and said he had to get back to Miami for some scrimmage." She plopped down on the empty, leather love seat.

"A scrimmage? Against who?" Saudia prodded.

"Beats me. He wouldn't tell me any details. He claims he told me this last week, but I have no memory of it," Keera said.

"Well, what do you think is going on?" Jody was curious. It just didn't sound right to her. It used to be that Chance couldn't stand to be away from Keera. That was how they all became so close with him, too. Instead of being apart from Keera, he would join her in an outing with her friends. *Those were the days.*

"To be honest, I really don't know. Chance has been acting *different* for a while."

"What do you mean *different?"* Dani wanted to know.

"Well, he doesn't return my calls sometimes. He's gone for days at a time and can never give me a direct answer about where he's been."

"So he's cheating," Saudia blurted.

Everyone looked at Saudia as if to say "Nice going, Blabbermouth."

"Yes. I think so," Keera answered to everyone's shock. She had never before accepted the possibility.

"So, what are you gonna do?" Jody asked sadly.

"Well, tonight I'm going to enjoy my time here with you guys. Tomorrow I'll spend Thanksgiving with my dad and then first thing Friday morning, I'll head back to New York. There are plenty of jobs waiting for my return."

"How is good old Dad anyway?" Dani asked, changing the subject.

"He's fine, girl. I was mad at him cause he let Cruella whisk him out of the house last night before I could see him. But it's cool. She's gonna get hers one of these days. Daddy will wake up from this nightmare he's in and recognize. Then he'll kick her scandalous ass to the curb."

"Girl, are you two ever going to get along?" Queenie asked. She was aware that Keera and her new stepmother had been feuding since day one and it seemed it would go on until one of them was dead and buried.

"Not while I'm alive and breathing," Keera answered. "If I had the guts, I'd sick a hitman on her ass." Keera rolled her eyes.

"Ooh, Keera, you know you don't mean that." Jody responded. It scared her to hear people talk like that. It told her that the devil was at serious work.

"Hmmph. Think I don't?" Keera challenged.

"Damn, Keer, is it like that?" Saudia wanted to know.

"Yes, girl and that also goes for her demented son. He is really startin' to freak me out."

"Yeah, I'll agree with you on that one." Dani said. "Brotha got a screw or two loose for real."

"Didn't he work for you for a while, Keer?" Jody asked.

"Yeah, but not for long. Lettin' that crazy fool act as my bodyguard was a big mistake. He almost killed somebody for just lookin' at me."

"You are kidding?" Jody gasped.

The other girls nodded their heads knowingly.

"Yep. That's why I got this," Keera pulled the silver nose pearl handled .25 automatic pistol from her purse. "I can protect myself now."

"Oh, my God," Jody said fearfully. "Do you know how to work that thing?"

"Sure do. I took shooting lessons at the gun club for months before buying it," Keera said, as she placed the locked gun carefully back into her handbag. "Don't worry, it's legally registered *and* I have a permit to carry."

"Well, look out world." Saudia said in disbelief. She had never known a woman to carry a gun around in her purse. Let alone a friend of hers. *What has the world come to?*

"That's why we have God though. He is our protection and our strength. I don't know Keera. It's so dangerous." Jody said in a shaky voice. It was as if the words came out before she gave her approval.

"I know what I'm doin' and God knows, too. He knows that Keera's doin' what she needs to do for Keera."

Jody took that as her cue to leave the subject alone.

"Sometimes it's like that, Jody," Dani said, thinking of the two guns she herself owned. "Everybody doesn't have the same situations and challenges to face. Therefore you can't judge their actions and decisions."

"Yeah, shit. I got some lunatic who enjoys writing me sexually perverted and physically threatening letters. I can't allow myself to be victimized," Keera said.

She and Dani now sat side by side on the leather love seat. Dani leaned her tired head gently on Keera's bony shoulder telling her, "I'm here for you."

"Dang, Keera, your life is exciting," Saudia answered after slurping down the last of her drink.

"Is that what you call it? Exciting? Then, honey, I'll take boring any day of the week. Somebody else can have the stress."

"Girl, you know you love what you do. No matter how much shit you talk, you wouldn't have it any other way." Dani said, matter of factly.

Keera gradually allowed a huge smile and said, "You're right. I love my job and I would be crazy to give it up. I'm just talkin' shit but it is hectic dealing with some of the repercussions.

I have no time to myself nor to spend with my man who is now cheatin' on me, and I have stalkers. How can I not love my life?"

"Oh, Boo, you'll be all right." Dani said, putting her friend in a playful headlock. "Let me hook you up with some of my bomb ass chicken tacos. You'll feel a hundred percent after you eat."

"Now you talkin', Keera said rubbing her hands together. She spent all of her time and energy on Chance and trying to stop him from leaving that she hadn't taken out any time to eat.

"Y'all heffahs hungry or what?" Dani glanced the room at Saudia, Jody and Queenie and raised her arms in the air as if to say, "what's up?"

"Hell yeah," Saudia answered as they all rose and headed to the kitchen.

Keera tagged at the rear of the line asking, "And I know y'all Negroes left me some of them Pink Pannies!"

"Barely!" Dani answered from the start of the line to the kitchen. "But you can hook up another batch, don't trip!"

They all laughed as they each, except for Keera, prepared to fix a plate full of Dani's home cooked Mexican food. Keera wanted to make the drinks first. Their bridge night Mexican dinner wouldn't be the same without them. She emptied the last of the blended beverage into a glass and began to make another batch.

"So, how did everyone's evening end up last night? Despite me and Chances problems, the sex is still good."

"Gee, Keera, thanks for sharing." Saudia said bitterly. Even though Saudia had plenty of opportunities, she opted to pick up the kids from her dad and go home alone. She didn't dare tell her friends that Chance's married brother, Jeff, had practically begged for her number. No sooner had he sent his wife crying out of the club, he was hitting on her. He caught her alone when she had gone to the bathroom and complimented her on her looks. She was tempted but knew that if she succumbed she'd be labeled a tramp. He did manage to slip his number inside of her hand and she kept it just in case. *You never know.*

"Well, Keera, I think you are the only one who got some." Queenie sighed. Thomas was the only man she had set her sights on at the club and he was pretty clear about his disinterest. In a female anyway. She decided not to air her opinion about Chance's friend Thomas being gay. Especially since Chance and Keera were having problems. She didn't want to start anything, especially any false suspicions. And, regarding Chance, Queenie was sure they would be just that.

"Dani, how is Andrew?" Saudia asked, spooning a helping of black beans into her mouth.

"Well, I don't know. I got a letter from him yesterday and he sounds good. I haven't talked to him on the phone in days and not hearing his voice, let alone not seeing him, is killing me."

"He'll be home before you know it, Dani. Just wait and see," Keera assured her.

The phone rang and snapped Dani out of her vision of Drew being behind bars.

"Hello?" Dani answered the kitchen's cordless phone. To her surprise it was Jacobs.

"Hi, Mrs. Johnson, this is Jacobs. I hope this isn't a bad time."

"Oh, no, not at all." Dani had been waiting to hear some news about Drew's request for an appeal and she hoped Jacobs had something good to tell her." She put him on hold.

"I'll be right back you guys. I'mma take this in the office."

"Okay," said Jody, verbalizing the other ladies' silent head nods. Their mouths were too full to say anything.

Dani took the phone call in her office and closed the door. The last time she and Jacobs spoke, he was on his way to court to file the necessary paperwork to appeal Drew's case and she was anxious to hear the outcome.

"Thank you for holding, Jacobs. Do you have some good new for me?" She was straight and to the point. No room for chit chat.

"Actually, Mrs. Johnson, I do. The court issued a hearing date of December seventeenth," he said, matter of factly.

She sighed with relief and fell back in her leather recliner.

"Yes, that is good news, thank you. Does Andrew know this yet?" She asked, wondering what her husband was thinking and doing as she and Jacobs held conversation.

"Yes, I saw him yesterday morning. The facility is not allowing any privileges at this time. They were having disciplinary problems with the ummm-"

"Inmates?" Dani interrupted.

"Yes." he answered.

"Is he okay?" she asked, in sudden panic. "Is there anything that I can do?"

This fool makes it sound like Andrew's in a Catholic school or something. Disciplinary problems? What the hell did that mean?

He obviously sensed her worry. "Mrs. Johnson – Dani, Andrew is doing fine. There were a few incidents that occurred, but they had nothing to do with your husband. And when I saw him yesterday, he even asked that I let you know this personally."

"Okay, well, I appreciate your help. Are you sure he's okay?" She had to ask. Andrew had never been to jail before. *This was his first and his last time,* she thought. *At least it had better be.*

Before the call ended, Jacobs assured her that Andrew was fine and said that the lockdown would probably only last for a few more days, if that. If he only knew that for Dani, a few days without word from her husband ticked away like a few years. He dared not even mention The Shadow to her. He didn't want to have to lie to Andrew's wife unnecessarily. He assumed it slipped her mind because she hadn't mentioned anything about the hire of the ghetto's super sleuth.

"Damn, I forgot to ask him if he hired that investigator!" Dani said out loud after touching her forehead with the palm of her hand.

"I'll call him Friday morning," she said, as she wrote "Call Jacobs about PI" on her desk calendar.

If this appeal works out next month, Andrew will be home early. And if this investigator is brought in, he'll be home even sooner. But nothing was soon enough for Dani's satisfaction.

She knew that her husband was innocent and hated that he was locked behind bars instead of home with his family.

When she finished her conversation with Jacobs, she went upstairs to check on the kids. She giggled as she spied on them in DJ's room. They were all stuffed like piñatas and sprawled out on the floor watching one of DJ's many Disney cartoon movie classics. *Isn't this cute?* On her way back downstairs she could hear the doorbell ringing violently.

"Who in the hell?" Dani asked, looking at her friends who had all appeared from the dining room to see who was at the door.

She cautiously looked through the peephole, half expecting to see Trixxy who was due to pick Jasmine up at any moment. Dani had left her several messages and numeric pages, but had not heard a word from her all day.

To Dani's relief, it was only Tai. She opened the door quickly to stop her from ringing the doorbell again.

"Let the party begin, Tai is here!" she announced in full drama mode. "Hey, everybody! Do you know I had to practically run my ass in here! I thought this was a classy joint?" she asked, as she checked out her reflection in the mirror over the bar. Tai had such a way with words.

"What do you mean? What happened?" Dani was used to Tai's dramatics and was really just humoring her. She had never met more of a drama queen.

"Some fool was trying to follow me up here!"

"What did he look like? Maybe he's one of my neighbors," Dani asked curiously.

"Girl, if that fool lives in here, it is time for y'all to move. He looked like he belonged in cellblock H, for homicide. He had a long perm, pitted skin and very bad teeth. I sized him up in case I had to take off on him. He was a lot bigger than me, but y'all know I know when I dated that martial arts instructor I learned me some moves." Tai demonstrated some karate movements. "And he reeked of alcohol, too. I can still smell it."

All the girls were almost in tears from laughter.

"He was probably lost. Visiting someone in Las Flores for the first time can be a bitch," Dani suggested, trying to ease Tai's nerves. She seemed abnormally jittery when she talked about the stranger.

"Well, I sure feel sorry for whoever he was trying to visit!" Tai said, finally settling down. "Whatever. Does anybody wanna hit this shit?" She asked, lighting her weed pipe and grinning from ear to ear.

Tai was in a good mood. Chris had popped by The Boutique just as she was leaving. He gave her just what she needed to get her veins pumping. She was already so high that she took no consideration in the fact the weed she offered to her friends was laced with heroin.

After they'd left The Greenroom the night before, Chris told her between his bouts of laughter that he had given her a taste of the addictive drug. By then it didn't matter. All she wanted was more. Thankfully, the girls hated smoking from Tai's pipe and joints because of the way she drenched the tips with her saliva. Unbeknown to them, it would save their lives.

"It's the bomb, y'all!"

"Nope, I'm cool," Dani passed. Sometimes she didn't know about Tai. She was definitely one to keep an eye on.

"Naw, girl, I got my own," Keera answered.

"I'm not even talkin' to you, Jody, so don't even open your mouth," Tai said dismissing Jody with one sentence. "Saudia? Queenie?"

Saudia beamed a smile, "I don't mind if I do, but your stuff is probably too strong for me. Keera, I'll hit yours though." Saudia said, looking at Queenie for her to say the same.

"Yeah, same here, if you don't mind, Keer. Dang, it's been months since I've gotten high."

"Good, I don't want to waste my shit on y'all anyway," Tai was a little hurt, but was satisfied that she'd be left with more for herself.

Queenie turned to Dani. "Where should we do this?" she asked, pointing at the ceiling to the kids who were upstairs resting quietly after their meal.

"Oh, right, you guys can go out on the front patio and getya smoke on."

"That's cool. Let's go," Keera said, taking a leather case containing two rolled joints and a gold lighter from her purse.

"I might get down with it a little later, so save me a hit or two, will ya?" Dani said, giving Keera a knowing wink.

"Aiight." Keera gave her a thumbs up and followed Tai, Queenie and Saudia out the front door to the enclosed outdoor patio.

Jody watched her friends go outside to get high. She remembered the days when she smoked weed and drank alcohol. It wasn't a pretty vision for her. She wanted badly for her friends to stop the smoking, the drinking and the premarital sex and give their lives to Jesus Christ as she had. *Their time will soon come,* she thought to herself as if she knew something that they didn't. She hoped for their sakes that when His wrath did come that it wouldn't be a hard hitting hurricane in their lives. God was merciful, but He didn't play either.

"I got that, Jody. Just sit down and relax." Dani stopped Jody from loading the dishwasher.

"Girl, will you let me help for once? It won't kill you, you know," Jody said, fed up with Dani's overly generous hospitality. "I'm like family and family pitches in."

"Aw, youtoetweeeeet!" Dani said giving Jody a sisterly hug.

"Okay, if you really want to help, then be my guest. While you're doing that, I'll go and check on the kids again. They are unusually still up there."

"You know you're right. Usually they're climbing the walls," Jody said, as she rinsed the now empty salad bowl before placing it into to dishwasher. She had relaxed tremendously in regards to the kids and was no longer anxious about their well being.

When Dani got upstairs, she found all six children asleep while the TV, which played Hercules, watched over them. DJ and Jasmine occupied the bunk beds and Saudia's and Jody's little ones were sprawled on the floor sleeping soundly. She grabbed blankets from the linen closet and covered them all. Jasmine and DJ had been in their pajamas all day, but Dani let it slide. *It won't kill them to take their baths in the morning.* She could hear talking and laughter from downstairs, which told her that Tai, Saudia, Queenie and Keera had concluded their smoke out on the patio and had come back inside. Watching the kids sleep, Dani had second thoughts. *Maybe I'll take a toke after all. What the hell.*

Chapter Twenty One

Kilamunjaro ~ *Me Against the World*

The county jail was the last place Killa thought he would be on Thanksgiving Day or any other day in his near future.

Why did I even leave Dani's at all?

He wondered as he reflected on the events of the night before. He had been perfectly perched between the leaves and branches of a large bush near Dani's front door. He watched Dani and her friends through the holes of the patio gate and the partially open blinds flanking her living room. They drank, laughed and talked while Killa watched. He was in a personal heaven as he observed his queen's every move. The way she moved her mouth when she talked and her expression when she laughed turned him on. He couldn't stop himself when the urge came for him to pleasure himself in the bushes. In fact, he serviced himself several times before he had his run-in with the little blonde bombshell.

When the petite beauty approached the steps to Dani's, she had immediately caught Killa's eye. Not only because he was trying to lay low and had to be aware of his surroundings, but because she had a walk that could make a grown man cry.

By the time she got close to his stake-out post, Killa had devised a new plan. He would charm little blondie to gain access to Dani.

"Say, pretty lady, do you have a minute?" Killa slid from the bush. He had no idea that the leaves and twigs from the bush protruded from his wig-like hair. It reflected the image of the psycho hidden behind his shiny silk suit.

"No, but I got pepper-spray, muthafucka!" Blondie hurried into Dani's front patio and locked the wooden door behind her immediately. She hurriedly rang the doorbell, attempting to get inside before Killa could get to her. She was freaked out – so disturbed that she didn't notice her make-up bag tumble out of her purse and onto the ground.

It was not the response Killa had expected. *Why wouldn't she wanna talk to a suave brotha like myself?* After retrieving the small, sparkly bag, he ducked back into the bushes. He heard the loud mouthed woman make a scene to Dani and her friends, and didn't want to be discovered lurking outside of her window. He felt she might get the wrong first impression.

The whole incident had disturbed his groove. His next thought was that he needed another drink. He decided to make a fast run to the liquor store. He hated to leave his post, but he was all out of Hennessy and his forty-ounce of beer was down to the suds.

I'll only be gone a minute.

Or so he thought. He sped through the residential streets, wanting to hurry back to Dani. He didn't want to miss another heartbeat of hers. But when the sirens appeared in his rearview mirror, he saw the police were right on his tail. He was going well over the speed limit and his registration tags were expired.

Killa didn't immediately pull over. He screeched around corners and ran stop signs just until he could manage to get rid of his illegal assassin's knife during the chase. He wanted to throw his gun out, too, but he couldn't find it. Its' disappearance worried him, but he didn't have time to panic. When he did pull over, he was surrounded by black and whites.

"Get out of the car with your hands up!"

He didn't worry even when an Asian cop administered a breathalyzer to determine if he was under the influence. The policeman was not surprised when he failed miserably. Still, Killa wasn't troubled over that either. He figured he would be out by morning. He was off of parole and had no outstanding warrants. He was in the clear. Even when they ripped through the seats of his car, he didn't flinch.

They won't find shit, he thought as he cracked a knowing smile.

"Well, what do have we here?" asked a young Hispanic officer. "Looks like heroin. Tastes like heroin. Must be heroin," he announced in a sarcastic tone. "You're goin' to jail, Buddy."

"Hell naw! That shit ain't mine!" Killa yelled at the officer who held a foiled package of heroin in one hand and Blondie's sparkly make-up bag in the other. Now he was worried.

That bitch!

When he'd picked up the loud-mouthed blonde's glittered pouch, he had no idea that it was filled with drugs. If he had, he would have tossed it out the window just as he had his knife, since it could be traced back to many unsolved mysteries over the past year.

If I ever see that bitch again, her ass is mine, he thought, remembering her sultry walk and imagining the things he would do to her. *She needs to be taught a lesson, especially after she dissed me in front of Dani's house.* He couldn't wait.

The police station's holding cell was overflowing with pre-holiday drunks and petty thieves, which left no room for Killa.

"Looks like you get to spend your Thanksgiving in the County Zoo," laughed the officer as he got into the police car. "I'm sure you'll fit right in," he quipped, laughing even harder.

Oh, you think you so funny, huh? We'll see who gets the last laugh.

Killa remained quiet as they rode through downtown LA. It wasn't long before he arrived at the county jail facility. It wasn't his first time inside. It had been two years since his release from the place they called The Zoo. After he turned over his personal belongings, he was finger printed, photographed, then released into a large dorm of strangers. It was just as noisy, dirty and nasty as he remembered the prisoners' playpen to be.

He lay low on his cot so as not to be spotted. He checked out the faces in the large, overcrowded cell, but didn't spot anyone he knew. He needed to find out about Drew's state of mind so he would know how to handle him in case they crossed paths. He was well aware that Drew was close by and he didn't want to be caught off guard. He had no idea if Drew had become aware of his designs on Dani or if he would simply be recognized as *that crazy nigga from the block.* Nor did he want to find out.

Killa knew that because he was being held in the county's holding tank, it wasn't likely that he would even see Drew. He was well aware that Drew had been locked up for almost three months and would be in for at least another year.

A nigga doin' time like that don't get to come near the holdin' cell. Naw, I doubt if I'll see that nigga. But hell, if I do, I'll just have to kill em'. It'll happen anyway if he tries to stop me and Dani from bein' together so it really don't make a difference. Today, next year, when the fuck ever.

He had hoped to be out by morning, but was reminded that it was Thanksgiving and that the courthouse was closed. His arraignment would have to wait until the following day.

Another day without Dani.

Killa sighed. He knew that when he went to court, he had to play it cool. Protesting that the drugs were not his would be a lost cause. Instead he would tell the judge that he was using the heroin and be released under the conditions of admitting himself into an outpatient rehabilitation program. *No sweat.*

He used his phone call to try and reach Jackie but she didn't answer. *Good, I hope she stay gone.*

The thought of going home to her cramped his stomach. He couldn't stand her anymore and determined that her time was up.

No more Mr. Nice Guy.

He had to clean house before he could live happily every after with Dani, and the first hefty bag on the curb would contain Jackie.

The noise and the mayhem surrounding him slowly faded as Killa zoned into daydreams of Dani. He remembered how beautiful she was the night before and reveled in how close he was to finally being with her. He lay back, oblivious to his whereabouts and unzipped his slacks.

Slowly he began to pleasure himself and he dreamed that he was making love to his queen on her canopy bed. He stroked and caressed himself until hot semen exploded and filled the palm of his hand. He let out a long wind and closed his eyes tight.

We will be together, Dani. And that's a promise.

Chapter Twenty Two

Danielle ~ *I Can Love You*

It was five a.m. on Thanksgiving morning, and Dani had awakened in a cold sweat. *What is wrong with me?* She stared at the ceiling in the pitch darkness of her bedroom and let out a deep sigh. After two months of sleeping alone, she still couldn't accept that Andrew was not there. It was as if her heart wanted her to deny the truth that her mind knew all too well.

Lying alone in their big, half-empty bed, she would fantasize that he was downstairs in the office researching his next legitimate business venture or in the kitchen getting something from the fridge. And although none of her lonely nights had been completely restful, she had never had nightmares like the ones she'd experienced this morning. They were dark dreams filled with hollow cries for help and long hallways of endless darkness. They were vivid but, at the same time, foggy.

Dani strongly believed there was a hidden message, but didn't have the courage to try to decode it.

Please God, protect Andrew and bring him home safely. In the name of your son, Jesus Christ.

She wiped a single tear from her face, turned on her side and smoothed her hand over Andrew's cold, perfectly fluffed pillow. Her mind wandered to thoughts of her visiting him in jail. She saw him every weekend. He was allowed one thirty –

minute phone visit on Saturday and Sunday and that was it. Drew was agonized with having to spend time with his wife and son behind double-sided, bullet proofed glass. She didn't like the conditions either but to her it was better than nothing. This weekend would be no different and she couldn't wait. His tall, muscular build, rugged good looks and soulful brown eyes were what she missed seeing, but it was his intellectually stimulating conversation, his corny sense of humor and his warm smile that she missed most. Her need for him was undeniable. She physically aches, though, for the sex. After eight years of being together, it was still torrid. *Damn, it'll be goin' on three months already,* she thought and then sighed defeatedly.

She glanced at the clock on her nightstand and suddenly recalled that Trixxy had never come for Jasmine. *She is really trippin'.* She decided to try calling again, thinking that the early morning call would receive a live response. All night Trixxy's voicemail was all Dani could seem to reach.

"Hi, it's Trix. Leave me a message or if you have the pager number, hit me up. Peace."

Before the long beep could end, Dani hung up. Frustrated, she picked up her bedside Bible to search for answers. There was too much foul activity invading her sad, but otherwise manageable life and the weight was getting heavy. If one more situation that she was unprepared for were to arise, she feared she would crack.

She read a few passages in the Book of Psalms, which she always found comforting. Dani was eased by her faith that

God's shield was around her and her family and that the fears, which suddenly taunted her, were unwarranted.

I have a lot to be thankful for.

She smiled as she allowed herself to see the bigger picture. She had a wonderful family, irreplaceable friends, a great career and the strong belief that she was not alone. Ever. Her God was with her every step of the way.

So what am I trippin' off of?

These were thoughts that normally would be communicated as pillow talk with her husband.

Why stop now?

She propped herself up against the king-sized pillow which provided comfort against the wooden headboard. She opened the drawer to her nightstand and retrieved the expensive, yet simply stated stationary that she bought especially for her letters to Andrew. Her heart was full and she needed to relay its contents to her soul mate. Unfortunately, it had to be via the post office but it would do – for now.

After bleeding her feelings into a four-page letter, Dani rose out of bed to get an early start. It was Thanksgiving and the afternoon would be filled with house hopping and face stuffing. The kids would surely occupy her morning once they woke up, so she would use this quiet time to pamper herself. Whether it was to do her nails and feet, flip through a neglected magazine or even veg out on an old movie showing on cable.

Through Andrew's horrible experience, Dani had begun to realize that freedom was something they both had taken for granted. And it went beyond feeling free from the constraints of

White America, although that experience had yet to occur. This freedom was the ultimate freedom. What Dani felt that life was all about. Freedom from the chains within. The chains of doubt, the chains of fear and the chains of denying yourself the pleasures of loving others and being loved in return. Above all she was alive and healthy with windows of opportunity abound. Every minute counted and she was going to apply the lesson and make sure she used her time wisely.

Dani was glad that she and her girls had a chance to get together – all of them. Last night's Bridge Night was a complete success. Good food, good drinks and good conversation. They talked about their careers, kids, men, clothes, hair and everything else under the sun. Sometimes she forgot she had so many good friends. It felt like a breath of fresh air had blown inside of her while she was in the midst of enjoying their relaxed company. She realized how much she'd needed Bridge Night.

She frowned with concern as she remembered that Tai had come in all excited and nervous about some weird man inside of the complex. Then she broke out her weed immediately after her entrance. *Good old' Tai.*

Then her thoughts bounced to Queenie when she had confided to them a deep secret about a man she'd dated in New York and was now heartbroken over. *It's time a good man came into her life. She deserves it.*

Saudia talked about her dreams of becoming Mayhem Records' first female head of A&R. Jody wanted to join her, but she would only work with gospel groups. Keera talked about her fears that it was finally over between she and Chance. And she shared Dani's hopes of Andrew's being let out of jail before his expected release date.

At the end of the night, despite the fact that they smoked weed, drank liquor and cursed like sailors, Jody, who didn't partake in any of the above, led them all in a prayer of Thanksgiving and requests that each of their hopes be fulfilled. It was the perfect ending to the joyful evening.

Before leaving the comfort of her bed, Dani dwelled on thoughts of her mom. She was confused about why she couldn't commit to sticking around for Thanksgiving dinner. Dani hadn't seen her *once* in the two weeks that she'd been in LA.

She decided to dial Lena's number. The phone rang and rang. She hoped that her voicemail would pick up so she could give her mom a piece of her mind, but no such luck. Dani figured she was probably asleep with the ringer off. A usual scenario. Lena was a night owl and spent most of her evenings busy in front of the computer and a bottle of Chardonnay. Dani didn't know why she was surprised about her mom taking off. Not being around was her forté. She was more disappointed than anything else.

When they were able to spend time with each other, it was the best. She loved to hear about her mom's travels, her newest novel, even her new boyfriend. Embarrassed a little that Lena was still out there like that, Dani decided to give up and accept that her mom was a free spirit. Dani believed that her mom would never settle down. With her angelic beauty, she'd be mesmerizing men for decades.

Dani hoped that she'd inherit her mom's and Willie Mae's never aging good looks and energy. Everyone who met Willie Mae swore a resemblance to Lena Horne. Dani knew Willie Mae, her vibrant grandma, was compared to the gorgeous black starlet back in the day. It was probably the reason she named her only daughter, Lena.

Maybe she will find a good man someday and settle down.

Since Dani's father died in a car accident when she was just six years old, no one ever knew what was in Lena Kelly's mind. She had retreated into her own private world of fiction and only shared with family what she shared with the world. The words in the pages of her best-selling novels. Everything else in her life was guesswork.

In two hours, Dani had done much of nothing. She skipped the manicure and pedicure deciding to leave that to The Boutique's talented Lisa. Instead, she listened to a new jazz CD and started to read the mystery novel that had been sitting on her dresser for weeks.

She had gotten deep into the spy thriller until being surprised by a bouncy DJ and giggly Jasmine. It was nine a.m. and life began again.

"*Hi, Mommy!"* yelled DJ, as he pounced on her bed.

"Hi, Stepmommy!" giggled Jasmine, who was in a terrific mood.

Dani loved to see her stepdaughter happy. In the very beginning Jas was very distant and reclusive, as if she were trying to physically hide herself inside of her silence. It didn't take too long for her to open up to Dani though. Dani would do things like tickle her mercilessly just so she could hear something out of her. The laughter that was buried so deep. When the shell of sadness and silence was broken, she blossomed like a flower. Jasmine looked so much like Drew, it was easy for Dani to put her crazy mother out of her mind when she looked at the little girl. Her wide smile, reddish brown skin and almond shaped eyes. She even had a dimple in her chin like Drew.

"Who wants pancakes?" asked Dani.

"Meeeeeee!" they both cried.

"Okay, but first you two rugrats need baths. You guys are stinky, stinky, stinky!" Dani held her nose and pretended to smell a foul odor. The kids cracked up with laughter. "Who wants to go first?" They both looked at each other and pointed.

"Okay, we'll do the polite thing and let the little lady go first. What do you think, DJ?"

"Yes, good idea, mom," he answered in a much older tone than one would expect for his four years.

"Do I have to?" Jasmine asked softly, her expression suddenly serious.

"Yes, you have to, sweetie. You guys spent all day yesterday in your pajamas, and the night before at Willie Mae's I know you didn't bathe."

"Can I stand up, please? The water burns me sometimes," Jasmine whined softly.

Dani gave her a puzzled look as she stroked DJ's freshly cut hair.

"What do you mean, sweetheart? What burns?"

Jasmine was silent.

"Are you hurt somewhere, Jasmine? Do you have a cut or a sore that you don't want wet? Because if so, I'll be careful when I bathe you, I promise."

Jasmine was still quiet, but in her eyes Dani saw she wanted to say something. Instead Jasmine looked at DJ who stepped up to the plate.

"Mommy, Jasmine got boo-boos." He pointed to his own backside as if he were the one hurt.

"Really, Jas? Let me see."

Jasmine got down from the bed slowly and pulled down her flannel pajama pants just enough for Dani to get a glimpse of the torture that Jasmine had endured for so long. There were welts, cuts and bruises all over her bottom. Dani's heart nearly stopped and she clutched her chest in an attempt to catch her breath.

"DJ, sweetie, go in the den and watch TV while I have a little talk with your sister. We'll be out in a minute, okay?"

"Okay, Mommy. Is Jasmine in trouble? He asked, as if he was afraid he had done a bad thing by telling his mom what was wrong with his damaged sister.

"Of course she's not in trouble, honey. Mommy just want to fix her up and make her feel all better."

"Okay, I'm gonna watch Pokémon," DJ said as he trotted out.

"Jasmine, how did this happen?" Dani managed to stay calm. She knew the answer, but wanted to hear Jasmine's version.

"I fell down," she answered softly looking down at her stubby little toes.

Dani was beyond furious. And the pain she felt for Jasmine was excruciating. There was nothing she could have done to deserve that. A dog didn't deserve that.

"Okay, let me see what's going on here."

Dani pulled off the little girl's pajama top and was immediately filled with horror. The cuts, welts and bruises not only covered her bottom but her back as well. It was obvious that underneath the fresh lacerations, many layers of old ones were buried. Tears rolled down Dani's cheeks without permission and she was glad Jasmine was turned around so she wouldn't see her pain.

So this is how Trixxy treats Jasmine at home. And, this is probably why she suddenly stopped letting us see her. I'mma fuck her ass up when I see her. And wait 'til Drew finds out – let alone the police.

Dani wiped her tears just as quickly as they appeared and pulled Jasmine's pants back up. She had to think.

What do I do? Who to call?

Dani recognized that Jasmine had already been through the ringer and had enough compassion for her to know that grilling her about who and what happened wasn't a good idea. It wouldn't have been good for either of them.

In silence, Dani led Jasmine into the bathroom where she gently applied calamine lotion to the cuts and bandaged the ones that were freshly opened. When she was finished, she turned Jasmine toward her and gave her a kiss on her forehead.

"Everything is going to be okay, Jasmine. I'm going to keep you safe."

Jasmine smiled and hugged Dani tightly. Obviously her way of saying "thank you" to her loving stepmother.

"Jasmine, sweetie, do me a favor and go watch cartoons with your brother. I'll be in there in just a few minutes."

"Okay, but do I still have to take a bath?"

"Not right now." Dani managed a smile.

Jasmine gave Dani a strong hug and walked out of her room to join DJ in the den.

Downstairs in the privacy of her office, Dani sobbed while squeezing the cordless phone in her hand.

Who should I call first? The police? Willie Mae?

She calmed herself so she could think and quickly decided to call her mother-in-law and Jasmine's grandmother, Francine.

"Mom, it's Dani," she said solemnly.

"Hi, sweetie. I was just telling Richard that I was looking forward to us all being together tomorrow."

"Yes, my plan was to come to dinner but something has happened. I don't even know how to tell you this."

"What's wrong, Dani? Is it Andrew? Is he okay?" she asked frantically.

"No, it's not Andrew, it's Jasmine. She spent the night last night and this morning I discovered bruises and welts all over her backside. It's really bad. You should see her, Mom. I'm still in shock. I knew Trixxy was deranged, but I never thought she would hurt Jasmine like this."

"My poor baby," she gasped. "Dani, I'm on my way over."

"No, Mom. I don't want Jasmine to get freaked out."

"Where's Trixxy anyway?" Francine asked, angrily.

"I don't know. I've been calling her house since last night. She still isn't answering the phone."

"Well, Sweetie, don't waste any more time. Call the police to make a report and get a lawyer. It's time that you all take Jasmine in for good."

"You're right. Let me make some calls and I'll call you back."

"Are you sure you don't want me to come? I promise not to upset Jasmine."

"Mom, when you see Jasmine's scars you will flip out. Jasmine will know that you are upset and I don't think she should be feelin' that right now."

"Okay, sweetie, but what about Andrew. He'll want to kill Trixxy when he finds out."

"Yeah, I know. I want to kill her myself, but the difference is that Drew would actually have the thought carried out. I have to tell him, Mom. I just don't know how or when. He'll be devastated. Especially since he won't be able to reach out to Jasmine like he would want to."

"This is a terrible mess. Okay, well, go ahead and make your calls and call me when you're done. Trixxy has a lot of nerve putting her hands on my grandbaby like that. I'm going to have to pray on this. That girl needs to be the one locked up." Francine let out a deep sigh. "Dani, tell my grandbabies that I love them."

"Of course, mom. But I can assure you that they already know."

Francine was just as hurt and upset as Dani. She agreed that action must be taken and that was what Dani needed to hear. She instinctively went to dial Jacobs but she hung up before she finished. She didn't want to distract him from Andrew's case. She then went to her Rolodex and flipped to MATHIS, C.; attorney at law. She came upon this lawyer when she and Andrew had first considered getting legal custody of Jasmine.

When Dani dialed the number on the card there was a voice mail saying that Carolyn Mathis was unavailable. With all of the excitement, she had forgotten that it was Thanksgiving. Dani was surprised and pleased to hear she was a woman and had a good feeling about her. Ms. Mathis left her pager number on the recording in case of an emergency.

"This is definitely an emergency," Dani mumbled as she dialed the local number.

Trixxy is gonna pay for this.

Little did Dani know Trixxy had already paid her price. And the proof was in Trixxy's cold, stiff body, which remained undiscovered in the trenches of Los Angeles.

Chapter Twenty Three

Tai ~ *My Downfall*

Tai couldn't believe that she had taken a client on Thanksgiving Day. *What I was thinking?* But deep down she knew why. She never turned down money.

Besides, Mary is a faithful customer. I wouldn't diss her just so I can sleep in. She convinced herself.

Tai was running a few minutes late because she couldn't find her make-up bag.

I hope I didn't leave it at Dani's. Oh, please no.

She filled her weed pipe in panic. In her sober state, Tai couldn't bear to face her friends again if they found out that she used heroin.

I would absolutely die.

Tai called Dani more than once but the line was tied up.

Damn. I guess I just have to cross my fingers on it.

In the meantime, she had to get with Chris so he could hook her up until she found it. She would arrange to have him meet her at Grits n' Greens a few blocks away from The Boutique. She preferred for him not to come near her place of business but it was the only way.

During brief moments of inflection she hated and despised Chris. She was ashamed of what she did with him and severely hurt that her addiction was because of him. Therefore, she kept him at arms length, until she needed him.

When Tai first met Chris he was not only fine but he was also driving a brand new Lexus. As far as Tai was concerned, she had hit the jackpot. As much as she loved being a single and independent woman, she was constantly looking for the man who would save her from it.

She met Chris backstage at a rap concert – one of many that Saudia had gotten tickets to through her job at Mayhem Records. Tai was immediately attracted to him. He had that look that drew her in each and every time, but his self-confidence was the clincher.

This nigga think he's the shit, Tai remembered thinking to herself.

He carried himself as if he owned the joint and she loved it. When Tai wanted something, nothing could stop her. That same night, after Saudia dropped Tai at home, she couldn't resist paging Chris. Little did she know that that very page would eventually result in a heroin addiction.

Tai continued to search every nook and cranny of her house for her drugs. She was late for a client but couldn't tear herself away.

I just know that shit is here some fucking where, she insisted.

As much as she hated to, she called Queenie, Saudia and Jody to see if they had possibly picked up her make-up bag by mistake.

I knew I shouldn't have put that shit in there!

She stomped her foot in frustration as she sat on her unmade bed and dialed Jody's number. She was her last hope until Tai could get a hold of Dani.

"Hey JoJo, Happy Thanksgiving." Tai fronted as though she were in a good mood when she actually felt like shit.

"Girl, same to you. What are you doing up? I thought you would be sleeping in this morning."

"No such luck. I have a client today if you can believe it," Tai said. "But it's Mary and you know I can't let her down."

Jody didn't buy it. Everybody knew that Tai was money hungry and would take a client on her death-bed if it were possible. She hoped that Tai would someday see that the money and the jewelry didn't come with you to heaven. She knew though that it would take a big brick and a good arm to knock some spiritual enlightenment into her.

"Well, Mary is blessed to have a beautician who is as flexible as you are. Not many would work on this holiday. I hope she remembers you while she's giving thanks this evening over that turkey and dressing."

Yeah, yeah, Tai thought.

Jody never missed an opportunity to get her preach on.

"She's a sweetheart. I don't mind doing it," Tai stated. "But I don't want to keep her waiting too long so let me go. But before I do, have you seen my make-up bag?" Tai crossed her fingers.

"Make-up bag? What does it look like?"

"It's silver and black with rhinestones, and it's by MAC."

"Nope, sorry, I haven't."

"Damn!" Tai couldn't hold her reaction.

"Dang Tai, is it that serious?" Jody wanted to know. Tai had been acting strange lately and her reaction just cemented the notion.

"No, it's not that serious, but I just bought a gang of new make-up. That shit ain't cheap." Tai was convincing.

Jody could feel her on that one. She hadn't been able to splurge on make-up in a long time. Not that she would now anyway.

"I hear you girl. Did you call Dani? Maybe you left it over there last night."

"Yea, I called but I didn't get through. I'll try her again from the car girl. I gotta get outta here."

"Okay then. Call me later." Jody said. "I'm sitting here waiting on Marcus to bring the kids. We're going to church this morning."

Tai wasn't impressed. "Aiight, then, I'll talk to you later."

No sooner could she hang up before the phone rang. It was Chris.

"It's about fuckin' time you called me back, Nigga. What took you so long?" Tai was not in the mood for his bullshit this morning.

"Slow your roll, woman. I called when I could."

"I need you to meet me at Grits n' Greens."

"Whatchyu need?"

"The usual," she answered, impatiently tapping her foot as she stood holding her cordless phone to her ear.

"Aiight, but it won't be till later," he replied, nonchalantly.

"Later? No, I need you now."

"You do realize that it's Thanksgiving, don't you?"

"And?"

"And? I'm chillin' today. I'mma hang with my peeps."

"Puh-leeze, nigga, it is too early in the morning for this shit."

"If you want to hook up, you gotta come over here," he insisted.

"Come over there? Where you stay at?" Tai didn't want to argue. She knew that Chris was not going to come until he felt like coming and she couldn't wait that long.

"865 Selby off of Lincoln. Ay, and come by yo'self, ya heard? Not everybody know where I stay and I wanna keep it like that."

"Aiight, damn. You mean Lincoln by those new movie theaters?"

"Yeah."

"I'm on my way. And have my shit ready cause I got a client waitin'," Tai didn't wait for a response. She hung up the phone, grabbed her purse and keys and hurried out the door. Chris had her exactly where he wanted her.

Chapter Twenty Four

Saudia ~ *Deep Inside*

When Sam called, Saudia wasn't as thrilled to hear from him as she usually was. For the past few days, she really thought hard about what she was doing with him in her life. She knew he wasn't going to leave his wife, but the truth was, she didn't want him to. She simply enjoyed his attention. Almost as much as she enjoyed being able to send him home when she felt like it. He couldn't act too much of a fool about it for fear of being caught by his wife. *I don't want to live my life like this anymore.*

Instead Saudia made a conscious decision to concentrate more on her children and her sick father and stop worrying about what every man thought about her. She looked at her friends and how successful they all were in their own respects. She desired the same for herself.

For Saudia, life at Mayhem Records was blissful. She met all sorts of cool people. There were also lot of perks: free concert tickets, VIP backstage passes, free CDs. The list could go on and on.

The only thing that she could complain about was the weak pay. Because of it, Saudia was very thankful that she had the ability to make a penny into a nickel if she had to. Her good savings sense had saved her ass many times. She'd been the receptionist for the past three years and was ready to move up, or move on. She was sure that if she could show somebody her skills she would get the promotion she felt she was due. She just had to figure out exactly what her skills were. She had a good ear for music, she was good with numbers, good with people, extremely organized and dependable. If she could put a little bug in the ear of the big boss, Marvin Melody, she felt she'd be in for sure. Melody was the president and CEO of the company. You couldn't go any higher up than that.

The twins, Damon and Daria, were still asleep. They were worn out from hanging with other kids at Dani's the night before. That worked for Saudia because she had always been an early riser and the kids had definitely inherited that trait. She was relieved to be able to for once, have a peaceful morning to herself. *I should keep them up past midnight every Friday,* she joked to herself.

It would've been nice if their dumb ass daddy would've bothered to contribute to their upbringings. Preferably, financially, but hell a phone call at this point would be a step in the right direction. But Saudia wasn't tripping off of him. In her eyes he was just a no good, coward ass, little boy. Aside from the fact that he beat her to make himself feel masculine, he thought he was "Mack of the Year." That is, until he found out that she was cheating on him. Then he ran home cryin' to his mama. *Punk bitch.*

Daryl was blind to the fact that Saudia was well aware of his little flings and sordid affairs. She would've had to have been deaf, dumb and blind not to have known. He was careless – so careless it was as if he *wanted* to get caught. She never confronted him about any of them during their five-year marriage. She just let him keep thinking he was "the man." When her self-esteem began to diminish, she looked for fresh meat of her own not only for approval, but satisfaction and revenge. That was what her therapist had told her, at least.

Saudia lay in bed and flipped channels with the remote control until she settled on a televised parade. There was nothing else on TV but football and after she and Daryl split up she vowed she would never again watch the violent sport. Many times during her marriage, his addiction to the game was the source of many fights in their household. Fights that ended up with her having a black eye or a busted lip. Nothing that she wanted to be reminded about. She was down for her soap operas though. Her stories were her escape from the life she considered to be hum-drum. She loved watching other people's drama since she had none of her own.

Bored with the parade, which had yet to display a face of color, she turned off the TV and got out of the bed with the intention of cleaning her house. Since she'd been with her friends for the past two days she hadn't bothered to wash a dish, let alone pick up after the kids had run wild with the sitter. She was supposed to go over her dad's for dinner, but she never knew with him.

Many times she'd get to Ebenezer's following an invitation and he'd forgotten that he even invited them over. He'd had two strokes in the past year. After her mother passed, he seemed to have just given up on life. The only times he seemed happy was when he was spending time with the kids or reminiscing with Saudia about her mama and the good old days.

It made her sad to see him that way. Not long ago, she offered to move in and take care of him, but he wouldn't have it. Her dad, Ebenezer, could be real stubborn when he wanted to be. She made sure they visited him at least three times a week. They were all he had left, with the exception of his sister who was almost as ailing as he was. Saudia refused to let him down no matter how hard he tried to push her away. She wasn't going anywhere.

She called Dani to tell her and DJ happy Thanksgiving but her line was still busy. Saudia reflected to her earlier phone conversation with Tai, when she called to ask if Saudia had seen her make-up bag.

She was trippin'.

Saudia wondered about Tai sometimes. They were good friends but Saudia felt that she never really new her.

After her unsuccessful attempt to call Dani, she continued her "Happy Thanksgiving" phone call list by dialing Queenie.

"Hello?"

"Hey, Q, it's Saudia."

"Good morning, Saudia, darlin'. Happy Thanksgiving."

"Same to you. What are you doing today? You wanna come to my dad's and eat?"

"Girl, I would, but I'll be in the office until late tonight."

"You goin' to work?"

"Yes and I know it's bad but this is our busiest season. Besides, it's just not the same with Mom and Dad living in Atlanta."

"I know but we're family, too. You don't have to be alone," Saudia said, reassuringly.

"Oh, I know that. It's just that since I've been away from home, I always made sure to spend the holidays with my family. I don't know. This year I just wasn't feelin' it."

"But now you miss them, right?"

"I do. I tripped by not going and they're pissed too. They swear up and down that I'm hiding a man over here."

"Are you?"

"Hell, I wish," Queenie laughed.

"Hey, have you talked to Dani or Keera?" Saudia was curious. "I already talked to Jody, she's about to go to church."

"That sounds like our Jody," Queenie chuckled.

"And Tai called looking for her make-up bag, as if I would have it," Saudia complained.

"Really? She called me too. That girl is losing it, I think. She needs to leave that weed alone," Queenie declared.

"Fo' sho'," Saudia laughed.

"But, no, I haven't talked to Keera or Dani yet. Let's call on the three way," Queenie said. "Hold on." She clicked over to dial Dani's number.

"It's busy," Queenie announced as she clicked back over.

"Dang, still? It was busy when I called, too."

"Hmm, that's strange. Why would it be busy if she has two-way calling? Queenie wondered.

"I don't know. Maybe she has Drew on the line and she doesn't want to be disturbed. You know you can cancel call waiting if you press star seventy on your phone."

"Is that right?" Queenie was enlightened. "Damn. You learn something new everyday. Aiight, let me call Keera. She's at her dad's but we'll try her cell phone first. Hold on," Queenie clicked to the other line once again.

"Hello, this is Keera. Leave me a message and I'll call you back in a minute," her voicemail prompted.

"Hey, Keera, it's Q and Saudia calling to wish you and yours a happy Thanksgiving."

"Yeah, and give your daddy a hug for me," Saudia added.

"We'll talk to you later, girl." Queenie hung up.

"Should I call the house?"

"Yea, why not."

"Okay, hold on again," Queenie clicked over to dial Keera's dad's number where Cruella picked up on the first ring.

"Hello?"

"Good morning, um is Keera there?" Queenie asked, not expecting Cruella to answer the phone.

"You must be mistaken. She doesn't live here anymore." Cruella said sternly.

"Right, but she's visiting..." Queenie paused trying to find suitable words.

"Visitors do not get phone privileges. Try her on her cellular phone, deary," she said, and promptly hung up.

"Daaang. She is a trip," Saudia said in disbelief.

"O-kay? You think she would have at least taken a message. What if it was important?" Queenie was not pleased.

"Ooh, Keera, is going to be pissed when we tell her. She already doesn't get along with the bitch – obviously for good reason," Saudia concluded.

"Knowing Keera she won't be up till the day is half over anyway. I'll page her in a little while to see how she's doing."

"Yeah, hopefully she made up with Chance and is back on cloud nine." Saudia was optimistic.

"Yeah, hopefully. So did you cook?" Queenie wondered. Saudia was a gourmet in the kitchen.

"Nope, not this year. Aunt Sis and her little helpers from the church cooked. You're still welcome to come you know. Fuck going to work on a holiday. I wish Mayhem Records would have the nerve." Saudia rolled her eyes at the thought of going to work on a paid holiday.

"I know, I know, but I really do have to go in. Christmas is coming and I have to have all of my ducks in a row. I'm still being watched and I'm sure somebody in corporate is just waiting for me to screw up."

"Yeah, girl. You doin' the right thing. Don't ever let them catch you slippin'."

"I'mma get a little more sleep in before I go though. No need to rush. It's gonna be a long day."

"Aiight, Q. I love you, girl. And hey, I'll save you a plate."

"Cool, and I love you, too. I'll get with you tomorrow or by the weekend at least."

"Okay, I'm off tomorrow, too, so I'll be here."

"Lucky dog," Queenie joked.

"Yeah, right. I wouldn't say all that."

After Saudia's conversation with Queenie, she turned on the radio in the living room and put on her rubber gloves. Cleaning house was a bitch but somebody had to do it.

Chapter Twenty Five

Jody ~ *There will come a time...*

Jody peered out of her living room window, anticipating the arrival of her kids. Even with Yolanda Adams rejoicing from her speakers, her mood was funky, in a big way. She was dressed and ready to go to church, eager to be on her way. *I can't be late for the special Thanksgiving day service.* She removed the pink satin scarf, which kept her up-do in tact, twisting it between her fingers. *Marcus always does this,* she thought, as she paced the floor waiting for her ex-husband to get there with Chelsea and Xavier. Back in the day she would've already called and cursed him out. *He better be glad I gave my life to the Lord. Ol' sorry fool.* She had expected them over a half an hour ago. *I told his so-called girlfriend that I was taking the kids to early morning prayer service. It is Thanksgiving Day after all.*

Before she could express another thought, the doorbell rang.

"Praise God!"

She knew if she were patient enough they would come. The kids dragged in drowsily as if they were just pulled out of bed.

"Why aren't they dressed, Marcus?" she asked, already tired of the same old argument. "I sent their church clothes over for a reason. I told Shelby that we had to be at church by ten o'clock this morning. It's almost that time now."

"Jody, you the only person I know that gets up at the crack of dawn, on a day off from work, to go to church. You didn't bring the kids over 'til late last night anyway. You might as well have let them stay. What is it with you nowadays? You need a man."

Now, he had really crossed the line. Jody tried to keep calm.

I thought I had a man, she wanted to say but instead she said, "I don't need a man, Marcus. I have my children and I have God. I suggest you and Shelby find God, too. Especially if you're trying to have kids."

"Who said anything to you about that?"

"Me and Shelby talk. It's no big deal. I've accepted your relationship long ago. She's even accepted my invitation to join me and the kids to next Sunday's service."

"Well, count me out. I'll be at home watching football."

"Shelby has already informed me of your Sunday activities. Missing one day of football won't kill you." *Some things never changed.* Jody thought remembering that Marcus wouldn't miss a football game to save his life.

"Hey, I don't smell anything cooking. Don't tell me you guys are eating Thanksgiving dinner at church."

"And what's wrong with that?" Jody wanted to know.

"Nothin', if you don't have family to spend the evening with, but you do. Why don't you go to your mom's and spend time with your family? Your brothers and sisters aren't that bad."

"They're not that good either. I'd rather the kids be in a more positive environment," Jody said, with thoughts of her family who smoked weed, drank liquor and cursed at the dinner table with no shame. The thought alone made her nerves twitch.

"Well, the kids can stay with me and Shelby if you want. She's cooking as we speak and it will be a feast fit for a king, I assure you," Marcus said, smiling at the thought of his beautiful mate.

"How wonderful for you, Marcus. No, the kids will be with me at church as planned," Jody Said, deciding that she was ready for Marcus to leave. "Xavier, did you get all of your things from the car? I need you to go take your bath."

Turning back to Marcus, "Knowing you as well as I do, I ran some bath water."

"They had a bath right before bed. I think they can skip one this morning. Anyway, I'm out. It's back to bed for me."

"You are still a lazy..." Jody began.

"Oh, no, I'll be putting in work, believe me!" he said, with a sly laugh.

"Okay, okay, no need to go into detail. See you in two weeks."

"Bye, kids! Behave in church and I'll talk to you later!" He yelled toward the back of the house where the kids' room was.

The situation was funny to Jody. This was the house that she and Marcus had once shared together, but now he'd barely step into the doorway. The kids both came running to give their daddy a hug and tell him goodbye. Jody couldn't help but watch as he drove off. She wondered if her feelings for him would ever die.

While helping her kids get ready for church, she tried calling Dani. She wanted to invite her and DJ to church but never got through. Jody's personal mission was to slowly but surely, bring her friends back into the church. She was sure they got tired of her preaching, but it was purely out of love. She was especially working on bringing Dani back.

The first time Jody visited Best Baptist, her church home, Dani came with her. Jody remembered Dani saying that she and Drew were going to start going to church. They were both raised in church, but like so many others, including herself, they drifted away from the Lord's house. Jody knew that Dani was very spiritual so her concern was more for the souls of Saudia and Tai. Positive that they both would have declined her invitation to attend service this morning, she didn't even bother. The last time she invited them to church, they both got real ugly attitudes. Tai specifically said that Jody sounded like her mama. Jody was saddened by their responses and felt that the rejection was a real shame because they both need The Lord.

I won't give up on them though, ever.

Chapter Twenty Six

Queenie ~ *Reminisce*

Everybody she'd talk to about her Thanksgiving day plans responded the same. "Have you lost you mind?" Were her big sister Nina's actual words.

Queenie reflected back on her those words and didn't see what the big deal was. Thanksgiving was just like any other day to her.

I give thanks to God each and every day so why was today so different?

Driving in to work on Thanksgiving day was an incredible breeze. The usual freeway traffic was absent. So, as Queenie cruised along, many thought s occupied her mind.

As much as she complained about LA, while living in New York, Queenie truly missed being here. She appreciated the fact that although it was the middle of fall, the sun beamed as if it were summer.

When her family moved to Atlanta there was nothing to hold her in LA. She knew that wherever she dwelled, her family and her friends would always be there. So when she was offered a bigger and better position as senior buyer for Bloomingdales in New York, she jumped at the chance.

Queenie was happy with her choice to move. Living in New York was an experience she'd never forget. In her opinion, New Yorkers knew how to dress and spoke her language. She considered fashion to be her life. Therefore, life in New York had been a refreshing change from LA, which Queenie considered to be fad frenzied. On the other hand, she always represented her taste, which earned her the nickname, Queen Bee.

Where are the classic styles? Where's the individuality? She asked herself this whenever she saw style-starved people while out and about. She'd dreamed of working independently, as a freelanced fashion artist. She wanted to change the world and everyone's outlook how to gear up for the day. She often fantasized an assignment such as dressing all of the hip-hop artists for a music award show. Hip-hop was her choice because it was her culture. It was her family. The very entity, which assisted her parents in her upbringing. She was also sure that hip-hop artists would have the necessary exposure to the masses and would represent her designs to their fullest.

Queenie's decision about making that big move to New York was not only about the experience but also about her independence. Her parents tried to talk her into moving to Atlanta with them, but she had to explain to them that she was an adult. A grown woman. No more following Mommy and Daddy around the store. She wanted them to see that she could handle her business and prove that she had listened to all of the heart-warming conversations and stern lectures as a young girl.

After weeks of battle her folks finally gave in and offered full support. The very same way that they always did when Queenie had her mind made up about something. "Spoiled

Ass," is what her foul mouthed father would say after defeat. He would have it no other way.

Queenie did nothing but work, work, work when she first moved to New York. Her work habits had so consumed her life that her then boss insisted she take a few days off and go see the city. She gave Queenie a list of places to go and a week off with pay.

Queenie thought the idea was quite considerate of her. Real cool, in fact. And she had a ball indeed. In the beginning, she felt lonely and sorry for herself. She had even considered flying to Atlanta to visit her family. But when she weighed the pros and cons, she decided not. She still had to prove her self-government, and running home to her family would admit failure.

Instead she spent the week visiting museums, art shows and, finally, her first Broadway play. *Madam Sunshine,* she remembered fondly. As she reflected on the magical evening she realized that it was that very experience when New York captured her heart. *Emilio De Shay.* She can't seem to separate the two. Emilio and her New York experience went together like a tea bag and hot water. He was gorgeous and when Queenie first saw him her jaw dropped to the floor. He was an actor in "Madam Sunshine." He didn't have a lead role, but his character was very significant to the story. She was consumed with his every word.

When Queenie was introduced to Emilio backstage after the play's end she almost died. She'd been invited back after she bumped into Kerri Simmons, a colleague who happened to have the VIP hookup. "Come back and hang out with me. It'll be fun," were Kerri's exact words. After Queenie's and Emilio's introduction they exchanged brief yet heavy conversation. Queenie had found that he was as beautiful inside as he was on the outside. His dark skin was as smooth as butter and his bald-head was a perfect compliment to his dangerous smile and over-all good looks.

Thoughts of the night she met Emilio still made Queenie crazy. When she complimented him on his style of dress, he returned the favor with a seductive gaze. He licked his lips and pouted them in a knowing smirk. A smirk that she later learned to adore. She also found pleasure in reminiscing their many, very intense conversations. She never knew a man could be so intellectually stimulating. They became a hot item and Emilio wasted no time in professing his undying love for her. Two years ago, she was naïve enough to believe him. Just before he crushed her heart into tiny fragments. So microscopic that to this very day she still felt that some of the missing pieces would never be recovered.

Upon arriving at her Century City office, Queenie looked around and got a reality check on how blessed she was. *Hey, why am I trippin' over Emilio? I'm smart, attractive and successful. I have a good life with goals that I look forward to accomplishing. I cannot allow his hurting me to stunt my growth.* Now that Queenie was back in LA she vowed to make a fresh start. She planned to enjoy the industry parties, shopping on Melrose and spending restorative afternoons at her favorite day spa. Queenie made a firm decision to reap the benefits of her successful career as well as to pamper herself in colossal proportions. *Emilio who?* She laughed out loud at the revelation and allowed a capacious smile to sweep across her gorgeous face, captivating those she passed on her way to her third floor office. Her new outlook and positive mind frame had made her glow with anticipation for the future. *Look out world here I come!* They didn't call her "Queen Bee" for nothin'.

Chapter Twenty Seven

Keera ~ *In the Meantime*

Keera's dreams were crowded with Chance. But they weren't the usual. Unlike her previous dreams, these were not ones that envisioned her and Chance walking down the aisle, or playing in the park with their yet to be born children. No, in these dreams, she and Chance were anything but happy. Chance appeared to be an alien beneath the mask of a human face. The mask began to melt during a lovemaking session and the terror of his true identity came to light.

Keera struggled to understand her dream because she believed that dreams were the key to one's life. Dreams were secret messages given by a higher power to be decoded in one's conscious state, was what her now deceased mother taught her as a young girl. Her quest to learn all she could about dream interpretation was one of the key reasons Keera chose to major in psychology at UCLA. She read every related book she could get her hands on. This dream though, about Chance, seemed clear as a bell. He wasn't being real with her about something. *What is he hiding from me?* Keera clutched the bedcovers, dreading the answer she'd already acknowledged but wasn't ready to deal with.

The mixed aromas of turkey and coffee slivered under Keera's bedroom door. The fact that it was Thanksgiving Day hadn't even crossed her mind in the half an hour that she lay still thinking about Chance. She glanced at her crystal travel clock, which rested on the nightstand, then propped herself onto one elbow. Her pager and cell phone both lay on the floor next to the bed; both displayed new messages.

Keera hoped Chance had called, but to her disappointment, none were from him. She hadn't heard from Chance since his abrupt departure to Miami and now, the following morning, still no word. *Damn him.* Keera sat up straight in the cozy queen-sized bed and smoothed her soft, curly locks down with both hands.

The blanket dropped to her waist exposing her bare breasts and stomach. She viewed the somewhat messy room to find her bathrobe hanging on a top hinge of the closet door, where she usually chose to hang her clothes after shedding them.

She walked her svelte, nude body over to the door where her robe hung. After tying the robe closed, she kicked on her fuzzy slippers and reached for the door handle. She would go and see her dad before hopping into a steamy shower.

Kevin lay on his stomach and watched as Keera left her bedroom. For hours, he'd been spying on her through the ceiling as she slept – or as she tossed and turned, to be more accurate. He was pleased when she finally woke up and even more when he saw that she slept in the nude. He had always suspected that she did, but now he finally saw for himself. He drooled so profusely at the sight of her in the raw that his thick saliva almost escaped through the vent and onto the floor below him. To his relief he had it all on tape. It had taken him weeks to figure out a way to spy on Keera on the rare occasions when she visited them and actually slept over in her old bedroom. When he found the old home's floor plan in the attic, he was like a child at Christmas. He wasn't going to let a little drool ruin it for him.

"Hey Daddy, what's shakin'?" Keera leaned and gave her dad a kiss on the cheek. He sat in his favorite recliner in front of the big screen TV, a gift from Keera, and watched football.

"Happy Thanksgiving, Sweetheart," Mr. Sanders said, his voice rough and gravelly. "How did you sleep?"

"Fine," Keera lied. "Where's Cruella?" she asked as she realized the kitchen was empty.

"*Mary* had to run to the market for a few things. You are staying for dinner, aren't you?" Mr. Sanders knew his daughter too well.

"Yes, but only to spend time with you. Where's Kreepy Kevin?"

"Child, where do you get these nicknames? I don't know, I'm sure he's around here somewhere." He couldn't help but chuckle.

"Daddy, do you want me to get you anything out of the kitchen before I take my shower?"

"A beer would be nice."

"I'm sure it would, but you can't have one." Keera was stern with her dad in regards to his eating and drinking habits. She feared his diabetes would begin to eat away at him as it had done in the past.

"Has Cruella been letting you drink Daddy?"

Keera worried about his new wife's leniency with his diet. She felt that her evil stepmother was plotting her future days as a well to do widow.

Not if I can help it.

"No, Baby, now go take your shower and stop worrying about me. I'm just fine."

"Okay. But I'm comin' back 'cause I see my Cowboys are playin' and I know they're whoopin' that ass," Keera was never hesitant about cursing in front of her dad and he'd long ago given up on scolding her about it. She smiled and looked forward to relaxing in front of the game with her dad like old times.

"Them Cowboys ain't no good. Baby, I thought I taught you better than that. You know that the Forty-Niners are where the money's at."

He loved to taunt Keera about her team picks.

"Okay, Daddy, we'll see. I'll be back in a few."

It felt good to be spending time with her father. Time alone at that. It had been too long.

Chapter Twenty Eight

Andrew ~ *When I Get Free*

This sure wasn't the Thanksgiving holiday that Drew was used to. He'd never craved his mom's turkey and dressing so badly. Instead, a tray of dried mystery meat and watered down potatoes was inedible.

"Ay, Homie, you want this?" Drew asked, hoping to give his untouched food to his withdrawn cellmate.

"Naw, man, you got it," the usually intensely quiet man answered.

Drew was surprised that he had uttered a word. Usually he would just nod his head when answering a question and rare was the occasion when he asked one.

When Drew introduced himself two days ago, the man returned the introduction by asking Drew to call him god. Drew laughed and said that he'd have to settle for "G" because there was only one God in his life.

Since that small exchange of words, there had been nothing. G kept his head buried in books, his body in yoga inspired positions and his mind in meditation. Drew thought nothing of it at first – in fact he was glad that his cellmate's interests kept him silent. But then Drew began to wonder what was really going on. What was in those books that kept his cell mate so tranquil?

Drew's questions seemed to create an opportunity for him to discover the answer. G had been escorted from the cell to go on work duty. As he sat alone, Andrew couldn't help but think of his family. It was Thanksgiving Day and he was in the worst place he could possibly be – just short of being in a casket.

The book's cover was worn and tattered. *Key to Yourself* was its title but the author's name had worn off. Drew scanned the table of contents, then flipped curiously and cautiously through the barely adhesive pages.

Finally he landed on chapter ten, entitled FAITH, and began to read.

"*If we would only understand that God is not some far-off deity; not a stern judge, but the beneficent force that we recognize as nature – the life principle that makes the flowers bloom, and the plants grow; that spreads abundance about us so lavishly.*"

Andrew found the text interesting and continued. *"If we could recognize that there is no lack, limit or restriction in the Universal Mind. The supply is limitless, inexhaustible and free-flowing to all God's children and creatures."*

By the time G returned to the cell, Andrew was immersed in the book with the cloud filled sky on its cover. He didn't even look up to acknowledge G or the fact that he had confiscated his property.

"I see you found the *Key To Yourself,"* G said to Andrew who was sitting on his bottom bunk with his face in the book's pages. It was the first time he had actually spoken outside of necessity since his arrival.

"Yeah, man, I hope it's not a problem I was just a little curious," Andrew said, forcing himself to look up.

"It's cool, man, but you gotta have an open mind for that stuff. It's deep. Go ahead and read it. I'm interested in your thoughts about it."

Andrew lay back on his bunk and started from the beginning. Chapter 1, Thought Law.

"Thinking is the true business of life. Thinkers rule the world. They always have and they always will." It had Drew's full attention already because he was a thinker and he was somehow going to have to think himself from behind the steel bars, which now enslaved him.

Maybe this book is the answer. Danielle, sweetheart, I'm comin' home.

Chapter Twenty Nine

Danielle ~ *No More Pain*

It was a day of enlightenment and major stress for Dani. She was enlightened about how Trixxy was *really treating* Jasmine at home. She'd endured major stress when she took action to make sure that Jasmine wasn't subjected to any more animal-like treatment - ever again.

After she spoke with Carolyn, her new attorney, she made several phone calls before deciding how she would handle things. The police were at Las Flores within minutes. They took a detailed report after examining Jasmine's scars then questioned Trixxy's whereabouts. Dani couldn't help them. She, too, wondered where Trixxy was hiding. She was supposed to have picked Jasmine up the day before, but Dani hadn't heard a word. She paged Trixxy and continued to leave messages on her home machine.

It was a good thing for Jasmine that her mother hadn't shown up. Otherwise, no one would have become aware of the horrific treatment she'd suffered.

The police were very genuine about their concern for Jasmine's well-being. Dani had honestly explained she and Andrew's situation. About him being in jail and all. After hearing Dani's side of the situation and observing Trixxy's absence, they immediately contacted Family Services to have an investigator sent over. The attorney, Carolyn Mathis, sent her colleague, Mike Maxwell, to stand in for her until she returned to LA the next day. Apparently, the Thanksgiving holiday didn't stand in the way of a child's cry for help and Dani was appreciative of everyone's efforts.

Do I want to put Jas' mother in jail? Would that hurt Jasmine more than it would help her?

She prayed about the situation, which always helped Dani regroup, and came to a clear decision. She was more than willing to take Jasmine in full-time, and would do all that she could to make it happen. *She should be with us anyway.* And just like that, it had been settled.

Finally, hours later, the police and acting attorney Mike Maxwell were gone. During the interim of all of the discussion, the kids had escaped to the family room to watch a videotape and had eventually fallen asleep on the couch. Dani had hoped that Trixxy would call, or even better, show up. *It would have been sweet for her to have walked right into police custody, so they could take her to ass jail where she belongs.*

Dani wanted badly to hurt Trixxy the way that Trixxy had hurt that sweet, innocent child. She sat back and visualized how she would "whoop" Trixxy's demented ass.

Later, Francine called to say, "There's plenty of food here at the house," but Dani wasn't up to visiting. Francine had at least a few dozen people over and she wasn't in a very sociable mood.

She called Alfred and Willie Mae throughout the day to keep them posted on Jasmine and the situation at hand. They wanted to come over but she insisted it was not necessary.

They don't need to be dealing with this madness. Lord knew they'd dealt with more than their share raising me, let alone my mother who was hell on wheels.

Speaking of Lena, she was still no where to be found.

Francine had sent food over by way of her new boyfriend, Richard. Dani had heard about Richard, even spoke with him briefly on the phone once, but she'd never met him in person. He was young, at least twenty years Francine's junior, and very good-looking. Charming even. Dani was surprised to say the least. Not because Francine wasn't deserving of such a good find, but because Dani viewed her mother-in-law as an elderly church-going grandmother. One would have never expected her to hook up with a man the likes of him.

He came in briefly, saw the kids and then asked to use the phone. Judging by his polished looks, Dani concluded that Richard was definitely a businessman. She was also sure that Drew was not going to be happy about his mother having a boyfriend. Especially, a young stud like Richard.

Dani woke the kids from their late nap so they could eat dinner, then afterwards she sat them down for a talk. She explained to them that because Jasmine had endured such horrible abuse, which was absolutely no fault of her own, Jasmine would be living with them then on.

"You mean foreva, Momma?" DJ asked, with wide-eyed anticipation.

"Yes, Baby, forever."

She bent down and embraced the two children who squeezed her with all the might they could. When they pulled apart she smiled warmly.

And, felt instant relief about finally unloading what was going on to the children. Jasmine stood still and wrung her little fingers together anxiously.

"Foreva?" was the word she managed to let escape from her thoughts. She wanted reassurance.

"Yes, Sweetie? Are you okay with that?"

Jasmine shook her head "yes" and smiled broadly. The single tear, which welled never did flow down her cheek. Instead it disappeared into the sparkle of her joyful eyes.

They jumped for joy and bombarded Dani with hugs and kisses. Dani, dropped a tear or two, and then sent them upstairs to play. They would talk in more detail later. Pleased that Jasmine responded well to the sudden changes in her life, she could breathe again.

She wanted to talk about everything with Keera or Queenie but decided against calling. Instead, she ran a hot bath and prayed silently as she soaked in the sudsy water. She was beyond worn out and needed badly to relax. After her bath water was done she prepared for her relaxation with music and candlelight. She turned on the radio in her bathroom, turned the dial from The BEAT's hip-hop to The WAVE's contemporary jazz, for the soothing sounds that her mind was craving. Then, she lit the lavender-scented candles around her giant Jacuzzi tub and was just one step away from heaven when the phone rang.

She let it ring. She was sure it wasn't Andrew because of the late hour. She wondered if it was Trixxy. She had already decided she didn't want to talk to her. First, she needed to figure out how she would handle her when she showed up at the door to claim Jasmine. Dani wanted to avoid any confrontation so that her record could remain spotless. In order to do that, she would need to keep her distance until all of the paperwork was filed and Family Services had come to investigate further.

She'll never get her.

Dani wasn't having it any more. Enough was enough.

After her long soothing bath, Dani went to look in on the kids. "The Little Rascals" movie was on, but they were knocked out. They had fallen asleep again, one on each couch and each clutching a McDonald's Happy Meal toy. She covered them with blankets and turned off the TV. They looked as if they were out for the night and she wasn't about to carry them into their bedrooms. She then kissed both of them good night and said a silent prayer over them. They usually prayed together and Dani felt that just because they were asleep, they needn't be deprived of it. It had been a long trying day for all of them and they all needed a good night's sleep. It was obvious that the kids were already in dream-land, but Dani had a feeling that her trip wouldn't be as trouble-free.

Chamomile tea, here I come.

Chapter Thirty

TAI ~ *Let's Get High*

Thanksgiving Day flew by for Tai – of sound mind she was not. The plan was to meet Chris for a quick fix then head to The Boutique to do some Thanksgiving Day hair. It sounded good but didn't quite work out that way.

Chris waited for Tai, as the Coyote would for Roadrunner. He decided that when she got there he would have a little fun. He would test her to see just how hooked she was on the drug and at the same time get his kicks.

When she pulled up she was beautiful, as always. Her short blonde hair, spiked and stylishly messy on top, was sexy and her blue jeans and midriff sweatshirt were casually seductive. She never appeared desperate to get a hit and always carried herself as if she didn't give a damn.

She hopped across the cement foot-stones which lay a path to the front porch. Tai glanced around cautiously and stepped quickly. His neighborhood was nice enough and his home well groomed but the vicious hounds that barked and growled visciously were scary as shit. Even worse, they were not in plain view, which made her an easy target. The last thing she needed was to be mauled by a pair of heathen dogs. *Unh-unh, my name is not Alpo.*

The sound of the doorbell was hard for Tai to hear above the loud music coming from inside. If she didn't know better she would have sworn there was a Jay-Z concert goin' down.

After banging a couple of hard knocks against the iron bar door, she finally got a response.

"Chill on the bangin' girl! You got me buggin' an' shit!"

"Whatever. You got my stuff ready? 'Cause I gotta go." Tai stood just inside of his front door, jingling her keys. Suddenly she felt a tad uncomfortable.

"Aw, come on, Tai. You got a minute to kick it, don't you?" Chris asked, having already started his fun and games.

"Nope. Sorry, my client is probably already at The Boutique," she said. Tai glanced around the room to check out how Chris was living. *Pretty nice.*

"At least come in and smoke one wit a nigga." Chris gave Tai the puppy dog eyes and held his arms out wide.

She couldn't resist. He held her hand and led her into his partially empty home. He'd lived there six months and even after he unpacked his moving boxes, he still hadn't completely filled the space. Besides the leather furniture that smelled brand new, there was a glass coffee table and an entertainment center against a large bare wall.

The entertainment center was home to a TV, VCR, stereo and CD player, and a Sega Dreamcast. On the floor next to the coffee table lay a stack of *Code, Hustler* and various other male-friendly magazines. And, against a wall were CDs and an array of video game cartridges. There was no art on the walls, no nick-knacks, no pictures of family or friends. *A true bachelor.*

She sat perched forward on his dark green, leather sofa and watched him as he lit the hypnotic cigarette. Her waiting client was no longer an issue; neither was her full Friday morning schedule, nor Thanksgiving dinner with her sisters and their kids.

An entire day evolved while Tai and Chris smoked, drank and had sex. All it took was a few hits of "that shit," some Alize' and some R. Kelly to make Tai lose her mind. She shrugged off the nagging voice in the back of her head that told her, "Get up and leave. You still have time to save yourself." But she was not trying to hear it. She was feeling too good to stop and return to her boring life. The fact that she had no man in her world at that particular time made Chris look like a dream with his new home and Lexus Coupe parked in the driveway. The good looks and charm didn't hurt either.

She bought into the illusion that he would actually make a good man, despite the fact that he was a drug dealer – her drug dealer.

Their sexual encounter the day before was frightening for Tai. After an intense smoke out everything seemed cool. They laughed and talked and even slammed some dominoes. But then all at once, everything went into super slow motion. She felt numb, cold and even a little dizzy. She had a vile taste in her mouth and her tongue seemed to be swelled. Her high was out of control.

They smoked Chris' stash and finished off half a bottle of Gran Marnier. She was tossed. They both were, but Chris didn't consume nearly as much as Tai did. He only pretended to. He noticed that she would only take a hit if he did, so he faked it. He was having the time of his life watching Tai go through her changes. He enjoyed the feeling that he was in control.

"You alright?" he asked her after she lay back on the couch and closed her eyes as if in agony.

"Yea, I'm alright. Damn, ain't it hot in here?" she asked, sitting up and fanning her face with one of Chris' magazines.

"Nope. I feel great," he boasted with a straight face.

"Well, I'm hot." Tai began to strip off her clothes – first her shirt, then her jeans. There she sat in her Victoria Secret's bra and panties, sweating bullets.

"Chris, quit playin' turn off that damn heat," Tai said accusingly. He hadn't turned on any heat, but he did turn her on to a drug that had begun to take over her life. After the hot flashes came the paranoia, which still lingered.

"Chris, somebody's at the door," she insisted. First, she thought it was the police, then her sisters who she felt were surely looking for her. After all, she had never gone to The Boutique, or shown up for the family's Thanksgiving dinner. Now, it was the next morning and she still hadn't talked to anyone.

I'd better get home.

Chris was finished with his little experiment and no longer cared whether she came or went. He was worn out from his binge with Tai and wanted to sleep for the rest of the day. He turned off his pager and all of his phones just before dragging himself to the door to let Tai out.

"Don't forget my shit, mothafucka," she told him as she walked out his front door. They had smoked all of his stash and she still needed to buy her weekend supply.

Chris agreed to have it ready for her when she returned after work. She'd be doing hair well into the night and would be more than ready for another rendezvous when she was finished.

Friday was usually one of Tai's busiest days, but this one was different. She'd gone straight from Chris' house and had neither the energy nor the desire to go to The Boutique. She still had a little time before her first appointment, so she lounged around the house just a little longer. She had taken a bath and washed her hair but still felt dirty.

Although she enjoyed her smoke-outs with Chris, it never failed that afterward, she felt guilty and remorseful. She wanted to stop because she could already see that her life would become tragic if she didn't. She had already soured a few relationships with some of her faithful regulars at The Boutique by not showing up for their appointments. She also knew that her bank account would suffer if she continued this trend.

She looked around her tastefully decorated, yet, filthy house and decided that enough was enough. Her home was usually spotless, but even it had fallen by the wayside. She opened all the windows and got busy. To start, she picked up the piles of dirty clothes and separated them into loads. As she prepared to throw her first load into the washing machine, she felt faint and almost passed out. A heavy dizziness came over her and the walls began to close in around her, surrounding her like an army brigade. Her vices called out to her enticingly, waiting just in the next room.

What the hell, if I finish my stash it won't kill me.

Before succumbing to her urges, she went back and forth with herself about kicking what had obviously become a habit. But the drugs prevailed. She was ashamed and would die if any of her friends saw her. She knew none of them would have ever gone the route she'd chosen.

Every hit of the pipe was as good as the first and every gulp of liquor as good as the last. She used to never mix her alcohol with her smoke, but there were no more rules when it came to her drug use. She no longer felt dizzy, but she did have an urgency to finish cleaning the house. It was as if the sight of the dirt and the mess reflected her image of her rotten and decayed insides.

Tai got a lot done around the house in an hour. She washed a load of clothes and planned to finish the rest when she returned home from work.

"Shit, I'm late again," she said aloud. She had gotten so involved with cleaning that she had totally forgotten about her ten a.m. appointment.

It took her only a few minutes to shower and dress. She called The Boutique from her cell phone to check in. Lisa, her resident manicurist, answered the line.

"The Boutique, how may I help you?" she answered in a professional tone.

"Hey Lisa, it's Tai. Is my ten o'clock there yet?"

"Yet? She's been here and gone, girl."

Tai didn't appreciate her tone but she let it slide.

"She left already? But it's only ten thirty, damn."

"Yeah, she was pissed too. She mentioned something about this being the second time. I offered to give her a manicure while she waited but she stormed out in a huff."

"Whatever, she'll be back. Can't nobody but me hook up that nappy ass kitchen she got anyway." Tai laughed at herself but Lisa, who sported dreads, didn't think it was funny.

"Hey, I'mma stop at Grits n' Greens for some breakfast. Do you want anything?" Tai asked but hoped Lisa would say no.

"No thanks. Charles and I had something delivered earlier. We're cool."

"Okay then. I'll see you in a few."

I guess I fucked up again. Shana's naps were too much to be dealin' with this morning anyway.

Tai convinced herself that there was a reason for everything. She had another two hours until her next appointment so she chose to eat her breakfast inside the diner, Grits n' Greens, and flip through the latest issue of *Essence*. It had been in her car all week, along with mounds of other neglected mail. She had a lot of paperwork to catch up on and bills to write out but she would do that when she got to her office. For now, she would just sit and enjoy her *Essence* and her usual breakfast of scrambled cheese eggs, toast and coffee.

Grits n' Greens was unusually quiet. There was also a handsome new waiter Tai had never seen before.

I need to start eating in here more often.

She didn't flirt with the man, as she normally would have. She didn't feel all that great and she couldn't put her finger on what the problem was. She felt yucky as opposed to her usual, sexy, spicy self. Her period was late but she could tell it was coming. Her breasts were tender and she was retaining water around her stomach.

When she finished her *Essence* magazine and her half eaten breakfast, she left a huge tip for Mr. Cute Waiter. She didn't flirt with him today, but when she felt better, she would be back.

At The Boutique she found Charles and Lisa in an intimate conversation. They were leaning against the doorframe of Charles' massage room, whispering like school kids. It wasn't a big surprise to Tai that the conversation ended as soon as she walked through the door.

I know they're talkin' about me but I don't give a fuck. As long as they stay within their boundaries and pay me my rent, we are all good.

Tai broke the ice by asking, "Did I have any other pissed off clients this morning?"

"Nope, just that one," Lisa answered in a smart-alecky tone.

"Good, and how about you all? What are your schedules like today?" She knew her question would irritate Charles because he rarely had a client. It puzzled Tai that he was able to pay his rent.

"Hello?" Tai said when her question was ignored. "Am I talking to myself or what?"

She was well aware that she was being a bitch, but felt that because it was her establishment, she had every right.

Let them get their own shop where they can do what the fuck they want. Puhleez, manicurists and masseuses are a dime a dozen.

"I have three clients scheduled to come in today then I'm off to do my VIP housecalls," he bragged.

Yeah, right. The only house you'll be visiting is your own, propped in front of your TV with yo mama, watchin' soaps and Ricki Lake.

Tai's thoughts were vicious.

"And Lisa. What about you, Sweetie?"

"Who me? Oh, I have back-to-back appointments today. My schedule is mad crazy," she answered matter-of-factly.

"All right, well I'm waiting for a shipment of hair products this morning. Can you sign for it? I'll be in my office going over bills."

"Yeah, girl. No problem," Lisa answered, seemingly preoccupied.

Lisa could be cool at times and a straight bitch at others. Charles, on the other hand, had been catty from day one. Tai was sure that he wasn't getting any. And even more sure that getting pussy was not on his agenda.

Before Tai settled into work mode, she went to her car to get a quick fix. She had one good drag left. She couldn't resist the urge to smoke drug that she began to despise. It was taking over her life.

Tai returned to her office on full buzz and lay on the couch. Her high came on good and strong, then she was back on cloud nine. She daydreamed about her night with Chris – what she remembered, at least. She'd had a few blackouts as of late and sometimes couldn't remember certain events. Her stomach was queasy and before she could make it into the bathroom, her breakfast was all over the floor.

What the fuck?

This was the second time this week that she'd thrown up. Before that she hadn't earled in years and couldn't make heads or tails of why she had now. She felt vile. Before she could begin to clean herself up, Lisa buzzed on the intercom.

"Yes?" Tai asked, sounding as annoyed as she felt.

"Tai, there's a walk-in client out here for you. She says she would like a trim and a blow style," Lisa announced. "Can you take care of her?"

Before she could think straight Tai answered, "I'll be right out." She thought about the clients she had recently lost and decided to do it.

She cleaned up her bathroom floor using rubber gloves and disinfectant. Then she cleaned herself by brushing her teeth, gargling with mouthwash and washing her face. Lastly, she dabbed on some Eternity perfume and felt she was good to go.

Her stomach felt better but her high was still on full blast. She amazed herself with the fact that she could still function while performing normal tasks.

Did Chris give me some bullshit or what? Why am I so sick?

Tai thought that because she hadn't been eating right, her stomach had acted up. She would order a healthy lunch after she worked her new client and was sure it would put her on track. She refused to believe that the drugs were the problem. Anything but the drugs.

The walk-in client's name was Mindy. She was a large woman with a head full of thick red hair. Tai began to comb through her thick mane and she swore she could hear Mindy having a full conversation with herself in the mirror.

Wonderful. A crazy bitch with a full head of frizzy red hair. Looks like an all day job. I'll only do what the bitch asks for. Nothing more.

Tai glanced at Mindy's mother who sat in the waiting area reading *Jet* magazine.

She could use a relaxer her damn self. If I wasn't feelin' so shitty, I'd get her ass in my chair too. Mo' money, mo' money, mo' money. You know how we do it, baby.

Tai amused herself.

"So, Mindy, we're getting a trim and a blow style today?" Tai asked before beginning the process.

"Bitch!" Mindy responded in a loud brash voice.

"Excuse me?" Tai swirled Mindy's chair around to face her.

No she didn't just call me a bitch.

Tai looked at her to try and get an understanding of what exactly was going on.

"Fuck you!" Mindy said in a louder, bolder tone.

"No, fuck you, Beeyatch!" Tai shouted right back at her. Mindy was completely out of line and Tai wanted an apology.

Mindy's mother tried to butt in and break up the controversy, but Tai was too charged up to listen. She was waiting on Mindy to say, "just kidding," or something like it. Instead, she continued with the insults and the name-calling. Lisa and Charles didn't help any. They just sat back and enjoyed the entertainment. Their laughter pushed Tai over the edge.

Everything was suddenly blurry. Without warning, Tai picked up her blow dryer and wrapped the cord around Mindy's neck, pulling at both ends as tight as she could. She was a maniac. Mindy appeared to be larger than life when she rose from the chair, lifting Tai at the same time. She picked her up in mid air and threw her across the room. Tai landed on her right arm and slid across The Boutique's freshly waxed linoleum floor. Underneath her, the bone in her right arm had cracked into pieces, but she was so amped that she felt no pain.

She managed to get up and run headfirst into Mindy, knocking the wind out of her. Tai rammed her into the wall so hard the whole place shook. Before Tai could finish Mindy off, her mother grabbed her and ran out of the shop.

Betta' had.

Tai was dizzy. She bent over in her chair and took deep breaths. Her arm throbbed heavily but it didn't bother her as much as it should have.

“Can you guys believe that shit?” Tai asked, turning to Charles and Lisa who still laughed uncontrollably. Tai was through.

“You know you guys could have helped. Hell, calling 911 would have been a good idea. You know what? Fuck both of y’all and get the fuck out! Y’all are both bitches!” She stomped into her office and slammed the door behind her.

It still smelled like the vomit that had gotten on the carpet. She should have left the window open to allow the small room to air out. The mixed odor of vomit and Pine sol made her feel sick again. Tai sat at her desk and used her left hand to grab her appointment book. She would cancel the rest of her appointments and get to the emergency room, fast. She was sure that her arm was broken. Luckily, she was able to contact most of her clients for the day. For those she didn’t reach she left messages that she was sick.

Next, she went to her liquor stash and found an unopened bottle of Hennessy. She pulled the cork with her teeth and began to sip. It helped a little but she was still jittery about what had just happened.

Who can I call? I can’t drive like this. How can I explain this to anyone? No one will understand.

She thought about calling Chris but decided a taxi would be better. She was through with him. She’d had enough. Before she could finish panicking there was a hard knock on the door.

“Tai Robinson?”

“Yea? Who is it?”

"It's the police. Open the door."

Fucking great. Tai opened the door to find two Caucasian police officers – one male, one female.

"Before making an arrest here, we need to hear your side of the story," the husky, male officer smirked.

"She attacked me! That's what happened!" Tai was out of control. "She broke my fuckin' arm! I can't even fuckin'work!"

Mindy and her mother wanted Tai arrested for assault. The police said that the bruises around Mindy's neck were enough to arrest Tai, but they wanted to hear her side of the story first. When Tai came completely out of her office, she saw Charles and Lisa giving a third officer a descriptive report of the incident.

Great. The perfect chance for those two losers to try and ruin me. I'm done.

When Tai came to, she lay strapped and handcuffed to a stretcher. She lay numb as they rolled her into the ambulance.

"She's conscious," the lanky, red-necked paramedic stated to a nearby police officer.

What the hell?

She was disoriented.

What is happening to me?

In the hospital, Tai lay with her left hand cuffed to her bed while her right arm rested in a porcelain cast. It was broken, just as she'd thought.

The doctor saw that Tai was awake. He came in and sat next to her bed.

"Well hello, Ms. Robinson. It seems you've had quite an exciting day," he said, smiling. His brown skin and gentle eyes were a comfort. It was obvious that he genuinely loved his work.

Tai looked at him and wondered what he meant by "exciting day." As far as she was concerned, there was nothing exciting about it.

"Are you aware that you put one of the police officers in the hospital? You took a real nasty bite out of him. Because of the nature of his wounds we were forced to do some blood tests on you to make sure, you know, that he wasn't infected by any disease that you may carry."

Tai frowned and listened intensely.

What is he tryin' to say?

"The good thing is, I'm happy to say, that you are disease free. But, you are pregnant. And judging by the way you have been behaving, with your drug use and all, I'm going to assume you did not know this." He looked at her like a father would his misbehaving daughter.

"You must be mistaken. I am *not* pregnant. That's impossible. Now go on back to your lab and re-check your results." She was tense and not in the mood for the okey-doke.

"No, Ms. Robinson, our tests are proof positive. And because the tests also revealed your heroin habit, I have no alternative but to demand that you be released into a confined rehabilitation center. If I don't, you will most likely go to jail and that won't help your situation."

You got that right.

She thought about her sexual escapades with Chris, back when they'd first met, and knew that her being pregnant was not that impossible.

Tai released a deep sigh. Her high was gone and so was her shield against the real world. She was ashamed and embarrassed. Her life had plummeted in a single day. *Bottoms up.*

"None of this is my fault. You have to believe me," Tai pleaded with the doctor. She needed for someone to listen.

"That, that woman called me names and then attacked me for no reason. I was just defending myself."

"Mindy Gaines has Turrets Syndrome. She had no control over her verbal attacks against you. It's a serious disorder. And I highly doubt that she attacked you physically. According to the arresting officer, you were on a rampage," he said with a sad expression.

Turrets Syndrome? Why didn't her mother tell me what was up? A person should be warned about that shit.

Tai had heard all about the disease on the Sally Jesse Raphael show. It was a disorder where one of the symptoms was uncontrollably blurting out obscenities.

"There is help available but you have to want it. You can use this experience to turn your life around. Do it while you still can." He was sincere.

The doctor had seen it many times before. It saddened him to see such a beautiful woman's life in so much turmoil. He would return later to see about her and talk to her more. In the meantime, he hoped she would think about what he'd said.

Tai let out another sigh and looked to the ceiling. The handcuff was tight on her wrist and it pained her to move it at all. Slowly, the tears dripped down her cheeks as she remembered the tragic events of the day. The fact that she was pregnant was a nightmare in itself. She no longer had use of her right arm, which meant she couldn't do hair; and she was on her way to jail or a drug rehab, which in her mind were one in the same.

Tai was up shit's creek without a paddle and there was nothing she could do.

Let God work it out? He never helped me before but I guess it won't hurt to ask. Dear God, I swear if you get me out of this mess, I will be your dedicated servant from here on out. I promise.

Sadly, her cravings for the joy powder consumed her. She balled herself into the fetal position and placed her free hand on her stomach rubbing it gently. She imagined the baby inside of her hungry for a fix as well. Terrified with speculations of "what-ifs" she cried herself into a deep slumber.

Chapter Thirty One

Saudia ~ *Next Lifetime*

As much as Saudia loved a paid holiday, she was just as happy when it was over. It was a given that she'd put on a few extra pounds. She always did during the holidays. She enjoyed food and food enjoyed her round behind. *The men don't mind it though,* she reminded herself just before finishing the last piece of Marie Calendar's lemon cheesecake.

She also reminded herself that she would soon face her thirtieth birthday and that she'd better watch it before she ended up like her Aunt Sis – all ass, coming and going. It was a pathetic sight, which made Saudia vow to lose ten pounds before the New Year. It was a never-ending cycle.

Other than the guilt of all of the food she inhaled the day before, she had a very nice family holiday. Saudia, the kids, her Aunt Sis and her dad sat and watched movie after movie and feasted on an eight-course meal cooked by Aunt Sis and her church friends.

Before dinner, they enjoyed watching Soul Food, which was Saudia's pick. Next, the kids voted on Dr. Doolittle. After dinner, Ebenezer, Saudia's dad, insisted that everyone watch football. Lastly, it was Notting Hill on the tube, which was Aunt Sis' pick. Her new favorite. The flick also put Ebenezer and the kids to sleep. The perfect ending to a flawless day.

Saudia worried about her dad. His attention span seemed even shorter and his memory was almost non-existent, which were the same signs that her mother showed just before she passed away one year ago. Soon after her death, Ebenezer's health began to gradually decline.

His doctor said that it was common for a longtime spouse to experience melancholia after the death of their partner. The doctor also said however, that in time Ebenezer would get better. Saudia was still waiting for the change. Her father was close to eighty years old and she feared that his time was near.

After her mother passed away, Saudia offered to move in with her dad but he refused. When she began to demand that she and the kids move in after watching her father lose weight and his interest in life, she saw a fire in him that she thought had long gone out. He ranted and raved until she pulled back to prevent him from having a heart attack.

Stubborn ol' fool.

She loved her father dearly and checked in on him every single day. She made sure he was fed, that he had clean clothes and underwear and of course that his house stayed clean. She wanted to hire someone to do the job because her hands were full with the twins and her own household, but her slim salary wouldn't allow for it.

Thankfully, her Aunt Sis, Ebenezer's much younger sister, lived nearby and helped out tremendously – that is when her own health was good. Saudia was very grateful to her feisty Aunt who never allowed anything to keep her down. She and Ebenezer had a falling out years ago over her choice for a husband. They hadn't spoken again until his health began to deteriorate. Saudia made the initial efforts to reunite them and so far things had gone well.

Her father was sometimes as much of a challenge as Damon and Daria, so she needed all the help she could get. Saudia cursed the twin's father for not being there because raising those two solo was no joke. At the moment she enjoyed a break because they were in the backyard playing with the kids from upstairs.

Her lower level duplex apartment was airy and spacious. It was her first home since becoming an independent woman and she has since made it into her castle. Over the years she enjoyed shopping for rare mantel pieces at antique stores and thrift shops and even made a few of her own treasures by hand. The abundance of plants was new to her, but when her mother died she felt she had to bring her "babies" home with her to nurture and care for. There was no way that Ebenezer would take on the role of a green thumb. She did however, leave a few with him because they were no doubt a large part of the woman he loved his whole lifetime.

She kicked back on her cushiony sofa and turned on the TV. Passing over court shows and boring news programs to finally settle on BET's music videos. Music was a big part of Saudia's life. She could easily see her receptionist position at Mayhem Records someday transformed into something bigger and better. If she got the promotion she felt that she was due, she would definitely be on her way.

Amongst her friends she felt inferior about her career. They were all so successful and glamorous. Even Jody had a good position at the bank, which allowed for her to maintain a seemingly financial free lifestyle. It scared Saudia that Jody chose to plummet so much of her money into the church. *To each his own*, was her final thought on the subject.

She was the only one of her friends who couldn't go shopping on a whim or dine at restaurants like EuroChow for lunch. They were all well-off: Keera, a successful model; Dani, an advertising executive on the rise; Tai, the owner of a beauty salon; Queenie, a Senior Buyer for Bloomingdales; and Jody, the loan manager at a Beverly Hills bank. Saudia no longer felt the same pride in her receptionist position that she had in the past. Not that her friends treated her any differently. As far as they were concerned, Saudia was on the same level as they were. But Saudia did have goals. One day she would be a top music executive. Big ballin' and shot callin' were her goals for the new year. Music ran through her veins and was pulling her slowly, but surely, into its' heart.

Just as the oven timer buzzed, which told Saudia that her dinner biscuits were ready, the telephone rang.

"Hello?" Saudia hoped that it wasn't Sam.

"Hello?" She repeated after getting no response. She heard what sounded like heavy breathing and asked again, "Hello?"

"S-Saudia? It's me. It's your Aunt Sis." The alarming tremble in her aunt's voice made Saudia panic.

"Aunt Sis, what's the matter?"

"It's Ebenezer, Sweetie." She paused uncomfortably.

"What, is it about Daddy?" Saudia was confused.

"He's gone, Baby. He's passed on." Her voice fell off and she began to wail.

"What happened? What do you mean he's gone? He was fine when we spoke this morning!" Saudia was in a panic.

"He had a heart attack." She paused. "Thank God I was here with him. I would have hated for him to have died alone." Aunt Sis had calmed herself.

"The paramedics just left. There was nothing they could do. Now I'm waiting on the corner."

"Oh my God, Daddy? My daddy is dead?" Saudia was in shock. She knew his time was coming but she didn't think it would happen so soon.

"I'm on my way over," she insisted.

"No, Saudia. I'll take care of things here. You just look after those kids. You're going to have to be strong for them and make sure they understand what happened. It's important that they know that his spirit is still alive. Do you hear me? You have to believe it too, Saudia."

Saudia knew her Aunt Sis was right, but it was all too much for her to digest. The thought of not having said good-bye to her father made her sick. The choice of staying at home while her dad lay dead in his home was a difficult one, but she felt it was best. She'd learned from rocking her mother's corpse for an hour after her passing that a sentimental visit wouldn't bring him back.

Somehow she managed to get dinner on the table that evening as well as get the kids bathed and tucked into bed just before she read them a story. What she couldn't do was talk to them about their grandfather.

First they lost their dad and now their Grandpa. It just isn't fair. My daddy is dead.

She cleaned the kitchen and took a shower as if nothing was different; but when she retired to her bedroom for a good night's sleep, she broke down and sobbed like a lost child. She had comfort in her belief that he was now happy with her mother.

Daddy was never the same after Mama died. And how could he have been? They were together for sixty-two years of their lives. Now he is at peace. I just know he is.

Still, her heart ached. With the exception of her Aunt Sis, her family now only consisted of the twins. She was lonely and sad and wished that she had someone there who could comfort her the way she needed to be comforted. Suddenly, Sam was on her mind and before she knew it she was dialing his pager number. It wasn't really him that she wanted, but she needed to feel close to someone and she knew that he could fill the void that she was feeling. Even if only for a few hours.

Chapter Thirty Two

Queenie ~ *Runnin' Thangs*

Thanksgiving had been an average day for Queenie. She went to work as if it were a regular workday. Today though, the store was crazy. It was the day after Thanksgiving and everyone who enjoyed a sale was at the Beverly Center's Bloomingdales. Her office was even more of a circus than the store. She met with her small staff of six about the designer fashion show they attended two nights before. She gave her personal tickets to her team of assistants and junior buyers. The tickets were courtesy of one of her many contacts in the fashion industry. The shows didn't excite her the way they had in the past, especially during her interning days, but her staff were excited and appreciative.

Queenie always had an ecstasy for clothes. Her ultimate dream was to be a designer with her own line. She carried the vision of a brand new funky outfit or elegant gown in her thoughts each night. The problem was that her sketches didn't always reflect the image she wanted to relay.

She loved her job though, as a Senior Buyer for Bloomingdales. It was a long climb up the success ladder, but it was well worth it. Her world was surrounded by her passion and she was grateful for her blessings. She was well aware that everyone didn't have it like she did. She knew she worked hard to get to where she was, but she also knew that if it wasn't God's will then it wouldn't have happened.

Today would be meetings, meetings and more meetings. In the morning, she had photographs of models to sort through, new designs to show to marketing and a photo shoot to dress for *In Style* magazine. There was more. After the photo shoot, she would head to Millennium Pictures' studios. Then she had an appointment to see a house her realtor just knew Queenie would "die for." It was the third "to die for" find that week.

Queenie was overwhelmed with anticipation in regards to working with Millennium Pictures. She received a call earlier in the week by a studio head who had heard of her reputation in the fashion world. Young and fresh was what they wanted and Queenie's portfolio of fashion picks was just that.

She was very excited to be offered the wardrobe consultant job for an upcoming Millennium Pictures' film. They were hot, innovative film studio that seemed unstoppable when it came to making blockbuster hits. Five independent filmmakers put their resources and talent together to create Millennium Pictures. It was now the top grossing studio for the second year in a row.

Queenie had no idea who referred her to the studio but she wanted to know. Whoever it was would get her deepest gratitude. The studio head wouldn't divulge who referred her, but he did confirm that the person was in the starring role of the tentatively titled film, "The Matchmaker," and that they would meet at the meeting.

She almost declined the offer when the mystery of it all began to scare her, but when they talked dollars, Queenie heard them loud and clear. She'd never in her life made as much money as they offered. The whole experience had widened her mind to a world of new possibilities. She never would've dreamed that her love for clothes would take her to Hollywood.

"Simone, can you make sure the valet has my car out front in exactly one hour? I have a lot going on today and I don't have a minute to waste." Queenie liked her new secretary and hoped that she worked out better than the last.

"Yes, Ms. Le Day. Is there anything else you would like me to do? I'm almost finished typing the check list for the photo shoot."

"Okay, great. When you've finished with that, give the list to Pam and Michael so they can go over the inventory in the van before we leave. And if I'm not back from my meeting with marketing, page me. Those guys can make a one hour meeting stretch until nightfall."

Simone smiled. She loved her new job as Queenie's secretary. She would do everything to make sure she did the best job possible. She wanted to go places and Queenie would be her guide if she played her cards right.

To Queenie's surprise, the meeting was smooth and brief. It seemed that everyone else had a busy day as well. She was right on schedule. The van had been inventoried and all of the clothes, shoes and accessories for the *In Style* photo shoot had been accounted for and were in route to the shoot's location. Queenie was right on their heels. She couldn't stand to be late.

Queenie went over a few last minute details with Simone then took the elevator to the main level where her Black

Mercedes S300 was waiting. She opened the sunroof and turned up the volume on the radio, which played an R&B slow song she loved; but she could never remember the name of the singing group.

Maybe they'll announce the song title and artist when the song is over.

She wanted to go buy the CD but didn't want to go through the embarrassing experience of having to sing the chorus to an unlucky employee at Tower Records.

The song's melody put Queenie in a relaxed mode. The sun was beaming and the traffic was light. Queenie enjoyed the road's tranquility.

If the rest of the day could go this smoothly it would be the bomb ending to a smooth ass week.

Chapter Thirty Three

Keera ~ *Can't get you off my mind...*

Keera lay in her bed and stared at the ceiling as she tried to dissect her recurring dream. In it, Chance was no longer Chance. Every time he blinked, he wore a different face – the face of another man. What does it mean? First he turned into an alien then he changed faces every ten seconds.

The strange string of dreams that she'd had for the past few nights were not her only concern. She hadn't talked to Chance since he fled to Miami late Wednesday afternoon. He didn't call her at all on Thanksgiving and here it was the morning after, and still nothing. The only pages she'd received were the same prank pages, which started weeks before. Probably from the same idiot who sent the sick letters.

Keera didn't put too much brainpower into it. The caller would breathe on her voicemail, page her with the numbers 666 and the number to an LA cemetery. *Fuck 'em.* She had a fearless nature and a pistol that was always at her side.

Come and get it, Mothafucka.

Thanksgiving was perfect. She spent the whole time with her dad. They played a few rounds of backgammon, watched football and had their annual Thanksgiving Day eating contest. Keera surprised both of them and won. Her diet was out the window on Thanksgiving, and when she was mad at Chance. Double helpings. Cruella and Kevin were not thrilled that Keera and her dad enjoyed each other's company, as if they were the only two in the house. Keera didn't feel guilty. She was making up for lost time.

"They get to see you everyday, Daddy. Can we just spend a little time, just us?" Keera asked her dad when he attempted to invite his new bride to play poker with them.

Cruella gave him the evil eye from the kitchen. She didn't know how to play and thought it insensitive of him to pick that particular game for her to play. She felt excluded and had complained to her husband on other occasions about how Keera monopolized him when she came home. This time she was once again the loser in that battle and she couldn't wait for Keera to go back to New York.

Kevin, on the other hand, had a different reason for his sentiment. Keera had barely spoken two words to him since she'd been home. He tried to strike up conversation. She ignored him. Since she wouldn't talk to him, he was suspended for hours spying on her from the vent in her bedroom's ceiling with his digital video cam rolling. His collection of unsolicited "Keera" film footage was growing and put to good during those lonely, late-nights. His time was also spent in his own room writing in his diary and plotting how he could get his job back as her bodyguard. He would do almost anything for the chance.

Keera had a long talk with her dad just before going to bed the night before. Sitting in front of the TV, they wore flannel pajamas and drank hot chocolate with marshmallows and whipped cream. Just the way they had when she was a little girl. It was once the only thing that soothed her at night after her mom's drug induced death.

These nights though, her mind was occupied with Chance. And just as she had done when her mom died, she pushed unwanted thoughts and questions to the back of her mind where she wanted them to stay. She actually wanted to forget about him altogether, but she knew that was not possible. He was a part of her. He was her best friend, her lover and her partner. At least she used to have it like that. Lately, she felt more like a fan.

It was she that always called him and sent him love letters and flowers, just because. He had stopped his romantic gestures long before, with the exception of the other night when he met her at the airport. They made love in the limousine then had a fabulous seafood dinner at Crustacean. She thought maybe he had snapped out of whatever he had been going through lately.

He behaved well at his birthday party too, except for his disappearing act. As a matter of fact, he disappeared a lot lately, but this had been the longest so far. Three days and not a phone call. That was strange to Keera because if nothing else, Chance would always call her after he'd landed. She did the same whenever she traveled. It was just something they'd done from the start.

"So now that he's stopped, does that mean it's over?" Keera asked her dad in a soft voice before sipping her mug of hot chocolate.

"Baby, I can't answer that. You need to ask Chance. It sounds to me like you all are way over due for a heart to heart. A good soul cleansing conversation." Mr. Sanders was firm with his answer. He hated for his daughter to be in pain but it was a part of life that everyone had to experience in order to grow and learn.

Keera valued her father's counsel. He was always straight to the point. He never psychoanalyzed or judged her about anything. He was her rock. It was as if Chance had thrown her in the ocean without a life jacket but instead of sinking, she swam the short distance to her dad, the buoy in the water. He was always there and always his same sensible, dependable self. It was her time with him that changed her mind about leaving for New York so soon. She wished it were just the two of them, but tried hard to accept her dad's new family out of love for her father. It would break his heart if Keera bitched and complained about them to him. Instead, she gave her dad the support he needed from her and treated Cruella and Kevin the best that she could. She didn't want to over do it though. Being phony was not her usual makeup and she wasn't going to fake the funk for anybody.

After they inhaled the Thanksgiving feast that Cruella had catered, Mr. Sanders had the bright idea that they all take a family road trip.

"It's settled. Tomorrow, we'll take a drive to Palm Springs. The weather is beautiful this time of year. There's plenty for us to do and we can be back home before nightfall."

Keera could smell the bacon being microwaved, which meant they'd be hitting the highway soon.

"We'll leave right after breakfast." Her father's words from the day before rang in her head.

Actually, a visit to Palm Springs would do me some good. I could call the Guest House Day Spa before we leave and make an appointment for a massage and skin treatment. I can enjoy being pampered while they go shopping.

Keera knew that Cruella would drag her father through the malls and she did not want to be a passenger on that ride.

She thought about calling her friends to see if any of them wanted to go too, but decided against it. Instead, she would take a few hours to be alone. *This would have been a perfect adventure for me and Chance.* She was always in his ear about spending more time with her dad so they could really get to know one another. After six years together Chance and her dad had yet to become closer than polite chit-chat between "hello's" and "good-byes". This would have been a good opportunity to get the ball rolling. She also wanted Chance to get a feel for Kevin and tell her that she wasn't crazy when she said he was weird. She could never get her dad to admit it.

Damnit, Chance. I'm going to get to the bottom of this 'cause this neglect shit is not cool.

She pulled the thick comforter to her chin and procrastinated her inevitable rise out of bed. She wasn't tired at all but liked the peace and quiet. She didn't look forward to fans asking for autographs during lunch at a restaurant, or tourists asking to have a picture taken with her. *It's not really me they love. It's my name and my face. Keera Sanders, Supermodel. Puh-leez, it's all bullshit. Why don't they see that?* She would be gracious though, and sign the napkin or pose for the picture that she would never see. But she didn't like it. She felt vulnerable when she was out in public. Even though she carried a deadly weapon, the letters and the prank calls did stay in the back of her mind. *What if someone is really out there?* She dismissed it with a shrug and decided to look forward to Palm Springs for the day.

Why not? If all else fails, I always have Kreepy Kevin.

She laughed and finally got out of her warm bed, ready to conquer whatever the new day would bring.

Chapter Thirty Four

Jody ~ *Get Gone!*

The bank was buzzing after the big meeting, which took place earlier this morning. All of the corporate heads had been meeting for the past few weeks and the rumor was that soon there would be a big lay off. The bank was merging with a bigger institution and there was no guarantee that anyone would still have a job once the merger was final.

Lord knows I can't afford to be laid off from work. I'm sure Marcus would love it. It would be just the excuse he needed to try and get the kids to move in with him and Shelby. Over my dead body.

If she allowed Xavier and Chelsea to move in with their father and his girlfriend, she feared that she would lose their hearts just like she had Marcus'. And that she could not bare.

Instead of eating in the break room, like normal, Jody visited her church during her lunch hour. All she could ponder was the possibility of being homeless. If she were to lose her job, she felt that her world would crumble. *It's in God's hands now.*

She tried to keep her faith that God would always make sure she was well taken care of, but her being jobless was still a likely scenario. It upset her that she was under someone else's thumb. She was frustrated with the reality that a corporate head could not only control the way she styled her hair but had the final decision on whether or not she would get paid at the end of the week.

She had already been frustrated with the fact that when she came into the Beverly Hills bank sporting braids, she was shunned. But not by only her white colleagues, but the black ones too. She had never felt so caged. But the idea that another human being could make or break another's stability with one meeting was a wake up call. They would decide who would be in the unemployment line, the welfare line, or the soup line. She had no control when it came to her job but she assured herself that when the time was right God would put her in a better place.

When Colette, her co-worker who was always in the know, told her about the possible layoffs Jody immediately panicked. Ever since, she tried to stay ahead of the next person. She kept late evenings to tie up loose ends and stayed on top of her workload. She lived from paycheck to paycheck and would've been in the hole a long time ago if she didn't get proper alimony and child support. It was a good thing for Jody that Marcus was a good provider and never missed a payment.

When Marcus left, Jody was devastated. His reason was that she gave more of her time and energy to the church than she did him. Before he left it was a constant battle for him. He fought until he felt he was out of ammunition. They grew in different directions and he had to accept it. He didn't want to hear any more of her revelations about being a saved Christian and living eternally free and happy with Jesus Christ. He believed in God and he felt that he was a good person, which was good enough for him. He didn't have a problem with going to church and he actually enjoyed attending as a family with the kids; but he felt that Jody took it to a whole other level. And when their bank account began to suffer because she increased her tithes on a weekly basis, he was through. Marcus couldn't take it any more. He said he would rather live apart than live a lie. He was miserable.

He left Jody but he didn't leave Xavier and Chelsea. They were his children and he loved them with all of his heart. Despite the split he took care of them just as much, and as well, as he did when he lived with them. He was still their daddy and Jody loved him for it.

Best Baptist was quiet and served as the perfect solace for Jody during her lunch hour. There were a few others who took advantage of the church's warm embrace, but as far as Jody was concerned, it was just her and God. She prayed from several Bible passages and recited the Lord's Prayer silently before she headed back to work. She didn't know if her prayers did the trick, but now she felt safe and ready for anything.

When Jody pushed through the bank's glass doors, all eyes were on her. The bank seemed unusually still. Usually after lunch on Friday, it was packed. So much so that she would sometimes be asked to leave her desk in the loan department to step in and assist on the teller line. But not today. Jody walked straight to her desk, ignoring the onlookers. *People always stare at my after-prayer glow,* she smiled proudly. But when she got to her empty desk, the lump in her stomach told her otherwise. Her desk was cleaner than it had been in months and she knew that the files weren't lost or stolen. They had been re-assigned.

The envelope, which sat lonely on her desktop, told the entire story. She glanced back and noticed that she was still in the spotlight. Her hands shook as she lifted the envelope slowly and held it to her chest. She exhaled a deep breath before carefully tearing it open.

"Notice of Lay Off" was what the bright pink slip of paper read in bold ink. Tears flowed to no end. She got the boot just like that. She plopped down in her old chair in shock. She had no room for embarrassment. Even with all of the whispering echoing as loud as if they were yelling at the top of their lungs, Jody sat despondent. Through her stream of tears she could see the sympathizers and the well-wishers walking towards her. She didn't want to be the guest of honor at anyone's pity party. She didn't give anyone the opportunity to tell her that God didn't close one door without opening another. That was her line to someone else in need. She never thought she would be telling it to herself.

Jody rose quickly and gathered the few personal items she had: a family picture of her, Marcus and the children, her Bible and a small plant given to her by a friendly bank customer. She didn't want a good-bye speech from her boss nor did she want to hear from others how messed up it was that it happened to her. *What's the point?*

With her arms full and her face streaked with tears, she walked out of the bank and didn't look back. She had fear in her mind and questions about what she would do next, but before she could deal with any of it she had to exit, stage right.

Chapter Thirty Five

Killa ~ *Me and my Girlfriend*

Friday took what seemed like forever to come, but it did indeed come. Just as Killa had hoped, he'd been arraigned in court first thing in the morning. After hours of waiting for his name to be called by the judge, he spoke his peace and was eventually released on his own recognizance. He still had to wait for all of the paperwork to be internally processed but overall he was satisfied. He was pleased with his efforts and even felt that he had the skills and charm that it took to be an attorney.

Killa's two-day stay in the county jail was sprinkled with incredible incidents. It still amazed him that he was locked behind bars for something as stupid as drunk driving, coupled with taking Dani's friends drug filled make-up bag with him to what he thought would be a quick trip to the liquor store. If only he'd known he would have never left his dream lady to be delivered into such a fucked up situation. Blondie was now on his list of paybacks. He was sure that he would run into her again at Dani's and couldn't wait to give her what he felt she deserved.

And Jackie was right behind her. She never did accept any of his collect calls. She didn't realize how much of a hassle using the payphone in the county jail could be. It was punk or get punked situation and you had to have balls to get yourself to the front of the line, which never seemed to move.

Killa couldn't stand that he was caged up like a zoo animal. His ulcer decided to act up too, which didn't make matters any better. The worse thing that he experienced was something he still couldn't swallow.

"Excuse me, brotha. Can I get that blanket?" Killa stared at the man before him and a chill covered his body like a block of ice.

He was a middle-aged man but appeared old and gray, obviously due to a hard life in the streets. His front teeth were missing and the ones that remained were rotted, on their way out as well. It was the tattoo beneath his left eye that caught Killa's interest though. Half of a broken heart with the letters LFL inscribed inside with cheap ink. It was the same tattoo that his mother wore on her right breast. Aside from the decayed features, Killa recognized him and his tattoo from the pictures that his mother showed him whenever he asked about his daddy. The daddy he would never know. He was a musician from what his mother told him and the road had always called him away from the family. She said that when he never came back home she was heartbroken, but not surprised. She had seen the day coming long before even though they both promised to be lovers for life. His leaving triggered a life of heavy drinking and prostitution for his distraught young mother, and Killa blamed his no account father for opening the door to her living hell.

I should shank this nigga right here, was Killa's first thought.

But when he looked in the man's eyes, he felt something that he hadn't felt since the loss of his brother Dimitri. His heart ached. With every crazy and mixed up thought that ran through Killa's head, all he could get the nerve to do was hand the man the blanket and watch him limp his way to the other side of the crowded holding cell. The old man curled into a fetal position and then talked to himself. It was obvious that he didn't recognize his son. How could he? They were strangers.

Should I talk to him? Should I beat his ass one good time?

Before he could ask question number three the guard yelled out his name.

"Kilamunjaro Washington! Let's go!"

I'm finally getting' outta this bitch. Here I come Danielle, baby. Here I come.

Chapter Thirty Six

Danielle ~ *It ain't easy...*

Danielle's morning was hectic, to say the least. After the discovery of Jasmine's abuse, Dani had many issues to consider. Number one was to make sure that Jasmine would never go home to live with Trixxy again. There were attorneys, the police and child welfare services to contend with; as well as the importance of making sure Jasmine knew that she hadn't done anything wrong. *She has love everywhere she turns.*

Dani knew she should've taken the day off, but being the workaholic that she was, she couldn't tear herself away. Willie Mae and Alfred offered to keep the children for her, which was a big load off of her mind. She didn't want Jasmine to feel abandoned and was confident that she would feel at home with Grammy and Papa.

She hadn't made any long term schooling arrangements for Jasmine yet, and wouldn't until the matter of her custody was resolved. With that in mind, she stopped by DJ's school on the way to the office and spoke to the principal about enrolling Jasmine. It was a blessing that she caught Principal Ryan. The school was closed but the principal was there and was nice enough to see Dani. Mr. Ryan was very understanding and agreed to let Jasmine enroll temporarily. She would start on Monday.

Dani had a long day behind her at the office but she would still work well into the evening. She called to check in on the kids throughout the day but had mainly focused on work. It had served as a good distraction from Drew's absence and it also allowed her to put the final touches on the ad campaign she and Scott had worked on for the past two weeks. She was pleased with the final production and would bring its attention to her advertising team during their Monday morning meeting.

The office was quiet. She decided to turn on the radio to ease her thoughts. As the hypnotic sounds of the rap group, Bone Thugs- n- Harmony (*Let's Change the World*) poured out, she stood at her office door, which was made of glass, and twisted the blinds just enough to see out. Of her team, everyone but Scott had gone home for the day. She reflected on how pleased she was with her team of copywriters, graphic artists and designers. Each one added a greatness to her creative ideas, in the same way that she inspired them. But it was she who needed the inspiration lately. Her life had definitely reached a new level. If only the elevator doors would open so she could get off on the next floor.

Scott was a young, ambitious brotha with a good head on his shoulders. Dani often teased him and called him Romeo because his lady co-workers held obvious affection for him.

He wore a curly, corporate Afro, stood at about five foot eleven inches, and was light skinned. He was very sweet and had an incredible sense of humor. He also cracked Dani up. They had become good friends in the six months that he'd worked for the company. Work projects brought them together and led them to conversation. Dani picked up a good vibe. He wasn't gossipy like most people at Kravitz Advertising. They'd had a few lunches together and through many conversations about life, got to know one another on a personal level. Of course, Dani told Andrew all about him. She felt it would be best since she and Scott would be working so closely together. When Andrew met him, he summed Scott up as a "little nerd" and was cool with him from then on.

Men are such a trip.

Scott even hung out at Mannigan's, the bar located in the lobby of her office building, with the two of them. Andrew would often pick Dani up from work and they would go there for drinks, appetizers and good conversation. She missed those days terribly.

Scott had just graduated, earning his Master's degree from Georgetown University. He was smart, funny and a genuine good guy. Dani had thought about introducing him to Queenie but decided against it. *Sometimes when you think you're doing a good thing the end result is wishing you had never bothered.* Besides, she thought Scott might be gay. The assumption wasn't a problem for Dani but she didn't think that homosexuality was a quality Queenie looked for in a man.

Dani hadn't talked to any of her girls about Jasmine. She was too damn exhausted. She was also positive that her machine would be full of messages when she got home. Messages that would most likely go unreturned, at least until tomorrow.

The clock struck nine and Dani decided it was time to pack up and head out to pick up the kids. Willie Mae had them fed and bathed, so all she had to do once they got home was put them in bed.

When she got to her grandma's, the kids were asleep. There was lasagna on the stove for her and she ate it like she hadn't eaten in a week. It was the bomb.

She stuffed her face to satisfaction, chitted-chatted with Willie Mae and Alfred, then got the kids into the car and headed home. Getting both of them in and out of the Jag was not an easy task.

Looks like I'm gonna have to start driving the Navigator.

To Dani's disappointment, there was no mail from her husband. The discovery of the empty mailbox was like a stake through her heart. After she got the children tucked into bed, she ran some hot bath water and soaked for about half an hour.

Just as she rose to get out of the tub, the telephone rang. To Dani's surprise it was Officer Smith, the policeman who was over the day before to take the report about Jasmine.

"Good evening, Mrs. Johnson. I'm sorry to disturb you so late but we've received some new about your stepdaughter's mother, Trixxy Boumont. You might want to sit down for this." He paused for a breath before stating the purpose of the phone call. As he did so, Dani wrapped a thick towel around her and walked to the chair in front of her bathroom's dressing table. The officer continued, "her body was found this evening. She was brutally raped and strangled."

Dani was stupefied. She didn't know what to say and was in a state of confusion. She heard his words clearly but it didn't make sense.

Does he mean that Trixxy is dead?

"So what are you saying? She'll be okay, won't she?" Dani pulled at straws trying to clarify the officer's statement.

"No, ma'am. She's dead. Her body was found near a freeway underpass downtown. A detective will be over in the morning to ask you some questions. It's routine being that you informed us that she was missing. Nothing for you to be concerned about."

"Do you know who did it?" Dani asked fearfully. She was suddenly afraid for her own life.

"Her killing matches that of three others in the past three months. We don't have the suspect in custody but we're on his heels."

"Well, you need to find him fast."

"We're working on it, ma'am. I wouldn't worry if I were you. You appear to be well secure where you are."

"Just catch the man. Your mother could be next on his list," Dani replied, angry that the officer was so jaded by the situation.

Dani hung up the phone and grabbed her heart to make sure it was still beating. *Trixxy is dead.*

All sorts of flashbacks of her past run-ins with her husband's crazy baby's momma ran through her head. She quickly realized that she never really knew the girl. Through all the years of fighting, first about Andrew, then about Jasmine, there was never even a decent conversation between them. Now, after everything that had happened, Dani would have to tell Jasmine that her mother was dead.

Although Dani felt nothing for Trixxy when she was alive, she had remorse about their constant bickering. *I'm sure somewhere in there, the girl had a heart.* Dani was hurt that she had suffered such a terrible death.

She didn't rush to make any phone calls. It was late and she didn't want to disturb Francine or her grandparents with the awful news of Trixxy's tragic death.

What will Drew say? How will he feel?

Dani prayed that her husband would call so she could tell him the news herself. She knew that despite his anger towards Trixxy about past incidents and circumstances, he too would feel pain about the news of her brutal murder. She debated on waiting to break the news to during her next visit. *I'll cross that bridge when I get there.*

She also had to determine the necessity of telling Drew the news about Jasmine's scars from on going abuse, at least for now. She knew it would be like twisting a knife in an already open wound. It was all too much for her to bear. She needed her thoughts to be clear and concise, but they weren't cooperating.

"Trixxy is dead," Dani said numbly. She felt dirty, like a film of crust had settled onto her skin. She stepped back into the still warm tub water, closed her eyes and breathed deeply. She directed her mind to God and began a conversation with Him about recent events. She wanted answers that would lead her in the right direction, or at least a different one from where she now stood. She knew that despite who she called, her God was the only one who would truly help her. For all Dani knew, she could very well be next.

Dani was afraid and she knew that sleep would be out of the question. Watching TV served no solace. Late night infomercials and talk shows filled with hatred and fighting were unappealing, to say the least.

She lay awake even though her eyes burned with exhaustion. Tonight, laying on her expensive mattresses was like being placed on pins and needles. She tossed and turned and turned and tossed. It was two a.m. and time seemed to stand still. She lay indecisive about her next move and decided to call Queenie to settle her nerves. Before she could pick up the phone, it rang. She picked up the receiver quickly.

"Hello."

There was no answer. Just breathing. Heavy breathing. She dropped the phone like it was full of bugs. She wondered if she should go to Willie Mae's. No. She wouldn't let some nut run her out of her home. She had her gun. She'd be fine. Finally, she dialed Queenie who answered the phone sounding comatosed.

"Hello?"

"Hi, Queenie, it's Dani. I'm sorry for waking you up but I really need to talk."

"Of course, girl. What's going on?" She was instantly awakened by the trembling fear in her friend's voice.

After giving Queenie a quick run down on Trixxy's murder and Jasmine's abuse, Queenie insisted on coming over. Dani didn't argue. It was times like this that she thanked God for her peeps.

Chapter Thirty Seven

Andrew ~ *Knowledge is Truth*

Andrew waited in angst for mail delivery. When he didn't hear his name called he sunk into an instant depression. "Mail call" was the most anticipated part of his day while in the joint. When he was at home he never even checked the mailbox. Dani always handled that. When he was on lockdown and restricted from getting his personal mail, he felt deprived. Cheated. Besides Dani's visits, mail was his only link to the outside world. Now it was broken.

Andrew felt isolated. He had no idea what was going on at home and he had a feeling that something wasn't right. He learned a true lesson about taking people and things for granted and he needed another chance so that he could put these lessons into practice. He believed that if anything happened to his family it would be all his fault.

He still hadn't been in contact with Jacobs. He had hoped that he would visit, but he never showed. Andrew wanted desperately to find out what had happened with the private investigator. He needed to hear some positive news because if his nightmares had any merit, something very bad was about to happen. The same dreams of his family drenched in blood invaded his head at night. He lay awake in his bunk and chanted the affirmations that he decided were best for him in this particular situation.

I am free. I am free. I am free.

His cellmate's book, *Key to Yourself*, had made a lot of sense to him about how the universe worked and he wanted to test his new knowledge.

Plant the seed by claiming your desire and visualizing it into being.

He chanted, "I am free," until he finally dozed off in a slumber with thoughts of himself as a free man. He saw himself at home with his wife and son, and in another dream he was surrounded by his mother and his brother, as well as Jasmine. His face told the story of the thoughts in his head. He smiled unconsciously because in his dream world, he was free and everyone he loved was safe and sound.

Chapter Thirty Eight

Queenie ~ *I Want It All*

For whatever reason, Queenie couldn't sleep. Maybe the day had been a little too much for her. She lay in bed and thought about her day while her Eric Benet CD whispered in the background. The *In Style Magazine* photo shoot went well. The models were pleasant and professional. Keera had recommended the agency, and as usual she was right on the money. Marco, the shoot's photographer, was in a great mood. This was a good thing because everyone knew that if the photographer wasn't happy, no one was. Queenie knew this too well.

From the *In Style* shoot she went straight to Millennium Pictures' studios. To say that she was nervous was an understatement. Her stomach was in knots. She had no idea who these people were. Out of the blue, she was summoned onto a movie set. Incredible. She racked her brain and tried to uncover the mystery, but using her mental Rolodex, she couldn't make the connection. She suspected everyone from Keera to her parents but couldn't pin point anyone who would have done her such a grand favor without telling her about it first. She did know that whomever hooked up the job had some insight and knew that it was her dream. Finally, she prayed about it and left it alone. She decided that the movie gig was just God doing His thing. The situation made Queenie think about Jody and something she would say, "Let go and let God."

When Queenie arrived at Millennium's studios, she was totally dumbfounded. She had been instructed to turn into the first driveway at Gower Street and tell the guard her name. That was the easy part. Renny, the guard, said to go left, make a quick right, then another right to stage five. She didn't know what he smoked for lunch but his directions had her all turned around. She had to ask the assistance of two men in alien costumes, a sitcom co-star and a soap opera actress before finally being properly directed to the right place.

She parked in a visitor's space outside of the soundstage that had been so hard to find. She was supposed to meet someone named Tracy so she could brief Queenie on the film and show her around wardrobe.

Tracy was not at all what Queenie expected. She had been looking for a petite, perky blonde, in her late twenties, early thirties. Instead, she was met at the entrance by one fine, tall and sexy man. He was white but there were no color lines where Queenie was concerned, especially since she hadn't been intimate with a man in close to a year.

Queenie was tongue-tied but Tracy was smooth. He was also very cool, down to earth and extremely friendly. He introduced himself as Tracy Millerton. He offered Queenie beverages and hors d'oeuvres then took her briefcase off of her hands.

"Let me take this for you," he said.

Queenie obliged gratefully. Tracy next gave her a quick tour before they finally settled in a small, very plush conference room. He apologetically told her that Max, the producer, was on his way from the Commissary.

"This is going to be one extraordinary film. The director is hot and the cast is hotter," he said in a deep mellow tone.

Before she could respond, his pager went off and he quickly excused himself. He told her to make herself comfortable and said he'd be right back. *Thank God.*

She had started to feel queasy from her intense anxiety. To contain it took grit. She wanted to ask him questions but didn't want to appear completely stupid. His eyes were spellbinding. They were such a deep green, she felt she could get lost in them for sure. And his smile was killer. The kind you'd want to wake up to in the morning. Lastly, she got a peek at his ass. *Dayumm.* Was all that could be said. *I know I'm lonely because drooling is not my style,* she joked to herself in an attempt to ease her nerves.

Queenie was all alone in the magnificent room. The deep maroon carpet was thick as her grandma's lawn. The mahogany wood table was so polished that she could clearly see her reflection. There were posters on all four walls of recent Millennium movie releases and stars. It was the type of environment she could definitely see herself surrounded in, someday.

She flipped through the latest issue of *Entertainment Weekly* twice before she heard a slight tap on the door. Before she could blink there he was. He stood before her like a vision in a dream. It was Emilio.

All Queenie could do was stare in awe. She couldn't believe it was him. Emilio was the very last person she'd expected or wanted to see. Even still, he was just as fine as when she had last seen him.

When he came over to greet her, she wanted to hold him and kiss him. Instead, she gave him the coldest look she could muster.

What the hell is he doing here? This is my meeting.

He graciously asked the others who came in behind him to give them a few minutes alone. Deep down inside she was happy, but at the same time she was totally pissed off. Confused would be a better analogy. She didn't know how to react or what to say but she had to think fast because her icy stare would only last so long.

"What are you doing here, Emilio?" Queenie asked while staring into his warm eyes.

"I'm here to see you, Sweetheart," he answered with his trademark grin. "Aren't you happy to see me?"

The ice had already begun to thaw but she wouldn't dare give him the satisfaction of knowing.

"I am not your sweetheart. Uh uh, Emilio, this is not cool with me – at all," she said sternly with her arms folded and foot tapping.

He interrupted by saying, "I miss you Queenie." Then he boldly walked up to her and held her hands tightly in his own.

She snatched her hands away and demanded an explanation by asking, "What the hell is going on? Is this some kind of joke? Haven't you toyed with my feelings enough, Emilio? I am a very busy woman and I don't have time to be playing games with little boys all day."

She snapped up her briefcase and attempted to walk past him and out the door. He wouldn't let her leave though. He'd waited what he felt was an eternity before attempting to re-position himself into her life. He wasn't going to give up without a fight.

Tears began to well in Queenie's eyes. She fought so hard not to blink so that the teardrops would not flow down her cheeks. But the emotion was too strong. She was angry beyond words but she expressed herself loud and clear. Her voice was low and her tongue sharp. She hated to be in such a vulnerable position.

Mentally she kicked herself for not further investigating the job offer. *If I had any idea that he was behind this meeting I would never have come.*

"Don't be mad, Queenie. I'm not playing games. This is an opportunity that has your name all over it and I wanted to be able to open this door for you. I remember the dreams you shared with me. I remembered you wanted to some day explode onto the entertainment scene. You wanted to 'dress the stars', as you put it. This is your chance. At least stay and hear what we have to say. It's the chance of a lifetime. Don't let your anger with me stop you from fulfilling one of your dreams, Queenie, please."

Queenie thought about what he said without uttering a word. She wanted to slap the shit out of him but instead remained cool. He was right. If this was business she would handle it as if it were business, personal feelings aside.

"Okay, Emilio. I'm willing to listen. You're absolutely right. Working on films has always been one of my dreams." She rested her briefcase on the floor. "Let the others in so we can get this started," Queenie said as she dabbed her face with the Kleenex tissue that was propped on the conference table.

She tried her best to be hard, to be tough, but Emilio saw through it all. He always did. He didn't say a word in response. Instead, he came closer to her, slowly and gently. He held her face with his big, strong hands and pulled her into him. She tried with little effort to push him away at first, but eventually gave in to the embrace.

They kissed feverishly. He whispered into her ear and told her how much he missed her. While they exchanged a passionate French kiss, he slowly backed Queenie into the wall and pressed his body against hers. He wasn't much taller than her so when he pressed against her she felt his private at attention. Still kissing, she moved her hips from side to side. He was quick to follow her lead. The rhythmic motions were as if they were dancing but without music. She moved his hand underneath her skirt and placed it between her thighs. She knew he would take it from there once he felt that she was soaking wet. He rubbed it around and around until she couldn't take it anymore. She placed her hand on his and slid his middle finger into her love canal. She in turn lifted her right leg and rested her high heel onto the chair in front of her.

There was a knock at the door, but it felt so good that it did not break them apart. It took the voice of the film's producer, Max Jeffries, for them to become de-hypnotized. Queenie was totally lost in Emilio.

She straightened her clothes, fixed her hair and took a seat at the conference table as Emilio went to open the door. She was nervous and excited at the same time. She couldn't believe that they were about to have sex right here in the conference room.

What was I thinking?

Emilio saw her uneasiness and gave her a wink and a warm smile as if to say, "It's all good." It helped.

As the others came in they were introduced to Queenie, one by one. First, there was Max. A short, balding but distinguished black man wearing a very nice suit. When he came closer to greet Queenie, she noticed the bold jewelry and the stench of cigars. Big turnoff. Max was one of the producers of the film. His money funded the film's wardrobe, hair and make-up.

Next, there was Chamille Rourke. She would star opposite Emilio in the movie. She was a tall, lanky woman with chiseled jaw structure, big brown eyes and obvious breast implants. Her caramel skin was unreal and, unfortunately, Queenie thought the same about her tired weave. Hopefully her hair will be whipped when shooting the film. Bad hair could make an entire outfit look bad. *I see I'm gonna have to hook her up with Tai.* All the same, she was extremely beautiful – breathtaking even. She looked familiar too. Queenie thought she'd maybe seen her on TV.

Finally, Tracy returned to the room. He seemed annoyed that she and Emilio had locked themselves in the conference room. He had major attitude. Queenie assumed he was jealous of Emilio being with her, but then again Tracy had not given her any indication during their brief encounter that he was in the least bit interested in her. She couldn't call it.

Once again, Emilio had Queenie under his spell. He was the best sex she'd ever had (not that there were very many to compare to) and he was a definite Hot-Boy. *Not a bad dilemma.*

It was uncovered during the meeting that it was he who insisted on her being hired as wardrobe consultant for the film. Even though Queenie had no prior experience on a film set, Max agreed to hire her. It was obvious they wanted Emilio bad for this role. It was said that they'd seen him in his last few Broadway hits and were blown away by his talent. Emilio had a knack for "blowing people away." Queenie was gone from the first moment she saw him.

Chamille was very pretty but not very warm. It was clear that she was not pleased with Queenie being chosen for the job. She sat during the entire meeting with her arms folded and a bratty smirk on her face.

Max described the duties that would be expected of Queenie as wardrobe consultant. They went over the budget for the clothes, material and props that Queenie was to shop for. They also presented her with some sketches of a few ideas that had been discussed. Queenie was so thrilled that someone was actually giving her money to do her absolute favorite thing in the world: shop.

Queenie asked a lot of questions but had already made up her mind to take the job. How could she not? She would've been a fool. The gig had flexible hours and she was assured that it would not interfere with her permanent position with Bloomingdales.

When do I start?

Tracy handed her a contract and suggested that she go over it with her attorney before signing. He also handed her a copy of the script, outlining how the characters should look for each scene. Queenie overlooked Tracy's sudden funky attitude. Instead she gazed at Emilio who was smiling from ear to ear. He knew that he had done well and that he was back in Queenie's life. She was captured by him, yet again. It seemed that her life had taken a turn for the better in just one afternoon. She never believed life could throw such good curves. Right over the plate.

After all of that, she lay in bed unable to sleep. She went over the day again and again, unable to let go of the past events. She wanted to relive them again, especially when she and Emilio almost made love in the conference room. Queenie hadn't had sex in months and was bursting with desire.

Queenie jumped when the phone rang. It was two a.m. and Queenie just knew it would be Emilio servin' up a booty call. She had given in and gave him her number after the meeting. Hesitantly she answered to find that instead it was Dani.

Something had gone wrong and Queenie quickly dismissed all other thoughts to concentrate on her good friend and her dilemma.

"I'll be right there," Queenie assured her after listening to her trauma.

What Dani had to say didn't sound very good and Queenie would do anything she could to help her. Lately, Dani's world seemed to be crashing around her. Her husband was in jail and now she had a serious situation regarding her stepdaughter. Queenie was puzzled because it seemed that all of the good people had the most difficulty. In her opinion, Dani deserved much better.

Chapter Thirty Nine

Keera ~ *Not gon' cry*

Hanging out with her dad and his new family was a day Keera would never forget. The day trip to Palm Springs turned out to be a success. She thought she would regret committing herself to an entire day with Cruella and Kevin, but she actually had a lot of laughs. She could go as far as to say she had fun.

She underestimated her dad as of late. She thought he had lost some of his spunk and zest for life since he'd remarried, but he'd showed Keera that he was still a fun loving man. She hated that his life was being wasted with Cruella and her lurch of a son, but it was what her dad wanted and he was the boss.

Keera still hadn't spoken with Chance and she was furious about it. She had concluded that he was cheating, but hoped for his sake that he was either in a bad accident or dead. He had never gone this long without calling and she was seriously concerned. She called his family and a few of their mutual friends but no one had heard from him. She even went so far as to contact his coach but she wasn't able to reach him. Chance would be pissed at her for going through those channels, but he left her no alternative. She had debated about stopping in Miami on her way to New York on Sunday. She ultimately decided that if she still hadn't heard from him by then, she would try to find him.

Keera had been invited to a few parties tonight but she chose to stay home and soak in a tub of relaxing bubbles. She bought a ton of CD's while shopping in Palm Springs and listened to a few as she relaxed in the tub. Her love for music showed in her collection, which contained everything from rapper DMX, to singer Macy Gray, to Sting. She never felt she had enough. Once in the bed, she loaded her portable 10 disc CD player and hit random. Now all she needed was a hit of her blunt that was left over from Bridge Night at Dani's, but she would never disrespect her father's house.

At two a.m., as Keera lay wide-awake in the bed listening to music, her cell phone rang.

"Hello?" Keera answered.

"Hello?" She asked again.

"Asshole," she whispered as she hit the end button, disconnecting the line.

Dang, don't people have better things to do than play on the phone?

It was the tenth call of its sort that day and Keera was beyond irritated.

Tired of wondering, she decided to call Chance again at his house. No answer. When her phone rang right back she just knew it would be him.

"Hello?"

"Hey, Keera, it's Queenie. Dang, I didn't expect you to be awake this late."

"Hey, Q. What's going on?" Keera was puzzled by the two a.m. phone call from her friend and hoped everything was okay.

"Actually it's Dani. Brace yourself, she just called and told me some crazy news."

"I'm listenin," Keera wanted to get it over with. If it had to do with Chance she would just die.

"Trixxy was raped and murdered a few days ago."

"What? You are lyin' girl!" Keera sat up in her bed. "Did they catch the killer? How is Jasmine?" Keera had a ton of questions.

"I don't know but I'm in the car on my over there."

"Say no more, I'm on my way too." Keera wasted no time. The news about Trixxy was frightening to her so she could imagine how Dani must have felt.

She threw on a pair of sweats and some tennis shoes, put her hair up with a clamp and headed over to Dani's. Keera had never known anyone who had been murdered, and even though she didn't know Trixxy very well, it was still too close for comfort. She sped through LA's streets and reflected on the fact that tomorrow is not promised to anyone.

Chance better recognize because he will lose me if he keeps this up. Life is too short to be wasted on bullshit, especially somebody else's.

Chapter Forty

Jody ~ *best friend*

I know it was God who made me call Saudia last night.

Saudia had been on Jody's mind all evening, so she called. When she did, Saudia cried like a baby. It took the longest time before Jody could decode the words between her friend's heavy sobs. She was forced to play twenty questions with Saudia before she discovered that her father had died.

Ol' Ebenezer has finally joined his wife Milly, in heaven. Now he is finally at peace.

When Jody got the news, she called Marcus to ask if she could drop off the kids. He was in the shower but Shelby said it would be fine. Jody didn't insist on talking to Marcus like she usually did. Her mind was too pre-occupied with Saudia to focus on any other drama. She packed the kids' bags and dropped them off without so much as two words. She did, however, manage to tell Xavier and Chelsea, good-bye. *But why did Marcus have to answer the door in a tank top and boxers? The man still looks good.* She also bet that he still felt good too, and silently prayed that she would someday find out.

When she arrived at Saudia's, it was an eternity before she finally opened the door. It only took five seconds for Jody to see that Saudia was completely plastered.

"Yes, I'm dr-unk and I don't wanna hear no got damn shit about it! If Jesus could drink wine, then so can I, dammit!"

Saudia could barely stand up straight. She told Jody on the phone that her Aunt Sis had picked up the kids. Jody was glad of that because they surely didn't need to see their mother like this.

Jody warmed up a couple of plates of Saudia's turkey and dressing leftovers. She had drunkenly confessed to not eating and Jody felt that the food would help to sober her.

It took a lot of work but Jody finally got the girl to swallow enough food to soak up some of the alcohol in her stomach. Saudia showed her the bottle of Alize' Red she guzzled from and it was completely empty. She couldn't figure out how Saudia's eyes were still open. Jody would have been passed out had she even smelled as much alcohol in one sitting. Saudia had always been one who could hold her liquor, except for tonight.

Saudia had eaten with only a few threats of vomiting. Afterwards, Jody was finally able to get her to talk sensibly. Jody then got a pen and paper to write down a "to do" list for Saudia. She offered to help with calling friends and relatives to notify them of Ebenezer's death, but Saudia was not in the right state of mind to make those calls. She said something about "in the morning" and "Aunt Sis," then went back into her bedroom where she lay buried under the covers.

Jody thought about the bank and being laid off earlier that day, but quickly pushed it to the back of her head. She didn't want to deal with it and would not mention it to a soul until she figured out what she was going to do.

She watched Saudia sleep. Her dear friend clutched her pillow as if it were a man. Jody felt sad for her. Saudia's dad was a big part of her world, especially after her mom died, last year. She became her dad's caretaker as well as his loving daughter. She made sure he was fed and she read the Sunday newspaper to him. She'd go over and clean up after him almost every day, if she could make it in time, before he went to bed.

Jody had always admired Saudia for her dedication to her father. Now both of her parents were gone and Jody couldn't imagine how that must feel. When Jody's own parents moved to Florida three years ago she felt completely lost. Thank God they moved back.

Jody wondered if this experience would get Saudia to finally change her ways. She wouldn't pressure her about going to church like she had in the past though. She now realized that it was a step she would have to take on her own.

The following morning Jody was up bright and early. She didn't wake Saudia though because she knew she needed rest after her alcohol binged evening.

It wasn't until Saudia's Aunt Sis had called that she decided to check on her friend. After several raps on the wooden door went unanswered, Jody made her entrance. What she saw shocked her horribly. Saudia had a man in her bed. They lay naked with sheets intertwined between them and despite the intrusion remained sound asleep in the spoon position. Jody felt uncomfortable having walked in on them so she backed up slowly and quietly. When she turned forward to walk out of the door, she ran smack into the wall.

"Ow!" She couldn't help but blurt out in pain.

Instinctively, she turned to make sure she hadn't woken them.

"Ooh, excuse me, my bad." Jody said, to the bald, stocky man as he looked at her with an odd expression. He frowned the same way a confused dog would. It was as if he didn't remember where he was.

"Shit! I gotta go!" He realized that he had actually spent the night, which he never did. He would have a lot of explaining to do to his wife. Especially since he slipped out at two thirty a.m. between her hard snores.

Jody scurried out just before the man hopped his hairy chested, naked behind from under the sheets. She was embarrassed to have invaded Saudia's privacy and at the same time ashamed of her.

How did she slip him in last night without me hearing anything?

It was beyond Jody how Saudia could have made a booty call, while she grieved for her father.

She sobbed internally for her girlfriend. Jody prayed for her. She mentally held her hand and touched Saudia's forehead like a church evangelist would. She imagined cleansing her friend from her sinful ways forever. The whole experience gave her an invigorating rush.

The phone rang shortly after Saudia's lover made his exit. Jody hid herself in the kitchen until she was sure he was gone. It amazed her that Saudia remained asleep. On the phone was Saudia's Aunt Sis calling back to check on her. Jody assured the sweet, elderly woman that Saudia was asleep and that she would be by her side so that she need not worry. After she hung up with Aunt Sis, she dialed Tai's number. There was no answer, so she called Dani.

"Hello?"

"Hi, it's Jody."

"Hey girl, this is Keera. What's up?"

"Hey Keer, um, I have some bad news."

"What is it?" Keera wanted to know.

"Well, I'm at Saudia's," she paused to inhale and exhale a deep breath. "Ebenezer passed away last night."

"Aw, shit." Keera sighed deeply. "How is she? Where are the kids – ?"

Interrupting, Jody said, "She's still asleep. She drank about as much as she cried. The kids are with their Aunt Sis. I've been here all night though, watching over her."

"That's good. She probably needs the rest. Both Dani and Q are still asleep too. Are you gonna be over there all day?"

"Yes, of course. The kids are with Marcus and Shelby."

"And Shelby? That's the first time I've ever heard you add her name onto a sentence."

"That was before I had Jesus. You should try Him. It will make a difference."

Ugh. No she didn't just preach to me, Keera thought to herself.

"Well, we've had some drama over here as well, but I'll let Dani tell you guys all about it herself. I'll wake Dani and Q up and we'll be over in just a little while."

"That'll be perfect. She needs all of us, especially now."

"Tell Saudia we love her."

"I will. See you guys soon."

"Bye, Jody."

Jody was joyfully surprised that Keera was at Dani's. She thought she'd gone back to New York already. She found satisfaction in the fact that the girls were coming over. It was much better, in her opinion, for Saudia to have all of her friends near, in her time of need.

She wondered what had happened with Dani and hoped that it was good news about Drew. If anyone deserved something good to happen, it was Dani.

Jody wanted to talk to the kids but she didn't wake up in time. According to her home answering machine, Marcus and Shelby had already taken them to breakfast and then to the park.

The smell of breakfast woke Saudia from her sound sleep. Saudia dragged herself into the kitchen looking like she needed a few more hours of rest. Her eyes were almost swollen shut from crying.

"Good morning Sleeping Beauty." Jody looked at her friend with concern. She wanted to chastise her about her sleep over but had the better sense not to.

Jody poured a glass of Cranapple juice as she sat at the table slowly and carefully. It was very clear that Saudia had a hangover, but that didn't stop her from wolfing down the pancakes, bacon and eggs that Jody whipped up. Saudia grubbed.

While she ate, Jody gave Saudia her messages from her Aunt Sis and told her that the girls were coming over. Jody was glad she was able to do something for her. For a while, she had felt rather helpless.

Saudia had been a good friend to Jody. She was always supportive and kind, although she could also be harshly blunt. But whether it was giving advice about life or just putting a smile on her face, she had always been there. Jody never really had the chance to show Saudia how much she appreciated her friendship. She was just sorry that her assistance had to be during such a sad time. Even with her own problems creeping back and forth into her mind she was happy to be there. She was so sorry that Saudia had lost her father and she wanted to give her as much sisterly love as possible in her time of need.

The news of her dad's passing had definitely gotten out. The phone rang off the hook with sympathies and condolences. Saudia didn't take any of the calls. She didn't want to talk to anyone. She seemed okay at breakfast but now she looked numb. Jody tried everything she could to get her to talk, but nothing worked. This was why Jody was so surprised when Saudia took the phone from her to talk to her friend Angie.

The conversation was brief. When Jody heard that Angie would be dropping by too, she perched her lips. This outta be interesting.

Jody had heard a lot about Angie from Saudia. She learned that she was an intern at Mayhem Records and that they had become friends over a short period of time. It began with office lunches, then Happy Hours after work, and finally night-clubbing. Jody was ashamed because she realized that she was actually jealous. Saudia was her best friend. They used to do those things together, but when Jody changed her habits and her way of life, she didn't indulge anymore. *I would be a hypocrite,* she constantly reminded herself.

Jody felt that Angie had taken her place in the passenger seat of Saudia's ride. She was curious to meet her and see what she was all about. *I've lost my husband, I can't lose my best friend too.*

Jody would always warn her friends, and even Marcus, that they needed to serve God and not their sinful cravings. In the past she'd even pleaded for them to stop drinking the alcohol and smoking the weed, and especially to stop the sex before marriage. It shocked her when Marcus announced that Shelby, who then was his new girlfriend, had moved in with him. That had been a challenging time for Jody but she overcame by plunging deeper into her church.

She didn't understand how anyone had sex these days anyway, with AIDS, herpes and other stuff being passed around. Admittedly, it was hard for her to quit her bad habits cold turkey, but she did. Jody never cared too much for smoking weed even though she would puff on it along with everybody else. Therefore, marijuana was not very hard for her to give up. But drinking was another story. She had really binged when Marcus left, and if it weren't for her religious convictions, she didn't know where she would be right now.

Angie arrived first. She was not at all what Jody expected. Aside from being gorgeous, she was as sweet as pie. Her southern accent was adorable too. *Now I'm jealous.* Her complexion was like hot cocoa. She was tall and shapely with pearly white teeth and long braids. She was the ultimate Nubian queen. Her eyes were slightly slanted and she had perfectly arched eyebrows. She introduced herself to Jody after giving Saudia a hug. She brought Saudia a plate of food that she said she cooked herself. She sat Saudia down and talked to her about being strong for herself and for the twins. Apparently, Angie had lost her dad six months ago and by Saudia's reaction to the news, Jody could tell it was the first time she had heard about it. They hugged and cried and then laughed while Jody sat across the table and listened quietly. She felt like an outsider all of a sudden.

Jody hadn't been able to get the smiles and the laughs out of Saudia as Angie had, and she felt deficient. She felt as if she failed somehow, which led her to thoughts of her job. All of her life's inadequacies that she tried to ignore had surfaced. She suddenly realized that she needed support, just as Saudia did. For the past few days, she had lived in an imaginary world and was oblivious to the fact that she was in deep shit. Procrastination was not her style when dealing with problems, yet, she embraced it like a sick child. It wasn't until after she gave all of her sympathy to Saudia, leaving none for herself, that she realized she had better wake up about her circumstances before it was too late.

Chapter Forty One

Keera ~ *Love is all we need...*

"I have so much on my plate sometimes, that I just want to stay in bed with the blinds closed. Do you feel me?" Dani paced the room and then plopped on the bed next to Keera.

"Just take it a day at a time, girl. That's all that any of us can do." Keera rubbed Dani's back for comfort. "And of course, we're here for you no matter what, D. Even if it's two a.m. and you just wanna talk."

Keera referred to the scenario, which led her and Queenie to Dani's and they all knew it, smiling at her comment.

"Of course, y'all are my sistas. I know that I can count on you guys. Now shut up before I start crying," she laughed as she dabbed a tear from the corner of her eye.

"O-kay?" Queenie and Keera chimed in agreement with Dani.

They all looked at each other and fell into laughter. For the moment, Dani had forgotten about Trixxy, Keera about Chance, and Queenie about Emilio. After the giggles and the playful banter ended, Dani, Keera and Queenie stayed up until dawn and seriously discussed their individual feelings about Trixxy's death, life and love.

Dani and Keera were excited about Queenie's new side gig at Millennium Pictures. They reminisced about their younger years and compared those problems free days to the present. Dani had made huge mugs of lemon chamomile tea and Keera kept the marijuana joint lit. It was an interesting combination. By six a.m., they were all passed out on Dani's oversized bed.

DJ and Jasmine bounced into Dani's bedroom, bright and early. They found Dani, their Aunt Keera and Aunt Queenie sprawled out, comatose. The kids, who were hyper and just plain happy, jumped on the bed in an attempt to wake up the sleeping beauties.

"It's too early, little ones," Dani mumbled just before burying her head underneath a goose down pillow. "Can you go back and play in your rooms for just a little while? Please?"

"Okay!" They both giggled as they jumped from the bed and raced out of the room.

"Let's watch Rugrats!" DJ said to Jasmine.

"Yea, let's watch Rugrats!" She repeated gleefully as she chased behind him.

Keera, awakened by the kids, got up to relieve her bladder. She noticed the time on the way into Dani's modern, yet elegantly decorated, bathroom. She wondered if she had any messages from Chance on her pager or cell phone. When they parted four days earlier, she left him with the impression that she would be returning to New York before the weekend. Here it was Saturday morning and she was still in Los Angeles. She knew in her gut that something wasn't right with Chance and she wanted to get to the bottom of it.

After she used the bathroom, Keera trotted down the stairs to get her purse. The kids, who watched her pass them by, followed right behind her.

"Auntie Keera, can you please make us some cereal?" DJ charmed his aunt.

"Yes, please?" Jasmine was right behind him.

"Anything for you two munchkins?" Keera turned and began to tickle them mercilessly.

They both chose Cocoa Puffs out of about ten other choices. Dani and her cereal. Keera laughed to herself thinking of their college days when Dani ate nothing but Fruit Loops and Frosted Flakes, morning, noon and night.

Keera poured them both a big bowl of cereal, sat them at the table, then flicked on the kitchen TV to Nickelodeon, per their instructions.

As soon as the kids were situated, Keera slid into Dani's office with her pager and cell phone in hand. There were no messages from Chance on either. She wanted to call him badly but resisted the temptation.

Fuck him.

She did have a message from her agency. Keera had alerted them, after Chance had gone, that she would be returning sooner than planned, eager to work. She forgot to call them back to renege after deciding to stay in LA a while longer. She called from Dani's office phone.

"Hello, is Frederick in the office? This is Keera."

"Hello, Keera. Yes, he is in and awaiting your call. I'll connect you," said the peppy receptionist, thrilled to have a job at a top-modeling agency where she was able to exchange words with famous models, like Keera Sanders.

“Keera, darling. Good morning!” Frederick was always on.

“Good morning, Frederick. What’s up?” She asked, dryly.

“We have a terrific assignment for you. It’s with the new Brazilian designer, Fontana. You need to be at her Manhattan studio first thing in the morning.

“On Sunday? Anyway, that will be impossible because I’m still in Los Angeles and won’t be flying out until Monday Morning.”

“Oh, come on, Keera. This job will boost your career sky high. I’ll have Cynthia make arrangements for you to return to New York tonight.”

“Nope, sorry Frederick. I have family situations that I’m dealing with and it is not going to happen. You can tell Fontana that I will be available on Tuesday. If she can’t accept that, then find a replacement.” Keera was not backing down.

“Keera, this is not a good idea.” Frederick’s tone was stern.

“Frederick, I love you babe, but are ya deaf or just stupid? I said that I won’t be available until Tuesday. Take it or leave it.” And with that, she hung up. *Agents.*

Next, she decided to call home and check on her father. She had a sudden craving to hear his soothing voice.

“Hello, Kevin? Where’s my dad?” Keera had no time for his usual babble.

"They went to breakfast. Are you coming home soon?" Kevin was focused on her being there with him while the house was otherwise empty.

Keera was boggled by his interest in her whereabouts. It was none of his business where she planned to be. He was no longer her bodyguard and needed to recognize.

Smith and Wesson are my bodyguards now, Mothafucka.

Ignoring Kevin's question, Keera said, "Can you tell my father that I called, please? And tell him that I will see him later." She hung up before Kevin could say anything else. The very sound of his voice disturbed her.

No sooner had she hung up the receiver did the phone ring. It was Jody. Keera listened as Jody explained about Saudia's father's death and assured her that she, Dani and Queenie would be there soon.

After the short phone call, she stepped out of the office and stood and watched the kids. They hadn't noticed her as they ate and watched cartoons in their own happy little worlds. She envied them and wished that she could be a kid again too. She was sick of Chance's bullshit and wanted him to get his act together, but also knew that it was on him. She had no control over what he did and regardless of what happened she would still have to live her life.

Back in the kitchen, Keera poured herself a bowl of Honey Nut Cheerios and joined the kids at the table. Before she knew it she was laughing at The Rugrats right along with them. She didn't realize it was so easy to actually feel like a kid again. Gradually her anxiety and curiosity about Chance had disappeared and she eased herself into a comfort zone. And, with the exception of Thanksgiving Day with her dad, she felt safer than she had in a long time. She glanced over at a giggling Jasmine and sensed that she felt the same way too.

Chapter Forty Two

Danielle ~ *Where my girls at?*

She would have gone crazy had she stayed at home alone. Dani embraced her friends' company, happy that they came to her rescue. She called Queenie who in turn called Keera and now they were all together like the old days. As kids, they would always have sleepovers on the weekends. The situation which brought them together this time, though, was something each would've never imagined: murder.

Both Keera and Queenie had come to the house and talked with Dani until sunrise. All over, her fears subsided, for the time being at least. She still couldn't believe that Trixxy was dead. *Andrew, please call me today. I need to talk to you.* She sent her thoughts out into the universe with hopes that they would reach her husband. Remembering what Jacobs' told her about the jail being on lockdown, she called the information line.

"No ma'am the jail is on lockdown and they not allowin' no visits," the operator confirmed. "A guard was killed," she confided. Dani was disheartened and frightened by the news. But instead of allowing her fears to cripple her she kept her composure and prayed for his safety.

She also learned that Jody had called about Saudia's dad. It hurt when she heard the news. Saudia loved her dad to no end.

Why is death surrounding me? Dani knew that it was inevitable, but hoped that she wouldn't have to see death up close again for years to come.

Queenie was in the kitchen baking a cake to take over to Saudia's. They all had the love of chocolate cake in common. Especially Q's chocolate cake. Dani and Keera "helped" with the batter when Dani's doorbell rang. The girls looked at each other curiously then Dani spoke for them all.

"I wonder who that is?"

She licked her fingers of chocolate cake batter, quickly rinsed her hands in the kitchen sink and went to the door with the dishtowel still in hand.

Through the peephole she saw Reggie's big head. Not only was he one of Drew's closest friends but he was like a big brother to her, and she was glad to see him.

"Hey, what's up Reg? This is a pleasant surprise." He bent his tall, six foot eight inch self, down to give her a hug.

"What brings you this way?" Dani asked as she invited him inside.

She wondered if he had heard about Trixxy. She wasn't going to bring it up unless he did so first. She really didn't want to discuss it with anyone else until she spoke with her husband.

"You know I had to come see about my family. Why is it so damn easy to get inside of this so-called secured complex. All you have to do is follow another car inside and you're in."

Dani shrugged because she didn't understand it either.

"I don't know but I'mma bring it up at the next Association meeting."

"Yes, you do that."

Reggie was an attractive brotha. Mocha brown skin, a bald head and goatee, muscular build, and perfect teeth. He also did very well financially as the owner of an innovative Internet company. Dani had once thought about hooking him up with Queenie, but decided against it. The same way she'd thought about introducing her to Scott.

Mind yo' business, Dani, she scolded herself.

Keera, on the other hand, had always had a sly interest in Reggie. She always said that if it wasn't for Chance that she would definitely hook that up.

Reggie glanced around suspiciously. He heard voices and wondered who else was there.

"Don't trip. It's only Keera and Queenie," Dani said easing his mind of any unnecessary suspicions. *Like I would even have another man in my house.*

She led him into the kitchen and reacquainted him with her two beautiful friends. They each exchanged playful chit-chat until a serious toned Reggie said, "Dani, can I talk to you for a minute?"

She understood that he meant alone and told the girls, "I'll be right back y'all."

In her office they began their conversation.

"What's up?" Dani gave him a concerned look.

"It's about Trixxy," he said, as he took a seat on the sofa.

Dani walked over to her desk and sat down.

"I already know, Reggie. The police called me yesterday."

"The police? Damn."

"Yeah. I had made a report because I discovered that she had been beating on Jasmine."

"Word?" Reggie raised his eyebrows in shock.

"Yeah, it was a mess. By then Trixxy had been days late picking up Jasmine and the police were supposed to find her."

"Well, they found her all right. The news is all around the neighborhood."

"Does anyone know who did it?" Dani asked, in hopes that the answer was yes.

"Naw, but the cops been questionin' everybody about it. Not that they'll find out."

"Hmmph," Dani nodded in agreement. "Well let's pray for a miracle on this one 'cause whoever did it might just know about me and I ain't tryin' to go out like that."

"Naw, don't even sweat that. Y'all are in two different circles. She brought that shit upon herself. That shit is called karma."

Reggie was convinced that he was right. He knew well of Trixxy's selfish and vindictive ways and had always advised Andrew that as long as he didn't do anything stupid, things would work themselves out.

"Yea. I guess," Dani had her doubts.

When the phone rang, Dani answered limply.

"Hello?"

"AT&T with a collect call. Please say your name at the tone."

The recorded operator's voice was heaven to Dani's ears. It was Andrew and Dani couldn't have been more elated. She gave Reggie her trademark wide smile and whispered, "It's Andrew" as she pressed the number one to accept the collect call.

Reggie smiled back and took that as his cue to give her to her privacy. He left the room to join Queenie and Keera in the kitchen, which in his mind, wasn't a bad place to be.

"Hey you." Dani said with quiet joy. "I miss you so much."

"I miss you too, Baby. How is everything over there?" He was anxious to know. He had a bad feeling and he wanted to dismiss it by hearing good news.

"We're fine Sweetie but we need you. Jacobs told me about the appeal so I know you'll be home soon," Dani was optimistic.

"Let's hope," Andrew was trying to stay positive but he didn't want to be disappointed either.

"I'm surprised to hear from you. I heard the jail was on lockdown."

"It is. They turned the phone on but only temporarily. I guess somebody felt like doing a good deed today."

"Drew, there is something that I need to tell you," Dani was nervous. She didn't know how to tell him that the mother of his daughter was dead.

"What is it, Baby? Is DJ okay?"

"Oh yea, he's good and Jasmine is too. They're upstairs right now having a good old time."

"That's good. Okay, so what's up?" His heart began to beat fast.

"It's Trixxy."

"Oh, what she do now?"

"She's dead." Dani decided to just say it bluntly.

"Dead? How? Who?" Andrew was beyond shocked.

"The police found her raped and strangled underneath some freeway underpass. They don't know who did it."

Andrew's heart sank. He hated the things Trixxy had put he and his family through during the past few years, but never wished for this.

There was a deafening silence before Andrew spoke.

"Does Jasmine know yet?"

"No, not yet. I wanted to talk to you first," Dani could hear the hurt in her husband's voice. "Keera and Queenie came over and spent the night. Saudia lost her dad too, Boo. Queenie's baking her a cake as we speak. We're going over there in a little while. Oh, And, Reggie popped by just before you called," she informed him. She knew he would next voice his worry about her well being, and she wanted to let him know that she was not alone.

"Give Saudia my condolences. I'm sorry to hear about her dad. Dang, didn't her mom pass like last year?"

"Yup." Dani shook her head.

"Well, I'm glad you're not by yourself. It seems like a lot is goin' on out there." It eased him a little to know that she was surrounded by friends but he still worried.

"Baby, you know what happened to Trixxy was fucked up but we have got to move on. No need on dwelling on the past," Andrew was as level headed as always.

"Maybe you should talk to the kids?"

"Definitely. Put 'em on. And hey," he paused, "I love you."

"I love you, too, And, we're all gonna be fine. You'll see." Dani took the cordless phone upstairs expressing her feelings of love to her husband until she reached the den, where the kids had fallen asleep.

"They're knocked out. I guess they've had too much activity lately. Should I wake them?"

"No let 'em sleep. When the lockdown is over, hopefully in a day or two if not tonight, I'll call back. I only get two fifteen minute calls a day so we're going to have to have them scheduled so that they are not wasted on the answering machine."

"Baby, I can't wait to see you."

There was a quiet stillness. Then Andrew exhaled a deep breath. Dani listened. She knew Andrew thought thoroughly before he spoke and needed a moment.

"I'm trapped, Baby. A lot of shit is goin' down and I can't do nothin' from in here. They got me stuck. Whoever set me up has got me mad stuck."

"Don't worry, Baby, I got things under control over here."

"Oh, no doubt. You're a lioness, Baby. You can handle anything. That's partly why I knew you were *the one*.

If he had any doubts about the stability of his home, he put them to rest with his own words.

"Is that right?" Her voice was soft with affection. "What were the other reasons?"

Andrew laughed softly. The list was long, but the main reason was because she gave him feelings that he never knew existed. Warm, beautiful feelings.

"You make me complete. You know that." He told her, trying not to be too mushy.

"Did I tell you I love you?" She asked, softly in an almost hoarse voice.

"Yea. But you can tell me again."

"I love you," Dani blushed as gave him a kiss. He returned the affection.

"I love you, too."

After a long, intense pause, Drew realized his phone time was ticking.

"Baby, is Reggie still there?"

Dani sucked her teeth. "Yeah, he's in there flirtin' with Keera and Q."

"So what else is new?" Andrew chuckled. "Let me holla' at 'im for a minute, Baby."

Dani took the phone to Reggie interrupting his intimate conversation with Keera in the living room. While Reggie exchanged conversation with Drew, Dani turned to Keera with an inquisitive glare.

"What are y'all in here talkin' about?" Dani asked after handing Reggie the phone. She gave Keera a "you better behave" look. Dani knew her friend too well. She was mad at Chance and it was a fact that she turned into a big flirt when they were on the outs.

"Nothing. Not a damn thang," Keera smiled a devilish grin.

"His time ran out," Reggie said as he handed the phone to Dani. "He said to tell you he loved you and that he would try you later this evening."

"Cool," Dani answered. She was relieved to have finally spoken to her husband but was disappointed that he wasn't able to talk to Jasmine about Trixxy's death. She certainly didn't look forward to the job but if Andrew didn't call tonight she knew she would have to do the deed. *If it ain't one thing it's a damn 'nother.*

"Aiight, well I'mma get outta here. I have some runs to make. It was nice seeing you again," he said to Keera as he kissed her hand.

"Please, Casanova. Give me a break," Dani complained as she rolled her eyes.

Reggie gave her a sly wink.

"Bye, Queenie. I'll see you around!" He yelled out to Queenie who was busy cleaning the mess she had made in Dani's kitchen.

A faint, "Bye, Reggie," echoed back before he turned to the door to leave.

"I'll walk you out," announced Keera. She gave Dani a look to silently tell her to let her handle her business.

"I'll be right back, Mother," she joked to an evil-eyed Dani.

She didn't want Keera doing anything that she'd regret, but she shrugged it off. *She's a big girl.*

Dani went upstairs to get the kids packed to go to Francine's. When she called her about Trixxy's murder, Francine wanted to comfort her grandchildren. This was a relief to Dani because she wanted to get her thoughts in order before having her talk with them about Trixxy and the changes that would take place as a result of her death. She hoped she could handle Jasmine's reaction. She had no idea what the little girl would say or do. She also reflected on the fact that Saudia's aunt had picked up the twins and didn't want to bother her depressed friend with a hyped DJ and Jasmine. *The last thing a parent wants when their own kids are gone is to be bothered with someone else's*, Dani reminded herself. She knew this to be a fact.

Once she packed their bags for an overnight stay, she joined Queenie in her now spotless kitchen. Queenie sat at the bar counter and flipped through an issue of *Sister 2 Sister* magazine. Before Dani could speak, Keera came bouncing in and all eyes were on her.

"What?" she blushed. "What did I do?"

Queenie and Dani smiled and shook their heads, knowing their friend only too well. They felt it was useless to even speak on the matter. Dani especially knew that Keera always did what Keera wanted to do, period. *She's crazy but I love her.*

After the cake had been baked, frosted and cooled, the kids were awake. *Time to go.*

"You guys go ahead to Saudia's and I'll meet you there once I drop the kids off."

"Okay, that's cool," replied Keera.

"Yeah, and I'm going to stop at the drug store to get her a card." Queenie was always thoughtful.

"Well, I'll see you guys there. I'll probably stop to see if my dad is home on the way." Keera still had a yearning to talk to him.

"Has anyone talked to Tai?" Dani wondered aloud.

"No but I'm sure she's at The Boutique." Queenie was convinced.

"Yea, you're right. It is Saturday huh?"

"Let's call her from Saudia's." Keera suggested.

"Good idea." Both Dani and Queenie agreed in unison.

To Dani, it had been a long night and what seemed to be an even longer morning. She was more than anxious to leave her world to help put the pieces back together in Saudia's life.

Chapter Forty Three

Tai ~ *Only God can judge me*

The past few days were horrific for Tai. Her latest feat was faking imaginary pains so that the doctor would keep her under his care. Otherwise, she'd be released into the custody of a rehab, or worse, straight to jail.

She used her one phone call on her Uncle Sol. He worked for the FBI and was the only one that could get her out of this mess. Tai knew that he would find out more information about her situation than she really wanted him to know, but felt she could handle her Uncle Sol.

It had been hours since Tai's phone call before Uncle Sol finally showed up at the hospital. As he stood in the doorway he seemed much taller than he actually was. Sol was only about five-foot seven inches tall but suddenly he looked more like seven feet. Tai felt that it was his authoritative demeanor that made him seem bigger, or maybe she was still high and tripping.

Sol was Tai's uncle on her father's side. He looked as if he'd just come off an Indian reservation although he had only a quarter of Indian blood. Tai loved bragging to everyone that she was part Indian when she was younger. She had somehow gotten the idea that it made her better than her mostly all Black friends. Uncle Sol had gained tons of weight since Tai had last seen him. He had a serious potbelly and a receding hairline. Sol also looked a lot older than she remembered. It had been a few years since they'd last seen each other, and Tai was sorry that she had to call on him in such ridiculous circumstances. She knew he was going to give her shit for the rest of her life because of it; but she was no fool, she'd take his berating over jail any day. Her hope was that he'd feel sorry for her because she was all bandaged up. She would be sure to pour it on thick, just to make sure.

Tai's uncle and his crew spoke to the officer in charge. Then Sol handed them some paper work and voila, she was a free woman.

"Okay, Tai. You're going home in the morning. The doctor said he wants to run some more tests before you go." Sol spoke solemnly.

"Thank you, Uncle Sol. I just want you to know that – "

"We'll talk about this in the morning when I pick you up. Get some rest," Sol interrupted.

Just like that, her cuffed arm was released and her Inglewood police watchdogs followed behind her uncle as he left the room. The unclamping of the steel trap made the sun shine once again. It was good to know the right people in the right places. Jail was not for Tai and she was grateful that she wouldn't have to find out just how much.

Uncle Sol was her father's brother, but Tai was sure that he wouldn't tell him anything. FBI training went a long way and secrecy was part of the job. Now she had time to get her side of the story cleaned up before she and her uncle had that long car ride.

She thought the doctor had said that she'd have to wear her cast for six weeks and then wear a brace for another three weeks after that.

Nine weeks. I can't close my shop for nine weeks. What am I gonna do? Live off of credit cards the entire time? No can do.

She pondered solutions to her cash flow problem. She had money saved but not enough to save her. She would definitely have to cut some extra expenses but the main ones, mortgage and car, were the most costly.

Two months of not paying the mortgage on my house and my shop and two months without paying my car note? No more Mercedes? Oh, God.

She let out a deep sigh. Her head and stomach both ached terribly but the pain stemmed from her heart. She had to find a way, broken arm and all.

Tai thought morning would never come. She didn't sleep a wink. Worry and fear were her new companions.

My life is ruined. My shop is gonna close down. I'm gonna lose my house and my car too. I can just see going back up north to Mom and Dad's, driving my bucket to Burger King – the only place that would hire me. My arm will never heal and I'll be in a sling for the rest of my life.

That was all she saw when she closed her eyes so she chose to keep them wide open. The good thing was that she didn't have to go to jail. She would have killed herself if she had.

Uncle Sol got to the hospital bright and early. By his side was Tai's cousin, Marlena. They never go along, even when they were kids. In Tai's eyes, Marlena was a spoiled-assed brat. A prissy, know-it-all. She always thought that she was prettier than Tai because her mother was white and she had lighter skin and slightly better grade of hair. *Puhleez.*

The last thing Tai heard about her cousin was that she was attending law school somewhere. Tai was happy that she'd moved out of state and was not pleased about the reunion.

I may have a broken arm but if Marlena says one smart-ass thing to me, I'm gonna clock her with my left. POW! POW! Don't think I won't.

Tai visualized herself clocking Marlena over the head, knocking her out cold.

When Tai saw them, she went quickly into her porthole of a bathroom to fix herself up. This was the worst punishment Uncle Sol could have come up with. On top of Marlena being Tai's arch rival, she had the biggest mouth on the planet. *This'll get back to my parents, big time.* What was worse, they stood and talked to her doctor for five minutes and Marlena's brain was storing everything that came out of his thin white lips.

In the bathroom, Tai looked in the mirror and was startled. She resembled a living corpse.

I need to get myself a nice facial, manicure and pedicure. Then, soak in a nice hot bubble bath with a glass of wine and a ...no, no wine. I'm just going to take my bath and go to bed. My own big beautiful bed.

The nurse knocked on the bathroom door.

"Are you okay in there?"

"Yes, I'm fine. I'll be out in a minute."

"Okay. Your release papers have been signed and you're all set to go."

"Okay, thanks." Tai was filled with relief.

She splashed her face with cold water using her working hand, dried it and applied some generic hospital lotion. Tai came out of the bathroom to find Marlena standing there with her arms out like she wanted a hug. When Tai just stood there and looked at her like she was crazy, Marlena came over and embraced her as if she was truly happy to see her. Tai gently pulled away from her and caught the look of shame in Marlena's eyes.

"Tai, it is so good to see you!" Marlena beamed.

Tai was speechless.

"Daddy went to go pull the car around," Marlena said in a much calmer voice. She sensed that Tai was uncomfortable and didn't want to make matters worse.

For a moment, they both sat on Tai's hospital bed in silence. Tai sat dressed and ready to go. She was waiting on the nurse whom she was told had to wheel her to the exit. She wished she would hurry.

"Tai, I'm sorry about what you've gone through. But you gon' be all right, you know?" She patted Tai's knee for comfort. "I insisted to Daddy that I come with him this morning. Is there anything that I can do for you? Don't hesitate to ask. After all, we're family," she said with surprising sincerity.

"Wait a minute." Tai couldn't hold her tongue. "Is this the same cousin who used to put chewing gum in my hair when I was sleeping, steal all of my boyfriends in school – "

"Yes, it's me. But a new and improved me. Tai, we haven't seen or spoken to each other in about five years. I'm a different person than I was back then. All that stuff I did to you and all the nasty things I said to you were a result of pure jealousy and lack of happiness within myself."

Tai's mouth damn near dropped to the floor.

Am I dreaming or what? Could it be that Marlena has found some sort of spiritual awakening? Bullshit.

Before Tai could respond, the nurse came in to wheel her out. Tai sat in the wheel chair and didn't look back. This had been the lowest point of her whole life and she wanted it as far behind her as it could possibly get.

Marlena's new, pleasant disposition had proven genuine during the car ride to Tai's house. Uncle Sol seemed to have gotten a dose of it too. They talked to Tai about having peace within herself to create peace around her. Uncle Sol didn't even seem mad. Back in the day, she would have been yelled at and popped in the head a few times by now. Uncle Sol did, however, express how disappointed he was.

"Tai, the only thing I ask of you, is for you to take the necessary steps to get clean. And I'm sorry to say that if you do not go to rehab then you will be picked up and put in jail. I pulled a lot of strings to get you home safely and I want you to hold up your end of the bargain." He was firm with his words but the love poured out in each one spoken.

When they pulled into Tai's driveway, he handed her a piece of paper.

"Here's the name and number of a place that can help you. Call them right away. I can't make you do anything but I can't let you destroy yourself either. Listening to the doctor, it sounds like you are well on your way. Tai, you are my niece and I love you. Watching you go through this is like watching Marlena go through this and it hurts."

He gave Tai a hug and kissed her on the forehead.

"Tai, here's my number. I'm gonna be around for the next few weeks. Please call me. I miss you. I know you're gonna need help around here, and what about the shop? And if you don't call then I'll just have to be an uninvited guest," Marlena said.

Tai promised her she would call and insisted that they not come inside. She told them that the place was an embarrassing mess. They took her word that she would be okay and backed out of the driveway, slowly disappearing down the quiet, tree-lined street. Tai waved to them, with her left hand of course, until the car was no longer in sight.

The horror and shock that overcame her when she walked into her house was indescribable. An embarrassing mess was an understatement. Her house was wrecked. *What in the hell!* Her things were everywhere. Tables and chairs were turned over, dishes were broken and drawers emptied onto the floor. She got a freezing chill. *What if the person who did this shit is still here?* Her heart beat faster and faster and stronger and stronger. She felt sick to her stomach and became sweaty. Under all the mess, she couldn't find her trusted baseball bat; so she grabbed a butcher knife from the kitchen and walked toward the back of the house. Slowly, she tiptoed down the long hallway. The bathroom on the right side was empty.

She shook all over from her nervousness. There was only one more room to check out, her bedroom, straight ahead. The first thing she noticed was that her 32-inch TV, VCR and stereo were all gone. *Dammit!*

After she was sure that the thief or thieves had gone, she went through the wreckage in her house and tallied everything that was missing. Her jewelry, the cash that she kept stashed in various places and her drug paraphernalia box were all gone. They even took all of her liquor from the cabinets. *What if they come back? I have to get the hell up outta here.*

Her car was at The Boutique but she had a "get around bucket" in the garage. When she went to her "spare key" drawer for the key, she found them all missing. *Now these fools have the keys to my house, my shop, my cars, everything!* She was enraged. On top of all of the madness, it saddened her to know that her main concern was not about saving her life or her sanity, but that she needed a fix. Her urges overcame her every thought.

She called Jody but there was no answer. Then she called Dani and she wasn't home either. She thought about paging them but instead she weakened and paged Chris. She even left the code 911. She left a voice mail message as well and pleaded for him to come over right away. Ashamed, she lay balled in the fetal position in tearful agony.

Somebody help me. Somebody, please help me.

Chapter Forty Four

Saudia ~ *Better Days*

"Dear God, you have my mom and dad with you. Please give me the strength to carry on as they would have me to and be able to raise my children without them here. Thank you for everything you have blessed me with and for the blessings to come. Amen."

When she woke up, the first thing she did was pray to God. Saudia prayed in between streams of tears and dry heaves. She felt His spirit everywhere in the room. Her head hurt so bad.

That's my dad punishing me for drinking.

She wondered if she could live her normal life with the feeling that he were watching her. It was different from when her mom died. Now that they were both in heaven she felt like all eyes were on her. She knew if she continued to picture her parents watching over her from up above, it would motivate her to get it together.

When Saudia came out of her room she found Jody in the kitchen setting the table with breakfast.

"Good morning Sleeping Beauty."

"Hey, JoJo. You didn't have to do all of this," Saudia said in a gravely voice.

"Saudia, don't even start. You need to eat. Soak up some of that wine you drank last night," she said, looking like Saudia's mom would've looked.

"Don't forget that your auntie wants you to call her back. She mentioned something about meeting with the funeral director and the lawyer," Jody said hesitantly.

"I'm not doing any of that today. She's trippin'," Saudia said bitterly.

"She said you can leave the kids with her until tomorrow. She wants to take them to church with her and she wants you to drop their clothes by later." Jody finally sat down after cleaning the sink.

"Anything else?" Saudia asked after swallowing a bite of pancakes.

"Oh, and Dani, Keera and Queenie are coming over in a while. I hope you don't mind that I called."

"No, I don't mind. Y'all are all I have left now, besides the twins," Saudia said sincerely.

Just then the phone rang. Jody answered.

"Hello?"

"Hi there, may I please speak to Saudia?"

"Sure, who's calling?" Jody was curious since the voice wasn't familiar to her. She thought she knew all of Saudia's friends.

"Yes, it's Angie."

"It's Angie." Jody whispered.

"Hey Angie!" Saudia took the phone excitedly. "This is a surprise!"

"I didn't want to disturb you but I got the news about your dad's passing at work and I wanted to tell you how sorry I am."

"Well I appreciate you calling. I'm much better than I was last night but it's still a shock that he's gone."

"I know, but he's always going to be with you in spirit. Never forget that."

Saudia smiled. The tears tried to come but she refused to allow them. "Thanks Angie," was all she could manage to say.

"What are you doin' workin' on Saturday anyway?"

"You know an intern's job is never done, girl," she giggled.

"Well, don't let them work you too hard. Especially since there's no pay in for you." Saudia never understood that set-up.

"I won't girl. I love my job anyway, so it's no sweat. By the way, if you're not too busy I was hoping I could stop by a little later."

"Oh, I would love that." Saudia was pleased at the gesture.

"Okay, so I'll see you a little later. Did you need anything?"

"No, I'm fine. My girl Jody is here taking real good care of me. I can't wait for you to meet her."

Jody blushed and was happy to have been acknowledged.

"Okay then, I'll see you a little later."

"Bye, Angie." Saudia hung up the phone and sat back down at the kitchen table.

"So, Angie's stopping by, huh?" Jody asked.

"Yeah, she's a real sweetie. I can't wait for you and the girls to meet her. I know she will fit right in."

"Yeah, I can't wait." Jody said hiding her resentment.

Saudia thought it was real sweet of Jody to come over and take care of her. She was the perfect example of a true friend. Way back in high school, at St. Paul's, Dani introduced Jody into the clique, but Jody connected with Saudia from the very beginning. Saudia felt the others might have been a little intimidating because Jody was so shy at first. Throughout the years, her demeanor stayed passive, until Marcus came along. Since their divorce she'd gotten a little bit more backbone. Jody had also become much more church going. *Whatever floats your boat.* Saudia felt that being involved in church was cool for Jody, but it wasn't her time yet. Saudia did have God in her life. He was her life.

When Angie arrived, Saudia could tell that her warm disposition had won Jody over. And when the rest of the crew joined them, it was clear to Saudia that she had an irreplaceable set of friends. They were all mothering her in their own ways and Angie melted into the scene like warm butter. Jody suggested that they pray and meditate for a moment or two, which proved very helpful.

Queenie set the mood by telling them about her second job as wardrobe consultant for an upcoming film called "The Matchmaker." She explained how she shopped with other people's money. Saudia thought that Queenie had such an exciting life compared to her own and she wanted the same for herself. *If I could only get a promotion, I will be on my way.*

In the middle of Queenie's story a production assistant paged her to tell her that there was a meeting called for later that afternoon, so she had to split.

Although Saudia had just lost her dad, she had an unbearable urge to go out. Getting dressed up and being around crowds, especially crowds of men, always remedied whatever ailed her – if only temporarily. She had heard about a party at The Terrace Supper Club and everyone wanted to go. Each had something that they wanted to escape from that evening and a party at The Terrace was the perfect place.

"I'll be back in a few hours. Should I bring my clothes for tonight or should I stop home and change first?" Queenie wanted to know.

"Change first, Q," was Keera's answer. "We're all going to have to go home first to change."

"Yeah, then we'll all hang out here before hand and go together," Saudia finalized.

"Sounds good. I'll see y'all lata. And save me some cake." She specifically spoke to Keera who was already stuffing her face with a big chunk.

Soon after Queenie's departure, everyone left to get their lives in order in preparation for yet another evening out, leaving Saudia with her thoughts. Her heavy dreams from the night before were still with her. She had a lot of work to do if she wanted to get to the next level. She finally called her Aunt Sis and told her to arrange for the funeral director and the attorney to meet her the following morning. Even though it would be Sunday, she wanted to get all of the formalities over with. No need in moping around feeling sorry for herself. Aunt Sis assured her that all would be fine, then said a prayer with her over the phone. Any other time the gesture would have irritated Saudia, but because of the circumstances she embraced her aunt's efforts.

Saudia also reflected on the conversations that took place just before the girls' left to get ready. Dani filled Saudia and Jody in on what happened with Trixxy. They were both in shock.

"That was one crazy bitch. Somebody needed to put her out of her misery," was Saudia's response. The others thought her statement was mean but she didn't care. She believed what she believed.

While Queenie handled her business at Millennium Pictures, Keera and Dani shopped for party gear. Keera had a suitcase full of crumpled clothes and Dani just didn't want to go home. She still feared that whomever killed Trixxy might be waiting for her too. She wanted so much to go out and get her mind off of things that she didn't even think about the possibility of missing a call from Andrew.

Jody and Angie would both go home to get themselves together as well. And Saudia would go to her aunt's to spend a little time with Damon and Daria.

When the girls met back at Saudia's, everyone looked beautiful, as usual. Dani was dressed flyy in an elegant, black

Calvin Klein pants suit and Keera had on sexy black leather pants with a beaded halter by BEBE and a pair of Christian Louboutin sandals.

That's why I can never shop with them. Way out of my budget, Jody thought as she guiltily envisioned herself someday shopping in Beverly Hills on a whim. *But how could I with all of the starving children in the world?* She finally settled comfortably with the resolution that she could do both; live lavishly and feed the poor. She was conservative, as usual, wearing a beige Rayon dress that buttoned up the front. It looked more suitable for church than the trendy supper club but Jody was Jody no matter where she went and no one else thought twice about it.

Angie was the last to arrive wearing a red suede mini dress with matching thigh high boots. The girl had an outrageous sense of style.

Saudia was unusually frumpy. She didn't feel as much like dressing up as she thought but she did want to get out of the house. Sam had done her justice when finally he came over at three a.m. She was thrilled that Jody, who was sound asleep on the sofa, didn't wake up and try to interfere with her needs being fulfilled. Even if she had, Saudia was sure that her urges were stronger than her friend's holier-than-thou influence and would have won the fight that would have surely occurred.

"Has anyone talked to Tai?" Jody asked.

"We thought about her just before heading over here. I'm a little worried about her. She hasn't been the same these past few days," said a concerned Dani.

Everyone sat in Saudia's living room and looked at each other expecting someone to have an answer, but no one did.

"Tai has always been different. Besides, it's Saturday. You know she is packed with clients until at least one a.m." Saudia said.

"Yeah, she's never up to hang out on a Saturday night because her schedule is so hectic," added Jody.

Keera called the shop to be sure but there was no answer.

"Dang, she must be busy. She didn't even answer the phone. I'll leave her a message to page me if she wants to come. She can always meet us up there."

"Good lookin' out," said Dani. In her opinion, there was always something missing when Tai didn't accompany them on an outing.

"Y'all ready?" Keera stood up and grabbed her car keys. She'd be chauffeuring everyone in the new Lexus Landcruiser that she recently bought for her dad.

With last minute primps in Saudia's living room mirror, everyone followed Keera out the front door and into another girl's night-out adventure.

Chapter Forty Five

Queenie ~ *Caramel Kisses*

Queenie was kickin' it at Saudia's when her pager went off. One of the production assistants called to inform her that there was a meeting at three o'clock. *You think I'd get a little bit of advanced notice.* She thought about telling them that she couldn't make it, but she didn't want to screw up a good opportunity. She still couldn't believe it was true. She actually had a job on a film and would be in charge of dressing the actors. *Unbelievable.*

Clothes were her absolute favorite things to play with. Even when she was a little girl, she wasn't happy unless she was dressed to the nines. It had nothing to do with parental influence. She just wouldn't have it any other way. She would refuse to leave the house unless she was coordinated from head to toe. At times, she even got her butt whooped for being stubborn; but no matter how red Queenie's face and eyes were from crying, she always walked out of that house looking like the princess that she believed she was.

She often wondered what ever happened to the "I'm a princess" state of mind that she once had. It got lost somewhere in my gawky teen years, she supposed.

Going to The Terrace for dinner and drinks sounded good to Queenie. The past week had been dark and filled with tragedy. It saddened Queenie to conclude that at the same time

Dani found out about Trixxy's murder, Saudia's dad passed away.

Saudia was in a better state than Queenie had expected. Saudia believed that Ebenezer was in a better place and that he was no longer suffering. And it was that belief that kept her sane.

Queenie couldn't imagine losing even one of her parents, yet Saudia had lost both of hers in just a year's time. She could see though that Saudia would be fine. Her pain was obvious through her expressions, but so were her strength and perseverance.

It took Queenie no time to stop at her place to change into something more appropriate and then get to Millennium Studios. She didn't think her DKNY jogging suit, even with matching baseball cap and cross-trainer sneakers, would've made a good, first impression. Although designer Donna Karan was the bomb, but not quite the first impression she wanted to make. Queenie had to meet the designers and a few more of the movie's financial backers; therefore, she needed to look like she knew what the hell she was doing.

Everyone in the room was cool except for Chamille Rourke, the film's female lead. She had been such a snob. She seemed to have a strong opinion on what styles her character would wear from frame to frame.

Queenie set the tone by assuring her that her ideas were more than welcome. After all, she'd be the one wearing the clothes in front of all America.

Queenie pumped her ego a little because she was smart enough to know that it would benefit her in the end. Chamille would eventually gain trust in her and things would be smooth sailing from there. Queenie had no doubt that she would have Ms. Rourke looking her absolute best and that she would come begging for more.

Just as the meeting wrapped, Emilio walked in. Queenie had no idea that he would be there and did not complain. Her heartbeat was so loud, she feared the whole room could hear.

Damn, he looks appetizing. Those dark eyes, that smooth brown skin and perfect smile. And that body. Please help me.

Emilio leaned seductively against the frame of the door and motioned for Queenie to come to him. She could feel the stares and hear the intense silence that swarmed the room. With a deep breath she got her sketches and notes together and placed them in her briefcase, closing it firmly. She smiled and thanked everyone for being patient with her. She sweetly told them that she looked forward to working with them and charmed her way out of the room's awkwardness.

The gesture unfroze their curious expressions; and shortly after, they all started moving about as if they were under hypnosis and the hypnotist had snapped his fingers again.

Finally, they were all gone and it was just she and Emilio. He turned off the lights and didn't hesitate putting his arms around her. He embraced her so passionately, it was like the first time he ever held her – or the last time he ever would. She hugged him back and didn't say a word as he slid his big strong hand up the front of her skirt.

Not wearing pantyhose today was a good thing, she thought to herself. He felt so good to Queenie. Pure ecstasy.

She prayed time would stop and everyone else in the world with it, except for them. She unbuttoned his shirt and kissed his chest like it was dipped in chocolate. They were all over each other until the phone rang.

The receptionist called over the intercom to ask if the meeting had cleared out. There was another meeting scheduled right behind Queenie's and the party was waiting to be allowed into the room. The sound of Paulina's voice over the intercom freaked Queenie out. She jumped up and quickly started to fix her clothes and hair. Emilio took a hold of her wrists and pulled her into him.

"I've missed you, my Princess," he said softly in her ear.

"I've missed you too, baby, but we can't fool around here. They'd fire me on the spot. I'm not a big shot like you, Mr. Movie Star," Queenie said smiling and stroking his face. He had such a beautiful face.

"I want you to stay with me tonight, Queenie. I'm at the L'Mirage Hotel until I get a permanent spot. We can take my car. You shouldn't be driving alone at night anyway. LA's no joke."

What is that supposed to mean? Did he forget I spent two years alone in New York, let alone that LA is my stomping ground? Men.

Dismissing his comment, Queenie said, "Yes, Emilio, I'll come with you but I'll drive my own car. I have to be back at my girlfriend's house in a couple of hours. She lost her father last night and she needs me." She didn't bother mentioning that they were going to The Terrace. For what? Besides, he might want to tag along and this wasn't exactly the best time to introduce him to everyone.

"Whatever makes you happy, Princess. Any time I can spend with you I will treasure," he said with the look that Queenie could never resist.

In less than thirty minutes they were in his hotel suite wrapped in nothing but each other and bed sheets. They kissed, grinded and even mildly bit on each other until they couldn't take it any more. Queenie got on top of him and worked her magic. She served him the "Queenie Special," where she rode until the horse fell with weakness. Then he got "Queenie's Delight," doggy style on all fours. The ultimate orgasm when handled right. She got a perverted kick using names for her sexual positions. She, Dani and Keera laughed about it one day when they shared with one another how they put it on their men, making them revert to little boys. Sometimes even babies. They were so cute when they were helpless.

During their harmonious lovemaking, Emilio panted in Queenie's ear, professing his love for her. He told her that he and his wife's divorce was final and that he left her back in New York to pursue his film career. He said all of the right things. Before Queenie knew it, she had called the girls to apologize for not being able to go out. She felt real bad on one hand, but on the other she felt so damn good.

Chapter Forty Six

THE TERRACE ~ *Men all pause*

The supper club was packed. There were fine men everywhere. Angie and Saudia were practically salivating. Out of the twenty dinner tables there weren't very many brothas, but the ones who were there, were top choice.

"Saudia, you came through on this one girl. It looks like we got all these gorgeous men all to ourselves," Keera commented as she surveyed the delicious eye candy.

"O-kay! What is goin' on up in here?" Saudia was intrigued with the all male company. She thought back to the tickets that she pilfered from one of the staff's mailboxes at Mayhem records. She didn't remember seeing that it was a men only event.

Even with the tickets in hand the ladies had a hard time getting into the door. The party was private, by invitation only, but Keera worked them in with her fame. It was strange though, when the doorman said, "I don't think you ladies will have that good of a time in there tonight," with a chuckle.

Nevertheless, they were hooked up with a table. It was located in the very back of the small banquet room, but a table nonetheless. As the ladies were escorted to their seats, they sensed a strange ambiance. It looked more like a convention than a party, a convention for fine men everywhere. The ladies got a lot of stares too, and they definitely weren't the stares of adornment that they were used to.

Finally, Keera asked the waiter what the occasion was and the answer was shocking. He said it was a celebration for TCOC. He then explained that it stood for "The Coming Out Club," as in, out of the closet. The girls were grossed out, to say the least.

"All of these fine men in here are gay?" Saudia wanted to know.

"Isn't it wonderful?" The waiter sang as he placed a glass of cold water in front of each of them.

Keera complained that she should've pulled a Queenie and stayed at home. Although she wasn't looking for a man, if she did find one, she wanted him to pay her some attention and make her feel like the queen that she was. *Don't think that'll happen tonight*, Keera thought to herself as she looked around the room at all of the well dressed men.

It was obvious to Keera that it was an entertainment industry function. She saw many familiar faces in the crowd but none that surprised her. It soon became a game of "Who Will I Spot Next?" The girls exchanged notes on who knew whom, but nothing could have prepared any of them for what happened next.

Saudia did a double take when she saw Sean Melody walk up to the podium. He was her boss' son and also the newest R&B sensation to hit the music scene. Saudia and Angie couldn't believe it. At Mayhem, he constantly strutted around pretending to be such a ladies man.

"Thank you all for being here this evening and your donations for our AIDS awareness program are even more appreciated. You know we've got to educate our youth." He glanced over the room between the massive clapping.

"The first thing on our agenda before our delicious eight course meal begins is to introduce the newest member of our organization. You all know him well as a highly talented basketball phenomenon, as well as the face in many commercial endorsements. Please give a warm welcome to Chance Walker!"

The loud claps and the standing ovation were all a blur to Keera. Though she sat there cool as a cucumber, mentally she had passed out.

"Do you want to leave Keera?" Dani stood up and bent near her friend's side. "Keera, are you okay?" She was concerned about Keera's blank stare. "Come on, y'all. Let's get her out of here." Saudia, Jody and Angie all got up from the table to help, but Keera would not budge.

Chance, oblivious to Keera's presence, rose to the podium and spoke.

"Thank you all for having me. I'm honored to be here. I'm going to do all I can to help raise awareness. And as I venture into acting, I will make sure that I open doors for as many of my TCOC brothers as I can."

He then put a fist in the air, and then he stepped down to take his seat. Saudia noticed that he sat next to his friend, Thomas, whom she'd met at his birthday party.

Humph, Queenie was right all along about him.

Saudia was tweaking. Aside from Sean Melody and Chance being there, there was Percy Cannon, the famous comedian and Sydney Shepherd, the football star.

And, Jody also spotted a white boy named Tracy Millerton that she went to Santa Monica College with. She'd heard from mutual acquaintances that he now had a good job with Millennium Pictures, which made him fine and successful. *And gay?* She wanted to cry. Jody looked around the room in amazement. She couldn't believe how many men she recognized from sports, TV and movies. She got a sudden chill. *What is the world coming to?*

Without warning, Keera stood up and shouted, "You lyin' muthafucka! Who in the fuck do you think you are? You are not gay! You can't be gay!" Keera was crying and bursting with fury. She was hurt and betrayed by her boyfriend of six years. *How dare he!*

By this time, four big brawny bouncers had come into play. Keera had long since stopped yelling and screaming but she had picked up a knife from a nearby table and began to charge toward Chance. She didn't get very far.

Once outside, Keera cried while her friends tried wholeheartedly to get her into the closely parked Lexus Landcruiser.

"Wait! Keera, wait!" It was Chance.

Dani walked back toward him to give him a piece of her mind.

"Chance, I don't know what's going on with you but my girl is hurt. You better come clean and stop playin' games. This is the kind of shit that could end up on the news if you know what I mean," she threatened.

Dani was smooth with her tone. She knew that the heavily guarded restaurant had not alerted the press of their little "underground awareness meeting" and that the club members wanted it to remain that way.

Before Chance could answer, Keera walked up and cold-socked him in the jaw. He tumbled backwards, eventually falling hard on his backside. Keera walked toward him and hovered over his expensive suit and defeated eyes.

"Why, Chance? That's all I want to know. Why?" Keera's voice trembled and Chance just sat there.

He didn't even bother to get up from the ground. He felt lowdown and dirty so he stayed on the ground where he thought he belonged.

When Thomas made it through the on-lookers, things got worse.

"You don't have to explain shit to this bitch." Thomas' tone was bitter. "He don't love you anyway, he loves me. I wanted to tell you on the plane but it wasn't my place." Thomas helped Chance up from the ground.

"Keera, let's go, Sweetie. You don't need this."

Saudia knew that if they didn't leave, she would be throwing punches at Thomas. He had really gotten to her and she was sure that Keera felt the same way.

Keera didn't argue this time. She let her friends pull her away from the scene and lead her to the car.

"Give me the keys, Keera," Dani insisted. Keera was in no state to drive.

In the truck, Keera's face was the picture of devastation. The ride to Saudia's conversation free. No one said a word. It was a rare awkwardness that they'd never experienced before. Dani drove fast and Keera, also in the front seat, played the music almost deafeningly loud. She put in 2-PAC's Makaveli CD. It soothed her because 2-PAC's angry lyrics mirrored her own emotions.

Dani pulled into Saudia's driveway.

"Keera, I'mma follow you to your dad's." Dani said just before getting into her black Navigator SUV. Even though Keera insisted on being alone, Dani knew what was best.

Saudia, Angie and Jody all got out of the truck in silence with the exception of solemn "good-byes" to their friends. They stood on the sidewalk as Dani and Keera drove off into the night.

Saudia definitely didn't want to go home so she talked Jody and Angie into going to a bar in the Marina. She felt like mingling. They wound up at a joint called "The Piano." She had heard about it but had never been before. It was a nice place with a dark, cozy setting accented with loud chattering and clinking glasses. There were crowds of people, Mexican, Black, White, Asian and every other ethnicity in the house.

Of course all three of them talked about what happened at The Terrace. Jody was in tears. You would have thought she saw Marcus. Being in that scene would convince a single woman that she had no chance in hell of ever finding a man who will love her and only her.

Angie was pumped when she realized there was a Karaoke machine.

"Ooh, I love to sing!" She lit up like a Christmas tree.

After Saudia and Angie had a few drinks, Angie finally got the nerve to go on stage. She swore it was her first time but it sounded like it was her livelihood, something she did all of the time. She had the most angelic voice Saudia had heard in a long time, and she heard a lot of music working at Mayhem Records. People wanted record deals so badly they'd call the company and serenade Saudia over the phone in hopes of being discovered. She was in no position to help them, but she could help Angie. This was fate. When Angie was finished singing Teena Marie's "Portuguese Love," she got a standing ovation. Afterwards, a whole lot of men bought her drinks and Saudia didn't mind helping her with the excess. Saudia kept the singing thing in the back of her head until Jody dropped them off at the house.

"All right you guys, I'mma head on home now. I still feel like I'm in the Twilight Zone." Jody said in an exhausted tone.

"I feel you on that one." Angie agreed.

"Okay Jody, Honey. Be careful driving home and I'll talk to you tomorrow." Saudia bent down and gave Jody a hug through her open car window.

"Okay. And Angie it was nice meeting you. I hope to see you again soon."

"Definitely. It was nice meeting you too. I had no idea Saudia's friends were so fun and, um, interesting." Angie struggled for the right words to summarize the dramatic evening.

“To say the least.” Saudia added with a smile.

“Bye you guys.” Jody said just before backing out of the driveway.

“Angie, can you come inside for a minute?” Saudia’s tone turned serious.

“Sure, girl. What’s up?”

Angie followed Saudia inside with her arms crossed and her ears wide open. It didn’t take much convincing for Angie to agree to make a demo after listening to Saudia’s ideas. She had gotten Angie pumped about the possibility of signing a deal with Mayhem. Marvin Melody, the owner, was always looking for new talent. Saudia was positive that he would be just as hyped as they were, once he heard Angie blow.

She wasn’t wasting any time in plotting the steps to make it happen. She would make a few phone calls to her industry contacts and try to get a demo made before work on Monday morning. She had twenty-four hours to work her magic and the clock was ticking.

It was a windy but sunny Sunday morning and Saudia’s dad’s attorney, Mr. Henry Boss, pulled up at her Aunt Sis’ at the same time as she did: eight a.m. on the nose. He was about sixty year old, Saudia guessed. He was tall and thin with black leathery skin and a creased forehead. His eyes were a pale gray and his demeanor, strictly business.

Aunt Sis and the kids had just finished breakfast. Saudia was glad that her aunt arranged for an early meeting. Now her day would be free to get Angie’s voice on tape.

Mr. Boss had been her dad's lawyer since her mom's passing. He was a no nonsense man who got the job done. Her dad had some legal issues to battle with against his wife's family and Mr. Boss came through in resolving matters. The situation was a big reason why Saudia was not close to her mom's people at all.

When he laid everything out to Saudia, she almost fell out of her chair. Ebenezer had left everything to his daughter. It was more than enough to take care of her and the kids for the rest of their lives. She could even quit her job if she wanted. Mr. Boss was quick to point that out to her. *If this thing with Angie works out, I might just do that.* Both of her parent's had invested in life insurance policies as youths and now Saudia was the sole beneficiary of her father's and her mother's insurance. There was all of that money, plus what he had invested over the years.

Mr. Boss gave Saudia some paperwork to sign and her hands shook the entire time. She had no idea her daddy had it going on the way he did. He was a bit of a miser and never discussed his finances.

When he left, the funeral director was on the front porch. After a few hours of deciding, they arranged a nice dignified service for her dad. He would be pleased. His burial plot had already been arranged and he would lay right next to his beloved wife. Saudia didn't hesitate to use some of her new money to pay for a special ceremony but she realized she would need a financial expert to help her manage her new wealth. She refused to go out like Hammer.

After spending more time at her aunt's than she had planned, she called Angie to tell her that she was on her way. Aunt Sis appointed herself in charge of looking after all of the arrangements they had made that day. She had more experience with it than Saudia did and it seemed important to her. Saudia had no problem with it.

The kids were watching one of the videos that Saudia had brought along with the rest of their things. It was a relief that they handled everything so well.

Angie was still at the nail shop when Saudia was done so she made a trip back to Mayhem Records. The office was dark and quiet. She hadn't been there after hours in years. Without a second thought, Saudia went straight to her Rolodex and made some phone calls. There were some struggling rappers and a couple of up and coming producers that she had become real cool with. They were always hungry for work. She even used some of her new money to let them know that she meant business.

Rocky and Bullwinkle, two talented and hungry producers, said they were messing around in their basement studio at the house and agreed that she and Angie would come on over. Saudia swung around to the nail shop where Angie was waiting and they were on their way to a new beginning.

When they got there, Quan, a rapper with GrandStand Entertainment, was already busting mind-boggling lyrics. Angie wasn't shy and slid right in after she looked over some music that Rocky gave her. Her experience in the church choir came very much in handy when it came to reading music.

They didn't leave that studio until seven a.m. the next morning. They both went straight to work from there, with energy to burn. The demo turned out real hot. It was the bomb. Even the guys said it sounded good enough for a radio release. Saudia accessed Melody's schedule while in the office the night before and strategically put them in at two o'clock. She had that much confidence that they would be ready. Angie was so amped, she was going to go for it if she had to go in there and sing a cappella. She thanked Saudia for her encouragement and for helping her to get to this point. She confessed that it was always something she wanted, but never pursued to her fullest potential. If all went well, they agreed that Saudia would be her official manager. Angie had no problem with signing a contract that Saudia would have Mr. Boss draw up. Business was business.

Two o'clock took forever to come. In the meantime they had a talk with company's attorney, Allison Blue, and she agreed to sit in the meeting and represent in case Melody wanted to negotiate. He thought the girls were playing games when they sat to talk, until Angie stuck the demo into the tape player and blew him away. He signed her on the spot. Allison hooked Angie up with the best offer she could ask for. Of course, Melody figured out that he would need a new receptionist. He told Saudia he'd never find one as good as her. She thought it was real nice of him to say considering that she didn't even think he'd noticed. Saudia felt like she was in a fairy tale. The reality that money would no longer be an issue removed a lot of weight from her shoulders. All of the pain she felt when she found out her dad had died was still there, but she would use the pain as a stepping stone, instead of as a brick upside the head.

Later, regrouping at home, she picked up the kids and headed straight back to the house. She spent some time with them and read them a few stories, fed them, bathed them, then tucked them into bed. In her room she did the most praying and praising that she'd ever done in one sitting. She was truly thankful and she wanted Him to know that.

Chapter Forty Seven

Jody ~ *Hangin' on a string*

The events that took place over the past few days were unbelievable to Jody. Saudia's dad passed away, Dani found out that Trixxy had been killed and Keera found her missing boyfriend at a gay party. And last but not least, Jody was now jobless. She had been buried so deeply into everybody else's problems that her own had become hidden underneath her denial.

After coming in from a long evening with the girls, she called Marcus to let him know that she was home.

"Hey, Marcus. I made it back. How are the kids?"

"Sound asleep. How's Saudia doing?"

"She's doing better, much, much better."

"Why don't you let the kids stay through the weekend? I'll get them to school on Monday morning too."

"Okay, that's fine."

Jody would have normally refused his offer but she knew that after church in the morning, she would have to hit the Sunday paper's want ads. She had to find a new job and fast.

"While I have you on the phone, there's something I've been meaning to tell you."

Marcus decided to tell Jody he and Shelby's news while she seemed to be in a mellow mood. He also wanted to tell her before the kids did.

Jody sat in silence, waiting for the bomb to drop.

"Jody, Shelby's pregnant. We're having a baby."

Somehow Jody got a "congratulations" out of her mouth and it actually sounded sincere. The news sank in her stomach like a bag of cement. Now she knew she had truly lost him.

The next day, Jody went to church and then spent the rest of Sunday evening combing through the paper for jobs. She circled a few possibilities and planned to follow up on them in the morning. All that night, Jody thought about Marcus, Shelby and their new baby. The only thing she could do was pray for them. She wanted to believe that Marcus would leave Shelby just as he'd left her. *She'll see. Some dogs never learn new tricks.*

During the night, Jody tossed and turned. She had never felt so alone. The house was quiet and the only thing that she heard were Marcus' words echoing in her head. *Shelby's pregnant. We're having a baby.* She also revisited the scene in the bank when she was given her lay off notice. Jody's panic and fear swarmed her body and took over all of her good senses.

She got out of bed and went to her kitchen cabinet where she kept hot chocolate and tea, and pulled out the bottle of Vodka that was stashed way in back. She hadn't touched a drink since Marcus left three years ago. She never thought that it would be him who pushed her once again over the edge. This was the last bottle left when she finally got the strength to quit drinking altogether. She saved it as a reminder of how bad things could get. She had no idea that it would help take her to a place equivalent to her idea of hell. Without thinking twice, she opened the bottle and put her lips right to it. The liquor burned but not nearly as much as her pain. *I lost my husband and my kid's father and now my job,* she sobbed heavily.

"Fuck them! Fuck all of them! Yes, I said fuck! FUCK! FUCK! FUCK!" Jody was out of control.

She cried for what seemed like hours before she needed something besides the liquor to relieve the pain. She then remembered the sleeping pills prescribed to her when she had constantly complained to her doctor about back problems.

She took pill after pill until she felt satisfied with the results. She was limp, like she had no joints or muscles in her body. She lay there like an inflatable doll with all the air let out. Finally, there was only darkness. Pitch, quiet darkness.

When she woke up in the hospital, she had a very scary feeling. Jody didn't remember anything from the time she gulped down her first sleeping pill. When she opened her eyes, Saudia and Marcus were at her bedside. She was more embarrassed about that than anything else.

"Hey, Jody. How do you feel?" Saudia was terrified for her friend. She stroked Jody's hair and tried to give her a sip of water.

"I'm okay. How did I get here?" She asked groggily.

Saudia explained to Jody that she called the bank and was told that she no longer worked there. She remembered Jody telling her about the possibility of being laid off and quickly rushed to her house. She saw Jody's car in the driveway and knew she was there, so when she didn't answer the door, she went around the back and broke in. She'd warned Jody about getting new locks in the past but was relieved that she didn't.

When Saudia found her lying on the bathroom floor with an empty bottle of Vodka and prescription pills, she called 911. She then found Marcus' pager number in Jody's phone book. When he called back she told him to meet them at St. Luke's hospital.

Marcus gave Jody a hug and told her that everything would be okay.

"Jody, please don't worry about the kids. Me and Shelby will keep them until you get back on your feet."

All she could do was crack a smile and breathe a soft thank you.

"Yeah, girl. Now it's my turn to take care of you. You have nothing to worry about, Saudia comforted.

She then relayed to Jody that she packed her bag and that as soon as she was released, she would be coming home with her.

She didn't know why, but right then Jody knew that she would be just fine.

Chapter Forty Eight

Keera ~ *Mo' money mo' problems*

Every time Keera thought about what happened with Chance at The Terrace, she wanted to throw up. At first, when she saw him she didn't even put together that he was at a gay party. She was initially just pissed that he was hanging out in LA and didn't even bother to get in touch with her.

Who the fuck does he think he is? Hell, who the fuck does he think I am? Cocksuckin' mothafucka.

She wasn't pleased with how she handled the situation but didn't know what else to do. There was no way for her to know how to behave in such a situation. She didn't give a fuck. She called him every name in the book while he just stood there and looked stupid. It still didn't seem right. Her man, who did nothing but criticize and crucify gay men any time the subject was brought up? Her man, who could barely say the word gay without having to replace it with faggot?

"What in the hell is going on? Is the world coming to an end?" Keera wanted to know.

She did finally talk to Chance later that night. Before hand, Dani followed Keera to drop off the Landcruiser at her dad's. While she was there, she said good-bye to her sleeping father and got her things. She was so happy that she didn't run into Kevin. She was not in the mood for him and would have told him so had he infringed upon her, like he usually did.

Lastly, she and Dani got a suite at Embassy Suites Hotel near the airport. They didn't stay at Dani's because she was still freaked out about Trixxy's murder and Keera didn't want to be in her dad's face feeling the way she did. She wasn't ready to talk to him about what happened because she was still very confused.

When Keera paged Chance from the hotel, he called right back. He sat on the phone in silence for what seemed like forever. Then he just said it, straight out.

"Keera, I'm bisexual. I have been for a long time now. I hope you can forgive me. I still love you though, and I still want to be with you. No one else has to know about what happened. The club is sworn to secrecy."

Keera sat numbly. She'd heard enough.

Did he just say what I think he said? She wasn't sure so she asked him.

"Mothafucka, what did you just say? Did you say you were bisexual? First of all, that means you've been cheating on me. And with other men? You fucking sick, lying, faggot ass, mothafucka. Who gave you permission to waste my time? To fuck up my life along with yours? Six years mothafucka! Why didn't you say something? Oh, I forgot, only a real man would've done that. I don't ever want to see your sorry ass again! You disgust me! Oh and you can be sure that this shit will be all up in the news, so stay tuned mothafucka!"

She slammed down the phone and let out a barrage of tears. Dani sat by her side in silence not really knowing what to say to her distraught friend. Keera cried like she hadn't cried in years, not since her mom died when she was ten years old.

Keera had finally cried herself to sleep and didn't awake until late Sunday morning. Dani was already up, reading a magazine that she had bought in the gift shop and watching a movie on pay-per-view.

"So, how you feeling?" Dani asked.

"Still fucked up but I guess I'll get over it, right? I mean I'm sure I'm not the only girl in the world who found out that her long time boyfriend and love of her life is gay."

Keera tried to make light of the situation but it still hurt like hell. She just wanted to go home. Home to New York where she could bury herself in her work. She made arrangements to leave for New York on the first available flight, which turned out to be midnight. In the meantime, she and Dani hung out all day. They watched movies, ordered room service and spent silent moments in their own thoughts. Surprisingly, neither had a drink or even suggested getting high. That was a first.

Keera was thankful that Dani was with her. With her, she didn't have to mask the sadness that she felt. She didn't have to worry about doing anything stupid either, like calling the press. She wanted to be vindictive but knew that it would ruin her as well. They were vultures and would have loved to rip them both to shreds.

She didn't know about him but she needed her good name. She even somewhat felt like less of a woman because of her ordeal with Chance and wasn't sure if she'd ever overcome the feeling. She questioned the notion that she was not woman enough to keep her man satisfied. Dani convinced her that she had nothing to do with Chance's ventures outside of their relationship.

"Don't be crazy. Those are his issues and his issues alone with or without you in his life." Dani assured her.

As far as Keera was concerned, without her was definitely how Chance would be living.

Dani drove Keera to the airport an hour before her flight and sat with her until it was time to board. Keera had never been happier to leave LA. The weekend that she so looked forward to turned into pure hell and she would never forget it.

Earlier, Francine had assured Dani that the kids were fine and she talked to them briefly before concluding that they would be okay without her for another day. Dani decided to keep the room overnight and returned there after Keera's plane departed. She still had to have her talk with Jasmine about her dead mother and wasn't quite ready to deal.

When Keera arrived in New York early Monday morning, her Manhattan apartment was a wreck. It was just as she had left it the week before. She didn't sleep that good on the plane so she dropped her bags on the floor and climbed right into bed. Her eyes were so swollen from crying, she could barely open them. Her stomach ached so bad she knew the only cure was for her to get over the hurt.

I've lost my man.

But she never really had him in the first place.

My very, very best friend.

But if they were really best friends, she would have known about his sexual secrets when they were just a thought. She prayed and prayed for God to help her through this. She begged for a way out. A revelation. Praying was something Keera rarely relied on but now she felt it was her last hope for survival. If nothing else, it helped her to sleep when nothing else would.

Something told Keera to wake up but her eyes weren't listening. The loud bump in the other room got them to finally open. She soon realized that someone else was in her apartment. Someone was in her living room bumping around in the dark.

Who would be in my house? It could be a robber or a rapist, or even the creep that's been prank calling me for the past month.

She thought about Trixxy and how she went out. Her heart was beating fast and hard and she was scared as hell. Without hesitation, she grabbed her gun from under the bed. She was about to get up and investigate but it was too late, the intruder had already entered her bedroom.

Keera didn't move another muscle. The figure was a masculine one. A very big man. He stood over Keera like the shadow of death. She lay as still as she could so he wouldn't figure out that she was under the rumpled blankets.

She didn't know what happened next, it all went down like a flash of lightening. When he put his gloved hand on her throat, she closed her eyes tight and fired her pistol twice into his stomach. His rock hard body fell on her like a ton of bricks.

In the dark, she reached for her cordless phone next to the bed and called 911. There was no movement from the big, lifeless body that she slid from under. It took all of her strength. The blood was warm and plentiful. It dripped from him to her and then soaked through her mattress. She was scared to death. *What if there are others?* She was too scared to even turn on the light to see who he was, but for the sake of her sanity she did it any way. When she turned on the light, she wished she hadn't. She fell to the floor when she saw her stepbrother, Kevin, bleeding to death from the bullets she fired into his body.

"Kevin! Oh my God, Kevin! Is that you! Oh My God, somebody help. Somebody please help!"

Keera screamed and yelled knocking on neighbors' doors and pleading with God until she finally dialed 911. As she waited she sat with him. She stroked his head and prayed that he'd make it through. It hadn't even sunk in that he tried to take her life.

"Keera. I lo-ve you. I did it because I lo-ve you." He gasped for air between words. Then between syllables. "I will never leave you Kee-ra. Ne-ver." Those were the words he whispered with his last breaths of life. Keera was horrified.

When the police arrived the tragedy starved news media and paparazzi weren't far behind. It was a nightmare and it all happened so fast that she had yet to figure out how to digest it all.

Having to save face for the cameras had become so second nature that it was very hard to turn off the charm and just be herself. The flash of the cameras didn't invade her until now. Now they were intrusive and unwelcome. It momentarily took her back to her very first paparazzi experience years ago while jogging alone in the park. She was filled with apprehension but eventually grew to understand that a public image was all part of the game. The game of fame and fortune.

Keera flew back to LA the first chance she got. After the police, the only people she called were her dad and then Dani from the plane. Dani was still at the hotel and offered to meet at Keera's dads house. She assured Dani she'd call her when she got there.

"MODEL KILLS BROTHER IN SELF DEFENSE" was the newspaper headline. The news was all over the TV and the tabloids. Keera's agency and everyone else had been trying to get a hold of her. Even Chance. When she was ready to deal with the world she would, but she wasn't ready yet. She even thought about taking a break from modeling. With all that had happened with Chance and Kevin, she needed some time off to think about her future and where she was headed. Things had definitely gone off track.

It all made sense. Reading Kevin's journal back at her dad's in LA, she learned that he kept a log of every prank phone call, anonymous letter and plot that entered his mind to scare Keera. His plan, from what she read, was to scare her enough that she would give in to hiring him again as her bodyguard.

That confirmed to Keera that Kevin was a complete idiot. Such a way out scheme for such a simple job. She also discovered videotapes of herself that she had no idea even existed. All were carefully labeled with her name and the date of the taping. *Ain't this a bitch?* She dreaded to think what his intentions were for their use. *My bodyguard? Was that his life long dream? Gimme' a fuckin' break.* She was horrified by what happened in her New York apartment but she finally came to grips with it. The way she looked at it, it would have been either him or her. *I ain't goin' out like no sucka.*

Cruella was devastated, to put it lightly. She hadn't said a word to Keera since she'd come home. Cruella refused to believe that Kevin meant her any harm. Never mind that he broke into her apartment wearing a ski cap and black leather gloves, and that he was carrying a Swiss army knife and a Glock Forty-Five hand gun. Cruella was so spiteful and bitter that she immediately packed her bags and moved out.

"I'll see both of you in court!" was her promise.

Sayonara, Cruella.

Chapter Forty Nine

Tai ~ *Be Happy*

Marlena's phone number came in handy sooner than Tai had expected. Chris ignored her barrage of pages, so Tai found herself reunited with her Uncle Sol and Cousin Marlena. She didn't even realize that she was at a fork in the road. A crucial place in her life, which could have meant life or death.

Aside from her heroin addiction and her home being robbed, Tai had another serious problem to deal with: she was pregnant. She thought long and hard about what to do about her pregnancy. She was in no position to take care of a baby. She wouldn't even know what to do with a baby.

She could hear Jody loud and clear in her ear when she prayed her problems to God.

"God please give me the strength so that I can make the choice that I know is right."

She also asked for strength because she would definitely need it. That, and more clients. After praying about it and thinking about the pros and cons and the ifs, ands or buts, over and over again, she decided to keep the baby. *I'm going to be a mommy.*

Spending the last few days with Cousin Marlena had been truly enlightening. Tai discovered that her cousin had evolved into a really good person. At first, she was skeptical of Marlena's newfound disposition, but she was serious about the things she said and Tai had to listen.

“Tai, knowledge is truth and truth is freedom. You need to rebuild your mind in order to gain universal knowledge. There are so many different pathways in life and the pathways we end up on are a result of our thinking. Positive or negative.”

When she talked to Tai, she made her believe that she could have a fresh start. She closed her eyes and looked at her life over the past ten years. She felt dirty, like she needed an enema. She didn’t even feel she had to go to rehab after she embraced this new, positive outlook on life, but Uncle Sol insisted that she check in as soon as possible.

Tai also talked to them about her financial situation and as a result, her Uncle Sol agreed to help her out.

“I’ll give you what you need Tai and my only requirement for payment is your recovery. Get yourself healthy from the inside out.”

Tai realized that she did look bad. She was surprised that none of her girlfriends ever mentioned it to her. Or, maybe they tried to but she didn’t hear them. She had a problem with getting so wrapped up in her own web that things on the outside seemed invisible. *I’m going to work on that.*

Tai was shocked when she read the morning newspaper. Not only was Keera in the headlines for killing her brother in self-defense, but Chris was headlined as well. It was reported that he was involved in a police shoot out. They raided the warehouse where he had conducted a huge drug deal and now he was dead.

Tai called her Uncle and had him cross check the fingerprints from her robbed home with his. It didn’t surprise her a bit that the prints matched. She realized that she had left her wallet at his house, or either he stole it, during their drug binge. The rest was history.

Bad karma. I bet you all his thoughts were negative. I hope the baby doesn't inherit that. If so, I'll teach her what's right.

Tai finally talked to Dani who paged her from a hotel room. She was worried once she'd realized that no one had talked to Tai as of late. She wanted assurance that Tai was okay, especially with all of the drama that everyone else had endured. Dani gave her a brief run down on what everyone else had dealt with.

Tai was speechless. She thought she was the only one who had gone through some major shit. When Dani finished, it was then time for Tai to fill her in on her own crazy weekend.

Tai admitted to her that she got into a fight at The Boutique, she fired Charles and Lisa, her house was robbed, and that she was pregnant. Dani was completely floored. Tai left out the part about the drugs. She knew that her talking about it was inevitable but the time was not yet right.

"When is Ebenezer's funeral?" Tai wanted to know.

"I haven't heard yet. Saudia wasn't at home when I called but I'll find out and let you know." Before Tai could respond Keera had clicked in on Dani's other line.

"Tai, it's Keera. I'mma call you back in a little while. Do you need anything?"

"No, girl. My cousin Marlena is taking good care of me. Tell Keera I said to stay strong and I'll talk to you later."

The next phone call Tai made was to an in-patient rehab center in Pacific Palisades. She had an appointment at ten a.m. and actually looked forward to entering the program. Getting clean was the only way out of the grave she'd begun to dig for herself. She still had cravings but had managed to overcome them with prayer and positive thoughts. She wanted to banish them for good and knew that the treatments would help.

The Palisades rehab facility would be home for three months. While she immersed herself into getting her insides healed, the plan was to get her house back together and get The Boutique back in business.

I'm going to have to call all of my clients and kiss ass. Probably even lower my prices a little. I need to somehow gain new clients too. Uncle Sol told her she didn't have to pay him back, but she wouldn't sleep at night until she did.

She tried to call Jody but she wasn't home. For some reason, with everything going on with her, Jody had been on her mind heavily. She'd given her a hard time the last few years but now had an urge to talk to her and apologize. Jody, with all of her preaching and lecturing, used to get on Tai's nerves but Tai realized that she was a good person and only tried to do what was right.

I think I'm going to take her up on her invitation to go to her church. It was definitely time.

Chapter Fifty

Queenie ~ *Ex-factor*

When Queenie woke up in her own bed with the sound of the alarm clock in her ear, she thought it had all been a dream. Then she looked in the mirror. *Nope, the glow is unmistakable,* she thought, smiling. The more she looked the heavier the memories from the night before flooded her mind.

She left Emilio while she still had the strength. It was bad enough that she missed an evening out with her friends, she wasn't going to carry her hypnotic state over to the next day. She had to be at the office bright and early. Though it was Sunday, Queenie felt obligated to go in and prepare for Monday morning's budget and individual staff meetings. There were clothes to purchase and the big Christmas fashion show to get to work on. She would be there by seven.

Later in the afternoon, she and Chamille had a lunch date at Millennium's Commissary. Queenie figured since the prima donna actress was going to be under her skin, she may as well try to get to know her a little. They would be spending a lot of time together. Mostly shopping, but that could be a sensitive experience if it wasn't done right. For Queenie, shopping was an art.

Bloomingdales was a breeze. Queenie's head was so deep into *The Matchmaker* that she wasn't stressed or uptight about a damn thing. She floated through her budget reports like a sleeping fairy.

Chamille, on the other hand, was an experience in itself. First of all, she was twenty minutes late. She obviously had tried to make a statement, but she didn't have too much to say when Queenie's Chinese Chicken Salad and warm buttered Squaw bread was brought to the table just as she arrived. She was wrong if she assumed Queenie would wait on her. She had Queenie confused, but she would soon learn. Queenie talked to Chamille as if she actually liked her. She complimented her on her sense of style and her eye for colors. Queenie didn't lie, the girl could dress. In Queenie's book, there was nothing wrong with positively re-affirming someone's ideas about themselves. Chamille bought it hook, line and sinker. After lunch she ate from the palm of Queenie's hand. She went on and on about how she had always loved fashion and how she always wanted to be a movie star. She wasn't exactly there yet, but she was definitely on her way. Attitude and all.

Queenie decided that she did like her. In some ways, Chamille reminded Queenie of herself when she was a little girl. If Chamille Rourke were to sleep with a pea under her mattress, she wouldn't get a wink of sleep.

When their lunch ended, they parted with small Hollywood hugs and lots of giggling. Queenie was glad they talked. Chamille was not as bad as she initially seemed.

Soon after she returned to the film set to ask the resourceful Tracy a question about supplies and props.

As she approached his office door, she couldn't help but overhear a woman in tears asking if her husband were there.

She had a British accent and was very upset, even a little scared. Queenie didn't want to interrupt but she had to make her presence known, otherwise she would have been eavesdropping. If it were another day, she might have indulged, but she had to get back to her office at Bloomingdales. Queenie cleared her throat and gently tapped on the open door. There stood a tall, beautiful European woman with long, curly jet-black hair, startling green eyes and high cheekbones. She was also at least six months pregnant. Her eyes and nose were red from crying and she was extremely distressed.

Tracy smiled at Queenie as if relieved.

"Have you seen Emilio?" he asked hopefully. Queenie looked at him with a dazed expression and shook her head no. What he said next almost knocked her out cold. It sounded like "If you see him on the lot, tell him his wife is here." But it couldn't have been. Emilio was divorced and his ex-wife lived in New York. Queenie couldn't help but blurt out her thoughts.

"You mean *ex-wife*, right?"

The look on the woman's face needed no words. Emilio had lied. Queenie didn't pursue the conversation with Emilio's wife, nor did she turn around to answer her when the woman asked Queenie who she was. She was sure Tracy would fill her in, or maybe he wouldn't. It didn't matter anyway.

Emilio would now and forever be a piece of Queenie's past. He was not going to get away with dissing her a second time. The lovin' was good but she refused to let him bring her down. He was not worth it.

And she was pregnant? Emilio, you fucking lying bastard. Queenie would never give him the pleasure of knowing he had hurt her. No, instead, she would calmly tell him that she wanted to end their relationship. She would blame it all on work. She would say she couldn't handle him and both of her jobs. Regardless of which excuse she used, she would never speak about what just happened back there with his wife. She loved working on the movie and appreciated Emilio hooking her up. She was no fool. Besides, one day Emilio would be a big star with a lot of power. *Why burn my bridges?*

Queenie had a message on her pager from Tracy shortly after she'd returned to Bloomingdales. He told her not to worry, that Emilio's wife finally caught up with him and that she was going on location with him to Santa Barbara. He also made sure that Queenie knew that it was a two-day shoot. She didn't know if he thought she would follow them there, or if he thought she was genuinely concerned. He had to know that they had slept together. He'd caught them kissing on the lot more than once.

Queenie was glad Tracy left her the message. Now she knew that she had two days to get prepared for her round with Emilio. He could be seductively persuasive, but with the mental picture of his crying, pregnant wife burning in her head, his false charms didn't stand a chance.

Chapter Fifty One

Kilamunjaro ~ *nuthin 2 lose*

Yesterday, Sunday, on the way to Dani's, all Killa thought about was how she would love him forever for killing Trixxy. After all, he did it for her. He talked himself into going straight to her door and be the bold nigga that he knew he was.

Before his journey to her house he'd called Dani continuously but she never answered the phone. The more Hennessy Killa drank, the more confidence he got to actually talk to her instead of hanging up like he normally did. He turned the TV to the porno channel and got himself off until he became sore. The Hennessy must have really fucked him up 'cause he began to think about Jackie's fat ass, but that bitch was through. She got the boot.

After Killa came home from his two-day stint in the county jail, he confessed to Jackie that he had found himself a new woman to take care of him. He told her all about Dani and how classy and beautiful she was. He even went so far as to confess to her the lengths he'd gone to be with her: that he had her husband put in jail and had killed her rival, Trixxy.

He tried to put a scare into her, but when Jackie refused to leave, he beat her like a slave. It didn't matter that she begged and pleaded and cried, or even that she threatened to kill herself, he just wanted her out of his face and out of his life, for good. *She's nothin' but trash compared to my Dani.*

Saturday morning, he woke up sick. He threw up and had diarrhea all day. His mouth was stuck together as if he had eaten an entire jar of peanut butter. He thought back to the night before and remembered the food he had eaten at Jackie's.

That bitch poisoned me.

He would bet his life on it. He should have known better than to eat her cooking after he had done her the way he did.

He spent all of Saturday detoxing his system from the foul catfish and greens he had digested. He drank water and stayed in bed with stomach cramps the whole day. *I'mma kills that bitch if I ever see her again.* But he was sure that he wouldn't. Naw, s*he ain't that stupid.*

Early the next morning, he felt like his old self. The first thing he did was call Dani again, but she still wasn't home.

I know she's not tryin' to disrespect a nigga by stayin' out all night, especially after the shit I did for her. Does she think I just kill people for the hell of it? She better recognize. She owes me big.

Now he was mad.

He knocked and knocked but got no response. He paced back and forth while he figured out what his next move would be and he struggled to keep his madness under control. For now.

I ain't never let no woman do me like this before. I put her so-called husband in jail, put her enemy in hell and she don't even want to be home to thank me?

The more he waited the more pissed off he got. Killa hid in the bushes that he'd grown to be so familiar with in past weeks. He couldn't believe his eyes when he saw that his piece was still there. He'd left it there on his last stakeout. He checked the chamber and it was full, but the way he was feeling he knew it wouldn't be for long. *I gotta let off some steam before she gets here. Even if I gotta pump some lead into them damn ducks out there. I don't wanna hurt her. I love her too much.*

Anxiously, he would sit and wait. *She gotta come home sooner or later.* The maniacle mad man felt it was due time that Danielle know just how much he'd gone through to be with her. And, if she didn't give him the love he felt he deserved in return...he couldn't bare the thought.

Chapter Fifty Two

Andrew ~ *One More Chance*

Andrew woke up out of a bad dream and realized he was living one. In the real world it was Monday, but in the county jail, it was just another day in hell. He had been waking up sweating all night wondering why he couldn't shake the nightmares. His thoughts were so scary they almost made him want to say, "fuck the system" and break out.

When the guard came to his cell and told him he was going home, he damn near passed out. Andrew kept his cool because he didn't want to wake up if it was all indeed a dream. They issued him his property so he could change into his street clothes and then he was escorted to the processing room where he signed his release papers. He wanted to ask, *are you sure? How did this happen?* But he was no dummy. Andrew Johnson was typed on all of the paper work that was handed over to him to sign, but he still didn't put it together. First, he waited for them to tell him that it was a joke and then drag his ass back to his cell. He was tripping, but he decided to think positive. *Maybe Jacobs pulled a miracle out of his hat and didn't have a chance to tell me about it.* He hadn't talked to Jacobs all weekend and thought that maybe he was busy arranging for his release. After signing about a thousand papers, he walked down the long corridor to his eventual freedom. Downtown LA had never been so beautiful. He didn't know what the hell to do next, but he was out and that was all that mattered. He quickly decided to get as far away as he could before they realized that there was a mistake.

He had just enough money from his property for a cab ride home and he didn't wait another second to get on his way. The seedy pay phone was heaven to Andrew. After calling for a cab he called Dani, first at home, then at her office. *She might even already know and be waiting on my call, he hoped.* The machine picked up, so he hung up. Next, he called Reggie.

"Ay, man. What's up?"

"Drew, is that you? What's up, man?"

"They let me out dawg! I'm standing here waiting on a cab right now."

"Get the fuck outta here! Where you at? I'll come and get you."

"Naw, it's cool. The cab is here now. Meet me at the house though. I still haven't talked to Dani and I might need you to roll with me somewhere."

"Bet. I'll see you in a minute."

Andrew pinched himself in the cab all the way home. He also kept looking in the rear window to see if the cops were on their way to try and drag him back.

The cab driver drove through the gates of Las Flores and parked. A chill ran up Drew's spine. Being home was only a dream the night before. He looked at his arms and noticed goose bumps.

Reggie was waiting like a good soldier would be. He didn't even wait until Andrew could pay the cabby before he started to fill him in.

"It was Killa, Man. That fool set you up."

"I'm listenin'. Andrew frowned and urged Reggie to continue.

"Late last night, Jackie, one of the whores in the neighborhood, came knocking on the homey, Rick's, side window. He thought she wanted to get her smoke on or something so he told her that he didn't have shit. She had to convince him that drugs was not the reason she was there. When she said she knew about your situation and who set you up, the homie knew he had to hear her out. He let her in the house and she told him the whole story. Rick paged me and told me to come right over and when I got there, she confessed it all."

"So Jackie told you that Killa set me up." Andrew repeated for clarification.

"Yeah, she said it was her man, Munjaro, the same fool we know as Killa from the neighborhood. That nigga Killa always been off his rocker, ever since he was little and his brother got killed. I've heard stories about him doing crazy shit, but those stories mostly came out of his own mouth so I never believed him."

Andrew was not amused. He knew of Killa well, but it still didn't make sense. *Is he jealous? Is that why he's fucking my life over? Because he wants what I have?*

"Man, I wanted to take him out right then but when Jackie let me in, he wasn't home. She said that he'd gotten out of jail, kicked her ass and then threw her out. Now, It's been days since anyone has seen him. She said that nigga's been plottin' and plannin' against you for a over a year."

Reggie had to catch his breath. His words were coming out faster than his brain could process.

"Where is she now? I need her to talk to the cops." Andrew was deep in thought. *She will testify if I have anything to do with it. My life depends on it.*

"I don't know, man. She said she had to leave town before Munjaro came back for that ass. She was real scared. She said the only reason she told us about him was so that somebody would kill him."

"Well, that just might be the solution because it's obvious he's playing for keeps. He obviously don't know who he's up against," Andrew spoke his thoughts out loud.

"Well, look. I need to make sure Dani is safe. I can't get into the house cause I don't have my keys. I think I'mma wait around here to see if Dani shows up. While I'm waitin' I'll plan that move we gon' make tonight. Ya dig? Drew made it known that revenge was around the corner.

"Okay, cool. I gotta pick up some things from the office but I'll be back. If Dani ain't here by then, I'll take you to your moms. Here, take this man, you might need it."

Andrew looked at the automatic weapon that Reggie handed to him.

"Naw, man. I don't want the cops to have any reason to lock me back up. I'll be all right. We'll deal with that when you come back." Andrew didn't want any trouble. He just hoped that his wife and kids were okay so he could go on with his life.

I'mma deal with Killa, Munjaro, whatever he called himself these days. There was no question. He had balls messing with Andrew's life and he would surely pay for it. *That fool won't even know what hit him.*

Chapter Fifty Three

Danielle ~ *Soon as I Get Home...*

The world's madness kept Dani in the hotel suite longer than she had planned. With everything else that happened over the past few days, even more drama had gone down.

Dani had learned about Keera's lunatic ass brother, Kevin, breaking into her New York apartment. As a result, he got two in the stomach. Keera seemed unusually calm about it all but Dani guessed that it was just her outer shell. She knew inside that Keera had to be suffering. She knew her childhood comrad better than that. She also took into consideration the numbness that Keera endured when she encountered Chance at The Terrace.

She was relieved that Keera flew back to LA as soon as the cops would let her. She needed her family and friends to help her heal. Dani would shoot over there as soon as Keera touched ground. In the meantime, she would go home to get some clothes and check on things. She hadn't even bothered to check her messages. Since Drew had to call collect, she knew there would be none from him and she had already spoken with the kids, Francine, Alfred and Willie Mae. Everyone and everything was fine. The only problem she was sure she'd have would be unspoiling the kids after their weekend with their grandma. She learned that Queenie had worked all weekend and that Tai had gone to hell and back but was seemingly in a better place. She hadn't spoken to Saudia but was sure she was doing okay. She was a strong woman and Dani admired her for it. Jody was surely at work and Dani hoped that her world was still on solid ground because everyone else in the crew experienced major earthquakes.

After she dashed to the house to get her life in order, she would go into the office for the rest of the afternoon. *Thank God for Scott. If it weren't for him, I would never be able to be so leisurely with my morning.* They had a meeting scheduled that she totally forgot about. She made a mental note to call Scott the night before to let him know she would be in late, but it got lost in the chaos that surrounded her and her girls.

Dani remembered her conversation with Tai.

"Girl, my house was ransacked and robbed over the weekend, so until I feel safe enough to go home, I'll be staying with my cousin Marlena and Uncle Sol."

Dani felt real bad that none of them had been there for Tai. She was relieved that Tai was okay though, and couldn't believe that she was pregnant. *Wow. Tai's going to be a mommy, unbelievable.*

It now made sense to Dani why Tai had looked so tired as of late and hadn't totally been herself.

Learning of Tai's house being robbed reminded her that she never called the security company regarding her defunct house alarm.

Damn. I'll make the call when I get to the house.

Dani checked out of the hotel much earlier than the check-out deadline and began her journey home. Driving the Navigator reminded her of times she spent with Drew. They were always rolling when he first bought it. Drew was like a little boy at Christmas. Just plain spoiled. If he were home now he would've gotten rid of it by now and bought something new. *Easy come, easy go.*

Dani was thankful that he treated his cars that way and not his women. She thought that if that were the case, she'd be a scratched out number in his little black book, as opposed to his loving wife. Andrew would be mad to hear her say that out loud.

"I've never been a player," is what he would lie and say. *Yeah, right,* Dani laughed. She humored herself with thoughts of her husband and the fun times that they shared. She couldn't wait to create new episodes to store in her memory bank. She was sure they would grow old together and wanted him to hurry home so they could begin their destiny.

Traffic was light but and that was saying a lot for Century Boulevard, near the airport, on a holiday weekend.

I need to hurry if I want to make it into the office today.

She debated on just going in with what she had on as opposed to stopping at home first. But she would risk the trip home. She had already bathed at the hotel so her pit stop would not take long at all. She had to maintain her professional appearance, no matter what.

Maybe I'll luck up and get a call from Andrew while I'm there.

With thoughts of her husband, she put in Biggie Small's "Ready To Die" CD, cranked "Big Papa," number thirteen, and sailed to the house.

Chapter Fifty Four

ANDREW ~ *Thank You Lord!*

Home sweet home was all he could think, as he inhaled deep breaths of fresh air and glanced appreciatively around the grounds of Las Flores. He felt fortunate to have been able to get through the gates, but not at all happy with how easy it was to get inside. How the cabby could follow behind a car that had driven through the gates just ahead of them was ridiculous. *It's way too easy to get into this joint. Time to move. Las Flores is plush but it's time to move on. If that fool Killa had me set up then he knows where I live. Shit, he was probably watchin' my every move. But why?*

He got a sudden pain in his chest.

Danielle.

He knew that chest pain well. It was the pain he got whenever he thought about his wife.

Danielle? He knew the pain was a message. *I should've taken Reg's cell phone. I have to find my wife.*

Less than twenty-four hours ago he was locked up, now he was at his front door. He now saw even clearer that he had taken his whole life for granted. He didn't know what it was about the streets but he could never stay out of them. Maybe his mind couldn't accept the fact that he was living well and could keep living well without them.

Environmental training. He now had trust that having true faith in God, love for himself and others, and that if attitude about life were straight, then everything else would be too. It was something he absorbed from one of the books his ex-celly, G, had let him check out. It spoke to his heart and gave him comfort.

He knocked on the patio door and prayed that Dani would answer. But after minutes upon minutes of silence, he gave it a rest. *She's gotta be at work.* He felt anxious, yet subdued. He was elated, yet disappointed. There was so much to do, yet time seemed to stand still.

Why do I seem to be the last person on earth?

The grounds were quieter than he'd remembered. The only sounds were those of birds singing and the voice in his head, which told him to "do something." He walked aimlessly on Las Flores' grounds until he reached the glistening lake. The beauty of the meadow was bewitching. The ducks and swans seemed to be out of a fairytale. The flowers were perfectly manicured and the green grass plentiful. He looked to the blue sky and noticed the sun peering from behind a cottony cloud. The air was clearer and crisper than his memory served. *Has it always been this beautiful here?* He had never noticed.

God, all I ask is that you keep my family safe. I don't know how I could live without my wife. She's my lifeline. After a long pause to appreciate nature's beauty he was jolted by that voice again. "Do something."

I need to find Dani. I'll use the payphone at the deli on the corner. I might as well order some grub while I'm there too.

When Reggie comes back I'll be able to see him pass by.

Andrew began on his journey to "Diana's," the nearby deli. As he walked he thought intensely about the quickest and easiest way to off his new arch enemy, Killa. He exited the iron gates, which opened automatically at the touch of a sensor. He walked up the deserted street with his mind heavy with aggravated thoughts and his stomach growling, anticipating a well overdue decent meal. Aside from all he'd endured the past few months, let alone this day, nothing could have prepared him for what he saw next. The moment was surreal.

Dani?

She swooped around the corner and onto their street oblivious to her husband's proximity. She looked like heaven, bumping Biggie Smalls and bouncing to the beat. He questioned his vision, as if he was experiencing a mirage in the desert. But there was no mistake, it was definitely her. To be sure, he glanced at the front license plate, which read "SHT CLLR," as big as day.

My beautiful wife. At last.

Chapter Fifty Five

Danielle ~ *Love No Limit*

Dani had gassed the Navigator all the way home. For whatever reason, she was determined to get there.

When she made her same old right turn onto her block, something amazing happened that blew her damn mind.

Drew?

Like a maniac, he had jumped into the street and began to wave his arms. He also did a little dance allowing his happiness to escape through his feet.

She pushed her sunglasses to the top of her head, squinted her eyes and peered out of the window as if she wasn't absolutely positive that it was her husband.

It was Andrew, he was home. She couldn't explain how. She slowed down and drove slowly toward him. The look on her face was classic. A definite Kodak moment.

When it finally sunk in that she wasn't dreaming, she jumped out of the still moving vehicle and fell into his arms. He felt so damn good to hold.

His lips felt so wonderful against hers, his tongue even better. His hands were stronger than she remembered, or maybe he'd never held her that tight before. They kissed for so long in the street, that cars formed a line behind them, waiting to gain entry into the gate. They were honking at them but she felt they were honking to cheer them, and not with impatience.

Drew was so romantic, he carried her back to the abandoned truck and drove them through the iron gates.

My man is home, where he belongs.

Chapter Fifty Six

Kilamunjaro ~ *Battlezone*

When Sunday turned to Monday, Killa was enraged. Smoking those sherm sticks he had in his pocket didn't help his mood. They were meant for a customer that he never bothered to hook up with. He hadn't smoked sherm in a long time and had forgotten the kind of head-trips that it put him through.

The hard heels against the cement alerted Killa. He rose out of the bushes, confident that it was her. When he saw a man standing there, wearing his Brooks Brothers suit, he just couldn't help himself.

"Dani ain't here, if that's who you come to see," Killa said, looking the man up and down, sizing him up for battle.

"Uh, do you know when she'll be back?" he asked, trying hard to conceal his well warranted concern.

"I came a long way, so if she won't be too long, I'll wait in my car."

This lil' nigga is pretty bold, tellin' me he's gonna wait around for my woman.

"She ain't comin' back for a while, so maybe you just need to bounce up outta here," Killa said in a threatening tone, giving the man a chance to save his life.

"And, you are?" The intimidated, yet curious man asked suspiciously.

That was all Killa needed before he hit him upside the head with the butt of his gun. He fell like Killa knew he would.

He quickly dragged the unconscious man onto Dani's front porch before any of her neighbors dared to be Superman and come to his rescue.

Just as he had opened Dani's patio door, Killa took the chance of picking the lock on her front door. *Easy as pie.* It was just his luck that her security alarm was still inoperative too. Killa dragged the little preppy man through the house and dumped his limp body down in the garage. There was plenty of duck tape and rope in the tool shed to tape and tie him, so Killa took the liberty.

He reached in the man's pocket to see what he had going on in his wallet. No cash, only a Corporate American Express from some advertising agency, and a Visa gold card. Killa put the wallet in his pocket and wondered if he should slice him right then. The gun would make too much noise. *Should I just kill him now, or wait till he wakes up to see what the hell he wanted with Dani?* He chose to wait for him to wake up. It would certainly prove to be entertaining.

While he waited for Dani inside of her home, he went upstairs from the garage to the kitchen and made a couple of jelly sandwiches, his favorite. He hadn't eaten all day and his appetite had grown tremendously since his stomach had healed.

He ate his sandwich as he looked at Little Preppie's drivers license: Scott Freeman, birth date July 18, 1972. Oh, a lil' young buck. He couldn't handle Dani if he wanted to. Killa refused to believe that Scott Freeman was there to get between Dani's legs, so he wondered what the fuck was up.

Killa next tried to open the briefcase that his victim carried with him, but it was locked solid. He could have opened it if he chose to, but he wanted to wait until Scott woke up. He wanted to have a little fun.

Scott was out for hours until Killa, in his angst for some action, kicked him awake. He was so mad about Dani being gone for so long he didn't know what to do. He didn't even really know how long she'd been gone but he was sure it had been overnight. *She should've had her ass home by now.*

He violently stripped Scott's mouth free of the duck tape but he couldn't get any information out of him. He did nothing but stutter. After taking a few deep breaths, coaxed between Killa's backslaps, he finally spit something out.

"Uh, I- I –I work with D- D- Dani-nielle. We- we- we're wor-king on a p-p-proj-ect t-t-to-gether. I – I-'m j-j-just drop-p-p-ing of-f-ff some-thing.

Killa laughed. He had a real good time with Scott.

"If you lyin' to me I'm gonna shoot you from your toes to your dick until you tell me the truth. What's the combination to the case?"

Scott gave it up immediately. "8 right, 12 left, 9 right."

Killa anxiously opened the briefcase.

"Nuthin' but a bunch of preppy paperwork," he muttered to himself. It hurt his eyes just to look at it.

Killa taped Scott's mouth back before he could scream while he poked at his stomach with the tip of his army knife. He wondered which part he should cut open first, but was interrupted by a loud noise just above. He secured the tape on

Scott's mouth before he headed upstairs to greet whom he was sure would be Danielle.

My Queen has finally come home. And just in time to watch me carve up a turkey.

Chapter Fifty Seven

Danielle ~ *My Life*

"Baby, how did you get out so soon? Why didn't you tell me? How did you get here? I missed you!" Between her barrage of questions she kissed him all over his wonderful face.

"Boo, I don't know how the hell I got released but they signed me out and walked me to the gate. I'm just happy to be home with you and – where are the kids?"

"They're at your mom's, Baby. We'll go inside and call to get their heads ready. They're gonna be so happy to see you! I can't wait for us to go and get them."

"I can't wait either. We'll call and tell them we'll be there in just a little while, but first we'll climb into a nice warm bath in the ja-cu-zi-tub," he said while he gave her lavish kisses. "And, you know – " For the moment all of his worries, Killa, the police, and everything else, subsided.

"Yeah, I know," a girlish giggle escaped, let's go," she said; more than ready. Two and half months without sex had been an interesting test, but not that interesting.

Andrew came around to her door and lifted her up again.

"I don't want my Princess to walk."

They laughed intimately on the way to the front porch. She struggled to get the keys out of her jacket pocket.

"Let me do that," Andrew offered with a sly grin.

"Handle it, Baby. You got it," she purred into his ear.

She then unbuttoned his shirt and kissed him all softly on his neck. He blushed like a fourth grader while she whispered seductive-*everythings* in his ear.

After unlocking both doors, they stumbled inside, intoxicated with happiness. Inside the house, Andrew looked around like it was his first time. Then he smiled warmly at Dani whom he still held in his arms, closed his eyes and kissed her softly on the forehead.

"I love you, Danielle. My wife, my everything – "

"I love you too, Andrew. Forever." Dani's tears trickled slowly.

"Don't you ever leave us again, Baby. We need you."

Andrew smiled down at Danielle and stroked her hair. She was more beautiful than he ever remembered. They held each other in silence enjoying the warmth of each other's bodies as they pressed against one another.

Danielle soaked in her husband's smell and his feel. She had missed them, among other things, while he was locked up.

Andrew broke the golden silence by saying, "I'm never leaving you guys. They'd have to kill me first, and even then I ain't goin' nowhere."

The blasts from Killa's raging gun rang out, one after the other. Before Dani and Drew stood a monster. A monster that had invaded their home and was now staking claim on their lives.

"Noooo! Ohhhh myyy Goddd! Noooo!" Dani screamed in horror. The deadly lead whizzed by her and penetrated Andrew with great force. One after the other he was pierced with what seemed like swords dipped in hot lava. And even though she hadn't been hit, she felt each and every one of them.

As Andrew fell, his weight knocked Dani on her back. All she heard was Andrew whispering her name again and again and again. He gasped for air and choked on blood. The monster's shadow loomed over them the way Dani imagined death felt like. Cold, dark, enveloping.

Everything happened so fast yet so slow. The monster screamed names at Dani while she screamed back in terror and anger. Andrew lay on top of her spouting blood the way a faucet would.

"You Whore! You Slut! You fuckin' bitch!" the monster yelled.

What did we do to deserve this! What did me or my Andrew ever do to this creature!

She almost had her hand inside of her purse when the demon pushed his gun harshly to her head. He leaned over her with his scarred face and his foul breath and whispered very intensely, "I love you girl but you not gon' play me like no sucker. All the things I did for you. Puttin' that no good husband of yours in jail, killin' that bitch Trixxy, following you around makin' sure nobody hurt you, and this is how you repay me?"

A flashback of the man trying to talk to her at a stoplight, while in her car, came clearly into her head. Tai's complaint of a frightening stranger outside of her door also echoed loudly. Dani shivered uncontrollably.

Killa continued, "No bitch plays me for a fool. I don't care who she is. You love that nigga so much I'mma make sure you die right wit' him!"

During his ranting, she prayed to God, *Let me win this, not this demon who's standing over me with so much madness in his dark eyes.*

With that prayer, she gained and used all of her strength to pull out the small pistol that had been her constant companion since she learned of Trixxy's murder. She expertly released the safety, then pulled the trigger until it's hollow clicks screamed out loud that the gun was empty. He was forced back about four feet before he stumbled backward, still screaming obscenities and vows of revenge. With a loud thump, he crashed down on the dining room table. He was through.

Dani felt no movement from her Andrew. No air came from his lungs, no life in his body. Strangely though, she felt his spirit run through her. It was warm and soothing – not at all scary. All she could do was let out a loud, long wail. She rocked him and cried over his body like a lost child.

Why did this happen! Why us! How are we going to live without him?

Danielle sobbed uncontrollably until the rest of the world woke up and came to her rescue. It took Reggie and almost the whole police squad to pull Dani away from Andrew. She felt that if she let go of him, he would be gone forever. The scene was horrific. Dani sat soaked with Andrew's blood and he lay soundly in her arms, almost as if asleep. For Dani, time had stopped simultaneously with Drew's pulse.

Munjaro, or Killa as he was more commonly known, lay spread-eagled on his back. He posed as still as a rock but with his eyes wide open. It was as if he were still there, alive inside of his bullet-ridden flesh; as though he wasn't finished with his mission, *whatever that was.*

Chapter Fifty Eight

Danielle ~ *The Aftermath*

After a pot of tea Dani finally calmed down enough to deal with what had just happened, piece by piece. She told the police that the monster, known as Killa according to Reggie, confessed to her about killing Trixxy just before a failed attempt to kill her. Reggie added what he knew in his statement: that the man he knew as Munjaro, aka, Killa was responsible for setting up Andrew and that his wife, Jackie, told him the whole story.

Poor Scott was found by the police in the garage secured by ropes, duck-tape and most of all, fear. He was hog-tied like an animal. Scott explained, in fright, how he had come by to check on Dani, since she'd missed a meeting with their boss and no one had heard from her. He also wanted to drop off some ideas for their project. He had a huge bump on his head and his pants were soaked with feces. The term "scared shitless" came to Dani's mind. He was caught in the middle of her mess. He almost lost his life for being a good guy. Dani apologized profusely. She felt like it was all her fault. *Everything.*

Keera was at the door just as the police finished up with Dani. They hugged and cried relentlessly. Keera was then able to let out her pain from her own recent tragedies. She cried hard and loud, reflecting the pain, which pierced her insides.

Reggie stayed to make sure Dani would be okay. He too was shaken up by Andrew's tragic death, but unlike Danielle, he was able to function normally despite it. He had been trained how to better deal with such tragedies due to his experience of losing not only scores of friends to street warfare, but his only brother as well.

He was stunned that the po-pos didn't have him in cuffs. With two bullet ridden bodies at the scene, he just knew he would at least be interrogated. *My bad, the murder victim and his dead killer are black. These crackers don't give a dayum. Two less brothas for them to worry about settin' up, harrasin' or killin' themselves.* He was well versed in the art of harassment by the LAPD. As a youth he'd come to realize that a Black man in America was a target. *Believe that.*

Dani insisted to Reggie that he go home, but only until she assured him that Keera would escort her to her grandma and grandpa's would he leave. She made a painful call to Francine who left the kids with Richard and rushed right over. Needless to say, she was devastated. She'd lost her son and she didn't even get to say good-bye.

Keera called Dani's office for her, then drove her straight to Willie Mae's and Alfred's. To Dani's surprise, they already knew everything. Keera had called and prepped them before hand. She was thankful for that because the strength they mustered up, helped her to the tenth power.

The kids were still at Francine's and keeping each other company. Richard stayed, keeping them isolated from the day's tragedy. Dani's talk would be more intense than she ever imagined. She promised them she would see them soon and after hanging up, said a silent prayer for them.

Dani talked with Keera and her grandparents until nightfall. Most of the time was spent in complete silence but Dani could feel the love in the room. Just the fact that they were there was a big comfort.

Andrew's death was senseless and evil. What makes a man kill another man in cold blood, really? Is it just plain hatred for that person or simply for themselves? I don't understand. I lost my life partner, his children lost a father, his mother lost a son... the world lost a great man. He still had so much to offer. And for what?

I promise I will go on a quest for these answers. A spiritual quest. One up and beyond anything that a psychologist or scientist can tell me.

When she closed her eyes, she saw his face. She heard his words, saw him smiling, as he told her that he was okay. It hurt, so bad, though. It really, really hurt.

EPILOGUE

U Gotta Believe

Two years later...

Danielle ~

The past two years have been full of realizations. Living in the world without my husband is surreal. As a young widow and mother of two, I had the weight of the world on my shoulders. For a long time I went to bed at night wearing a pair of Drew's boxers and a dab of his cologne. I also awoke every morning with my pillow moist from quiet tears.

I never realized how much I actually depended on him either, mentally and physically. It would be a hard journey but I'm getting there. I feel him strongly with me and can't explain it much more than that.

It turned out that Andrew had been released from jail by pure error. But, when he was identified to the police they alerted the jail that their "escapee" had been found. Instead of owning up to their goof, they instead put out a search warrant and claimed that he'd escaped. To me it was clear that the plan was to kill him once he'd been caught. How else would they have gotten away with such a ridiculous accusation? Fortunately, I had his release papers in my possession. They had been retrieved from the pocket of his soiled shirt and given to me by a police officer who was obviously out of the loop. The signatures proved that his release was their error, therefore clearing him of any wrong doing.

At first, I blamed the neglectful cops for Drew's death. If they hadn't of messed up he would have been in his jail cell and unable to have been the target for a parade of flying bullets. But later after embracing peace, I truly began to see that God sent Andrew to save my life. I came to accept that if he wasn't there, I would instead be the one dead. Those bullets were meant for me.

***

The week after Drew's passing, there were four funerals. Trixxy's obsequy, which I paid for, was small and sad.

Next was Saudia's dad's farewell ceremony, which I heard was a beautiful tribute to his life.

Kevin's interment was the very next day. Keera attended reluctantly only because her father insisted. He was kind hearted and felt they should at the very least, pay their respects. At the service, Cruella got the chance to show out and play the grieving mother who'd lost her mind, and Keera was forced to re-visit the grievous event of his death, one last time.

Saudia and Keera understood that I was in too much pain to attend the services of their father and stepbrother. My friends had been a major strength since Andrew's death. They were always tending to my needs, whether it be going out to breathe some of the life that existed outside of my home, or just a phone call to let me know they were thinking about me.

Andrew's funeral was last in the train of burials. The service was packed, to say the least. Because Drew was so well rounded and personable, he had friends and acquaintances in all realms of society. There were doctors, lawyers, teachers, professional athletes, gangsters, you name it, and they were there.

Frankie, Andrew's younger brother, and his mom Francine were strong and loving throughout the whole ordeal. They were my rocks. All in all, it was very uplifting to see all the love.

DJ seems to be doing fine since his dad's death. Maybe his being so young helps, or maybe he just hides it well. He is a true blessing.

Jasmine is also doing well. Everyone sees the difference in her personality. She is so much more bubbly and outgoing. She's been through too much for a child of seven, it's about time the clouds are lifted. I am sorry she wasn't able to spend more time with her daddy while he was alive. I have to make sure his memory stays alive in both of their hearts.

Although the children seem well adjusted, I feel sad for them, especially Jasmine. I had hoped that someday Trixxy would have come around and become a positive part of Jasmine's life. Wherever she is now, she can rest that her daughter will be well loved and well taken care of. I have wasted no time in obtaining legal custody and am now finalizing her adoption papers.

Me and the children stayed at Willie Mae's and Alfred's for a few months before finally settling into our own home. I barely left the house in the beginning. I spent much of my time reading the Bible and trying to really learn its' meanings.

The townhouse went on the market and sold immediately, but I wasn't ready to live alone. My mind and everybody with an opinion on my life said to get up and go back to work. But I began to listen to my heart. It clearly said, "Stay where you are until you are ready. Start your own company."

I spent my mournful days developing a business, my business. It didn't take very long before Seeing EYE Advertising was born. I'd started the development of my own company during the time I spent cooped up in my grandparent's house and at the same time took my life to a whole new level.

My dream has always been to own my own ad agency. Because of the long hours and stressful accounts, let alone the office politics, Kravitz had no longer fulfilled my creative hunger. It dawned on me that I could endure the same amount of pressure with my own agency. At least with my own company I would find passion in my work again. School wasn't going anywhere.

I'm not one to stay at home, go shopping and do lunches all day. Before I go that route I'd return to school full-time for my Masters degree or even attend law school. It had always been a thought.

Once the business had been established I didn't waste any time in recruiting my former colleague, Scott, onto the team. Scott's brilliant marketing strategies were a great asset. With Scott as my business partner, I knew we'd be unstoppable.

Seeing EYE Advertising is doing well for a new company. Many of our old clients from Kravitz's agency had been wooed over by our fresh ideas and low fees. Cyber-space has become a huge benefactor in the company's early success as well. It offers a universe of opportunities for growth.

When my wings mended, my heart began to heal, and my business got off of the ground, it had come time to move out. It was kismet when the perfect house had found me. Ironically I missed my turn coming home from work one day and happened upon a beautiful house for sale, located in the hills near Willie Mae and Alfred.

The landscaping and plentiful foliage is what at first drew me in. The front yard was filled with the most beautiful flowers. Once I arranged for a showing, it was then that I decided I had to have it.

There are five bedrooms, three and a half baths, a living room, dining room, and a bonus room. It's large and comfortable at the same time. Me and the children each have our own room. The two remaining bedrooms serve as a guest room, the other a workout, slash, game room.

In the back, a tiled staircase leads upstairs to a custom built office just over the garage. The walls of glass allow for a perfect view of the blooming garden in the backyard, which also houses a black-bottomed pool and a Jacuzzi. It was the perfect resolution for my need to move, and serves as the perfect locale for my home-run business.

I've been blessed with a life of luxury, which aside from my home, I choose to keep casual in regards to my spending habits. It is important to me that DJ and Jasmine understand that money is something that you earn with hard work. I am teaching them money management skills at their young age by opening interest-bearing saving accounts for them. They started and maintain their accounts with allowance money earned by doing chores. I hope by them learning to have respect for money and how to manage it at an early age, they will have discipline and good judgment when financing their funds as adults.

Having just paid off my own student loans, I wish I had done things differently. Debt has been a hard lesson, especially since I refused to let Drew pay off the bills I incurred before we met. I paid back every loan and paid off every credit card with my own hard-earned money. I revel in my debt-free life whenever I spend cash while shopping, as opposed to whipping out my Platinum Visa.

Free at last, free at last, thank the Lord, I'm free at last.

I find a certain freedom and peacefulness in my life in being my own boss. The weight of responsibility is grand but because I enjoy the work to the fullest, it's all well worth it. As a woman, I'm finally beginning to come into my own.

***

As for the rest of the ladies, they are also doing very well. As a whole, we continue the tradition of Bridge Night, gathering once a month. Every last Friday of the month we meet at one or the other's houses. We even meet for brunch at The Terrace after church service on occasion. Each Sunday is a renewed experience. I feel the church's pastor is a good teacher and I always enjoy the love from the choir.

As for our extra-curricular activities, we sometimes drink a mimosa or two at brunch, but the marijuana smoking is no longer a pass time. During the first Bridge Night we made a pact to be rid of the drugs and alcohol. "For Tai's sake, if nothing else," *was what I had asked of the girls. I felt that we should have Tai's back, after the frightening ordeal she'd been through.*

I couldn't imagine having been given heroin under the pretense that it was a chronic, marijuana blunt. What I didn't know was that they'd all thought about quitting cold-turkey as well and breathed a whole lot easier after the suggestion was made and the pact sealed.

Shortly thereafter, our vices had been gladly replaced by working out at the gym, running in the park and eating healthy meals. And for those who had a significant other, sex is still fair game, for now. Jody would continue to work on that one, I'm sure. All in all, it's time for new beginnings. Good beginnings.

Keera ~

Well, ya'll I was blessed to have been given the opportunity to audition for the lead role in the anticipated film "The Matchmaker." The actress who held the starring female role, abruptly quit. It seemed that Emilio, had sexually harassed her to the point of no return. For her replacement, the directors then wanted a fresh face with at least some acting experience. Queenie had confidence that I was perfect, so she pulled some strings and hooked me up with an audition and a screen test. My face was well known but it was fresh on the movie screen. And my acting skills were tight. I got the part after only one callback audition.

Out of respect, Queenie warned me about Emilio and his sleazy ways. I assured her that she need not worry. He was a piece of cake compared to what I had dealt with in the past.

The film wrapped in eight months and debuted with glorious reviews. I prevailed just as everyone predicted I would. I wasn't as sure as they were but I'm glad they were right. Soon after, the Hollywood buzz was that this A-list model turned actress was a shoe in for an upcoming Golden Globe award. And guess what, they were right again. Now what?

I had thrown myself into the role because it helped me to heal the wounds that both my stepbrother and my ex-boyfriend left with me. Nevertheless, it paid off and I'm extremely happy with my new life.

I have a new man now too. He's a young and talented, black Hollywood director. Not only is he as fine as he wants to be, but he treats me the way I deserve – and he's straight. So much for empty vows of staying singe for life.

Saudia ~

I am happy to say that I am the proud owner of Lyrical Management. The talent management company specifically geared toward music talent, for now. Once Angie, now known as Angel, blew up on the charts, I kept scouting new talent and hit the jackpot time after time. I have a small office in Century

City where both myself and Jody work endlessly. I have no time for a boyfriend and that's okay. When I'm ready, I'm sure God will hook me up.

Jody ~

I'm having the time of my life! After being fired from my job and a failed attempt at killing myself, Saudia came to the rescue. She offered me a job to assist her in running Lyrical. I protested at first for many reasons but she was convincing. Especially, when my bills began to pile up and Saudia offered me a hefty pay advance. I also came to accept that God made sure that Saudia was in my life at that moment, for that reason. I am grateful beyond words.

My children Xavier and Chelsea are shared between me and Marcus and Shelby, who are now also the proud parents of a new baby girl they named Summer.

The shared custody arrangement works well for us. They love spending time with their baby sister. No longer am I the over protective mother or the doting ex-wife. I have a life of my own now. A beautiful life, which I thank God for every single day.

Do you remember Daniel, the wheel chaired ex-football player, whom I met at The Greenroom? Well, he is now my fiancé. He is wonderful! We are wonderful! The blindfold has been removed when it came time for me to see that family additions are not such a bad thing. I was even whole enough to attend Marcus' and Shelby's wedding. I loosened up a whole lot and opened my mind to the idea of being happy. So far things are flawless.

Queenie ~

I'm in love with my new career. I live and breathe as a celebrity stylist. It all began with Chamille Rourke. With the aid of her hit sitcom, she became a major player in Hollywood. When she quit "The Matchmaker" it was the best career decision she'd ever made.

Chamille loved my style so much that she called on me to help her shop and dress for every major dinner, lunch and brunch that she had on her schedule.

Soon other celebrities were calling. I was so busy with shopping for celebs and the film, I was forced to quit Bloomingdales.

Another added blessing for me was meeting Dani's friend and business partner, Scott. One date turned into every Saturday night. We fit together like legos and have been an item for over a year now. It's clear to us, and all who know us, that we aren't going anywhere, except the alter. Hallelujia!.

Tai ~

I think I've changed the most out of everyone. Before my admittance into the rehabilitation facility, I had a long talk with my friends and family about my heroin addiction. They were all ashamed of themselves for not seeing that I was in need of help. Their unyielding support had overflowed and I embraced it. It had even become my lifeline at one point during my road to recovery.

Although, I haven't been on the drug for very long, it had found a home in my cells, my veins, my bloodstream, my thoughts and my dreams. Withdrawals were gruesome but my will-power was mighty. I kept my unborn child my priority. The sight of my ever-growing belly kept me disciplined. I got plenty of rest, ate the right foods and kept a light daily exercise regimen. I also took the time to read and sing to my unborn baby.

The birth of my little girl, Chastity, was miraculous. She had no scars from my addiction. My silent premonitions of my unborn baby's deformities were proven false. Instead she was pure and untarnished. A precious jewel.

I'm a new mommy and loving it. I had always said that I never wanted children but now I couldn't imagine not. Unfortunately, Chastity's father died before she was born. Then again, he was the sleaze who got me hooked on heroin in the first place. Maybe it's not so unfortunate after all.

The love I feel for my daughter is something I've never experienced before. I want to protect her from the world. *I know it will be a big job but I can't wait to tackle whatever comes our way.*

Upon my release from rehab my worries about my livelihood overwhelmed me. I had to ultimately close The boutique. It had been proposed several times by several people that I should allow someone else to temporarily take over the lease. I struggled with the decision during sleepless nights, but *ultimately felt the shop was linked to all of the things I wanted to leave behind. So I made a clean break.*

I came home from rehab, clean as a whistle. Drug free, craving free, and burden free. Because my friends had so much love for me and faith in me, they pooled their resources and acquired a building for "Tai's Place" my new salon and day spa in Beverly Hills.

I am happy and humble. I vowed to pay everyone back in spades but it wasn't necessary. Their shares in the business and lifetime guarantee of free service was good enough for them. Dani, Keera and Saudia took the roles of "limited partners" in the business and allow me full control of the salon. I couldn't have asked for better.

I created my new boutique to be fit for a queen. It was extravagant and classy proving my uniquely exquisite taste. I even hired a contractor who added a baby-safe day care facility. The day care offers reading, writing, art, a computer, and a selection of movies and video games. To work in the center and to help with tasks in the salon, I hire unemployed teenage mothers, who are the focus of one of the many non-profit organizations to which I'm devoted. I provide the underprivileged young mothers with the necessary *training for the job in the center I named Chastity's Corner. And those who I feel aren't quite right for the job, I put to work with either a bottle of shampoo and a waiting client, a broom or an appointment book instead.*

Motherhood made a lot of changes in me. I not only have love for my Chastity, but for every baby in the world.

Tai's Place had a grand opening that was out of this world. I'm happy to report that it's the city's new "it" salon specifically for Black hair care. But not just anybody can get in. It 's like that.

My move to Beverly Hills proven to be fruitful. Me and my staff of hairdressers, masseuses and manicurists have a clientele full of money spending celebrities. Actresses, models, singers, rappers, all thanks to Keera's, Queenie's and Saudia's industry contacts.

Tai's Place also caters to female athletes, behind the scenes movers and shakers such as writers, directors, company presidents and CEO's – courtesy of Dani and her agency's contacts and plenty of word of mouth.

And, of course, there are the socialites. This group is made up of drop-dead, gorgeous women who know everybody who is anybody in the industry, and have the little black books to prove it. They are the fortunate ones who are born with silver spoons in their mouths, or glamorous and cunning enough to persuade a rich entertainment industry hot-shot to spoon-feed them whatever their hearts desire. Nevertheless, their money is green too, and more than welcomed at Tai's.

I live a much more peaceful life than in past times. I'm very fulfilled. The chaotic episodes, I can't believe I lived through. It was almost as if I was sleep walking through life, blowing wherever the wind did. My eyes were closed and as a result I fell into many ditches. The last ditch took my last breath to climb out of. I had no choice but to finally open my eyes and face the world. The view from up here though, is mad wonderful. God is good!

***

Danielle ~

This past year, I've spent memorable moments with Lena. She hated me to call her by her first name, but "Mom" doesn't quite fit our relationship. We've become friends more so than mother and daughter. DJ and Jasmine have also spent time with her and love her to death. Maybe one day she'll slow down enough to be an at home grandma to them. It's a long shot but, all things are possible.

As for me, I don't know if I'll ever settle down with a man and feel as safe with him as I did with Andrew. If the right situation comes my way, then cool, but I'm not dealing with any bullshit. I've learned that the pathways in my life will be full of many surprises, some good, some not so good. The answer will be how I deal with the situations I'm given, and learning from my past mistakes. The key is that I maintain a powerful faith in God. My knowledge that I can have anything and everything I desire, permanently, if I return His love and welcome Him into my daily life, is soothing. I even look at people differently. I recognize that God lives in them as well as in me, and treat them as such. I work hard to train myself to have the most positive of thoughts, the most positive of words, and the most positive of actions. I pray that my life will be blessed the same in return. Can I get a witness?

ACKNOWLEDGMENTS

Thank you for reading my story. This has been a true journey. These events that took place in my imagination have served as not only a blessing but as therapy. Please look for "The Kismet Continues," part two, because my story does not end here. (see the back of the book for a sneak peak.)

Thank you, God, who has carried me such a long way, spiritually and mentally. Thank you for the strength and the courage to listen to You when you speak through my heart. Releasing the reigns of my life and following my spirit is a challenge but it's what makes life, life.

Thank you to my husband Patrick. I know you've been looking out for us big time from heaven. I still feel you Boo.

Mom, thank you for absolutely everything... Paybacks should be coming in real soon – in spades.

To my editor, Tai Shabazz, thank you for lending your skills and giving me encouragement as well as much needed guidance. And to Noel Barker, Kismet's co-editor, thank you for all of your assistance. You are treasured for pitching in the way you did.

Serge and Corinne, both of you are a God-send! Thank you for all of your help. And, Iris, your typesetting services were heaven sent, as well. Thank you so much for your hard work and kindness.

And finally, to all of my friends and family, you know who you are, thanks for all of your support. A special holla' out to my girl, Yvette. Proof that real friends actually do exist. You were a huge rock during the craziness I endured, while sculpting Kismet for it's public debut. Thank you for that.

To the rest of my goddess circle sisters, I love you all. What more can be said? The o/g's: May and Petal, what could I do without you guys? And, Coco and Cori, you ladies came in right on time.

And a very, very special thanks to you, Patrick, Jr. You are my sunshine. Thank you for your love, encouragement, and especially your patience. If nothing else, I hope watching me dedicate my time, heart, soul and energy to my work shows you that your *can* make your dream a reality, with lots of hard work, courage and faith. I love you, Mom.

Excerpts from Key To Yourself by Dr. Venice Bloodworth, courtesy of DEVORSS Publications.

What's Next?

The Spring 2001 Release

Of

THE KISMET CONTINUES…

But for now, turn the page for a

Sneak peek….

Chapter One

CHANCE

Chance Walker paced the room nervously while he silently recited the over-practiced announcement inside of his head. He rang his sweaty hands together regretting that he'd ever initiated the press conference that was about to take place – but he had no choice. The rumors had become too thick and they hit too close to home.

He met with Coach Baldwin last week and then with the team as a whole just last night. Coach had been surprisingly sympathetic. He'd expected more support from his friends and teammates but instead he received the cold shoulder. Even from Timberland Humphries, his best friend. Tim's words still rang in Chance's memory.

"You on your own with this one man. I can't afford to be caught up in no bullshit. How could you let this happen anyway?" Timberland asked almost with tears in his eyes. He shook his head and walked out of the locker room leaving Chance alone to cry in anguish.

Chance heard the voices buzzing outside the door and he knew the time had come. The reporters hovered outside like piranha. Chance had never known them to be so vicious. At least, not with him. He'd been the darling of the NBA for the past five years. The press had loved and adored him. Now he was nothing more than a tabloid scandal.

“They’re ready for you Chance. Have you had enough time to prepare? I don’t think I can hold them off any longer,” said Chance’s agent and publicist Michael York.

Michael York was the best in the business. It was because of his utmost insistence that Chance came clean to the public about his situation. He assured Chance that it would be better for him in the long run.

“Yeah, I’m ready,” Chance answered. “I thought about sneaking out the back door but I guess that would be pretty dumb at this point,” he said with a dry chuckle.

“Take a deep breath and just get it over with. This day will come and go, you’ll see,” Michael answered in a disappointed tone.

Chance gave him a look that could have easily translated, “that’s easy for you to say,” then followed Michael into dreaded pressroom...